SCHOLAR OF THE CROWN

THE HEIRS OF WILLOW NORTH, BOOK THREE

MELISSA MCSHANE

Night Harbor Publishing

Night Harbor Publishing

www.nightharborpublishing.com

Cover design by Jay R. Villalobos www.coversbyjuan.com

North sign and shield designed by Erin Dinnell Bjorn

Dedicated to Elizabeth "Tish" Simone,
who taught me how deep a love of reading can run

THE SCHOLIA AND THE
TREMONTANAN CALENDAR

The Scholia in the year 807 Year of the Binding (Y.B.), when this story takes place, is a sprawling campus located two days' travel south of Tremontane's capital, Aurilien. It comprises fourteen main buildings in addition to its many stables and other outbuildings. The main buildings are as follows:

Godfrey Hall: Administration

Merriwether Hall: History and Philosophy schools

Richfield Hall: Math and Natural Philosophy (science) schools

Covington Hall: Literature and Linguistics schools, as well as the Scholia infirmary

Saunders Hall: Architectonics and Devisery schools

Lyton Hall: Law and Library Sciences schools

Four dormitories: Patience, Honor (women); Fortitude, Temperance (men)

Two instructor residences: Justice and Mercy

A refectory

The bethel

The Tremontanan calendar is made up of four seasons, each ninety days long, with four extra holidays corresponding to the solstices and equinoxes (Wintersmeet, Springtide, Midsummer, and Harvest). Each season is fifteen six-day weeks long.

Originally, the six days were named for six of the minor lost gods, but in later times (beginning around 775 Y.B.) the days came to be referred to simply as Firstday, Secondday, etc. The exceptions are the third day of the week, called Haransday in honor of the traditional day when Haran received her revelation about ungoverned heaven, and the sixth day, known as Endweek.

*V*eronica stood in the hall outside the east wing drawing room and listened to the Queen of Tremontane argue with her Consort. Eavesdropping wasn't something she'd planned on, but she had come back from an early morning ride to find the argument going strong, and interrupting other people's conflicts had never been something she was good at.

She didn't bother trying not to listen, pretending to stare at the walls reflecting on whether the wallpaper needed replacing. She already knew the subject of the argument and how it would end. Elspeth and Duncan had said everything that needed saying a dozen times in the last week. But love expressed itself in so many ways, and the sound of two people trying to sacrifice for each other could be loud and acrimonious. And Veronica knew intimately the pain they both suffered, though it had been...sweet heaven, almost thirty years since she had been in their position? Her memories no longer stung, but she remembered.

"This isn't over. We have options," Elspeth was saying.

"Only one option. It's the obvious one," Duncan replied. His voice was strained, as if he was suppressing a shout.

"*I am not divorcing you*," Elspeth said, her voice equally strained. "I haven't given up, and neither should you."

"Two years without conceiving is beyond what my faith will bear." Duncan's voice was louder now. "Dr. Ambrose was clear. You just want to believe in a miracle."

Elspeth's words cut across his. "Is that a slur on my faith?"

"Damn it—" The shout escaped Duncan finally. "You know it isn't," he said, more quietly if not more calmly. "This isn't about religion, it's about practicality. I can't have children."

"What Dr. Ambrose *said*, if you'll recall," Elspeth said, biting off each word precisely, "is that your fertility is low, and it's going to take time."

"Time the Council—the country—isn't likely to give us. Elspeth. I feel like less of a man already. Let me do this."

"This has nothing to do with your manhood unless you decide it does!" Elspeth's voice, never shrill, rose sharply. "Duncan, two years isn't so long."

Duncan let out a short, bitter laugh. "Tell that to everyone who whispers where they think we can't hear. Tell it to the people who think it's hilarious to joke about whether we know what it takes to get a child."

"Those people are idiots, and not worth listening to. *You* told me never to let rumor rule my life."

"I'm having trouble remembering that."

There was a pause. Then Elspeth said, "Adoption—"

"Elspeth!"

"There's nothing wrong with adopting. Heaven looks kindly on those who embrace children who need a family."

"The implications of adopting the heir to the Crown are beyond fraught. You ought to know that."

"Worse than a foreign-born woman dedicated to a religious life taking the Crown? Tremontane will endure, Duncan. I think we should consider it. And I haven't given up hope that I'll bear your child."

Duncan sighed. "I could leave, you know."

"You wouldn't do that." Elspeth's voice shook.

"No, heaven help me. It would break my heart to leave you."

Silence again. Veronica realized she could have left the east wing instead of eavesdropping, and wondered what hidden motive had kept her rooted to the spot, listening to her niece's pain. Then Duncan said, "I should change my clothes. High court is in an hour."

"I don't know if I can bear listening to cases when my personal life is in turmoil." Elspeth's voice was quieter now, as if she were moving away.

"We don't have personal lives, Elspeth." Duncan's footsteps sounded on the parquet floor, gradually fading.

Veronica waited half a minute before walking forward into the drawing room. She came up short as Elspeth looked up from where she had been staring into the enormous fire in its hearth of polished river stones. Elspeth's eyes were red, her cheeks flushed, and between that and her red hair she looked scorched. "I heard the door open," she said. "I'm sorry you heard that."

"I apologize for violating your privacy," Veronica said, and instantly regretted her excessive formality. She never felt capable of offering comfort in a way grieving people would appreciate. The best she could ever do was listen awkwardly and maybe offer a pat on the shoulder. Hugs made her uncomfortable.

Elspeth waved a hand dismissively. "You already know what's happened. We haven't been discreet. I just...for Duncan's sake...you probably heard how sensitive he is about it."

"Men and women handle infertility differently," Veronica said.

"Yes, and I can't convince him it doesn't matter. To me, I mean. Not when he knows how much it matters to Tremontane that we've had trouble conceiving. He blames himself." She laughed, one short, brittle *hah*. "I suppose he's right in a literal sense, but it's not as if he chose this...problem."

Veronica nodded. "I understand. I told your Uncle Landon he should divorce me when it turned out I couldn't have more than one child. The North family had such a fragile grip on the Crown, and I thought he, as King, needed a dozen heirs."

Elspeth sat in the nearest overstuffed chair, her eyes on Veronica. "I'd forgotten that. And he refused, because he loved you."

"He did." She hadn't realized he actually loved her until that night. The memory made her heart constrict. "Duncan just needs time. I take it there was no healing Dr. Ambrose could perform?"

"She said it was beyond the scope of magical healing. I love him, Aunt Veronica. I'd rather see the Crown pass from the Norths entirely than give him up." Elspeth rubbed tears from her eyes. "But I know it won't come to that. I have to believe we'll find a solution."

Veronica nodded, not meeting Elspeth's eyes. Her niece's religious faith had never made sense to her, given that heaven had never paid the least bit of attention to any of Veronica's pleas. It had taken Landon in such a horrible fashion, and then her son Francis had died of influenza despite the groove Veronica's knees had worn in her floor, praying.

"There's always adoption," she said. "There must be hundreds of children with no parents in Aurilien alone, not to mention the rest of the country."

Elspeth let out a deep sigh. "But how many of them have no family bond at all? Duncan is right that adopting an heir is complicated." She rose. "It's a busy day, so I'll see you at supper, yes?"

How busy a day, Elspeth had obviously forgotten. Well, it wasn't as if the fifty-second day of Summer meant anything to anyone but Veronica now. "You'll find a solution," she said, and for a moment she actually believed it.

She went straight to her bedroom suite and stripped off her riding clothes as steaming water poured into the enormous claw-footed tub. She had had these rooms since Landon's death, because she couldn't bear sleeping in their big bed alone. The bathroom's pale yellow walls were a nice contrast to the cornflower blue tiles, and although she hadn't chosen the décor, she felt it suited her.

She sank into the hot water and let her mind drift. Memories rose unbidden from where Time had stowed them. Five years ago today... Landon had still been alive, and they'd celebrated her birthday with a picnic in the royal family's private garden, just the two of them. He'd given her a silver ring set with polished amber and teased her about having plebeian tastes in stones. "Not even a stone," he'd said, "hardened tree blood!" But she loved the warmth of amber and the way it felt when she touched it, and Landon knew that. She'd put away her wedding band a year after his death, but she'd never stopped wearing her birthday ring.

She scrubbed herself clean, rinsed off, and stepped onto the mat to rub away the remaining water. Movement caught her eye, and she realized it was her reflection in the full-length mirror that had also not been of her choosing. Unlike the walls, she didn't care for it, didn't like having it in the bathroom instead of the dressing room, but it was set into the wall and removing it was a non-trivial task.

Now she walked across the wet tiles to examine herself. *Too thin*, she thought, and chided herself mentally. That was a criticism that only made sense in comparison to others, and comparing was a fool's game. Instead, she looked more closely at her face, at the fine lines clustered at the corners of her hazel eyes and the faint, almost imperceptible pale brown splotches on her cheekbones, and wondered when she'd started getting old. Surely she wasn't more than twenty-two, at least in her heart? But today was her fiftieth birthday, and if that wasn't a landmark, she didn't know what was.

Her hair was a lighter blonde than it used to be, something others usually put down to either sun or artifice. Veronica never told anyone it was a profusion of white hairs. She'd made a fuss out of finding the first one, years ago, and Landon had said— what was it? That vanity would be her downfall, and white hair was dignified. Then he'd kissed her, and she'd never plucked another white hair again.

She cast another look at her body, feeling she was doing penance for some unnamed sin, and went to the dressing room to find something to wear. She had two maids, but although she'd called on Mary as usual that morning to bring her breakfast, she didn't want to summon Iris to help her dress now. Iris might divine the importance of the day and comment on it, and Veronica felt a sudden desire to make it through the day without celebrating.

Though... Her hands slowed in buttoning her high-waisted, narrow-skirted gown, made of a soft cotton printed with pansies in a faded lavender not at all like the vibrant, real flower. It wasn't as if she had plans. She helped in the paupers' hospital every morning and didn't see any reason to skip that just because it was her birthday. She was to have lunch with friends, or at least acquaintances, and in the afternoon there was the dog breeders' show she'd agreed to judge, as if she knew anything about dogs beyond the obvious. And supper with Elspeth and Duncan, of course. But those were *appointments*. It surprised her to discover that with the exception of supper, she had no desire to fulfil any of them.

Veronica sat slowly on the edge of her bed, her hands falling to her side with the neck of her gown still open. They were all good and meaningful pursuits, but were they what she wanted to do? Did she even know what she wanted? Confusion, and fear, rose up within her, followed closely by anger. She was the former Consort—she refused to think of herself as a Dowager—with resources and connections anyone might envy, and here she was sitting in her bedchamber feeling sorry for herself because...she wasn't even sure where this feeling had come from.

Frustrated, she rose and paced the length of the room, buttoning her gown with shaking hands. She didn't know what she wanted. She did know she was tired of this rut she had fallen into since Landon's death, drifting from one worthy cause to another, smiling and nodding and being polite because being assertive made her feel uncomfortable.

She and Landon had complemented each other. Left to his own devices, Landon had been brash, outspoken, loud, and verging on boorish. Veronica had been a steadying influence on him, an anchor that reminded him he didn't need to behave badly to conceal how anxious he always was in company. And Veronica might be silent, withdrawn, and unable to carry a conversation with strangers, but Landon's warm presence had comforted her and given her the courage to speak. They'd needed each other, and now Landon was gone and Veronica had retreated. Not all the way, she had good manners and knew how to interact with others, but she had very few friends and no one she was truly close to but Elspeth.

She hadn't always been this way. Before meeting Landon and being swept away by him, back when she was Lady Veronica Chastain, she'd had a path and a goal. She'd been a Scholia student, intent on taking the robe of a Master, and she'd been confident in academic circles as she hadn't been in society. Veronica restlessly moved some things on her dressing table without seeing them. Those years at the Scholia were so distant it was as if they'd happened to someone else.

She realized she'd stacked several flat-topped pots of rarely-used cosmetics into a pyramid. Building things. She'd loved building things since she was a child, making extraordinary constructions of wooden blocks or books or her mother's hatboxes. The act of creating, the moment when you set one block atop the other, the act that held contained within it the distant moment when the last block was laid, was like nothing in the world. She'd given it up because Landon, as Crown Prince and then as King, had had too many demands on his time that spilled over onto his Consort, and studying at the

Scholia was incompatible with that. But she'd never lost the passion.

She pulled a pot from the base of the pyramid, making the rest tumble into a pile. A strange new thought grew within her, one she didn't dare look too closely at for fear it might turn out to be stupid. Instead, she let other thoughts circle around it. Why *shouldn't* she make a change? Her usual occupations were worthy, yes, but anyone might help at the hospital or judge a dog show. And she had wealth settled on her by her parents, and the remains of Landon's personal fortune, so she could afford to do almost anything she wanted.

And if what she wanted was to return to the Scholia, who would tell her no?

Her hands automatically tidied the dressing table as more thoughts sleeted through her brain. She had completed three years of a five-year course of study when she left. It was possible the Scholia Masters might make her start over, but some of her knowledge had to apply still. On the other hand, it had been... she counted mentally...twenty-eight years since then, and maybe that was too long to try to pick up where she'd left off.

Fifty years old. She'd be the oldest student there. Discouragement set in, and her hands stilled in the act of replacing her hairbrush. The oldest student, and likely the most famous— she shuddered at the thought of being conspicuous among all those young faces. Suppose the Masters didn't take her seriously? Or worse, suppose they treated her with servility because of her rank?

She gripped the silver handle of the hairbrush so tightly it made her palm ache. No. She was tired of making decisions out of a desire to avoid notice. Either they'd have her, or they wouldn't, and however they treated her, she would not let it prevent her doing what she wanted. True, she had no idea what she would do with a Master's robe and a degree in architecture, but that wasn't important, was it? It was the getting it that mattered.

Veronica set the hairbrush down precisely between a comb and a phial of perfume she couldn't remember acquiring and let out a deep breath. It might be a slightly mad idea, but that made it even more appealing—the idea of doing something no one, least of all herself, would expect. And at worst, the Scholia would turn her down politely, and she could go on as she always had. The thought of that made her shudder again. The idea of returning to the Scholia had gripped her so hard everything else seemed pale and dull by comparison. No, she would *make* them accept her, and then...anything was possible.

She smiled at herself in the dressing table mirror, deepening the wrinkles at the corners of her eyes, and saw for the first time in ages her twenty-two-year-old self looking back at her.

2

———

When Veronica had last been a student, the Scholia had still been housed in the palace, in the cold, high-ceilinged rooms Kerish North had claimed for it over a hundred years before. Now, as her carriage took her over the low, rolling hills of central County Cullinan, she leaned out the window and stared, wide-eyed and astonished.

The Scholia wasn't just one building, as she'd half expected despite knowing the truth; it was more than a dozen buildings of warm, golden stone similar to the walls of Aurilien, solid and reassuring. They looked more like bethels than houses or even businesses, with their arched and spired roofs reaching to heaven. The tallest tower housed a gleaming copper bell Veronica could see even at this distance, which meant it must be enormous.

Emerald lawns as fresh as if fed by the rains of Spring beckoned to her to run barefoot across them, though the gravel paths cutting across them indicated a more conventional kind of traffic. There weren't many people outside at the moment, so classes must be in session. Despite her resolve to be forthright and assertive, Veronica felt relieved that her arrival wouldn't be a grand entrance. The former Consort grants the Scholia the honor of her presence...no, today she wanted to be only one prospective student among many.

An arched stone gateway stood athwart the road, grayer than the many Scholia buildings. There was no wall surrounding the campus, and no gate, just an opening that curved to a point in a tall stone tower with the Scholia crest carved into its face. It was symbolic rather than defensive, and Veronica liked the idea of passing from the outside world into a dedicated place of learning. It made this venture feel even more like starting something new.

She leaned back in her seat and waited for the carriage to come to a halt outside the largest of the buildings, then allowed the driver to help her down, though she didn't need assistance. She'd already discovered the woman felt honored to drive the former Consort, and Veronica didn't mind giving her a chance to feel she'd done something to exercise that respect.

"I'll wait here, Lady North, if that's all right," the woman now said. "Unless you think it will be a while?"

"I don't know how long this will take. Please rest yourself and the horses, and I'll send someone if it's likely to be longer than an hour." Veronica's attention was already on the building, which was constructed in the Valantine style of some two hundred and fifty years previous. She examined the spires, which weren't as tall as the bell tower but were more ornate, and admired the flying buttresses. Valantine architecture wasn't her favorite period, but she had to admit the construction allowed for enormous stained glass windows in walls that no longer had to support the whole weight of the building as the earlier Harandan style had required. This building had two of those windows flanking the enormous double doors of new oak, depicting a man and a woman engaged in study. A little obvious, but the deep jewel-like colors were beautiful.

She put her hand to the door and discovered it swung open as easily as if it weighed nothing at all. So, the builders had adopted more modern design elements instead of slavishly imitating true Valantine construction. She approved of that.

Beyond, a dark hallway made darker by her light-accli- mated eyes extended deep within the building. A handful of people occupied it, going in and out of doors or walking toward or away from her. She stood aside for two people to exit. Neither of them did more than nod. She wasn't as conspicuous as she'd feared.

She removed her bonnet and let her eyes adjust before walking forward. It was cooler inside, a welcome change from the heat of the Summer day. More heavy oak doors, these smaller and banded with iron—another Valantine touch— lined the hall on both sides. Veronica's feet in their soft shoes made almost no sound on the dark floor, which felt smooth despite the rough-hewn look of the stones.

A wide staircase at the far end rose to a landing ornamented with another stained glass window, this one depicting a host of people surrounding a giant book. That was even more obvious than the other two. Passing a few more people, each dressed in the dark robe and red stole of a Master, she ascended to the second floor. It looked just like the first, though the floor was of plain wooden slabs instead of stone. Each door was set into an arch flanked by wooden posts carved to look like pillars twined with ivy. The pillars were Valantine, the ivy a whimsical touch, and Veronica felt a growing desire to meet the craftspeople responsible.

She counted doors until she came to the fourth on the left. None of the doors were labeled. Presumably, if you belonged here, you knew which door was whose. Veronica, still alien—for now—had to rely on the instructions the Magister had sent her. She knocked lightly, then, when there was no immediate response, knocked again hard enough to make her knuckles tingle. A muffled response came from within, and Veronica decided it was an invitation.

The small, cubical room beyond was windowless, but the light of several lanterns illuminated it almost as brightly as sunlight. Paintings of landscapes from all over Tremontane hung on every wall like little static windows on the outside world. The furnishings, a desk, a glass-fronted cabinet, and three chairs, were neither modern nor Valantine, but a more baroque style Veronica put at about fifty or sixty years old, near the beginning of the Sylvestran period. It was an odd choice, but the furniture was elegant and expensive, and Veronica recognized someone's personal taste in the decision.

One of the chairs was occupied by a man who looked barely an adult. He had a blank book balanced on his knee and was scribbling furiously. Veronica didn't look to see what he was writing, though his intensity roused her curiosity. A young woman sat behind the desk. She wore her hair piled high on her head in a haphazard manner, secured by two sticks in the Veriboldan fashion, and looked rather harried. She didn't look up as Veronica entered. "Yes?"

"Veronica North to see the Magister," Veronica said.

The youth's head came up abruptly, and his pencil made a black line across his writing. The woman's expression went from harried to astonished and stopped at embarrassed. "Oh! Lady North, I apologize, I forgot—" She shuffled through a stack of papers as if she hoped an excuse for her rudeness might spring out of them. "I do beg your pardon. You're to go right in, of course."

Veronica smiled and nodded. She'd found, over the last thirty years, that calmness and a reluctance to take offense could carry someone far. "Thank you."

The second door looked the same as the first, iron-banded oak, so it was only her imagination that it glowed with promise. Veronica knocked, just to be polite, and then opened the door.

Bright sunlight met her eyes, making the secretary's office seem dim by comparison. The light came from a row of windows overlooking the lawns and the bell tower. Though they had heavy maroon curtains, all the drapes were drawn back, and between the windows' size and the gleaming brightness of their panes, the effect was similar to that of Queen Genevieve's old drawing room near the top of the palace, which had floor to ceiling windows on two of its walls. It felt as if the outdoors was only waiting for an invitation to enter.

The furnishings matched the ones in the secretary's office, the desk and cabinetry ornamented with so many curlicues and carved oak leaves they looked more like art pieces than functional furniture. The carpet was Eskandelic and floral and perfectly matched the ornate desk and the maroon curtains. A brass chandelier hung from the high ceiling, unlit and doing nothing to illuminate the room, but its crystals caught the sunlight and fractured it into tiny rainbows.

Donald Montgomery, the Magister of the Scholia, rose from his seat behind the desk. "Lady North, welcome," he said in his thin, wispy tenor. "Please, have a seat."

The Magister's manners were as old-fashioned as the décor, Veronica reflected; he knew not to offer his hand to a lady, as it had formerly been the lady's decision whom to shake hands with. Veronica extended her hand for him to clasp. His grip was firm, and his skin was as dry and inelastic as her own. It was so strange to realize he was only a few years older than she.

She sat in one of the two spindle-legged chairs, also of the same baroque Sylvestran era, pulled up to face the desk. Its cushion was firm and well-compressed, not soft, which confirmed her guess that all this furniture was antique, not modern copies. Someone had spent a fortune equipping these two rooms.

"Your letter was quite a surprise," the Magister was saying. "I didn't realize you had been a Scholia student."

"It was a long time ago," Veronica said. "I left because I married and had a child, and there were other demands on my time. But I loved my studies."

"Yes, I'm sure the Consort must be very busy." The Magister leaned back in his seat and folded his thin hands atop the desk. "But now...I apologize if this is rude, but surely your time is still occupied? One hears of the Dowager Consort opening charity hospitals, supervising different organizations..."

Veronica suppressed her irritation at his term of address. He was only being polite. "I enjoy helping others, of course, but much of what I do could be done by anyone. I feel drawn to complete my course of study—surely that's not so unusual?"

"Of course not, of course not. But the Dowager Consort—"

"Please, I would prefer you call me Lady North." *Veronica* was far too informal for their proposed relationship, though she doubted she could have gotten him to use her first name even if they were to be colleagues. "And my title is irrelevant when it comes to scholastic pursuits. When I was a student, I had any number of colleagues who were noble. One of them later became the Baron of Hightop. And the instructors treated us all the same."

The Magister nodded. "Certainly. My apologies." He sat forward. "You realize, with the interruption to your studies—the time that has passed—you'll have to repeat some of the coursework."

"I expected that. I had thought...perhaps some sort of evaluation, to know where I should be placed?" Veronica's heart beat faster, and she felt like kicking herself. Becoming nervous over something so simple as taking charge of her own education! She should have done this years ago, if she had grown so timid.

"I intended to propose that, yes." The Magister's hands flexed once, his bony fingers extending and relaxing. "I am certain you won't need to repeat much. Architecture, after all, stays where it's put, yes?" He chuckled, and Veronica laughed with him, though it hadn't been much of a joke.

"Yes, and it's been a hobby of mine over the last thirty years, observing new trends in construction," she said.

"Excellent, excellent." He smiled. Veronica's eyes were drawn to the gleam of sunlight off his bald head. He might be a reflective surface in full daylight. She silently chided herself for the cruel thought, but not very hard. "If I may be direct, the fees are not small."

A reflective, greedy surface. "I can afford them. And I intend to make a bequest to fund another student as well. Someone deserving who otherwise might not be able to afford schooling. I'm sure you know of someone who fits that description." She knew it came close to bribery, but she did not intend to be denied, and if her money could grease some wheels, all the better.

The Magister's smile deepened, making him look like a hairless cat who'd found the cream pot. "Your generosity is astounding, my lady."

"It's nothing, really."

"Then I suppose it's just a matter of scheduling," the Magister continued. "You'll want to arrange for lodgings in Knightsbury, which is the closest—"

"Actually, I had hoped to stay on campus," Veronica said. "I understand you have housing for students?"

The Magister's mouth fell open slightly, and his fingers jerked again. "Why, yes, but...surely the Dow—Lady North would prefer...they're not luxurious, and I don't know—"

"I know I am not your usual kind of student, but I would rather not draw any more attention to myself than necessary." Veronica leaned forward a little, a gesture that invited the Magister to lean closer as well. "Please, Magister. I may be royalty, but that does not make me any better or worse a student than someone who came up from the gutter on a scholarship. Or on *my* scholarship. Surely you can indulge me in this one whim?"

The Magister now looked as if the cream pot had been unexpectedly full of vinegar. "Certainly, certainly," he said, not sounding very certain. "If you...that is, it is an additional expense, but there are always rooms...of course you know your own mind."

"I do." Veronica met his gaze directly. She refused to entertain the discomfort she always felt in confronting someone. This was nothing. It barely qualified as a confrontation. And she would not let her own stupid diffidence interfere with getting what she wanted—what she was increasingly convinced she needed.

The Magister smiled, some of his good humor restored. "Then...welcome to the Scholia, Lady North. The Autumn term begins in approximately five weeks, during which time your instructors will determine your revised course of study."

"Thank you, Magister." Veronica rose, prompting the Magister to mimic her. "I appreciate your willingness to accommodate me."

"Not at all, not at all. I am certain you will make a fine Master someday." The Magister smiled again. The expression made his words sound less patronizing. Veronica shook his hand again without saying anything, and excused herself.

The carriage driver rose from where she'd been seated on the ground when Veronica approached. "That was quick, my lady," she said. "Where else can I take you?"

"I'd...actually, I think I'll take a look at the buildings," Veronica said. "Do you mind waiting a little while longer?"

"Of course not." The woman leaned against the carriage as if to suggest she could comfortably wait all day. "Take your time, my lady."

The gravel paths were laid out in a random way Veronica suspected would show a pattern if observed from the air. If so, the birds were the only ones who appreciated it. Students in ordinary shirts and trousers and a few black-robed Masters crossed the lawn more directly, ignoring the paths in favor of getting from one place to another as quickly as possible. Veronica stuck to the paths, feeling even more like an outsider despite the Magister's words. She also felt, superstitiously, as if walking the paths invoked some kind of sympathetic magic that bound the students to this place, invoking the lines of power on their scholastic behalf. It was an odd thought, but it satisfied her.

Almost all the buildings resembled the main one, with towers and arches that led nowhere and fluted columns and many, many stained glass windows. Veronica had heard Duncan complain, not very sharply, about how much of the treasury had gone into building the Scholia. Now she understood his concerns. The architects had outdone themselves if what they wanted was to recreate Valantine architecture on the scale of the palace, but more unified, and it must have cost a fortune. If the Crown had paid for even half of what she saw, it would have been an unparalleled expenditure.

But it was beautiful. Valantine architecture en masse was an awe-inspiring sight, even to Veronica's eyes. The few buildings that didn't match, set well back from those circling the courtyard, looked like stables, a dairy, and perhaps housing for servants. Even those were beautiful, if modest. Veronica suspected they were intended not to draw the eye away from the main part of the campus.

The lone building near the courtyard that did not match the others still bore the marks of the architects' vision; it had only one spired tower, was low to the ground, and had no stained glass windows, only rows of square four-paned ones in plain brown wooden frames. Even so, like the outbuildings, it didn't look out of place. It looked, Veronica mused, like the younger brother of all the other buildings that would eventually grow to look like them.

The sound of an argument drifted toward her on the warm breezes, coming from an open window in the low building. Veronica altered her course so she wouldn't come close enough to eavesdrop, but she could still tell it was a man and a woman who were very angry. The idea that anyone might feel inclined to argue in this peaceful place disturbed her. Then she laughed at herself. Of course people still argued. This was the Scholia, not heaven.

She left the argument behind and headed for the center of the pattern of paths, where the second largest building stood. Though it was smaller in size than the Magister's administration building, it was the tallest, with the bell tower a slim finger pointing to heaven. The oak doors stood open, revealing an open space filled with pews. Veronica had not expected to find a bethel on the Scholia grounds, at least not one so large.

She entered, curious to see this unexpected sight. No candles were lit, and the warm Summer air filled the space, which would otherwise be cool and dark. Veronica sniffed the air, but smelled nothing but the warm green scent of grass and the darker smell of wood from the pews aligned on both sides of the central aisle. The niches in the walls for private prayer were all empty, and the dais at the head of the bethel's main room bore rows of upholstered chairs, also unused. The room felt completely unoccupied. Veronica had heard others speak of sensing heaven's presence in a bethel, but that had never happened to her.

She walked around the periphery, looking into the niches. Each was equipped with a padded kneeler and a copy of the *Book of Haran*. Veronica wasn't sure how anyone could consider this private, given that you would have the entire bethel at your back and the niches were shallow, but again, worship wasn't something she cared much for. It was a very nice bethel, though, less ornate on the inside than the Magister's office, and she wondered how much use it saw.

When she exited the bethel, the green lawns and pebbled

paths were crowded with people. Surprised, she stood with her hand on the door frame and watched for a few minutes. Students laughed and chattered at top volume, or strode along in conference with black-robed figures wearing red or blue stoles. Some of them ran, dodging others, from one building to another. Veronica felt overwhelmed at the noise and commotion. Then she remembered she'd chosen this, and her disquiet faded. She would learn to be part of this institution, and all of this would be a commonplace.

Even so, she waited a little longer until the paths cleared before making her way back to her carriage. She had five weeks to prepare, and so much to do in that time. Including telling Elspeth what she had in mind; she hadn't informed her niece she intended to return to the Scholia, just in case the worst happened and they wouldn't have her. Elspeth hated injustice and was likely to have come down hard on the Magister to get him to change his mind, and Veronica didn't want that kind of help.

"Back to Knightsbury," she told the driver. As the Magister had suggested, it was the closest city to the Scholia, only a mile away, and she'd taken rooms there after the two-day journey from Aurilien. "Thank you for your service."

"It's my pleasure, my lady," the woman said. "May I ask— were you successful?"

Veronica settled herself in the carriage. "I was," she said. "I'm a Scholia student again."

———————————

3

*M*aster Catherine Lansing's office was the mirror-reversed twin of the Magister's, on the opposite side of the central building where the administrative offices were. Its wide windows, in shade at this hour of the morning, looked out over nearby Knightsbury, which was a pleasant young city vibrant with traffic whose distant noises filtered through the open window in snatches of sound. The furnishings were of the same Sylvestran style as the Magister's, carved all over with grapes and pears and apples so the desk looked like a greengrocer's wooden nightmare and the handles of the sideboard cabinet were invisible.

That was where the resemblance ended. Papers and cardboard folders covered almost every inch of the desk and were stacked several inches high in four piles on the sideboard. Stacks of paper nearly doubled the height of the short, utilitarian table, unornamented and modern, that stood beneath the center window. Inkwells and jars crammed full of pens occupied whatever space on the desk the paper didn't take up. Even the chair Veronica currently sat in had had a box on it before Lansing removed it, with many apologies.

Now Lansing sat behind her desk and regarded Veronica with wide hazel eyes the same color as Veronica's own. Veronica judged her to be in her mid-thirties, young to have earned four black bands on the blue stole indicating a Master who was pursuing the advanced degree of a Magister. She wore her dark brown hair cut short to brush her chin; at the moment, it was in disarray, wisps of it flying everywhere as if she'd been running. "It's an honor to meet you," Lansing said. "Please excuse the mess. I'm afraid it builds and builds—so many things to keep track of, and not enough filing space..."

Her voice trailed off. Veronica waited politely for her to finish her thought, but it appeared after a moment or two that she was done speaking. "I admit this is all very new to me," she said. "We didn't have tutors in—well, thirty years ago." The room was too warm for comfort, despite the open windows, and Veronica hoped she wouldn't sweat; it might make her appear nervous. She *was* nervous, true, but she didn't want that to show.

"Oh, no, that's a new development," Lansing said, rather eagerly. She leaned forward, shoving a few stacks of paper to one side to lean her elbows on her desk. "The courses of study the Scholia demands are rather intensive—well, *you* know that —and it was discovered that students became overwhelmed with having to juggle all the requirements. Now a student's tutor keeps track of their advancement, assists in planning the course of study, answers questions..."

"That makes sense," Veronica said, though she didn't remember ever having trouble keeping up with the Scholia's academic requirements when she was a student. She hadn't liked that rather personal "*you* know," as if Lansing wanted to establish their relationship as equals or friends rather than that of tutor and student. "And we'll meet once a week?"

"That's right. Though of course I'm available at any time if you have problems." Lansing sounded rather as if she hoped Veronica would have problems needing her intervention. "Now, I've discussed your situation with the Magister and gone over your academic record. You were twenty-two courses away from achieving the robe when you left."

"That's right."

"And your primary course of study was architectonics."

Veronica nodded. They'd just called it architecture or engineering in her day. Inwardly, she winced at how old that made her sound and resolved never to use the phrase again.

Lansing opened a buff-colored cardboard folder and sorted through its contents. "Your work was excellent. Really, with these marks, I don't think you should have to repeat any courses, just pick up where you left off..."

When Veronica realized the fading pause meant Lansing was once again finished speaking, she said, "I'm not sure that's fair. I've been away from serious study for twenty-eight years, and I'm sure some things have changed since then. And I know my mathematics skills are rusty. I don't want to find myself in classes whose basics I've forgotten." She also didn't think her work had been all that spectacular. Better than average, certainly, and she was exceptional at understanding the underlying principles of architecture, but she was no genius.

Lansing's eyes widened again. "Oh, but really, *you* shouldn't have to repeat—"

"I want to earn the robe, Master Lansing," Veronica said,

feeling for once no embarrassment about interrupting, "not have it given me. I assure you I'm not upset at having to take some classes again. Now, what kind of course of study does that require?"

Lansing blinked. "Well, if you're sure..." She shuffled through the papers again and withdrew two. "There are five classes you should probably repeat before proceeding further in architectonics. And it seems you have some fundamentals pending. History, natural philosophy, a law course...you lack eight fundamentals and fourteen discipline classes. With the repeats, that's a total of twenty-seven classes." She sounded almost apologetic. "That's two to three years of study, depending on how rigorously you intend to tackle it."

"I thought I should make this first term a sort of experiment, to see how difficult it will be." Veronica heard herself speak in the soothing tones she'd used on Francis as a child when he became anxious, and she felt uncomfortable. This was a grown woman, her Scholia superior and tutor, and it wasn't Veronica's job to make her feel at ease. Surely that ought to go the other way around?

"At any rate," she went on, trying to sound brisk and certain, "I was thinking five classes this Autumn term, and evaluate whether I want to continue in Winter term next year or take a break until Spring." She had no intention of taking it slowly; she felt impatient with herself for having waited this long, and any delay felt like hooks embedded in her flesh, dragging her onward.

"Five classes—that's ambitious," Lansing said, her eyes wide once again.

"I don't think so. It never was a problem before." Veronica's impatience rose, startling her. She wasn't an impatient person, but Lansing's eagerness, and now her reluctance, felt like the Master either didn't want her there or wanted her there too much. She briefly considered asking for a different tutor, but that would mean stirring up trouble, and that wasn't the sort of person she was.

"But...no, you're right, Lady North, it shouldn't be a problem." Lansing took up a pen and dipped it in one of the open inkwells that threatened to spill all over the sea of paperwork. "If you'll allow me...?"

Confused, Veronica nodded. Allow what?

Lansing proceeded to write on the topmost paper she'd removed from Veronica's folder, with many pauses and staring off past Veronica through the windows. "A balance between discipline and fundamentals...let's see...I want you to retake the third mathematics class, which will assess your skills and give us an idea of how to structure the rest of your mathematics study. I think you should also retake the second architectonics class, fundamentals of engineering. It's perhaps more basic than you need, but if you can pass that with high marks, you won't have to retake the third class."

Veronica nodded. Lansing, despite all the pauses, suddenly sounded confident. It was much more as Veronica had hoped her tutor would be.

"As to the other classes, I believe a balance of three of your remaining fundamentals would be best. Principles of Devisery...a history course, probably, yes, art history—have you a preference for an historical era?"

"I've always liked Harandan architecture," Veronica said.

"We offer a class on Harandan era iconography and the transition from abstract to representational art I think you'll enjoy. And...I believe there are still seats in Master Tyndale's fundamentals of law course. He's a demanding teacher, but you did say you wanted to experiment..."

Veronica was coming to realize Lansing ended most of her sentences with that drawn-out, fading sound. "It sounds excellent. Thank you."

"We're all very excited to welcome you as a student, Lady North. You're such an inspiration." Lansing was back to sounding too eager again. Veronica's anxiety deepened.

"Am I? How is that?" she said, trying to maintain a light, curious tone even though she felt she knew what was coming.

"Well, of course! Returning to your studies after nearly three decades away...you're an example to everyone that education doesn't have to be limited to the young." Lansing leaned forward again, beaming. "And the Dowager Consort—you could choose to do anything. Your presence honors us."

Anxiety coiled like a writhing snake in the pit of Veronica's stomach. Being conspicuous had never come easily to her, not even when she had been the Consort and public appearances were the norm. Briefly, she wondered if she'd made a mistake. Too old, too famous—these next two to three years might become a nightmare. Then she took hold of herself and gave herself a mental shake. She'd endured far worse than standing out in a crowd of twenty-somethings, far worse than being a novelty and a figurehead. This was nothing.

"I prefer to be simply Lady North," she said mildly. "And... thank you. But I hope I will not receive preferential treatment because of my rank. I know I can't be just an ordinary student, but I don't expect favors."

"Of course not." Lansing's tone of voice was surprised, but the look in her eyes, that reverential look she'd worn when Veronica had entered her office, told Veronica her tutor would bear careful watching. She did not want Lansing crippling her education in a misguided attempt to give the former Consort what she believed was Veronica's due.

Veronica rose. "Thank you again. I look forward to classes starting."

"I'll have a copy of your class schedule sent to your rooms," Lansing said, rising as well and extending her hand. "I understand you're staying in the student dormitories?" She sounded curious rather than judgmental, which was a relief after the morning Veronica had already had, trying to arrange for her housing. Everyone else had looked at her as if she were mad.

"That's right. I'm supposed to see my quarters after this." Veronica hoped her demands had been taken seriously, though she knew "demand" was the wrong word for how diffidently she'd approached the housing administrator and the dormitory chatelaine. She really needed to learn to be assertive.

"Very well. Good day, Lady North, and remember—I'm here any time you need assistance, or if you want to talk about anything..."

Veronica nodded. Yes, Master Lansing wanted to be Veronica's friend. More accurately, she wanted to be the Dowager Consort's friend. Veronica supposed that was possible, but she'd had too many years of deflecting sycophants to be much interested in pandering to Lansing's desires.

She left the central building and crossed the yard, staying carefully on the paths. It was the fallow time, the space between terms when no classes were held, and she had the yard to herself though she knew there were still students and Masters around somewhere. She still wasn't familiar with all the fourteen buildings of the Scholia and its outbuildings, but she could find the refectory—the low-roofed building with all the square windows—and she knew which of the edifices were the women's dormitories.

All four dormitories looked very similar, with towers rather than spires at their four corners and tall, arched windows that gave the three stories a very startled look. Smooth-sided pillars formed roofed colonnades that encircled each building, providing welcome shade on this sweltering late-Summer day. Most of the windows stood open, which wouldn't have been possible in a true Valantine building. Veronica felt grateful that the unknown architects hadn't thought themselves bound to tradition over comfort.

The dormitories were named for virtues, Honor and Patience, Fortitude and Temperance. Veronica wondered if the names had any influence on their characters, or on the characters of the people they housed. If that were so, the one she'd chosen, Patience House, ought to stand her in good stead.

Patience House was the one on the left. Veronica entered and knocked on the first door she came to. It didn't open immediately, and she stood with her hands clasped before her, feeling awkward again. Finally, Mistress Holyoak, the dormitory chatelaine, appeared. "Lady North," she said. "I wasn't expecting you."

"You did say to return at noon," Veronica said. Mistress Holyoak's gaze withered her, made her feel ten years old and caught snitching pastries from the kitchen. She could hear her voice growing smaller and quieter and made herself stand up straight and face the woman directly. Mistress Holyoak was shorter than Veronica, with gray-streaked black hair braided and coiled around the back of her head in an iron-hard construction rifle balls could probably bounce off. Veronica had yet to see her smile.

"I did," Mistress Holyoak said, her frown deepening. The implication that she had expected Veronica to change her mind stiffened Veronica's resolve.

"You said you would have a room ready for me by noon," she said in a louder voice. "I hope it's not an imposition."

"Of course not, Lady North." Mistress Holyoak—Veronica would never dare address her by just her surname, even in the privacy of her own head—pushed past Veronica and walked away without another word. Veronica hurried after her.

They climbed stairs to the third floor, where the hall split in two directions. Traditional Valantine architecture dictated a central well and no interior rooms, so Veronica judged the hall would make a rectangle, with rooms on both the inside and the outside. She hoped the antagonistic chatelaine hadn't put her on the inside. There would be windows regardless, but Veronica didn't want hers looking out on a depressing courtyard three stories below.

But Mistress Holyoak led the way to a door in the right-hand corner on the outside. "I'm afraid this is all we have," she said, opening the door. "You can always take rooms in Knightsbury."

Veronica entered and suppressed a gasp. This was a tower room, perfectly round, and was fully furnished in a modern style that appealed to Veronica's expert eye. A small ash table and two chairs were drawn up between the arched windows, while a sofa and armchair upholstered in blue and silver brocade promised comfortable seats for anyone wanting to read or chat with a friend. A tap over a basin and a small single-burner stove made a kitchen nook next to the table. The room was stuffy, the windows closed, and there was no fireplace, but Veronica loved it instantly.

An archway to the left proved to contain a spiral staircase, its old stone niche cooler than the sitting room. Without waiting for Mistress Holyoak's invitation, Veronica mounted the stairs and found herself in a dream of a bedroom, a small, cozy chamber made cozier by the large four-poster bed filling most of it. A wardrobe had been crammed into the remaining space, and between that and an old-fashioned wash table, there was barely enough room to move around.

It was, if anything, even hotter than the sitting room, and Veronica sidled around the bed to open a window. Then she stood for a moment, breathing in the delicious scent of warm grass and soil. The mattresses were bare, and the wardrobe door hung open, revealing that it was empty. Veronica pictured the bed covered with her own favorite quilt, the wardrobe full of her clothes, and could easily see herself living here for the next two years.

She descended the stairs to find Mistress Holyoak standing with her arms crossed over her capacious bosom. "The furniture upstairs can't be changed," the chatelaine said. "We can't get it out without taking it apart. We had an Eskandelic princess studying here last year and she had a thing for Tremontanan styles, insisted we indulge her."

"Eskandelics don't have princesses," Veronica said absently. Her mind was already on how she would decorate. No fireplaces in either room, but she could buy Devices to heat them when winter made that necessary. And no drapes to hide the beautiful arches of the windows. It was unlikely anyone could see into the tower rooms, anyway.

"I'm sure you'd know better than I, Lady North," Mistress Holyoak said. Her tone of voice was bland in a way that concealed disdain, but Veronica discovered she no longer cared what Mistress Holyoak thought of her. Probably the woman had given her these rooms as a punishment—they were no doubt smaller than most, and the stairs might be considered an inconvenience—but if she'd intended that, she'd shot wide of the mark.

"I can move in immediately, yes?" Veronica had brought only her personal possessions, intending to purchase furniture in Knightsbury, and she was glad that wouldn't be necessary.

"Of course." Mistress Holyoak handed her two large iron keys, perfectly in keeping with the rest of the architecture. "Your room key, and a key to the outer door, which we lock at midnight. I've got a spare copy of your room key for emergencies. There are four washrooms on every floor, so I hope you don't mind sharing, and commodes outside each washroom. We have the latest Devices installed. No men beyond the common room and study rooms downstairs, and no women in the men's dormitories either. I'm sure *you* won't need the reminder."

The way she said it made Veronica want to find a man and drag him into her bedchamber. How dare Mistress Holyoak, who had to be nearly her own age, imply she was too old for romance? All right, she probably was too old for assignations, but Mistress Holyoak's tone of voice, that dismissive, scornful tone, hurt Veronica in a way she'd thought she'd left behind forever at Landon's death.

"I wouldn't be so inconsiderate, no," she managed to say in a polite voice.

Mistress Holyoak sniffed. "There are study rooms on the ground floor in addition to the common room. You can meet with your study group there if you wish, but near the end of term you'll have to schedule their use. As I said, I lock up at midnight, and even though you can let yourself in, we look sharply at anyone who returns late night after night. There's no curfew, much as I think there should be. Students aren't sensible enough to be trusted with that responsibility."

"When I was a student before, I lived in my family home in Aurilien. This is very different." Veronica hoped she still sounded polite. She had never liked people like Mistress Holyoak, fond of enforcing rules at the expense of treating people like people.

"Very different, yes." Mistress Holyoak turned and left the room, forcing Veronica to hurry to keep up as she strode down the hall. "That's the washroom—all the washroom doors look the same. For an extra fee, a maid will tidy your rooms once a week, and if you're honorable, you won't make much work for her by leaving food all over the place."

"That won't be necessary," Veronica said. She liked the idea of caring for those perfect, small rooms herself.

"I see," Mistress Holyoak said as if Veronica had suggested something vulgar. She glared at Veronica briefly. "Any questions?"

Veronica couldn't think of anything she wanted to ask the hostile chatelaine. "Not at the moment. I'm sure if I think of anything—"

"That's fine, then. Welcome to Patience House, Lady North." Mistress Holyoak disappeared down the stairs without waiting to see if Veronica would follow.

When the chatelaine had disappeared, Veronica turned and walked slowly back toward her rooms. *Her rooms.* It made everything suddenly feel more real.

She realized, as she passed the washroom, that she needed to use the commode. Curious about what Mistress Holyoak meant by "latest Devices," she entered one of the two cubicles flanking the washroom door. It turned out the commode was a rugged porcelain Device that would be freezing in winter, but it whisked her waste away and emitted a puff of flowery air as it did so. Very modern. When she considered the kind of toilet conditions a real Valantine edifice would have, she was even more grateful no one had felt impelled into slavish imitation.

When she emerged, it was almost into the arms of another woman leaving the washroom. "I beg your pardon," Veronica said, her voice pale with embarrassment.

"It happens," the woman said. She wore a dressing gown of patterned Veriboldan silk and house slippers, and her wet brown hair draggled over her shoulders, darkening the silk. Her eyes had an exotic tilt to them that made her look like a cat, but rather than giving her a sly look, they made her lovely face seem even more approachable. "You're Lady North, aren't you?"

"I am. I suppose I'm unmistakable." Veronica smiled and hoped her inner turmoil didn't show.

"I didn't expect to see you in Patience House, but everyone knows you've enrolled for Autumn term, and—forgive my rudeness, but you're older than the rest of us and very recognizable." The woman shifted the woven bag she held that seemed to contain toiletries and a face cloth. She didn't sound judgmental, just curious, and Veronica's anxieties eased.

"It's not rude. I know I'm different. I hope it won't matter," she said.

The woman nodded. "Samantha Wilde," she said, extending her free hand. "I'm just down the hall that way."

"I have the...I think it's the southwest corner tower," Veronica said, examining a mental map.

Samantha's catlike eyes widened. "Arakelian Jennea's aerie? Did you anger Mistress Holyoak somehow?"

Veronica's lips twitched in a smile. "I think she resents me wanting to be a Scholia student at my age."

"Well, she certainly intended to punish you. That place freezes in winter. You don't have to put up with that, you know. I'm sure there are other empty rooms."

"She said this was the only one."

Samantha scowled. "That can't be true."

"It doesn't matter. I love it."

Samantha let out a short laugh. "We'll see how much you love it come Wintersmeet."

"I don't see why. Haven't any of you heard of heating Devices?"

To her surprise, Samantha's brow furrowed briefly before the woman said, "I...don't know that any of us are accustomed to throwing that kind of wealth around. We're not poor, exactly —can't be poor if we can afford a Scholia education—but those Devices aren't inexpensive."

Veronica's heart sank. And to think she'd come so close to making a friend. "I'm sorry, I shouldn't have presumed—I didn't think—"

Samantha shook her head and smiled. "No, I'm being foolish. Why should you be embarrassed just because you're the Dow—"

"Please don't call me that," Veronica said, feeling a little desperate. "Just...it's just Veronica, really. Since we're both students."

"I suppose Dowager does conjure up images of a little old lady in a lace cap and mittens," Samantha said with a grin.

"Very well. Veronica. Let me get dressed, and I'll help you with your things—you are moving in now, aren't you?"

"I have to go back to Knightsbury, but yes."

"Give me a few minutes, and I'll go with you. Then I can show you around the place, maybe introduce you to some people. I know it's quiet now, but wait until the dead day."

Finally, something Veronica remembered. The dead day, the last day before the new term started. Counter to its name, it was the busiest and loudest day of the term. "I can imagine."

Samantha smiled again and hurried away, saying, "At least you have rooms to yourself. Last year I had a dormitory sister who snored."

Veronica laughed and followed Samantha more slowly. Her anxieties had all but disappeared. True, not everyone would be as friendly as Samantha, but she'd begun to hope she might eventually fit in here, after all.

4

The mirror inside the wardrobe door was narrow and too short to show all of Veronica's body at once, but it was sufficient for her to make sure her gown was straight and her hair tidy. She smoothed hair behind her ears for the fiftieth time, then closed the door with a deliberate click so she couldn't obsess over her appearance anymore. It wasn't so much that she cared how she looked; making dozens of little changes was a substitute for giving in to the anxiety that gnawed at her insides.

She plucked at the skirt of her gown, a lightweight, pale gold muslin with no lace trimming and a wide ribbon for a waistband, high above her actual waist as fashion demanded. Fashion. Hah. She had no idea what passed for fashion among the students. Possibly she should wear trousers, but she'd always preferred dresses, and maybe her comfort was more important, given that nothing else about this day was comfortable.

She sat on the edge of her bed and squeezed her eyes shut. Her intellect told her *everything is fine, you're just another student, everyone else is so concerned about their own problems they won't care what you do.* Her emotions, and her churning anxiety, knew her intellect was a fool, like those confident people who never worried about making mistakes in public and didn't care that they were stared at. Fifty years old was old enough not to let other people's opinions affect her. But her heart couldn't stop throwing up scenarios in which she made herself ridiculous with her mistakes.

Her watch Device chimed the hour. Ten o'clock. Her first lecture was in half an hour. Automatically she rose and descended the spiral staircase to her sitting room. She gave herself a moment to enjoy the sight. She hadn't brought much from the palace, just a few decorative touches, but they made the place feel home-like.

Her statuette of the famous sculpture *Giselle* by Harvey d'Arnot stood atop the bookcase she'd bought in Knightsbury. The sculptor had caught the little huntress, clad in an impractical length of cloth draped around her waist, leaping into the air and shooting past herself at an unseen prey. Veronica loved the pent-up energy of the original, which stood in a public square near the palace, and had been delighted when d'Arnot had presented her with the bronze miniature. It marked one of the few times she'd felt being Consort was a benefit.

She drew in a deep breath and let it out. She was getting worked up over nothing. Whatever happened, she wasn't likely to leave the Scholia over it, and if she made mistakes, they'd soon be forgotten. She was uncertain, she was diffident, but she wasn't a coward.

She gathered up her satchel, bought new in Knightsbury

the day she'd ordered the bookcase, and checked its contents once more. Pencils, a penknife for sharpening them, and five blank books for note taking, one for each class. Uncertainty crept over her again. She didn't know if lectures had changed since she had last been a student. Maybe—

No. Not a coward. She was going to approach this as she always had approached her studies, and if no one else did it that way, well, it wasn't as if she intended to do their studying for them. She slung the satchel on its long strap over her shoulder and left the room, locking the door behind her and dropping the key into the satchel's outside pocket.

The halls of Patience House were remarkably empty, with only a few young women passing Veronica or using the stairs. All of them glanced at Veronica and then looked away quickly in a way that suggested they would stare when she couldn't see them anymore. This no longer bothered her after ten days of living in the dormitory, with increasing numbers of students arriving for Autumn term. Thanks to Samantha's intervention, she'd even gotten to know some of them. Staring was fine; she knew she was a novelty. Eventually, her novelty would wear off.

The yard, by contrast, was full of students taking advantage of the half-hour between lectures to mingle with friends. The sound of hundreds of conversations washed over Veronica like a dry tide. Strangely, it didn't overwhelm her. The knowledge that none of these people were interested in her comforted her, made her feel more at home. Even so, she stayed on the gravel paths. The small round rocks crunched pleasantly under her soft shoes, though the sound was inaudible thanks to all the voices. The sensation was enough.

Her anxiety had led her to explore the campus thoroughly in the days since arriving. She knew which schools were housed in which buildings and every classroom and lecture hall her classes were held in. She knew how long it took to get from any of those rooms to the others and had allowed extra time to pass through the crowds. She was as prepared as it was possible to be. Her anxieties still thought she'd forgotten something.

Lyton Hall, home to the law school and the library studies school, was one of the larger buildings on campus. It reminded Veronica that Scholia-trained questioners and law-speakers were the most highly regarded in Tremontane. Duncan had received his training in the old Scholia, though he had chosen not to take the robe. It occurred to Veronica that she and Duncan never spoke about the Scholia despite their common experience. She wasn't sure what to make of that.

She passed through Lyton Hall's great double doors, thrown open as if in welcome. More silent stares, more hushed whispering whose content she could guess. She stiffened her spine and pretended not to notice. None of them meant any harm.

Master Tyndale's lecture hall, windowless and oppressive, was on the ground floor, but the tiered seating that curved around the lecture platform made it reach a full two stories tall. Veronica, in her explorations, had discovered some of the lecture halls had balconies, but hadn't yet learned if those were for students or for interested guests. The seats here were high-backed wooden chairs on tiers deep enough that someone sitting on one chair could kick someone sitting beneath them in the back of the head. The image increased Veronica's anxiety. Naturally she would never do that on purpose, but suppose in an idle moment her foot connected with someone's head?

She crossed the lecture platform to the nearest aisle, which rose a few steps at a time to the top of the lecture hall. Small square landings at each tier relieved the steep stairs, and she climbed to the second landing and made her way to a seat near the center of the row. She'd given this choice far too much thought over the past few days until she became impatient with herself. Not too high, not too low, and in the middle because she anticipated arriving early and didn't want to inconvenience other students by making them climb past her. There was no way to know how her choice would look, so she decided she didn't care. It wasn't true, but she was firm enough with herself that she believed it.

She settled her satchel, withdrew a blank book and pencil, and sat watching the other students as they entered. The lecture hall was filling up fast, to Veronica's surprise. She remembered what Lansing had said about there being a few seats left in this class and guessed it wasn't so surprising. If this Master Tyndale was as good as Lansing had implied, it made sense people would want to take his class.

She surreptitiously looked at her watch. 10:22. Someone approached along her row and took a seat next to her. He was a short, stocky young man with thick black hair who moved with a contained impatience as if he wished he could run instead of walk. He nodded at her with no sign of recognition, removed a penknife from inside his vest, and began sharpening a pencil. Wood shavings flicked everywhere. Veronica watched him covertly, fascinated by the swift energy with which he shaped the tip. He didn't seem to have a blank book on him, so she didn't know why the pencil mattered, but he certainly wielded the knife as if the pencil was the most important thing in creation.

Someone on her other side gently bumped Veronica's foot and apologized. It was a young woman dressed in shirt and trousers who gave Veronica a smile before turning to converse with the woman next to her. Veronica's tension grew. She hadn't guessed how it would feel to be completely ignored. She told herself it was better than being stared at and opened her blank book, her eyes focusing on the white, unmarked first page. The impulse to doodle struck her, but she suppressed it. Time enough for doodling when she knew what this class held.

Distantly, she heard the great bell in the bethel toll the start of the next class hour. The lecture hall was nearly full now. Veronica had just congratulated herself on her foresight in coming early when a door at the back of the platform banged open and Master Tyndale entered. He carried only a thin book bound in black leather, twice the size of her blank book, which he set on the lectern at the center of the platform. Instantly, the hushed conversations went silent, replaced by the smaller sounds of people shifting their weight or tapping pencils against armrests.

Tyndale rested one hand on the lectern and regarded the students. His blond hair shone in the light from the Devices illuminating the room, but from her position Veronica could tell he was about her own age. That was unnerving, but the thought of instructors even younger than she unnerved her more than that. He was also attractive, which realization made her feel even more uncomfortable. Being attracted to her instructors was inappropriate, and certainly nothing she'd ever felt the last time she was a student.

She crossed her legs at the ankles and made herself look at him dispassionately. His attractiveness was marred by the stern set of his jaw and an unusual, shallow look to his green eyes, as if they were made of glass and could express no deep feeling.

"The study of the law is a noble profession," Tyndale said abruptly, not opening his book. "It is the field in which humanity most nearly approaches the divine, as we judge and are judged. It is also a solemn profession, requiring diligence of thought and clarity of intent. The law is pure reason, dispassionate and logical. It is also the instrument of pure mercy. In this class you will gain an understanding of the fundamental principles of legal reasoning. While most of you will not pursue the law as a vocation, you should leave this class with an enhanced ability to reason and judge appropriately."

Veronica's assessment of his attractiveness dwindled as he spoke. He didn't sound bored, or angry, or pleased; instead, his voice was a steady near-monotone that suggested his listeners didn't deserve to be addressed by him. And yet she didn't think it was arrogance, which implied he wasn't entitled to his superior attitude. It was more like an utter certainty that he knew what would happen in the next moment, and the next, and the next, all the way into tomorrow and next week and beyond, and was unimpressed by anything he saw in the future.

She listened to him lay out the structure of the class and took careful notes, though she seemed to be the only one near her doing so. The man on her right glanced at her book once, then at her, and then returned his attention to Tyndale. The woman on her left ignored her completely. Veronica soon became absorbed in Tyndale's words as the introduction turned into a lecture. His voice avoided being truly monotonous just enough that she wasn't inclined to drift off or become distracted.

Then a phrase caught her attention. She raised her hand in a mute request for permission to speak. Tyndale did not at first notice her. Then, as his gaze swept the lecture hall, it fell on her —and he stopped mid-sentence. There was a pause. Then Tyndale said, "Yes, Lady North?"

The entire lecture hall, which had been quiet before, went as perfectly still as if every person in the room had suddenly frozen. Not a breath, not a cough, not a slither of cloth against cloth sounded. Veronica swallowed. She rose as she had been taught to do and said, "May I ask a clarification of your last statement?"

Another pause as Tyndale regarded her. His glass-green eyes showed about as much emotion as a shark's might. "You may," he finally said.

The silence broke as hushed whispers went up here and there around the lecture hall. Veronica knew instantly she had made a mistake. Well, there was nothing for it but to brazen it out. "You said law-speakers have a duty to know the law with specificity and depth. I was wondering what 'specificity' means. It sounds at odds with 'depth'."

Tyndale's regard was starting to make her nervous. "Those terms refer to what one might call the axis, or axes, of the law," he said. "Depth refers to a knowledge of how laws relate to one another. Specificity means an understanding of the details of a certain law. The minutiae, if you will."

Veronica nodded. "Thank you." She resumed her seat and discovered her hands were shaking.

Tyndale nodded in return. "I must ask that you direct any further questions to Master Herewiss or Master Averill Cates after the lecture is concluded," he said, and picked up his lecture where he had left off without a pause.

Veronica's heart sank. Not left off. Been interrupted. It seemed she had inadvertently broken a rule about not asking questions in class. She wished now she hadn't chosen this seat right in the middle of everyone, because it was impossible for her to flee as she wanted to do. Stupid, stupid, stupid.

She took more notes, sporadically, when her humiliated brain caught hold of something she thought she might need later, and when the Device bell over the door rang to signal the end of class, she stayed seated when everyone else rose. Should she apologize to Tyndale? No, he'd already left by the same door at the back of the platform. She didn't know who Masters Herewiss or Averill Cates were, as if she would dare ask any more questions. Maybe she could sit here until the room was empty and avoid the stares and muffled laughter at her mistake.

"That was bold," the young man at her left said. Veronica looked up. His dark, amused eyes were fixed on her, but the amusement didn't seem to be at her expense. "I guess you didn't know we're not supposed to interrupt the lecture."

"That's so different from the last time I was at the Scholia," Veronica blurted out. "We—the classes were more like a discussion."

"Definitely different." The young man extended a hand. "I'm Ian Frost. I'm sure that's not the first impression you wanted to make, Lady North, but I promise no one will think less of you. We've all made mistakes in public. Though it's a wonder Tyndale didn't eviscerate you. I wouldn't have guessed him as a respecter of royalty."

Veronica shook his hand. "Are you a law student?"

"No, I'm a Deviser, or hope to be in a year or so. I put off taking this fundy and ended up in Master Tyndale's class, more's the pity." Frost rose and ran a hand through his hair, disordering it further. It occurred to Veronica that he was about the age Francis had been when he died, and although Francis had been lean and tall like his father, he'd had the same dark eyes Frost had. The similarity sent a pang through her.

"Is it a pity? I understood this class to be quite desirable."

Veronica rose as well, but Frost was between her and the stairs, so she stayed where she was rather than rudely push past him.

Frost shrugged. "It's not like Tyndale doesn't know his stuff. He's just a prick. And he doesn't like students. Why he's teaching here instead of making a fortune as a law-speaker in Aurilien, I have no idea. He's certainly got enough arrogance for five law-speakers all wrapped up in one body."

Veronica thought this was a cruel thing to say, but she didn't like to reprimand someone she'd only just met. "I see," she said, feeling somehow as if she'd betrayed Tyndale, though she owed him nothing. "And who are Masters Herewiss and Averill Cates?"

"Tyndale's assistants. They mark all the assignments and answer all the questions. Do all the work, as far as I'm concerned. Tyndale just delivers the lecture and leaves the rest to them." Frost pointed. "Abel Herewiss is over there, and Ellen Averill Cates is by the door—you can see the students surrounding them."

Veronica made note of the faces. She tucked her book and pencil away and lifted the satchel to her shoulder. "It's nice to meet you, Mister Frost."

"Call me Ian." Ian Frost regarded her closely. "Are you going into Knightsbury for dinner, or staying on campus?"

It hadn't even occurred to her that leaving was an option. How would she get to Knightsbury, anyway? Walk? "I'm eating in the refectory."

"Would you care to join me? I'll introduce you to friends— unless you have other plans. I suppose you're quite popular."

Veronica laughed before she could stop herself. "I know almost no one here. Just Anne and Renie and Samantha."

"Samantha—not Samantha Wilde?" Ian's voice took on an eager tone. "She's wonderful. Definitely worth getting to know."

"Oh. Are you and she...seeing each other?" Veronica didn't know if that was how people referred to courting anymore.

Ian shrugged. "We've stepped out together a few times. Nothing serious." His expression said it was more than a little serious, at least for him, and just as clearly said she shouldn't pry. Veronica decided to change the subject.

"I'd enjoy having dinner with you, Ian, if you'll call me Veronica," she said.

Ian's smile broadened. "Imagine me on first-name terms with you," he said. "The closest I've come to nobility in the past was sharing a dorm with Lord Michael Beresford last year. And he snored like a rusty saw. You seem much nicer."

"I hope so. Michael Beresford is very dull," Veronica said. She wondered if that was too catty, but Ian only laughed, and she reminded herself that if he had shared quarters with the young man, he certainly knew how dull poor Michael was.

"Then come along, and let's introduce you," Ian said. "And —don't hold it against me, but I have to admit I was hoping you'd agree to dine with me. I look forward to making my friends' eyes bugging out of their heads."

To her surprise, his words didn't rouse her anxieties. "I'm glad I can provide amusement," she said.

5

The refectory dining hall, long and low and brightly lit by dozens of small square windows, smelled deliciously of chicken and rosemary and roasted vegetables. Portraits hanging between the windows depicted men and women in black Scholia robes and red or blue stoles, red for Masters, blue for those studying for the advanced degree, three or four with the six-banded blue stoles of a full Magister. All of them looked stern, as if being a Scholia Master or Magister had sapped their sense of humor.

Brass chandeliers lit by candles rather than Devices hung low over the long tables, though the sunlight made them unnecessary. There were three tables, all narrow enough that the place settings on one side brushed up against the place settings on the other. The arrangement of tables was similar to that of the grand dining hall in the palace during state suppers, but those tables were ponderous oak rather than light maple and much wider. These left no room for platters to be placed, which made Veronica curious about how the food was served.

Ian strolled confidently to the far end of the middle table and pulled out a chair. "It's early, but these are the best seats," he told Veronica, gesturing for her to sit beside him. "Closest to the kitchens, you know."

Veronica settled herself. The place settings were simple, just a bowl and a bread plate with a glass of water, a knife, a spoon, and two forks, but the bowl and plate were of fine white porcelain decorated with the Scholia crest and the flatware was... She picked up a fork and examined it. Silver. The dining ware would not have been out of place in a noble's home.

She set the fork down and regarded the portraits as Ian said, "What discipline are you studying?"

"Architecture." Something was odd about the portraits, but she couldn't identify the strangeness.

"Interesting. It's not really something I'd picture you doing, building things." Ian waved at someone entering the hall.

"Why is that? I mean, obviously I wouldn't necessarily wield a hammer or a trowel." That was it. All the backgrounds were identical. Veronica was seized with a sudden urge to walk over to the portraits and see if the backgrounds had been put in by a different hand. The idea of the portraits being mass-produced amused her, as if it meant the Scholia turned out Masters in the same way.

Ian shrugged. "I don't know. It just seems so practical. I don't generally think of the nobility as being practical. Bec! Percy! Over here!"

A woman and a man approached, their arms linked. The woman was a few inches taller than the man, but they strode in tandem as smoothly as a couple of ancient litter-bearers. Their paces slowed as they neared, and both stared at Veronica for a few seconds before apparently realizing that was rude and turning their attention on Ian. "Something new for the new term?" the man said. "Don't we usually sit at the other table?"

"I felt like a change," Ian said.

"So long as we're near the kitchen, it doesn't matter to me," the woman said. "Ian, introduce us so I can stop pretending not to stare at Lady North."

Ian chuckled. "Veronica, these are my friends Rebecca Grayson and Percy Osgood. Bec and Percy, Veronica North."

Percy took a seat opposite Ian. "On first-name terms already? Lady North, don't let this fellow impose on you. He'd make friends with the world if he could."

"I'd rather you call me Veronica," Veronica said. "We're all students together."

"Then I'm Bec," Rebecca said, sitting next to Percy. "It's good to meet you. How are you finding Scholia life so far?"

"I've only been to one class, so I haven't had time to draw conclusions." Bec had an interesting, lively face, not quite beautiful, but compelling in its animated expressions. Percy watched her as she spoke, his half-smile full of fondness.

"Yes, and she made an impression on Tyndale," Ian said.

Bec's mobile face scrunched up in an expression of distaste. "Poor soul. How did that happen?"

"She asked a question mid-lecture."

Percy's mouth fell open. Bec gasped. "You did not," she said. "Did he tear into you?"

Veronica reddened. "No. He was very polite. I didn't know we weren't supposed to interrupt. It's not how they used to do it."

"I've seen Tyndale rip up at someone who didn't do

anything worse than approach him between classes," Bec said. "I guess being royalty has its perks. Though I wouldn't have guessed Tyndale would care."

"That's what I said," Ian said. He waved again, this time at a man who was looking around as if searching for someone. The man's eye fell on Ian, and a look of relief suffused his face, as if Ian had saved him from drowning and not just caught his attention. "Howard, get over here, they're about to serve."

"Has anyone seen Bridget?" Percy asked.

"I thought she started her course at the Royal Library this term," Bec said.

"No, that's not until Winter. Didn't you read the list? She's on our interdisciplinary team." Percy nodded at the man joining them. "Howard, have you met Lady North? Veronica, I mean?"

Howard, a thin, pale man with untidy fair hair and wintry blue eyes, jerked to a halt a few feet from their end of the table. "Your ladyship," he said, and bowed. Veronica felt her face heat up again.

"Don't be stupid, Howard, she's a student like the rest of us, and you're embarrassing her," Ian said. "Sit down already."

Howard took a seat next to Bec. His pale eyes never left Veronica's face. He was older than the others by about a decade, which still made him quite a few years younger than she, but his awestruck expression belonged on a teen. "Your—I mean, um, Veronica," he said. "You know Ian?"

"We're both in Master Tyndale's basics of law class," Veronica said.

Howard made the same face Bec had. "I'm sorry."

"No, it's...interesting."

Veronica startled as a woman slid into the seat next to her.

The newcomer was breathing hard and her face was flushed as if she'd been running. She shoved a satchel similar to Veronica's own beneath her seat.

"Bridget, will you ever not be late?" Bec said in amusement. "This is Bridget Armistead, Veronica. Bridget, say hello to Veronica North."

"Sweet heaven, the Dowager Consort," Bridget said. Her color was rapidly returning to normal, and she put a self-conscious hand to her red hair, which was coming free of its braid. "Though that title really doesn't suit you. Oh, heaven, that was rude. I meant you don't look like a Dowager anything."

To her surprise, the young woman's rapid talk eased Veronica's discomfort. "Yes, I'd prefer you call me Veronica."

"I don't know about that," Bridget said. "I can try. Why are you here—I mean, here at dinner—heaven, I'm babbling like an idiot. I promise I'm not usually this rude. It's just first day jitters, but I suppose you wouldn't get those, since it's not your first time at the Scholia."

Doors opened nearby, and a stream of white-clad men and women emerged bearing steaming tureens of soup. Veronica leaned back to allow one of them to ladle tomato bisque into her bowl. It smelled heavenly. A fat roll with a rich brown crust appeared on the plate next to it. Veronica hadn't realized she was hungry until she smelled its hot, yeasty scent.

Ian tore his roll into bits and dipped one in his soup, oblivious to good manners. "So, this is most of our interdisciplinary study group," he said, popping the dripping morsel into his mouth. "Not Howard, he's a Deviser like me. But the rest of us are a team this term."

"I don't know what that is," Veronica said. She sipped her soup. Normally she didn't have much of an appetite, but it seemed scholastic life had an influence on her stomach. She felt ravenous.

Bec waved her spoon in a lazy, tight circle in the air. "Starting in your fourth year, you'll be assigned to a project. Something the government wants, or a guild requests. Scholia students are highly desirable even before we take the robe. And the project team is made up of students from all different schools. It's so we learn to work together and appreciate fields of study other than our own."

"Personally, I'm not sure what the point is," Percy said, "given how much emphasis the Scholia places on the fundy courses. It's not like we don't get a thorough grounding in every field. But it can be interesting."

"And is this project interesting?" Veronica asked.

Ian shrugged. "Depends on who you ask. There's a bridge going up in County Harroden near Ravensholm. The government wants—well, maybe you already know, being who you are. The ferry traffic across the Snow River is always slow and congested, and it's past time they built a bridge."

Veronica shook her head. "I hadn't heard. So if it's interdisciplinary, does that mean you're all studying different things?"

"Like I said, I'm in training as a Deviser," Ian said. "Percy is studying philosophy, Bridget is in the librarian discipline, and Bec is on track to be an outstanding questioner."

Bec waved her spoon at Ian, making red drops spatter the white table runner. "Don't kid yourself. I'm already outstanding."

"Then you're a law student," Veronica said. "Does that mean you encounter Master Tyndale often?"

"Too often," Bec said with another grimace. "He's been my

tutor the last two years, and of course he teaches the advanced classes. I honestly don't understand why he has to be such a hardass. It's no wonder his wife left him. The real surprise is that he had a wife at all."

The bitterness in Bec's voice made Veronica uncomfortable. She wasn't fond of gossip, having been the focus of it, and Bec's description of Tyndale invoked in her not malice, but an unexpected sympathy. But these were still strangers, and Veronica wasn't good with conflict, especially conflict in which she imperfectly understood the situation. "I hope none of my other instructors are as harsh," she said, hoping to change the conversation. "I have an engineering class this afternoon...I don't suppose you know anything about Master Hunt?"

The mood eased. "Oh, she's all right," Percy said. "She doesn't turn most of the marking over to her assistants, and she's always available after class for answering questions. Jokes a lot. You'll like her."

"What else are you taking?" Ian asked.

"Basic mathematics, history of Harandan art, and the second basics of Devisery course."

Ian's eyes lit. "Devisery tomorrow? That's Master Varner's class. I'm her assistant. I promise not to go easy on you, though."

Veronica smiled. "I count on it. I don't want the robe given me, I want to earn it."

"Which you will," Bridget said. "I think it's amazing that you had the courage to pick up your studies again after so long— oh, heaven, that makes you sound like a crone—"

Veronica was beginning to get an idea of how Bridget's mind worked. "It has been a long time, though," she reassured her. "But...don't you think it's odd that I'm the only older student here? Surely I can't be the only one whose studies were interrupted."

"Howard's an older student," Ian informed her. "But he's only in his thirties, so I'm not sure whether that really makes him older."

Veronica was surprised to see Howard redden, as if Ian had said something insulting. "I didn't start young and return later, though," he told Veronica, leaning forward to add emphasis to his words. "I wanted to be a Deviser most of my life, but my parents needed me in the family business. It wasn't until three years ago I finally told them I wanted out."

"I think that's brave, too," Veronica said.

Howard shrugged. "The Scholia...actually, they weren't thrilled about taking me on at my age. They said they thought it would be too rigorous for anyone not of a young and flexible mindset. But Devisers are different, since you can't be a Deviser without the ability to manipulate source. Master Varner made a case for me being allowed to try for the robe, and eventually they gave in."

That sounded very strange to Veronica. "Nobody told me I was too old."

"Well, they wouldn't, would they?" Bec said. She leaned back for the soup bowl to be removed. "Not with you being who you are."

"Yes, but should that matter?" Veronica leaned back as well as a server deposited a heavenly-smelling plate in front of her. She picked up knife and fork and cut a piece of chicken with rosemary, releasing more delicious aromas. "If I'm...I don't know...too rigid of mind because I'm old, why should my being the former Consort eliminate that objection?"

Ian paused with his fork halfway to his mouth. "I hadn't

thought of it that way. You're right, though. Maybe the Scholia has the wrong attitude."

"Try telling the Magister that," Percy said.

Ian shuddered. "I wouldn't dare. Besides, he'd just look at me with that 'who are you, again?' expression. I doubt students register with him at all."

"Even famous Devisers?" Bec said in a teasing way.

Everyone laughed. Ian just went on eating. "Laugh all you want," he said between bites of chicken and roast vegetables. "I'm making advances in Devisery that will change the field forever."

"That's what you said about the automatic nose hair trimmer," Bec said.

"And the laundry folding Device," Percy said.

"That sounds very practical, actually," Veronica said.

"That's what I thought, but I couldn't get it to keep the seams straight," Ian said without a trace of embarrassment.

"And don't forget about the Canine Companion," Bridget said. She winked at Veronica. "That was a classic."

"Canine Companion?" Veronica glanced at Ian for enlightenment, but now he was blushing and had his attention focused on his plate.

"It was designed for walking dogs," Howard said. He sounded as defensive as if it were his Device they were discussing. "To help people with limited mobility. It attached to a collar and took the dog for a walk based on the route you taught the Device."

"But it was lighter than the dogs," Bridget said meaningfully.

It took a moment for this to sink in. "Oh," Veronica said, covering her mouth to conceal a smile. She didn't want to hurt

Ian's feelings with her laughter. "I...can see how that would be a problem."

"I haven't given up on that one," Ian muttered.

"Ian's brilliant," Howard said. "He's developed all sorts of Devices."

"Don't patronize me, Howard, I've told you I hate that," Ian said, but without rancor. "You all think it's hilarious that most of my Devices don't work—"

"Or work too well. Like the automatic nose hair trimmer," Percy said, grimacing.

"But even Kerish North had his failures. And you never get anywhere without trying." Ian grinned slyly. "Just wait. This new project is going to make my fortune."

"Yes, it's—" Howard began. Ian shot him a glare that could have melted iron. Howard subsided.

"You'll all find out once it's safely in development," Ian continued.

"If it's commercially viable, it makes sense that you wouldn't want to discuss it," Veronica said. "I've known Devisers who were loose-lipped about their Devisery and paid the price when someone else beat them to market. Isn't that what you're worried about?"

Ian didn't respond. He was looking off down the hall, his lips set in a hard line, his heavy dark eyebrows knit together. Veronica followed the line of his gaze and saw Samantha standing near the center of the hall, laughing at something her companion was saying. Her companion was an extremely handsome young man whose longish dark blond hair curled over his ears and collar. The style should have given him an effeminate look, but it set off the strong lines of his face, the curve of his jaw and the planes of his cheekbones.

Veronica looked at the others, wondering if they had noticed Ian's preoccupation. They were all looking in Samantha's direction, too. "I see Samantha's tastes in men haven't improved," Bec said, a little too casually.

"She's not actually interested in Carlton Dunn," Bridget said. "She was at the pub with Brendan Hogle two nights ago. He's much more her type." She blushed. "I mean—"

"I get it," Ian said. He sounded nothing like his carefree self. "You mean, not like me. It's not like it matters. We've made no promises."

"She wouldn't step out with you if she didn't like you, Ian," Percy said. "She's just not ready to settle down."

Ian shrugged and took another bite. "It doesn't matter," he repeated. "Speaking of the pub, we should take Veronica tonight. Show her what Scholia life is really like."

"I don't think I've been to a pub in thirty years," Veronica said, and immediately regretted her words. They'd all been talking in such a friendly, egalitarian way, and she had to go and remind them of their differences. But no one mentioned her gaffe.

As the others started talking about the pub, and who else might be there that night, Veronica cast one last look at Samantha. Her head was bent toward the young man, Carlton's, head, and she was smiling at him in her usual vivacious way. Veronica didn't know Samantha well yet, but based on what she saw, if Ian was interested in Samantha, he might be doomed to disappointment.

6

---

*V*eronica wrote a final line of text and set the paper aside for the ink to dry. She wiped her pen nib and flexed her hand to ease the slight cramping. Three weeks of classes had been more than enough to remind her just how much writing the Scholia required of its students. She'd already been into Knightsbury a few times to buy more paper.

Across the table from her, Samantha raised her head from her book. "Finished?" She spoke in a low voice so as not to disturb the other students in the study room.

"Yes. This represents everything I know about the earliest examples of Harandan art." Veronica stretched. "Master Kelson should have no complaints."

"He'll find something to nitpick. He always does. Kelson doesn't believe in handing out too much praise—thinks it will give his students swelled heads." Samantha closed her book on her thumb, marking her place, and stretched as well. "But he's a good instructor."

"I'm enjoying the class." Veronica's back ached from having hunched over the table for...actually, she didn't know how long it had been, but long enough to send a pain shooting up her spine and down her hips when she straightened. She always began a writing session with good posture, but the more intent she became on her work, the more her back curved. It was another reminder that she wasn't as young as she used to be.

Despite the lovely table and chairs in her sitting room, she'd found she preferred working in the west study room of Patience House. The sound of other people breathing, of pens scritching across paper, of the minute shuffling of chair legs, relaxed her. And she enjoyed the opportunity to chat with her fellow students from time to time. She'd always considered herself something of a loner, so this desire for company had been a surprise.

Samantha had opened her book again and was making a note on a sheet of paper. Her brow was slightly furrowed with concentration, her catlike eyes narrowed, and Veronica observed her covertly. Samantha fascinated her. Veronica had never known anyone so free with her emotions, so unafraid of being judged. Veronica would never have dared entertain more than one suitor at a time, so Samantha's ability to keep at least four men dancing to her tune intrigued her. While she didn't wish herself in Samantha's shoes—romance was the furthest thing from her mind—she did wish she had some of Samantha's confidence.

On the other hand, Samantha's casual attitude toward men meant pain for Ian Frost, and Veronica couldn't be happy about that. She and Ian always sat together in Tyndale's class, and ate dinner together with Ian's group of friends, and she was very fond of the young man. For his sake, she wished Samantha would settle down to just one man, even if it wasn't Ian. Much as she cared about him, Veronica couldn't feel certain Samantha would make him happy. But interfering in other people's lives wasn't in her nature, so she merely smiled and nodded whenever the subject came up.

The page was dry. Veronica shuffled the essay pages into the right order and tucked them into a folder. Then, sighing, she drew a blank book toward her and opened it to her notes from her law class.

"You are the most organized person I've ever known," Samantha said without looking up. "Folders for every class. Folders for every assignment. One blank book per class. And my biology instructors call *me* overprepared."

Veronica smiled. "It's how I was taught to study. Besides, I never lose things."

"I'm not saying it's bad, I'm saying it's amazing no one else does it your way. Maybe *you* should teach a class on organization. Or an evening lecture, maybe." Samantha made another note on her paper. "I can think of a number of people it might benefit. Ian Frost, for one."

Veronica held her breath for a moment, startled at the mention of someone she'd just been thinking about. "Ian...is a good friend of yours, isn't he?"

Samantha looked up again. "I like him a lot, yes," she said. "Though he's rather intense...I like him, but I'm not sure I'm comfortable around him, you see?"

"I think so." Veronica almost said *I know he likes you*, but that would not only be interfering, it would be a betrayal of Ian's friendship. Instead, she said, "I like him, too. He's made this law class bearable. I don't know if my marks will be high enough to pass."

"You're having trouble with Tyndale?"

Veronica shook her head. "He's not as bad as everyone keeps telling me. But his requirements are almost overwhelming, and I don't remember enough from the first law class I took thirty years ago to help."

"You should ask for a tutorial assistant," Samantha said. "You're smart enough, I'm sure all you need is someone to help you focus. And maybe direct you to materials that will enhance your understanding."

"I hadn't considered that. It's a good idea."

Samantha grinned, an impish expression that made her look even prettier than usual. "I got to know Brendan Hogle when he was my tutorial assistant in literature. Sometimes there are side benefits."

Veronica laughed and covered her mouth as a couple of nearby students looked up and glared at the sudden noise. "I don't think I should look for those kind of side benefits. Everyone here is at least half my age."

"Nothing wrong with seeing younger men," Samantha said. "Oh, all right, I know that's not anything you're interested in," she added when Veronica started to protest. "But some extra tutelage might help."

Veronica cast her eye over her class notes. She barely understood them, and she'd taken them herself. "Almost certainly," she agreed.

Two days later, when the Device bell rang to mark the end of law class, Veronica gathered her notes and rose hastily. Ian, moving more slowly, gave her a narrow-eyed look. "You're in a hurry," he said. "Planning to sit somewhere else for dinner?"

"No, I need to talk to Master Herewiss about a tutorial assistant." Veronica sidled past her friend more quickly than was polite and apologized. "I'll meet you in the refectory."

"I didn't know you were struggling. Do you want to study together?" Ian asked.

"You're so busy, I shouldn't impose. Besides, I think I need someone whose knowledge of the law goes beyond either of ours." Veronica gave him a little wave and hurried down the stairs.

Both Herewiss and Averill Cates were surrounded by students. Veronica's heart sank. She was terrible at being pushy, and it looked like pushiness was the only way she would get what she needed. She hovered at the outside of the crowd, shifting her weight awkwardly from one foot to the other.

She glanced toward the lectern and saw, to her surprise, Tyndale still standing there, riffling through his slim black book. Occasionally, he placed a sheet of paper between its pages. On a whim, Veronica approached him, saying, "Master Tyndale?"

Tyndale looked up. A flash of surprise flitted across his face, which then settled into his usual impassive expression. "Lady North," he said. It was not a question, but a salutation. Veronica's nerves twitched. No student ever spoke to Tyndale, and she'd never even seen his assistants address him. Probably this was another mistake. But she was there, and it would look even worse if she walked away.

"I'm sorry if this is...I mean...I was wondering..." Her mouth had gone dry in the face of his glass-green stare. She mentally slapped herself and said, in a rush, "I'm having trouble keeping up with the classwork. I wondered if you could recommend a tutorial assistant."

One of Tyndale's slim blond eyebrows curved in an arc. "A tutorial assistant," he said. "I wasn't aware you were struggling."

And I wasn't aware you knew anything about your students' work, Veronica wanted to say. But she would never be that rude. "I understand most of it," she said, feeling defensive, "but apparently my grounding in the subject isn't recent enough to be helpful. I was thinking...if I had someone who could guide me to the right foundational texts, it would be enough."

Tyndale continued to regard her. "You can request a class transfer, if it's too much."

That sparked Veronica's anger, an unexpected reaction. "It's not too much," she said, "and my work so far has been more than adequate, according to your assistants."

The eyebrow went up again. "Meaning that I don't have any idea what you're capable of?"

Since Veronica had meant just that, she didn't know why she blushed. "I'm not in a position to judge you," she said. "I'm just not used, yet, to the way classes are taught these days."

To her complete surprise, Tyndale smiled. "There are good reasons not to have students interrupt the lecture," he said. "Too much discussion leads to not covering the appropriate material in a timely way. But I can't say I disagree with you. I remember classes, when I was a student, where the discussion made a more lasting impression on me than the lecture."

It had never occurred to her that if Tyndale was of her generation, he would have been a Scholia student about the same time she was. "So do I," she said. "I remember Master Golden never could stick to a topic, but if you could get her going—"

"She had the most amazing stories," Tyndale said. "I hadn't realized you'd studied under her."

"Just the modern literature class. I'm not much of a reader, but she made books come alive."

Tyndale smiled again. "Her Harandan literature class was even better. I would have sworn she'd known Haran personally, and not just because she was old enough it could almost have been true."

Veronica laughed. "She was wrinkly enough to be almost seven hundred years old, certainly!"

For a moment, there was depth behind the glass-green eyes. Then Tyndale's features smoothed, and his mirth vanished. "I would be happy to make a recommendation, Lady North," he said, but not as severely as he'd spoken at first. "I have a fifth-year student in need of some teaching experience. His name is Carlton Dunn, and I think you'll find him exactly what you need. Tell him your requirements and that I recommended him —he lodges at Temperance House, and anyone there will be able to direct you to him."

"Thank you, Master Tyndale. I appreciate it."

"It's my pleasure." For a moment, Tyndale looked as if he wanted to say something else. Instead he merely nodded, gathered up his book, and disappeared through the door at the back of the platform.

Veronica watched him go. When the door shut, she realized they'd had an audience. All the students clamoring around the assistants, and the assistants themselves, were staring at her in varying states of astonishment. Embarrassment surged over Veronica, reddening her cheeks and making her heart beat faster. She told herself it didn't matter, that she hadn't done anything wrong, and left the room.

The crowds parted for her as she went, and she had the most unexpected memory of walking down the aisle of the coronation hall the day of her wedding, surrounded on both sides by the nobility of four countries. Then, she'd had Landon's steadying arm supporting her. Now she was only herself. It surprised her to discover she didn't feel afraid.

She was almost late to dinner, but her friends had saved her usual seat, and she dropped into it moments before the soup was served. "Well?" Ian asked.

"Master Tyndale recommended someone. I'll see if I can find him later." Veronica sniffed the clear broth in which fat egg noodles floated. It had been Francis's favorite food, chicken soup with noodles. For once, her memories didn't pain her.

She took a bite of soup and then realized everyone at her end of the table was staring at her. "What?" she said, then blushed at how abrupt and impolite she'd sounded.

"You spoke to Tyndale?" Bec said, in a tone of voice that might have more reasonably accused Veronica of eating puppies.

Veronica blushed harder and focused on her soup. "He was very pleasant," she said.

"Tyndale is never pleasant. Tyndale delights in making others cringe," Percy said. "I can't believe you dared approach him. You're braver than I."

The memory of her momentary accord with Tyndale was turning sour. "I don't believe he's so terrible," she said, "and he *was* pleasant. We—" She found she didn't want to share the details of their conversation. No doubt her friends would find a way to taint those memories, too. But defending Tyndale when she knew nothing more of him than that they'd had the same instructors thirty years ago was beyond her capacity. "It doesn't matter. He may be awful, but you can't deny he knows his field. I'm sure anyone he recommends will be excellent."

Ian, seated next to her, shrugged. "Who is it?"

"He said, Carlton Dunn."

Ian's face reddened. "Did he," he said, and applied himself to his soup as ferociously as if he thought it might try to devour him instead.

Veronica remembered Ian's reaction, weeks before, to seeing Carlton and Samantha together and wished she hadn't said anything. "I didn't know—I thought you and Samantha—"

"I'm afraid you and Howard will be on your own next week, Veronica," Bec said sharply. "Our team is going to Ravensholm to work on the bridge project."

Bridget, who'd been about to speak, shut her mouth. She glanced from Veronica to Bec. "But Carlton—" she began.

"Yes, we're leaving Fifthday afternoon, after Bec's literature study group," Percy said. "Though Bridget will probably be packing all the way up until we leave, right, Bridge?"

Bridget's expression changed. "That's rich, coming from you, Percy. You always pack far too much."

"Thanks, but you all don't have to tie yourselves into knots," Ian said. His face had resumed its normal color. "Carlton Dunn is Samantha's latest beau, Veronica. And it doesn't matter to me who Samantha sees. We're not together." He coughed into his napkin and dropped it back onto his lap.

"Oh," Veronica said, and couldn't think of anything else to add. She'd thought, from what Samantha had said, that Samantha still hadn't settled down to one man and that she cared about Ian. But if Samantha and Carlton were together, she could see why Ian wouldn't want to talk about it.

"You don't have to be so noble about it, Ian, we're all on your side," Bec said. "Carlton Dunn is a self-obsessed git who knows just how pretty he is and how far that will take him. But he is good at the law. You didn't say you were having trouble, Veronica. I could have helped."

"I didn't want to ask you because I know how much of your time goes into your project," Veronica said.

"And she's a terrible teacher," Percy said. Bec elbowed him not very sharply in the ribs, and he let out a dramatic *oof* of breath. "No patience at all."

"You don't have to be so honest, dear," Bec said sweetly. "Though he's probably right, Veronica."

"Anyway, don't feel you have to shun Carlton on my account," Ian said. "I really am over Samantha. I promise." He wasn't meeting anyone's eyes. Veronica decided not to push.

Ian coughed into his napkin again. "Sorry. Something stuck in my throat. Anyway, don't be too lonely, you two. It's just a week."

"We'll find things to talk about," Howard declared. "Veronica, you're interested in Devisery, right?"

Veronica wasn't really interested in Devisery, but Howard's interests were narrow and his ability to read social cues limited, and likely Devisery was all he was capable of discussing comfortably. And she liked him, for all his fawning over Ian became old at times. "I'm interested in your research," she said.

Bec and Bridget groaned. "You're going to bore Veronica to tears, see if you don't," Percy said.

"And no talking about my Device," Ian warned him, and coughed again. "I know you, Howard. You're likely to blurt out all my secrets just to impress her."

"I would not!" Howard protested.

"Ian, are you sure you're all right?" Veronica asked. "That cough sounds serious."

"It's really not. Just a tickle in my throat that won't go away," Ian said.

"It had better be, because I don't want to catch whatever it is you have," Bec said. "That would ruin this trip."

"I'm not sick!" Ian gave himself the lie by coughing even harder. He wiped his mouth and said, "I think that's got rid of it. So stop talking about it, all right? Who's for the pub tonight?"

"I have to study," Veronica said. "Maybe tomorrow." She'd had fun the few times they'd all gone into Knightsbury to the Lucky Star tavern, and didn't feel at all awkward going by herself now, aside from the feeling that going to taverns alone was something lonely, desperate people did.

"Your loss," Ian said with a smile.

7

When the meal was over, Veronica still had nearly forty-five minutes until her afternoon class. She decided to walk over to Temperance House and leave a message for Carlton Dunn. The men's dormitories were identical to the women's, down to the towers instead of spires, but Temperance House stood out because it was of a slightly darker stone than the other three. On this warm day, the door stood open, and Veronica entered, feeling as if she were doing something forbidden. Of course women were allowed inside, but she felt furtive nonetheless.

She knocked on the first door, hoping the dormitories really were identical and the dormitory majordomo had his office there. Immediately, the door opened, and a man said, "Yes? Oh, Lady North. Do you need something?"

Veronica was accustomed by now to being instantly recognized, and yet it still gave her pause to be addressed familiarly by someone she'd never met. The majordomo was built like a brick wall, wide in the shoulders and hips and muscular of chest and arms, an effect enhanced by his florid complexion and large, veiny nose. Wiry black hair covered both forearms and trailed on over the backs of his hands. He regarded her curiously but not antagonistically, not as if she were out of place, and that heartened her.

"I hoped to leave a message for Carlton Dunn," she said. "It's about a scholastic matter. I don't suppose you could send someone with a note?"

"Oh, Mister Dunn is on the premises. If you'll wait, I'll send a runner to fetch him." The majordomo shut the door behind him and beckoned to Veronica to follow.

He led her to a familiar-looking antechamber filled with comfortable sofas and a couple of chairs. In Patience House, the room was for male visitors to wait on their female companions. The idea that sitting here in Temperance House might suggest she was waiting on an assignation amused Veronica. She took a seat and nodded acknowledgment as the majordomo said, "Just a minute, Lady North."

Veronica entertained herself by comparing the room to its counterpart in the women's dormitory. Its layout was identical, of course, but the décor was plainer; aside from the sofas, which were upholstered in light blue brocade, there was only one painting on the wall, an oil landscape of the jungles of southern Eskandel, and a clock too small for the room. The realization that the dormitories really were all built alike led Veronica to consider who might have the tower room corresponding to hers. She hoped whoever it was had the resources to heat his rooms come winter.

Presently, footsteps approached, and the brick wall returned with Carlton Dunn in his wake. Veronica had only seen Samantha's new beau a handful of times, but she remembered well his handsome face and his long hair that curled around that face in an attractive, masculine way. Whether he was too proud of his looks as her friends had said, Veronica couldn't tell, but he looked at her curiously, without a hint of arrogance.

"You can use one of the study rooms if you like," the brick wall said, and moved off back toward his chamber.

Veronica rose and extended her hand. "I apologize for the imposition, Mister Dunn. I thought only to leave you a note explaining my situation, but...the majordomo, yes? He was very helpful. I hope I'm not interrupting you."

"Not at all," Carlton said. His voice was a pleasant baritone. "Though I am curious what kind of scholastic matter I might help you with."

"It's my law class, actually. I'm struggling a little, and when I asked Master Tyndale for a recommendation for someone who might help, he gave me your name."

Carlton's eyes widened. "*Master Tyndale* suggested me?" he said, his baritone voice becoming tenor briefly.

"Yes," Veronica said, nonplussed by his reaction. "He said you were in need of teaching experience and that he thought you would be an excellent choice."

"I can't believe *that*," Carlton muttered. He still looked stunned.

"Is...something wrong?" Veronica didn't want to ask if Carlton's relationship with Tyndale was so hostile he couldn't imagine the Master recommending him for anything, which was her impression of the young man's reaction.

Carlton jerked. "What? No. I mean...it's just I was surprised you approached Master Tyndale directly. He isn't known for his helpfulness to students."

He wouldn't meet her eyes, and between that and the nervous twitching of the fingers of his left hand, Veronica was sure he was lying. Well, it wasn't as if it mattered what he believed Tyndale thought of him. "It wasn't much," she said. "So, can you help me? My problem is that much of the foundational work this class relies on is unfamiliar to me. That's a lot of sources, and I don't know if I need to read everything, or which sources are most important. I'm afraid I feel terribly lost."

"Of course, I'd be happy to," Carlton said. The twitching stopped. "What is your Fifthday schedule like?"

"I don't have any regular study groups except the architectonics one, and that meets at ten o'clock in the morning. And I'm seeing my tutor at nine."

"I'm free around three. Meet me at Lyton Hall then, and I'll show you the law library and which books you'll need to start. Then we can discuss how you'll study them." *Now* Carlton sounded arrogant, but as Veronica really didn't feel confident in her law studies, she didn't mind his attitude so long as it taught her what she needed to know.

"Thank you, Mister Dunn," she said, extending a hand. "I'm so grateful."

"Thank me after you've passed Master Tyndale's class," Carlton said with a smile. "He can be hard on new students."

Again Veronica reflected on her own interactions with Tyndale. If he really was one of those impressed by royalty, as she was beginning to suspect, his treatment of her was a side benefit she couldn't regret—and yet the thought of being fawned over by him disturbed her, and she couldn't say why. "He is a demanding instructor, but I like being challenged."

"Let's hope you still feel that way by the time final essays are due," Carlton said.

He walked with her to the door of Temperance House and bade her farewell. Storm clouds filled the sky, and Veronica hurried to Saunders Hall and her afternoon class without looking back. She felt sure, however, that Carlton would still be there, watching her go. So, he disliked Tyndale and thought the feeling was mutual? Enough that he was surprised to learn Tyndale thought well of him, at least so far as his academic abilities went. Sympathy surged through Veronica, not for Carlton, but for Tyndale. She was beginning to think his perceived behavior wasn't everything he was. Suppose he just had trouble being himself around others?

Veronica laughed at herself as the first fat drops of rain fell. She was reading too much into a few interactions. He likely just treated her differently because of her rank, and her friends were all correct about what he was really like. But she couldn't help remembering their shared moment of reminiscence and wishing they were in a position to talk like that more often.

THE FOLLOWING AFTERNOON, VERONICA SAT IN THE MAIN lecture hall in Saunders and suppressed a yawn. She wasn't bored by the discussion, but she'd stayed up far too late studying and then reading an interesting book Master Kelson had recommended on the connection between pre-Harandan iconography and the revelation of ungoverned heaven. It was almost three o'clock, the end of her school day—technically the end of the class week, as tomorrow, Fifthday, was reserved for study groups and tutorials and Endweek was a holiday—and she felt more weary than she had since coming to the Scholia.

"And that's the key difference between Eskandelic Devisery and Tremontanan," Master Varner said. She was small-boned and petite, but her voice was that of a much larger woman. "In Eskandelic Devisery, artistic unity is of paramount importance. A Device that cannot contribute in some way to the beautification of the world is unworthy of an Eskandelic's time. Tremontanan Devisers, on the other hand, look to function over form. That doesn't mean Tremontanans don't care about aesthetics. It does mean aesthetic considerations usually happen after the Device is created and aren't generally integrated into the initial design."

She brushed her hands off on her hips as she always did at the end of a class. "That's all for today. Does anyone have questions?"

That was something else Varner did differently, though she still wouldn't take questions until her lecture was over. A few hands shot up, but Veronica's mind was already elsewhere. Knightsbury, at the Lucky Star pub, or even just back in her own bedroom. She was past ready for time off.

The Device bell rang, and Veronica packed her notes and pencil away. As she stood, she saw Ian approaching across the lecture platform. She went to meet him, nodding politely to Master Varner as she passed.

"Are you going to the pub tonight?" Ian asked.

"I planned to, yes. Samantha and I—" Veronica stopped mid-sentence, awkwardly conscious of how Ian's face closed off like a shuttered window. "I'm sorry."

"I told you, I'm over her," Ian said, not meeting her eyes. "Don't feel like you have to protect me from myself."

The anger in his voice made Veronica wish she could shrink in on herself. "I," she said in a small voice, and couldn't think of how to finish her sentence.

Ian's gaze flicked back toward her, and his eyes softened. "Oh, heaven, I didn't mean—look, I'm a sorry bastard who can't keep his tongue leashed. Really, it's all right. Samantha's your friend, and I don't want to interfere with that. I wasn't going into town tonight, anyway. There was something I wanted to show you, but if you're busy—"

Veronica shook her head. "I can go anytime. What is it?"

Ian coughed once, hard, and wiped his lips before smiling at her. "I've made a breakthrough, and—look, it's supposed to be a secret, but I can't stand not telling someone. Howard's no good, he'd just spill the news everywhere. But I know I can trust you not to talk."

His smile, and his infectious excitement, dispelled her unhappiness. "You mean about your Device? Of course I won't tell anyone, but is that really safe? I mean, I might give something away without meaning to."

Ian made a dismissive sound. "You're the most private person I've ever met. I'd believe you capable of keeping the secrets of heaven itself. Besides, this—"

"Mister Frost?" Master Varner said from across the room. "Could I have a moment of your time?"

Ian glanced at the instructor, then back at Veronica. "Come to my workshop around seven, all right? It won't take long, and you can still go to the pub."

Veronica nodded. Ian flashed her another quick smile and strode across the platform to join Master Varner.

She trudged across campus, feeling the ground squish beneath her feet. Dampness from the previous day's storm seeped between her toes, and she moved a little faster. Her shoes were pretty, but perhaps it was time to start wearing something sturdier. Winters on the great high plains of County Cullinan were harsher than in Aurilien, where the lowland weather meant more rain fell than snow. She would likely be more comfortable in trousers and boots than in dresses. That meant another trip into Knightsbury, but Endweek was just the day after tomorrow, and that would be plenty soon enough.

She heard her name being called—Lady North, not her first name—and turned to see her tutor, Master Lansing, waving at her from across the yard. Veronica changed course and met the woman just outside the bethel's door, closed now that the weather had turned colder.

Lansing's cheeks and the tip of her nose were rosy, but her smile seemed not to care about the chill in the air. "Lady North, I was just coming to speak with you," she said.

"Weren't we supposed to meet as usual tomorrow at nine?"

"This isn't about your schooling. It's about your scholarship." Lansing beamed as if she'd just given Veronica an unexpected treat.

For a moment, Veronica wondered why she had a scholarship, given how wealthy she was. Then she remembered. "Oh, yes, the bequest," she said. "Is something wrong? The funds went through all right? It's awfully late for problems to have cropped up."

"No, everything's fine. But we're organizing a supper for the Scholia benefactors, something to show our gratitude, and naturally you're invited."

Veronica's first thought was *And you couldn't send a note?* Her second thought was *What an excellent way to pander to your donors.* They were such nasty thoughts they surprised her. She wasn't a cruel or mean-spirited person, and yet looking at Lansing's eager face, she felt a cynicism that hadn't touched her since Landon's horrible mother Queen Genevieve had passed away.

"Thank you, but I want to remain anonymous in my donation," she said. "I don't require any special treatment."

Lansing's mouth made an O of dismay. "You didn't say anything about an anonymous donation, Lady North."

"Didn't I?" She couldn't remember, and discomfort like the seeping damp crept over her. Surely she wouldn't have forgotten to specify that...but she had been so nervous that day. "Well, I meant to," she concluded, awkwardly.

"If we'd known...but we've already publicized the donor names..." Lansing's voice trailed off as usual.

"Publicized, how?" Veronica's discomfort intensified.

"Oh, statements to the press, letters to our students' families...everyone likes to see their name in the paper, yes?"

Veronica remembered all too vividly the times when her name had been in the paper. The memories seared her heart. "I don't," she said sharply, for once forgetting her diffidence. "I assure you I am not in the least fond of publicity."

Lansing's wide hazel eyes narrowed in confusion. "But... you're the Dowager Consort! That's not—I mean, this is an honor, being recognized."

Veronica realized she'd closed her hand so tightly around the strap of her satchel it had gone numb. "I appreciate the honor," she said, "but I would prefer not to have a fuss made. I'm sorry I wasn't clearer about the conditions of the bequest." A horrible thought struck her. "Do you mean the student who received it knows who provided it?"

"Of course, Lady North." Lansing's cheeriness had disappeared, and now she sounded affronted. "We want all our students to be properly grateful to their benefactors. And the benefactors appreciate being thanked, naturally."

"That sounds—" Veronica controlled her outburst. "I understand. It's really not necessary." She couldn't ask Lansing to tell the poor student not to approach Lady North in fawning gratitude without sounding haughty or ungrateful. To think she had to worry about being polite about her own generosity!

Lansing straightened. "I'm sure you know your own mind, Lady North," she said, sounding as cold as the air. "The supper is Endweek evening, and you're welcome if you decide to join us." She turned and walked away, for once without a friendly goodbye.

Veronica watched her until she was a diminishing figure in the distance, then turned and resumed her course toward Patience House. Cold dampness chilling her feet made her realize she'd for once taken the shortest path between two points and was crossing the Autumn-pale grass. She didn't correct herself. Her talk with Lansing disturbed her enough that she didn't care that she'd broken with her tradition.

That interaction disturbed her, and it disturbed her further that she wasn't sure what had bothered her. Lansing's insistence on showing her honor wasn't new; the woman had found some-thing unctuous to say at every one of the tutorials they'd had since Autumn term had begun. But this wasn't Lansing's idea, it was Scholia policy, or possibly something the Magister had decided.

Veronica told herself it wasn't unusual for an organization to hold a banquet to honor its financial backers. Guilds did it all the time. But she'd always thought of the Scholia as above such pandering. She didn't know if they'd behaved this way when she was a student the first time, or if this was a change that had happened over time, like the no talking in lectures rule. In any case, it fractured her respect for the institution. Not much, maybe a hairline crack in the glass, but still a break.

She looked up at the ornate Valantine façade of Patience House and stopped, letting the dampness saturate her shoes. It was beautiful. All the Scholia buildings were beautiful. But she remembered the high-ceilinged, cold rooms of the old Scholia, deep inside the palace, and wasn't sure she thought the new campus was an improvement anymore.

She made it to her rooms without encountering anyone she might need to converse with and slipped off her ruined shoes with a sigh. Boots from now on, definitely. She had one pair that would handle the trek to and from Knightsbury tonight, and an old pair of trousers no one at the pub would criticize.

She slipped out of her dress and hung it in the wardrobe, then put on her dressing gown and lay on the bed without climbing under the covers. Tiredness had seeped into her joints, making her feel every day of her fifty years. She needed a nap, and she didn't care if that was something only babies and old people did. It wasn't even 3:30 yet; she could sleep an hour, maybe two, and still be on time for supper in the refectory. Yawning, she unfolded the soft woven blanket that lay at the foot of her bed, and was asleep almost before it covered her entirely.

She woke later, clear-headed and alert in a way that told her she had slept far longer than just an hour or two. The room was dark, the sky outside amber-tinged with the final glow of sunset. Veronica shot upright and fumbled for her watch, realized she wouldn't be able to see its face, and switched on the

Device lamp beside her bed. Her watch read 6:47. Supper would be all but over, and—

Veronica tossed the blanket aside and flung open her wardrobe, looking for clothes. Ian would be expecting her, and if she hurried, she might still meet him at his workshop. Forget the refectory; she could eat supper at the tavern with Samantha. Quickly she donned her trousers and a linen shirt too light for the Autumn weather—it was all she had—shoved her stocking-clad feet into her boots, and snatched her cloak from its peg by the door. She clattered down the stone steps and across the halls as she ran through Patience House.

The fourth- and fifth-year Devisery students were each assigned workshops in the basements and attics of Saunders Hall. The rooms were small and cramped, but Ian treated his as if it were the coronation hall, he felt that proud of what it represented. Veronica had been there two or three times and been unimpressed, but she would never have insulted Ian by suggesting it wasn't wonderful.

And maybe it *was* wonderful, she reflected as she ran across the campus grounds. It was certainly a mark of his success, that he was an accomplished enough student to deserve special treatment. She also knew from what Howard had said before Ian shushed him that the Saunders Hall workshop wasn't Ian's only workspace. Based on what she knew of her secretive friend, he probably had several, each housing a different part of his latest Devisery for security's sake.

Saunders Hall was only partially lit now that classes were over. The Device lamps over the main doors and the two secondary entrances burned brightly, and the lighted windows at the very top of the hall marked where other student Devisers were working late in their own workshops. A few lights near the foundation were more windows, these opening off the basement rooms. She'd wondered aloud why Ian's workshop was on the inside, without a window, and Ian had said only, "No chance of anyone prying into my affairs." Veronica hated windowless interior rooms. They made her feel like she was being interred. But Ian probably had a sound point.

None of the school halls were made to lock, the great doors lacking even a latch to keep them shut. It was a miracle of engineering that balanced the heavy oak doors so perfectly they swung open and shut with barely a push. Veronica slipped inside and hurried along the halls to the basement stairs. She'd never been inside Saunders Hall—inside any of the school buildings—after dark, and although the hallways were well-lit, she still involuntarily slowed her steps. Her footsteps and her labored breathing echoed off the stones as she walked, making her feel as if she were the only person in Saunders Hall that night.

One of the Devices lighting the stairs to the basement was out, and the remaining Device cast odd shadows across the steps. It made her own shadow stretch out, long and thin like nothing human. Veronica shuddered. She should rein in her imagination, if it was going to come up with such absurdities. But she took each step with care, rounding the landing and descending to the basement level as cautiously as she imagined a sneak thief might.

That the architects of the Scholia had not felt compelled to be perfectly faithful to the Valantine vision had never comforted her so much as it did right now. A true Valantine building the size of Saunders Hall should have catacombs beneath, dark stone arches dripping with condensation, torches imperfectly lighting the uneven stones underfoot. The actual basement, however, was dry and comfortably low-ceilinged without a single arch. Smooth flagstones made a reassuring foundation under her feet. Even the doors were lightweight and modern, not the oak slabs of the aboveground rooms.

Even so, the quiet unnerved Veronica. She knew there were people here, because she'd seen the lit basement windows, but the place was as silent as if everyone had gone home for Wintersmeet half a season early. She discovered she was walking as silently as her boots would allow in an effort not to break the stillness and felt impatient with her silliness. Stepping more firmly, she increased her pace. Ian would likely be wondering where she was.

Ian's workshop was about two-thirds of the way down one long hall, on the inside of the corridor. It was easy enough to find even if she hadn't been there before, because each room was labeled with its occupant's name. Veronica knocked on the door and waited. No one responded. She turned the knob and entered anyway.

The room was pitch-black, giving her a moment's unease. "Ian?" she said, though it was clear no one was there. She fumbled beside the door for the knob that controlled the room lights and turned it.

The lights came up slowly as they always did. For a moment, in the dimness, Veronica thought she was in the wrong room, after all. Nothing looked familiar except the table in the center of the room and the cabinets lining the far wall. She realized, just as the lights came on fully, it was because something had ripped through the room like a winter storm, tossing papers and chairs and bits of Devices in all directions. She gaped, confused at the mess. Ian always kept his workshop in perfect tidiness.

She became aware that she was staring at a shape her mind couldn't make sense of. It lay on the floor, a length of pipe curving around a sphere—and with that, the image clicked into place, and Veronica gasped and darted forward, falling to her knees beside Ian. Her friend lay with one arm flung over his head, his face turned away from it. Blood made a small pool beneath his arm and head, blood that stank with a horrible coppery wetness in the tiny room.

"Ian," Veronica gasped. Her voice made no more sound in the stillness than a bird's wings. She swallowed and tried again. "Ian, are you..." She put her hand on his shoulder and shook him, tentatively. Ian's body shifted, but he didn't raise his head. He didn't move his arm. He wasn't breathing.

Veronica clamped down on a scream that built in the back of her throat. Whimpering, she shook Ian harder, making his head loll like a puppet whose strings have been cut. His eyes were open, staring sightlessly at nothing. It was how Landon had looked, near the end. Past and present collided in her vision so hard she thought she might faint. She closed her eyes and made herself breathe until the moment passed, then once more looked at Ian, hoping she was wrong.

She wasn't wrong. Ian was dead.

8

---

*V*eronica reached out to close Ian's eyes, then stopped with her hand inches from his face. This was no accidental death. Something terrible had happened here. More memories surfaced: *Don't touch the body. Need to examine. No interference.* She swallowed bile and made herself focus. Based on the condition of the room, there had been a fight, or someone had searched for something. She didn't know how to tell from looking at Ian what blow had killed him, but someone would. So she shouldn't move him, shouldn't touch him at all.

She stood and stared blindly at the body of her friend. She didn't know who to tell. If Ian were only injured, she would immediately run to the infirmary in Covington Hall, but he was beyond their help. She needed the law. If this were Aurilien, there was the city guard, but this was the Scholia, and as far as she knew they didn't have even a token guard force. But she didn't think she could make it as far as Knightsbury without breaking down. And telling the Knightsbury guards about it without warning the Magister seemed wrong. She ignored the tiny, terrible part of her that wanted to run away and let someone else "discover" the body. She couldn't do that to Ian.

She was at the door before it occurred to her that she couldn't count on no one coming down here. And if someone else did enter the room before she returned with the authorities, that person might not be as cautious about the evidence as she was. She swallowed again and returned to kneel beside Ian. Carefully, she felt along the side leg of his trousers until she found a pocket slit. She'd seen him drop his keys, his spare change, bits of Device, and all sorts of things into it many times since she'd met him.

She tried not to be conscious of his inert form, how his flesh gave in a sickeningly non-living way as her hand felt around in his pocket. Reaching further, she lost her balance, and her hand landed on Ian's back as she caught herself. She let out a little cry of despair and horror and pushed herself upright just as her fingers wrapped around a ring of keys. She snatched them free, spilling a couple of brass gears that came with them onto the floor, and rose hurriedly, gasping for breath.

There were seven keys of varying sizes. Veronica's first guess at which one fit the workshop door was correct. She turned off the light, then, with a shudder, turned it back to full. She couldn't bear to leave Ian in the dark, like a... She shuddered again and locked the door behind her. Then she ran.

As she pelted through the halls and up the basement stairs, she frantically went over possibilities. The Magister was the obvious choice, but he lived in Knightsbury, and Veronica didn't feel any more up to that trip than she had ten minutes ago. By contrast, she could reach Master Lansing at any time, but she didn't strike Veronica as someone who would be good in a crisis, not to mention the argument they'd had that afternoon. She didn't know which of the other Scholia administrators had the authority to handle this situation. But she had to tell someone.

She flung the Saunders Hall door open and made for the instructors' housing. While the Magister and many of the high-ranking Scholia Masters and Magisters lived in Knightsbury, most of the instructors lived on campus in two houses, Justice and Mercy. Veronica had been amused by the names when she first arrived. Now, nothing seemed funny anymore.

Justice House was the first one she came to. She stumbled to a halt at its door and yanked on the knob. It didn't give. Her breath sobbing in her chest, she banged on the door so hard it hurt her fist. The pain startled sense back into her. She couldn't tell just anyone, but how was she, with barely four weeks' experience of the instructors, supposed to choose?

The door's lock ground open as if it were a hundred years old rather than two, and the door swung open. An elderly man peered out at Veronica. "Instructors' consulting hours are eight to nine in the morning and four-thirty to five-thirty in the evening. No exceptions."

"This is an emergency," Veronica gasped. "I need to speak with Master Tyndale immediately. Please. Can you just—will you take him a message that Lady North is asking for him? Just a message. And if he won't see me, I won't take any more of your time." She didn't know if Tyndale lived in Justice House, but his was the only name that came to mind.

"Lady North?" The man peered at her even more closely. His eyes, watery and slightly protuberant, reminded her of a couple of poached eggs with brown yolks filmed over by Time. "This is very irregular."

"*Please,*" Veronica begged. "I'll even wait out here."

The elderly man's lips drew up in a scowl. "All right," he said, and closed the door.

So she'd guessed correctly. Veronica wrapped her cloak more closely around herself. Shivering, she stamped her feet. She hadn't felt the cold in her dash across campus, and now she felt frozen from the inside out. Her memory of Ian's body returned, and she closed her eyes and suppressed a sob. Now was not the time for crying. Ian was dead, had probably been murdered—

Murder. She hadn't thought the word before, but it had hovered in her subconscious since the moment she realized Ian was dead. Someone had murdered Ian, destroyed his workshop, and—

Veronica became breathless for a completely different reason. Ian's body, she realized, had still been warm. He hadn't been dead for long. If she hadn't been late to their meeting, she might have stopped the killer. Or she might have suffered Ian's fate as well. Once more black spots rose up in her vision, and she breathed slowly until the dizziness passed.

The door opened. "Lady North," Tyndale said. "Come inside. You must be freezing." He looked so odd without his Master's black robe, in shirt and waistcoat and ordinary but well-made trousers but no neckcloth.

"No, I need—Master Tyndale, you must come with me immediately." She hadn't thought this through. She didn't want to blurt out the truth in public, not with that doorkeeper almost certainly hovering within earshot, but she hadn't worked out what she would tell Tyndale to get him to follow her. She didn't even know why she'd chosen him of all the instructors she knew. Maybe she'd felt a law-speaker was the closest thing to guard authority she could find.

Tyndale's glass-green eyes glinted in the light from the Device over the door. "Must I?" he said, arching an eyebrow.

His dismissive tone cut through her sorrow and turmoil and turned it to anger. "Of course not," she said, drawing herself up. She and Master Tyndale were the same height, part of her noticed. "But this is an emergency, and I need someone in authority to help me. I can't explain and I can't tell you details. I hoped you'd be willing to trust me, but if I have to run all the way to Knightsbury to fetch the Magister, I will."

Tyndale's expression didn't change. He turned away from the door, leaving it hanging open. Veronica felt sicker than before. Her bold words turned to acid inside her. Why she'd thought Tyndale was the best choice, she had no idea, but he was as awful and arrogant as all her friends had been telling her.

Then the door opened wider, and Tyndale emerged, pulling on a greatcoat. "Where are we going, Lady North?" he asked, his voice neutral.

Stunned, Veronica said only, "I'll show you. Please, don't ask questions. I don't think I could bear it."

Tyndale said nothing, but she caught the edge of the look he sent her way. He didn't look curious, or angry, or anything but impassive. She wondered if he experienced emotion like a normal person. Anyone else would have battered at her with questions regardless. To her surprise, she felt a rush of gratitude. His silent presence beside her reassured rather than intimidated her.

She led the way at not quite a run back to Saunders Hall,

which was as still as before. They passed a student on his way out; he looked at them curiously, but didn't pause. Veronica had a moment's panic—suppose he was Ian's killer?—before reminding herself Ian's killer was long gone.

The thought of a killer wandering free through the Scholia hastened her steps. Irrationally, she feared they would arrive at Ian's workshop and find nothing wrong, the room tidied, the body gone, and then Tyndale would think she was mad. Her wavering shadow beside Tyndale's mocked her as they made their way past the inactive light Device on the basement stairs. She felt as drawn-out and wan as her shadow, and knew she was on the brink of collapse. She reminded herself all this was for Ian's sake and focused on putting one foot in front of the other.

Tyndale looked at the name plate on Ian's door as Veronica unlocked the door with a shaking hand. "Mister Frost," he said. "Why do you have his key?"

Veronica shook her head mutely and pushed the door open, gesturing to Tyndale to precede her. Tyndale took two steps into the room and stopped, making Veronica bump up against his warm, solid back. Then he strode quickly to Ian's side and knelt as Veronica had. "Dear heaven," he said, then fell silent. Veronica shut the door and stood beside it, feeling as if she'd laid down a great burden.

Tyndale touched Ian's throat, then his face, and lifted Ian's head to examine the wound Veronica had guessed was there but hadn't been willing to touch. "When did you find him?" he asked, his voice intent in a way Veronica had never heard from him.

"It was only fifteen minutes ago. I think. I'm not sure." She looked at her watch and was amazed at how little time had passed. "I arrived a little after seven. I was late. We were supposed—" Her breath caught on a sob, and she sucked in a breath to keep from crying. "He had something he wanted to show me, and I was supposed to be here at seven. I wasn't that late, but I was late." She heard herself babbling and shut up.

Tyndale rose and turned to face her. "Did you touch anything? Move anything?"

"Just the—his body. I didn't move him, but I thought at first he was only injured. I took his keys so I could lock the door. I was afraid of someone else finding him."

"That was wise." Tyndale moved around the room, examining the scattered papers, the Devices and loose pieces of metal covering the floor, without touching anything. "Does the workshop always look like this, do you know?"

Veronica shook her head. "He's—he was always very tidy." She looked around more carefully. Despite the mess, she couldn't see anything extra that might have been what Ian was so excited to show her. Nothing big was missing, either. If the attacker had taken something, it would be small and easily overlooked.

Tyndale stepped carefully over Ian's legs. "Hmm." He bent to examine the central table. It was a plain, battered thing, scarred with burn marks and nicks from a hundred experiments by a hundred other Devisers. Veronica walked forward to join him.

"Look at that," Tyndale said, pointing. The corner of the table directly over where Ian's head lay was dark with blood. Veronica's gorge rose, and she turned away, clenching her back teeth together and swallowing desperately to keep from vomiting.

"I apologize," Tyndale said. "You're so calm, I thought you were inured to the sight of his death. Are you well?"

Veronica shook her head, but the urge to vomit had already passed. "I'm sorry, it's all right, it's just—he was my friend."

"I understand." Tyndale crouched beside Ian and lifted his head again. "It's possible he slipped and struck his head."

Veronica turned. "But what about the workshop? Ian would never let it get to this state!"

"I said it was possible. I didn't say it was likely. It would be difficult for someone to strike their head this hard just in a fall." Tyndale made as if to touch the bloodstain, but stopped with his fingers an inch from the table. "And you saw no one leaving the room?"

"I didn't see anyone leave Saunders Hall at all. There was no one in the halls."

"Have you any idea what he intended to show you?"

"None. But I don't see anything different in here. I mean, anything extra. Obviously the mess is different."

Tyndale stepped over Ian's body and came to Veronica's side. "Why did you come to me?" he asked.

He still sounded impassive, as if none of this mattered, and that angered Veronica. All her fear and grief came out in a swift, "I don't know. I'm starting to regret it. Don't you care that he's dead?"

Tyndale's expression hardened slightly. "I care that a student was murdered," he said, "and I intend to do what I can to bring the killer to justice. Is that not enough?"

Veronica's anger dwindled to nothing. "I'm sorry," she said, feeling small and fragile and unable to meet his gaze. "Of course it is."

Tyndale turned away. "You're grieving, and you're in shock," he said. "That was cruel of me to say. Go back to your rooms and get warm. I'll take care of this from here."

"Is that...something you can do? I didn't know who else to talk to. Is there a city guard in Knightsbury?"

"That won't be necessary. The Scholia takes care of its own." To her surprise, Tyndale put a hand on her shoulder. "Please, Lady North. You've done more than enough. Now, get some rest, if you can. News like this won't stay secret long."

Veronica wanted to protest, but she caught sight of Ian again, and finally tears threatened to flow. She didn't want to cry in front of Tyndale, so she said, somewhat thickly, "Thank you. Please tell me if there's anything else I can do to help."

"You should be prepared for questions as soon as it's known you discovered the body." Tyndale actually sounded sympathetic, but Veronica didn't want to look at him and see scorn or impassivity or anything else that might burst the dam.

"I know," she said. "I remember."

She turned and left the room, concentrating once more on putting one foot in front of the other. That kept the tears at bay all the way through the front door and halfway back to Patience House. Then she stopped beneath the bell tower of the bethel and let herself cry. The yard was dark, the bethel unlit, and she felt like the only person left alive in the world. Ian was dead. Lively, intelligent, talented Ian, fiercely dedicated to his work and loyal to his friends. And someone had taken his head in both hands and slammed it—

This time, she couldn't contain herself. She rushed to the ornamental bushes, spiky and leafless, that surrounded the bethel and vomited thin yellow bile all over the branches. Then she knelt, sobbing, until the damp soaked through the knees of her trousers and she was shivering too hard to control. She wiped her mouth and stood. Samantha would wonder where she was, but even if she had been up to a walk in the chilly darkness, she couldn't bear to face people just now.

She ran into Mistress Holyoak when she returned to Patience House, literally ran into her as she opened the door in the woman's face. The chatelaine exclaimed at the collision, saying, "Watch yourself, Lady North! Nothing's so important that you should ignore common decency."

"I apologize, Mistress Holyoak," Veronica said dully. The woman's hostility felt like it was happening at a distance, past a glass wall even sound barely penetrated. "I wasn't paying attention."

"I—Lady North, is something wrong?"

Veronica was already past her and headed for the stairs. "Nothing you need worry about," she said. "Have a good evening."

No one she passed in the halls looked closely enough at her to see her distress. That satisfied her. She made it to her sitting room and wearily shed her cloak and boots. Then she turned on the Device burner on her tiny stove and filled the kettle with water for tea. Peppermint tea wasn't traditionally something that settled one's nerves, but it soothed her, reminding her of when she was small and her mother would always make peppermint tea after a childhood tragedy. She'd never thought to try its efficacy against a true disaster.

She changed into her nightdress. Her trousers hit the floor with a muffled *clink*. Curious, she dipped her hand into her pocket and found Ian's key ring. She should have given it to Tyndale, but she'd forgotten she had it. Something to do in the morning, as if anything about this nightmare was normal.

She returned downstairs to finish making the tea, then filled a large mug and sat curled into one corner of the sofa. It was cold enough to justify turning on the heater Device, but any more movement was beyond her. The hot liquid coursed through her, restoring feeling to her numb body. It couldn't touch her mind, though, which persisted in throwing up images of Ian lying dead on his workshop floor.

To banish the images, she made herself think logically. Who would have wanted Ian dead? He'd had that breakthrough, the one he wanted to share with her—was it a breakthrough worth killing for? She'd never really taken his insistence on secrecy seriously, given that his earlier experiments with Devisery hadn't exactly been successful, but he *was* dedicated, and clever, and there was no reason he couldn't have finally succeeded with this mystery Device.

She drank down the last drops of tea and set the mug on the floor. That was just the most obvious reason. The murder could have been over something personal. But Ian was a friendly, like-able young man, and she couldn't imagine anyone wanting to kill him over a personal argument. If anything, she could see him—well, not *killing* someone, Ian wasn't that sort of person, but she could see him starting a fight over a woman. She didn't believe for a minute that he was as over his feelings for Samantha as he claimed, not with how he wouldn't look her in the face whenever Samantha's name came up.

But...no, that didn't make any sense. Why would one of Samantha's other beaux approach Ian in his workshop for them to get in a fight? It wasn't as if Ian would have asked someone else to join him, not if he expected Veronica to arrive shortly. Her brain must truly be muddled to have considered that.

It had to be the mystery Device. She needed to tell someone what she knew. The guards, probably, when they came to investigate. Except Tyndale had said something like "the Scholia takes care of its own," which meant...what? That he or the Magister or someone would try to find Ian's killer? That seemed like a bad idea. They should leave it to the professionals. That's what they were professionals for.

With those thoughts spinning madly through her head, she drifted off to sleep.

9

Veronica woke, stiff and aching, sprawled out on her sofa with her legs hooked over the armrest. Morning light, pale and chilly, filled the room. She sat up slowly, feeling like an unoiled Device whose joints had frozen. Various pops and clicks reminded her she wasn't thirty anymore. She yawned, stretched—and memory returned.

Her heart sped up as if she were still in Ian's workshop, crouched over his body. She breathed deeply to calm herself. She couldn't believe she had slept so soundly after that. Surely she should have had a restless night. But aside from the stiffness, which had begun to fade as she moved, she felt rested and clear-headed.

She checked her watch Device. Quarter to eight. She wondered if the news about Ian's death had spread yet. She was supposed to meet with Lansing at nine and with her architectonics study group at ten. Somehow, she didn't think much scholastic work would get done at either of those meetings if gossip had traveled as fast as it usually did.

Yawning, she made her way up the stairs to her bedroom, listening to her knees pop on the first steps. How she hated getting old. Her body was still hale, but there were all the little things that told her age was setting in—the lines and spots on her face, the way even a short run winded her as it hadn't before, the popping of joints. And yet her mind was as quick as ever, something her recent studies had proved true. Aging was so unfair.

She changed her clothes and felt slightly better at putting on a fresh shirt and trousers, though the old ones hadn't been dirty. Her bed was still rumpled from her nap yesterday; she hadn't tidied it in her rush to meet Ian. She straightened the blankets, fluffed the pillow, and then walked to the window. Her view from the tower was of the back of Honor House, the other women's dormitory, and of the fields behind the Scholia that extended south for several miles until it reached the next town, Brookside. From where she stood, no people were visible. She hadn't spoken to anyone but Tyndale and Mistress Holyoak since yesterday afternoon, and she felt a sudden urge to go where people were, to remind herself life went on.

Someone was knocking on her door, pounding really, when she came downstairs. She opened it to find Samantha, her dressing gown falling open over a silk nightdress. "Veronica, you won't believe this," she burst out. "Ian Frost is dead!"

For half a second, Veronica considered playing dumb, avoiding the barrage of questions that would follow if she told the truth. Then she remembered Samantha was her friend, and she didn't want to lie to her friend. "I know. I found his body."

Samantha's mouth fell open. "You—Veronica! What happened?"

Veronica ushered Samantha inside and took a seat on the sofa. "I went to his workshop last night and found him there. He'd hit his head on the corner of a table, and there was blood..." She drew in a calming breath. It seemed she wasn't as recovered as she believed.

"How awful for you!" Samantha sat beside Veronica and threw her arms around her. "I can't believe—" She let out a sob. "I feel awful. I was so unkind to him, and now...oh, listen to me, making this all about myself when you must be in the most horrid state."

"I feel better than I did last night."

"Such a terrible accident," Samantha went on. "You never imagine it happening to someone you know."

Veronica realized she'd inadvertently led Samantha to believe Ian had merely tripped and fallen. "Actually," she began, then went silent. It was possible Tyndale and the Magister didn't want anyone to know Ian had been murdered, in which case she had no business spreading the news around. "It was terrible," she agreed.

Samantha released her. "And everyone will want you to talk about it once they know you found...him. I'm so sorry. Do you need anything to help you sleep? I have a powder I can give you—"

"I'm fine, thank you." Veronica wished Samantha weren't quite so solicitous. "Really, I don't need anything."

"Oh, of course. I know how you hate being fussed over. Maybe you shouldn't tell anyone else. I mean, the news will get out eventually, you know what gossip is like, but if you're lucky, it will take a while."

"I'd really prefer not to talk about it, yes." Except to Tyndale or the Magister or whoever was in charge of finding the murderer. Her memories of Ian's body no longer sickened her. Instead, they filled her with a burning desire to see the killer brought to justice.

"Is that why you didn't meet me at the pub last night?" Samantha said. "I was worried about you, but I thought you'd just forgotten and gone to bed early. You did seem tired yesterday. I almost came to check on you, but I figured you would need sleep."

Veronica was so grateful she hadn't had to deal with Samantha last night. She might have told her everything in her turmoil. "It's all right. But I'm so hungry. I missed supper entirely."

Samantha rose and pulled Veronica to her feet. "Then let's go to breakfast, and you can pretend to be shocked by the news. Though really I think if we eat in a corner, no one will think to approach you."

It turned out Samantha was right. Everyone was too busy chattering to their friends to notice them. Veronica devoured eggs and sausage as if she'd never seen food before. Her appetite had certainly improved since she'd come to the Scholia. She'd put on weight for the first time since her pregnancy with Francis.

The refectory dining hall was abuzz with gossip. It didn't take effort to hear what everyone was saying: Ian Frost dead, accident in his workshop, what a tragedy. It seemed she'd been right, and the Scholia had kept it quiet that Ian had been murdered. Rather than relieving her mind, Veronica found the idea unsettling. She knew—oh, how well she knew—it was better not to inflame rumor with an even more dramatic story, but it still felt wrong to pretend it was only an accident that had taken Ian's life, like that pretense would keep his killer from facing justice.

She and Samantha ate in silence. Veronica thought Samantha might be listening to the gossip, too. That was confirmed when Samantha said, "I can't bear this. All these people talking as if they knew Ian well."

"He did have many friends," Veronica said.

"Yes, but..." Samantha drank from her coffee mug and grimaced. "I shouldn't talk. I wish I'd spent more time with him, but I don't know if that's because I really cared for him or because it's too late now."

Uncomfortable, Veronica said, "But Ian said it was over. Between you. I'm sorry, I don't mean to pry. I just thought he'd broken it off, or you had."

Samantha laughed, a brittle sound, and took another drink. "Ian and I have been on and off again for most of a year. He always came back. Does that sound hopelessly arrogant? I liked him, but he was just so intense, I couldn't deal with that. I should have ended it once and for all rather than leading him on."

Veronica hadn't thought Ian had behaved like someone who intended to go crawling back, but she'd known him barely four weeks, and who knew what his usual behavior was? "Don't blame yourself," she told Samantha, whose eyes were wet. "It doesn't matter now. And it's not like your relationship is what got him killed."

Samantha nodded and wiped her eyes. "I know. But you always consider the might-have-beens at a time like this, right?"

The memory of Landon's final moments gripped Veronica

so hard she couldn't breathe for a moment. "Yes, that's true," she said when she regained control of herself.

Samantha pushed her plate away and checked her watch. "I have to run," she said. "I'll see you at supper, all right? Maybe we can get some friends together and have a proper memorial down at the pub afterward."

Veronica nodded. When Samantha was gone, she looked at her own watch and discovered it was almost nine. The idea of meeting with Lansing depressed her. Either Lansing knew the details of what had happened, in which case she would burden Veronica with her well-meaning but uncomfortable sympathies, or she knew nothing and would want to talk about scholastic things. Veronica wasn't sure she wanted to think about her classwork. But that was foolish, because no matter what had happened to Ian, life went on, and he would have been the first to chastise her for letting his death interfere with her studies.

Lansing's office was as cluttered with paperwork as ever. The Master stood when Veronica entered and moved a stack of papers from a chair to the floor. "Such a terrible tragedy," she said. "I understand you found the body. I'm so sorry you had to witness that."

"Thank you." Veronica sat with her blank book on her lap, but didn't open it. "It was a terrible shock. Ian was a good friend."

"I didn't realize you knew each other." Lansing's hostility of the previous day had disappeared. "I didn't have much contact with the young man, but his tutor Master Blandings had nothing but good to say of him. It's a tremendous loss to Devisery, in addition to the personal loss, of course."

"I didn't realize he was such a valued student."

Lansing sat back and twirled a pen around her fingers. "Oh, yes. Of course, he hadn't invented anything viable yet, but according to Master Blandings, his failures were the stuff of genius. It was only a matter of time before he made a name for himself."

Veronica wondered about Ian's mystery Device again. "I know he was very excited about his latest project. It was why I was in Saunders Hall last night—he had some big break-through he wanted to show me."

Lansing perked up. "Really? Do you know what it was?"

"No. Ian was always closemouthed about his Devisery. He worried someone might steal it. I don't know how likely that was, but it definitely influenced his behavior, that fear."

"That's unfortunate. Don't you think it would be wonderful if he had finally achieved success? One wishes it might not be posthumous success, naturally, but it would be such a wonderful legacy."

"I suppose," Veronica said. She didn't think any Device was worth Ian's life, but it was certainly true it would be wonderful if he'd actually made that breakthrough. She wondered if Howard knew what it was. No, Ian had said he didn't trust Howard with the secret. But Howard might know *something*.

Lansing had opened a folder and was clearly ready to move on. "Now, let's see, Lady North. Your studies are progressing well, and I understand you've engaged a tutorial assistant for help in your law class. It's not too much for you?"

Veronica ground her teeth and managed not to sound annoyed. "No, I just need some direction, that's all."

"Very well. Then…"

Half an hour later, Veronica left Lansing's office and stood outside the front door of Godfrey Hall, the administration building. Instead of returning to Patience House, where she was due to meet with her engineering study group at ten, she turned right and headed for Fortitude House. She hadn't seen Howard at breakfast, and the idea of tracking down Ian's mystery Device had caught hold of her.

The majordomo at Fortitude House showed her in and said, "Mister Peterson hasn't left all morning. I believe he's ill. Would you like to leave a message?"

Veronica wondered if Howard's illness was actually grief, and she felt guilty at pestering him. Then she reminded herself that Howard was her friend, too, and they ought to be grieving together. Maybe it was wrong of her to decide what was best for him, but she knew Howard well enough to realize he would make himself more miserable if he wallowed alone. "Tell him Veronica North would like to see him," she said. "I think he shouldn't be alone. Ian was his good friend."

The majordomo nodded as if he, too, had known about Ian's death. Well, Ian had lived here; probably Tyndale had sent the news here first. "I'll be right back, if you'll have a seat, Lady North," he said.

Veronica settled herself into a chair and examined the clock on the far wall. Its case was crooked, like someone had thumped the wall hard with a fist and made it shift. She itched to straighten it, but it looked heavy and was too high for her to reach comfortably. So instead she just looked at it and wondered how long it had been awry. This room was just the same as its counterparts in the other dormitories, but the décor was more unified, and aside from the clock, it was in perfect order. Veronica wished the similarities weren't so overt. The resemblance left her disoriented, as if she might have been in any of the dormitories.

Presently, she heard someone approaching, and Howard appeared in the doorway. He looked terrible. His fair hair, never well-kempt, looked as if he'd combed it with a rake. His red-rimmed eyes regarded Veronica dully, as if he didn't remember who she was. But he said, "Veronica. You heard the news."

He sounded so miserable, so on the verge of tears, that tears came to Veronica's eyes. She stood and, without thinking, opened her arms to Howard. "It's so awful," she said. "I found him, Howard. I found his body."

Howard jerked. He came forward and embraced her. At any other time, it would have amused her to see how awkwardly they both did it, as if hugs were a language neither of them spoke. Now the simple touch merely comforted her. She patted Howard's back gently as he cried, hoarsely as if he'd already done a lot of crying on his own, and let herself weep more quietly.

When Howard's sobs wound down, he extricated himself from her embrace and said, "Sorry. I didn't mean to do that. It's just…"

"Let's walk outside. I need fresh air," Veronica suggested.

The day was cool and sunny, without a cloud in the sky. If not for the lingering dampness of the grass, Veronica would never have guessed the weather had been stormy the day before. She and Howard walked around the side of Fortitude House without speaking. There were no gravel paths on this side of the campus, but thousands of feet had worn trails in the grass around and behind the dormitories. Had there been trees instead of plains, Veronica would have suspected many of those feet had been interested in assignations, but there was nowhere for that kind of privacy.

Now, though, she and Howard were alone in the grassy

fields that stretched as far as Veronica could see. They walked in silent accord southward, past where the trimmed lawns grew to the untended fields where the weeds were tall and yellow as Autumn made them. Howard had his head bowed, and Veronica didn't think he saw anything around him. He seemed to be willing to walk in silence forever.

"Did Ian tell you he'd had a breakthrough?" she asked.

Howard nodded. "He wouldn't say what. Said I'd just blab." He let out a harsh laugh. "He was probably right. But I wish he'd trusted me. I do know—" His voice cut off abruptly.

"Know what?" Veronica said.

"Oh, nothing."

Veronica shot him a sharp look. His cheeks were pink, and his mouth was closed tight the way it went when he was lying. "That's not true."

"No, but it doesn't matter now, does it? Ian's dead, and his secrets died with him."

Impulsively, Veronica said, "Except for the secrets you kept. Howard, what do you know about this new Device?"

Howard shook his head violently. "Nothing anyone can use."

Veronica stopped, bringing Howard to a halt. "What if that's not true? Wouldn't it be wonderful if Ian's last Device lived after him? Howard, you have to tell what you know."

Howard raised his head to meet her eyes. "I'm nowhere near the Deviser Ian was," he said miserably. "But I helped him with his work sometimes. And I'm probably the only person still alive—" He choked briefly, then composed himself. "The only person who knows all of Ian's workshops."

"Did he have many?"

"Just three." Howard sniffed, then brought out a soggy

handkerchief and blew his nose into it. "Aurilien, Brookside, and Knightsbury. And here. I guess that's actually four." His face went pale. "I shouldn't have told you that. Ian would—" He sagged again. "Ian's not in a position to kill me for being loose-lipped. I suppose secrecy doesn't matter anymore."

Veronica patted his shoulder. "It's all right, Howard."

"Anyway," Howard went on, "there's the one in Aurilien, but he hadn't been back there in a season. Brookside was new, not much more than a room at the back of a tavern. But he spent a lot of time in Knightsbury these last few weeks, in the work-shop in Stowe Road."

Veronica's breath caught in excitement. "Maybe the rest of the Device is there! Or spread out over those places! Howard, think what this could mean!"

Howard's brow furrowed. "I thought his breakthrough was in his Saunders Hall workshop. Don't we already have that? It's the most important piece, I imagine."

Veronica hesitated. Almost she told Howard the truth about Ian's death. But Ian hadn't been exaggerating when he said Howard couldn't keep a secret. "The breakthrough means nothing without the rest," she improvised.

"Well, I suppose Master Varner can do something with it," Howard said gloomily. "I don't feel like much of a friend at present."

Veronica regarded Howard's miserable face, and something shifted in her head. The breakthrough, whatever it was, had disappeared, stolen by Ian's murderer. The murderer needed the rest of the Device for the breakthrough to matter. And Howard was the only person who knew where all Ian's secrets were kept.

Suppose Howard was the murderer?

Suddenly Howard's excessive grief seemed unnatural, faked even. Veronica held herself carefully still, willing her growing fear not to show. "You're a wonderful friend," she said, "and you shouldn't feel bad. It's not as if...as if you had anything to do with it."

Howard shook his head. "No, and you must be suffering more than I, if you found his body. I'm sorry. You know how bad I am at personal matters. I never say the right thing."

"It's all right. You know, I almost feel grateful that it was me and not some stranger? Like, at least Ian had someone who cared about him at the end." Veronica turned and walked in the direction of Fortitude House, carefully keeping her gait a steady stroll. No alerting the possible murderer to her suspicions. "Though I wish I'd been faster, because I might have been there when it happened," she added, keeping a close eye on Howard.

He didn't flinch. "Don't think like that. You'll start blaming yourself. It's nobody's fault, right?"

"Right," Veronica said. "Nobody's fault."

10

Veronica left Howard at the door to his dormitory and, when he'd gone inside, hurried across the strip of lawn that separated the student dormitories from faculty housing. She knocked on the door of Justice House and, when the elderly man appeared, said, "I'm looking for Master Tyndale. Is he in? I know it's after nine."

The man eyed her with his rheumy eyes. His jaw worked a couple of times as if he were chewing a particularly tough piece of gristle. Finally, he said, "Master Tyndale takes tutorials this time of Fifthday. Ask at his office." He shut the door in Veronica's face.

Well. That had been both helpful and rude. Veronica thought for a moment. She shouldn't interrupt Tyndale's work, but if he was the one investigating the murder, he needed to know about the possibility that Howard might have done it. Despite his words, she couldn't imagine he hadn't handed the investigation over to the Knightsbury city guard, but she didn't know any of those officers and couldn't walk into the constabulary in that city and start blithering on about murder and suspects.

Her watch Device chimed the hour. She was late for her study group. She scowled and headed across the yard to Godfrey Hall. Missing one study group wouldn't damage her marks in the class, where she was already at the top of the rankings. Engineering had come remarkably easy to her, despite the intervening decades. If anything, the study group would regret not having her there to guide them. She felt a wicked satisfaction at the arrogant thought. It wasn't arrogance if you really were good, was it?

The main office was crowded with students and a couple of black-robed Masters in blue stoles. Veronica waited impatiently for someone to notice her, wishing, not for the first time, that she was assertive and bold instead of diffident and shy. She hated being the focus of attention, and boldness guaranteed that. Elspeth was bold without being rude; it was too bad Veronica had never learned the trick of it from watching her niece.

Finally, someone at the wide counter that divided the room between the petitioners and the officials and secretaries said, "Yes, Lady North?"

"I have to speak to Master Tyndale. Could you tell me which is his office?"

The man nodded. "Third floor, fifth door on the right from the south stairs. But he might have left already."

Veronica thanked him and hurried away, inwardly angry with herself. Her stupid timidity was going to have serious repercussions someday. Suppose this had been a matter of life and death?

She trotted up the stairs and, breathing more heavily than she liked, walked down the third floor hall, counting doors. She didn't know why they didn't label them the way the Saunders Hall workshops were labeled. It would be so much more convenient for students—though maybe that was the point; students' convenience didn't matter. She wasn't sure how she felt about that.

She came to a stop outside the fifth door on the right and checked her watch again. 10:18. Typically, tutorial sessions lasted half an hour, starting on the hour and half-hour. Veronica decided to wait before knocking. More timidity, more adhering to polite behavior. She was almost disgusted with herself. And yet politeness and civility had gotten her safely through fifty years of life, so why should she change now?

She waited. People passed her, went into and came out of other doors. None of them did more than glance at her in idle curiosity. Finally, when the minute hand touched the six and no one had emerged from Tyndale's office, she knocked firmly on the door and heard a muffled "Come in."

Tyndale was alone behind his desk. Veronica took in her surroundings at a glance, noted the large painting—a Velasco, she thought, though it had to be a copy—hanging behind the desk, the little sculptures pressed into service as bookends on the two bookcases flanking the door, the soft Eskandelic rug beneath the chairs in front of the desk, and exclaimed, "Oh! You have a d'Arnot!"

Tyndale looked up from his work and lowered his pen. "I do. Most students don't recognize his work. You like it?"

"I—" She didn't want to blurt out that she was the great artist's patron. It sounded so affected. "Yes. The original is in the palace, in the southwest wing. I'd like it moved somewhere public so it can be appreciated. But Landon always had other demands on his time." *That* sounded even worse. She felt a blush beginning in her cheeks and spreading across her face and down her neck, and ducked her head so Tyndale wouldn't see her distress.

Tyndale half-turned in his seat to look at the quarter-scale replica of *Xavier*, turned so the warrior's blade pointed in challenge at whoever sat at the desk. "It's come with me everywhere I've lived over the last twenty-five years, like a true companion. But you didn't come here to talk about art. I presume." He gestured at the chairs. "Please, have a seat."

Veronica sat. Her blush had subsided enough that she could say, quite calmly, "I wanted to ask what the Knightsbury guards are doing about Ian's murder."

Tyndale's eyebrow arched in a now-familiar gesture. "The Knightsbury guards," he said, "have nothing to do with this investigation. I told you, the Scholia handles things its own way."

"But—surely they have experience in catching killers?"

"I wouldn't be so sure. They are a city constabulary at best, with nothing approximating the kind of experience needed in this situation. I assure you, I am more than capable of finding Mister Frost's killer."

Veronica felt a protest rising in her chest, and stifled it. She knew nothing about crime, nothing—almost nothing—about how murder investigations were handled, and Tyndale's certainty was rock-solid, not something she wanted to dash herself against. "Then I suppose you're the one I should talk to."

"About what, Lady North?"

Veronica stifled the feeling that she was being disloyal to

Howard. "It's about Ian's friend Howard. Howard Peterson. He worked closely with Ian and I think he might know something."

Tyndale's glass-green eyes glinted briefly. "Or might be the killer."

She felt even more uncomfortable. "I didn't say that."

"No, you didn't. You aren't the sort to want to believe evil of your friends." Tyndale leaned back in his chair and rested his hands on his desk, his fingers loosely interlaced. "I intend to discuss things with Mister Peterson this afternoon, once he's sufficiently afraid."

Veronica shot upright. "Afraid? Don't you dare torment him!"

"I would never do such a thing. My assessment of Mister Peterson is that he is the type to get worked up over any emotional crisis. I simply want him to be...pliable."

"Howard doesn't need to be pliable to talk," Veronica said sharply. "And if he's not the murderer, think what distress he's already in."

Tyndale raised an eyebrow again. "Lady North, I had no idea you could be so fierce."

Neither had she, really. "I just don't want to see my friends hurt."

"Don't worry." Tyndale nodded. "I intend my questioning to be subtle. If he's not the murderer, I don't want him spreading the news that Mister Frost's death was no accident. Best we keep that quiet—I assume you haven't mentioned it."

"How can you be sure?" Veronica felt vaguely comforted that he'd been confident of her discretion.

Tyndale smiled. "You strike me as a very private person, Lady North, and one who appreciates the value of a confidence.

To be honest, it never occurred to me that you might need to be cautioned to keep this secret."

That made her feel even better, though why she cared about Tyndale's approval, she didn't know. "Thank you."

He nodded again in acknowledgment. "Now, you're certain Mister Frost had something he intended to show you?"

"I am. And I didn't see anything out of place in the workshop, as I said."

"It's very difficult to prove a negative, Lady North. We have no idea what might have gone missing from that workshop." Tyndale's mouth thinned in a frown. "I understand from Master Varner that Mister Frost had more than one workshop. I'm hoping Mister Peterson might be open to sharing his knowledge of anything along those lines."

Veronica nodded. "He told me he thought he was the only person other than Ian who knew where all of them were."

"I hope he's right. If I can learn what Mister Frost invented, I might be able to work out who would be willing to kill to get their hands on that Devisery." Tyndale rose. "Now, unless there was anything else...?"

Veronica stood. "Will you tell me what you find out?"

Tyndale's eyes narrowed. "No," he said.

Startled at his curt response, Veronica exclaimed, "No?"

"You're already more involved in this than you should be, Lady North," Tyndale said, his voice as impassive as ever. "You are not an investigator. You're not even a law-speaker. There is nothing more you can contribute."

His words struck her to the heart. In that moment, she felt small and stupid, just an aging woman clutching a foolish dream that life hadn't yet passed her by. "I see," she said quietly.

Tyndale put out a hand, but let it fall before he touched her.

"I mean no insult," he said, just as quietly. "You are remarkably brave, and very good in a crisis. But this is not your fight. Please, allow me to pursue Mister Frost's killer. I assure you I will stop at nothing to see that your friend receives justice."

Veronica nodded. "Thank you. I understand."

She cast one last glance at the statue of *Xavier* before leaving the room. Now the sword seemed pointed in her own direction, threatening to impale her. It would be a lesser pain than the one that gripped her now.

She walked slowly down the hall toward the stairs, her head bowed, and thought of all the things she might have said to Tyndale if she were a different person. He was right, she didn't know anything about investigating a murder, and she shouldn't let that make her feel inadequate. But she wished she'd stood up to Tyndale. She wished she'd said *I'm already involved, so why shouldn't I help?* Or *I got the location of Ian's secret workshop out of Howard, didn't I?*

Her head came up, and she stopped with her hand on the newel of the banister. She hadn't told Tyndale about the Knightsbury workshop. It hadn't even occurred to her to do so. And—she put her hand on her trouser pocket—she still had Ian's keys, one of which might unlock that workshop. Why *shouldn't* she go to Knightsbury and see what Ian had hidden there? It had nothing to do with the murder and everything to do with preserving Ian's legacy. And she would prove to Tyndale that she wasn't a silly, aging woman with nothing to contribute.

Deep in her heart, she felt a nagging guilt that Tyndale hadn't called her either of those things, and had actually been quite complimentary, but she couldn't forget how she'd felt in the face of his criticism, small and awkward and at a loss for a rebuttal. She was tired of being the polite one, tired of being the one who always gave in for the sake of peace. She couldn't be bold for her own sake, but she could be bold for Ian's.

Swiftly, she trotted down the stairs and across the yard to the road connected to the highway leading to Knightsbury. There was a part of her that felt she was doing something forbidden, as if Tyndale's injunction against her helping with his investigation applied to anything connected to the murder. It was a foolish thought, and she ignored the guilty feeling. This was about Ian and his Device, not his murderer.

The warm Autumn day, filled with the scents of dry grass and, more distantly, of wood fires, cheered her further. The sun was bright, the fields full of chirping insects, the skies clear and blue, and she was able to forget her troubles for the few minutes it took to walk the mile to Knightsbury. She stepped aside to allow a wagon going the opposite way to pass, then waved cheerfully at a post rider on her way to the town. Aside from them, she had the road to herself. She felt independent in a way she hadn't before, even at the Scholia, and laughed at her foolishness. The former Consort, wealthy and connected, letting a simple walk in the fresh air give her confidence.

Knightsbury really was closer to being a city than a town. There weren't many farms in its outskirts, and other students had told Veronica this was because the business owners of Knightsbury and its appointed officials were buying up the land so Knightsbury could continue to expand. Since the Scholia owned much of the land east of the city, that meant Knights-bury bulged oddly to the north and west, away from the highway connecting it to County Cullinan's capital Treston and, beyond that, Aurilien itself. From the air, it likely looked like a water drop prepared to burst.

The stillness of the Autumn air gave way to the sounds of a city: people calling out to one another, wagons and horses clattering over the paved streets, the shouts of urchins selling newspapers. A whiff of manure came to Veronica's nose, a reassuring smell she associated with her father's stables from when she was a child. She increased her pace, eager to reach her destination and begin her quest.

Veronica would have known Knightsbury was young even if she hadn't been told it had been founded only fifty years before. Not only were there signs of new construction everywhere, that construction, and the existing buildings, were built in the latest style, with flat brick façades over storefronts with large-paned, curving display windows. Most of the businesses at this end of Knightsbury catered to travelers, but there were also stores carrying things students might need. Veronica knew one of them well.

She pushed open the door beneath the sign reading WATTLESFORD'S FINEST STATIONERS and breathed in a different comforting scent, that of new paper and pencil wood and the sharp bite of a dozen kinds of ink. Nothing relaxed her more than the smell of learning. Shelves filled with boxes lined two walls, while more shelves containing bundled reams of paper and blank books covered a third. A few customers browsed the wares, none of them students by their fine dress. Veronica had found early on that most students dressed in a style verging on sloppy that was instantly recognizable. Her continuing preference for dresses made her stand out among them even more than her rank.

Veronica gave a polite nod to the man who met her gaze and was amused to see a look of disdain cross his rather thin features. Well, she was dressed like a student today, but no one would assume someone of her age belonged to the Scholia. It was more likely the man thought she was a low-class worker who surely had no need of writing materials. People could be such snobs.

She crossed to the counter and rang the bell. Presently, Miss Wattlesford bustled out from behind the curtain screening the door to the back room. She was of average height and size and in a permanent state of bustling, always giving Veronica the impression that she held an invisible broom with which she swept herself a path. She smiled when she saw Veronica. "Why, Lady North! How are you this fine day?"

Veronica heard hushed murmurings behind her and wished she dared turn around to see the expression of the snobbish man. "Very well, Miss Wattlesford, and yourself?"

"Oh, I can't complain. My bursitis is giving me trouble, as usual. It's always worse come the colder weather." Miss Wattlesford rotated one shoulder in emphasis. She was younger than Veronica by about a decade, but had a host of physical troubles, some of which Veronica suspected were imaginary. But Miss Wattlesford was a very nice person who never traded on her ailments to gain sympathy, and Veronica liked her.

"I'm so sorry. I know that must be a dreadful inconvenience in your line of work, having to lift and carry so much." Veronica folded her hands together and rested them on the counter. "I came in for another blank book, but I also hoped you could help me with something."

"Of course. Jonas!" Miss Wattlesford directed this shout over her shoulder. "Do you want the usual, Lady North?"

"Please. And...perhaps a bottle of blue ink?"

The curtain moved again, and a mountain of a man came through. Miss Wattlesford's nephew Jonas was the biggest man

Veronica had ever known, taller by head and shoulders than she, who was nearly six feet tall herself. His chest was big around enough for two of Veronica, his arms looked like sides of beef, and he had shoulders broad enough for an ox. He smiled his usual friendly smile when he saw Veronica. "Lady," he said in his thick voice.

"Jonas, get the lady a book and blue ink," Miss Wattlesford instructed him. She enunciated her words more clearly than she'd spoken to Veronica.

Jonas smiled and nodded again, then lumbered toward the shelves. The other customers got out of his way, though despite his apparent awkwardness, he moved with great care. Veronica watched him carefully select a blank book from a stack and then fumble a glass bottle of ink from a bin. It looked tiny in his enormous hand.

The snobbish man, who stood near the ink displays, stepped back in obvious disgust. Veronica's dislike of him hardened into anger. Jonas couldn't help being simple-minded, and he was kinder and more caring than most of the people Veronica knew. She wished she dared confront the man, but he hadn't said or done anything overtly rude, and what would she say, anyway? That everyone deserved respect, even people who weren't wealthy and in possession of all their mental faculties? She still felt ashamed of herself, as if she'd somehow betrayed Jonas.

Jonas put the supplies on the counter and again smiled at Veronica. "Ink," he said. "For writing?"

"Yes, for writing," Veronica said. "I like it better than black ink. I think it's prettier." She could have gotten the things herself, but Jonas loved helping the customers so much she didn't like to deny him his pleasures.

"Prettier," Jonas said. "Like a butterfly. I saw one with blue wings like that before."

"So have I. I think they're called blue gossamers."

"Blue goss-gossmer," Jonas said. A look of distress touched his broad features.

"It's a hard word to say," Veronica agreed, knowing how Jonas prided himself on his diction. "You can practice it."

Jonas's face cleared. "Gossmer. *Goss-a-mer.*"

Veronica laughed. "I guess you didn't need much practice!"

"Gossamer. Blue gossamer." Jonas laughed his deep, slow laugh.

"All right, Jonas, it's time you went back to counting," Miss Wattlesford said. "He's been helping with the inventory. He's become quite good at notation," she told Veronica when Jonas left. Her voice sounded strained the way it always did when she spoke of Jonas, that pleading note that meant she felt defensive.

"I always like seeing him when I come in," Veronica said, and Miss Wattlesford's anxious face grew less tense. "Here's payment, and could I ask a question? I need direction to Stowe Road."

Miss Wattlesford accepted Veronica's money. "Stowe Road? That's in...it's not exactly a bad part of town, but I don't know as it's one you ought go alone to. Give me a minute." She ducked through the curtain. Veronica ignored the people she could feel staring at her. She hated being conspicuous, but unless she wanted to stop going out in public entirely, she had to put up with it.

Miss Wattlesford returned after a minute. "Jonas is almost finished with a crate, and then he'll take you," she said. "No, it's no trouble," she added when Veronica protested. "It will do him good to get out in the fresh air, after being cooped up in here all morning. And no one will molest you with him around."

Veronica had to agree. People who didn't know Jonas were always a little afraid of his size and muscles, though in truth Jonas was a gentle soul who to Veronica's knowledge had never intentionally hurt anyone, and who cried miserably if he hurt someone by accident. "Thank you. I appreciate it."

"It's no trouble, Lady North." Miss Wattlesford looked past her at the snobbish man, who held a box of pencils. It occurred to Veronica to wonder why someone who looked and acted like him was doing his own shopping. She smiled sweetly at the man and was amused to see him blush. She didn't know what had prompted that reaction, but she had learned from experience that rude people often were abashed by anyone who returned their rudeness with politeness instead.

Jonas emerged from the back room. "We go, Lady?"

"Yes, thank you, Jonas." With another nod to Miss Wattlesford, she and Jonas left the stationer's.

Jonas led the way down most of Knightsbury's main street. People got out of his way as they never did for Veronica except when she was conspicuously the former Consort. It was comforting, having him along to break the crowds, even though traffic was relatively thin at that hour. Come nightfall, the streets would be packed with citizens and students looking for amusement, and then Jonas's help really would be valuable.

The brick stores gave way to larger stone mansions, then they passed the wealthier district and turned a corner onto a narrower street. The buildings here were made of wood rather than brick or stone and were generally shorter than everything else Veronica had seen in Knightsbury to date. Though they weren't exactly run-down, they did have a weary look to them, their paint not quite fresh, their windows not quite clean. The smell of refuse was stronger here, though still not overwhelming, and the crowds had thinned out further. In the distance, a group of children ran past, screaming over some game that required kicking and throwing a red ball. The children eased Veronica's anxieties. If they could survive here, it couldn't be that bad.

Jonas stopped on a street corner and pointed. "This is Stowe Road," he rumbled.

Veronica looked up and down the road. It wasn't short. Her anxieties resurfaced. She had no idea how to find Ian's workshop in this place. "Thank you, Jonas, you can go back to your aunt now."

Jonas shook his head. It was like watching a mountain move. "Aunt says, stay with Lady and bring her back safe."

Veronica knew better than to argue with Jonas. Arguing either confused him or brought him to the brink of tears. "All right. Help me think. I need to find a place along this road. What should I do?"

Jonas scratched his head. "Ask?"

"I suppose that's the first option. But there isn't anyone here." Stowe Road looked like much of Aurilien's Lower Town, which Veronica had visited only rarely: all the buildings looked alike, but some bore signs declaring that they were businesses rather than the homes mixed in freely among them.

Jonas pointed. "Big store."

"Good idea. We'll ask there."

They crossed the street to one of the buildings whose storefront was larger than the others. It had a multipaned window several feet wide beside its door, but the view was blocked by an iron grille protecting the glass. Veronica pushed the door open, and bells jingled. The merry sound was so at odds with the grim appearance of Stowe Road Veronica wanted to laugh.

To her surprise, the place was a toy shop. Wooden toys and

cloth stuffed animals thronged the shelves, and larger toys such as a rocking horse and a dollhouse nearly waist-high to Veronica stood where they were visible from the window. It was so unexpected Veronica exclaimed, "Oh, Jonas! This is remarkable!"

"You need summat?" The voice came from a dark corner of the room, an elderly voice like a creaking hinge. Veronica squinted and saw an old man sitting in a rocking chair with a knitted blanket of blue and cream squares across his lap. He peered back at Veronica through spectacles with lenses thick enough to distort his eyes into huge dark pools.

"Oh," Veronica said again. "I...actually, I don't need a toy, I was hoping for information."

"Hmph." The old man sat forward. "Ought to make you buy summat first, but a pretty young lady, I guess I can help. What's your question?"

Veronica hadn't been called a pretty young lady in years. She smiled. "I'm looking for the workshop, or office, of a friend. It's somewhere on Stowe Road, but that's all I know."

"Your friend couldn't show you himself?"

An unexpected lump rose in Veronica's throat. "He passed away recently. I only just found out about this place, and I...wanted to help settle his estate." That was only a tiny stretching of the truth and not an outright lie.

"Sorry about your loss. Hey! No breaking the merchandise!" The old man's voice was suddenly sharp. Veronica turned to see Jonas holding a soft stuffed toy shaped like a duck. When he squeezed it, it emitted a tiny *squawk* that made Jonas's face light up.

"He won't break it," Veronica said, as sharply as the old man. "Just because he's big and not very bright doesn't mean he's not careful. But—" She turned back to Jonas. "Can I buy that for you? As a thank-you for helping me?"

Jonas brightened. "It's nice," he said confidingly, as if he were imparting a great secret.

"Then that's that," Veronica said, pulling out her pocketbook. "How much?"

"Two and six," the old man said.

Veronica handed over a few silver and copper coins and said, "So, can you help me?"

The old man hauled himself out of the chair, revealing a pistol Device the blanket had concealed. At Veronica's gasp, he chuckled and said, "Some folks not from around this street might think an old man an easy target."

He dropped the coins into a battered metal box he took from beneath the counter. "You said a workshop? Best ask at Garold Miller's manufactory. He's the biggest employer in these parts. Got his finger in a lot of pies—furniture, clothing, household things. If your friend had a workshop along about here, Miller would know about it. Keeps a close lock on his business, Miller does, you know what I mean?" He tapped the side of his veiny nose and winked.

"And where can I find this manufactory?" Veronica asked.

"Go west a ways. You'll hear the sound of the looms. The manufactory covers several buildings, but it's got Miller's name over the door where you might find him. Good luck, miss." The old man returned to his seat and settled his blanket over the pistol.

"Thank you, sir, I appreciate the help. Let's go, Jonas."

Jonas squeaked his toy all the way down the street until a rattling, clacking sound drowned it out. "You'd better put that away," Veronica said. "We don't want anyone thinking they could take it, do we?" She actually thought Jonas looked less intimidating holding a squeaky toy, and the place they now approached made her want someone intimidating backing her up. The buildings were dirtier and more run-down than before, and several windows at ground level were boarded up, not haphazardly, but in a tidy way that struck Veronica as somehow ominous.

"I won't let no one hurt Lady," Jonas said. He tucked the toy inside his shirt.

"I'm glad of that." Veronica had spotted the sign that simply read MILLER nailed above one of the doors. The windows flanking it were marginally cleaner, enough that Veronica thought someone might be able to see through them. She crossed the street with Jonas in her wake and, after only a slight hesitation, opened the door. Knocking might be more polite, but this was likely a business, not a house.

Beyond lay a tiny room lit only by the sunlight coming through the grimy windows. Its only furnishings were a single wooden desk that canted slightly to the left and a plain, well-worn chair. In the chair sat a heavyset woman with brown hair piled neatly atop her head in a fashion that would have suited a much younger woman. She was reading a book she hastily put away out of sight when Veronica entered. "Yes?"

"I'm looking for a workshop belonging to a friend of mine," Veronica said. "I was told Mister Miller knows everyone who works in manufacturing on Stowe Road, and that he might know where this workshop is."

The woman was staring at Jonas rather than Veronica, clearly impressed by his size. "Maybe," she said absently. "Mister Miller's time is valuable. He's not available to just anyone who walks in off the street looking for what might be confidential information."

"I'd like you to ask him to see me," Veronica persisted. "My friend passed away recently and I need to find his workshop."

The woman suddenly focused on Veronica. "Passed away? I'm sorry. What was his name?"

"Ian Frost."

The woman sat up straighter, her eyes wide and her mouth slack. "Ian Frost is dead?"

"You knew him?"

"He had business dealings with Mister Miller. He was in and out of here all the time. Sweet heaven." The woman dabbed at her eyes with a handkerchief she pulled out of her ample bosom. "Give me just a minute. I'm sure Mister Miller will want to talk to you." She pushed away from the desk and went through a door behind her, letting it close with a quiet *click*.

Veronica had barely had time to wonder why there were no chairs for customers when the door opened again and the woman stepped through. "This way," she said, beckoning.

Veronica and Jonas followed her down a short hallway and up a flight of stairs narrow enough that Jonas's shoulders brushed the walls thanks to his lurching gait. At the top, the woman opened another door. "Mister Miller," she said, gesturing.

Veronica entered the room and felt as if she'd stepped through a portal to some mansion in Aurilien's heights. The room was as opulent as anything she'd seen in the palace, from the chandelier blazing with Device lights to the mahogany desk and chairs to the gaily colored Eskandelic rugs covering the floor. Paintings crowded one another for space on the walls, and

Veronica was certain these, unlike the one in Tyndale's office, were originals. One look at the man behind the desk told her he would settle for nothing less.

Mister Miller sat leaning back in his leather upholstered chair, regarding Veronica closely. He might have been Veronica's age, but he looked older, his face seamed and craggy with hard living. Most of what was left of his hair was gray, and his hands, which lay flat upon the desktop, were gnarled and liver-spotted, the knuckles like walnuts. But his sharp blue eyes gave the impression of a clever man who was used to having things his way. Veronica felt herself grow small and insignificant before him and made herself stand up straight. She had a purpose, and she wasn't going to be intimidated by her own foolish fancies.

Miller pursed his lips. "Have a seat," he said. "What's your name?"

Veronica sat gingerly on the edge of the chair. It looked soft and deep enough to swallow her if she wasn't careful. "I am Lady Veronica North." She had a feeling she would need every scrap of significance she could muster.

Miller's eyes widened. "The Dowager Consort, come to tell me Ian Frost is dead? That's a strange confluence of events. How did you know Ian?"

Veronica was conscious of Jonas's steadying presence behind her chair, as he had chosen not to sit. He rarely did, because most chairs were too small for him. "We're—we were students at the Scholia together. He was a friend."

"I'm sorry to hear of his death. And you want to see his workshop? Why is that?"

Veronica didn't like the calculating way he looked at her. "I'm helping to settle his affairs."

"Hmm." Miller rubbed one gnarled hand over his chin, which had a patch of bristly hair he'd missed while shaving. "I suppose you want me to open it to you out of the goodness of my heart."

"It's not yours," Veronica said. "I just need to know its location."

"If Ian didn't tell you himself, why should I bother?" Miller picked up a pen and twiddled it. "It's on my property, that makes it mine."

For a moment, Veronica almost agreed with him. She almost stood and left the room, gave up on her quest. Then a rush of anger—anger at her diffidence, anger at this greedy man—supplanted her timidity. "Did he rent space from you?"

"More or less. I provided him with a workspace, he produced Devices for me. Anything in that workshop belongs to me."

"I don't think that's true." Veronica leaned forward. "You rented him a workspace, but unless you have documents attesting to a business relationship, the contents of that workspace are Ian's. So I'd like to see those documents. Now."

Miller's eyes narrowed. "You're bold, for a woman," he said. "Were you sleeping with him? Can't imagine why he'd confide in a woman otherwise."

Veronica regarded him closely. "That's interesting," she said, taking note of the way he'd gone still and how his gaze didn't waver, how his voice was more menacing than before. "Do you always pretend to misogyny, or is it just to throw me off balance?"

To her surprise, Miller threw back his head and laughed. "And smart," he said. "I suppose you're brave because of the mountain you brought to back you up? He's big, but I doubt he'd hurt anyone. I've known his type before. Employed some of them. Hard workers once they've learned a task."

He dropped the pen and laced his fingers together. "All right, Lady North. I won't play games with you. Ian and I had a business arrangement. You don't need the details. Whatever Devisery he got up to, I had first crack at, but on a purely profit-sharing model. He kept all the patents. He was even more a suspicious bastard than I am." He chuckled. "I can show you the workshop, but unless you've got the key…"

Veronica suspected there was an offer in that pause some-where to break down the door if necessary. "I have the key."

"Fine. I admit I'm curious. Let's go." Miller stood, pushing his chair back.

"This should be private," Veronica said.

Miller shook his head. "Ian's dead, Lady North. He's got no more use for privacy. And I'm more likely than you to recognize any usable Devisery. Besides, without me, you don't know where the workshop is."

Veronica hated the idea of letting this man anywhere near Ian's things, but she had to admit he had a point. "All right. But you don't take anything. His estate needs to be settled first." Stretching the truth got easier the more you did it.

Miller's smile was that of a predator. "Agreed."

They left the office and went back down the stairs. Halfway to the front office, a door in the hallway opened, and a lovely young woman no more than eighteen looked out. She had a heart-shaped face and enormous brown eyes like a deer's, and her rosy lips parted to say, "Father—"

"Later, Ariane," Miller said.

"But Flora said…is Ian dead?" The brown eyes went liquid with unshed tears.

"He is. It's no concern of yours. Lady North?" Miller opened the office door for Veronica.

Veronica looked at the girl, Ariane, and felt a wrenching sympathy for her; she looked as devastated as Veronica had felt only twice in her life, at the deaths of the two men she'd loved more than anything. She glanced at Miller, who was waiting somewhat impatiently for her to exit. He wouldn't put up with her interrogating his daughter, even though Ariane looked more upset than she should if Ian really meant nothing to her. Veronica smiled at the girl and went through the door.

Ian's workshop turned out to be in one of the buildings with the boarded-up windows. The building had the same small front office Miller's building had, but after that it was a maze of little unfurnished rooms, dusty and clearly unused for some time. Miller stopped at one of the doors that looked just like all the others. "Here."

Veronica fumbled through a couple of keys before finding the one that fit the lock. Miller betrayed no impatience, though he did cast a wary glance at Jonas from time to time. Jonas looked as placid as he always did. Veronica wondered what he made of all this.

She feared, in the moment before she opened the door, that the murderer had somehow managed to find this place. She braced herself against seeing the same destruction she'd seen in the Saunders Hall workshop. But when she turned the knob to illuminate the room, it was as orderly as she was used to seeing in all of Ian's possessions. She breathed out a sigh of relief.

The windowless room was sparsely furnished, containing only a worktable and a bookshelf knocked together from raw lumber, something so utilitarian it screamed "Deviser." Boxes and baskets were crammed onto the shelves, some of them glowing. Veronica tipped a basket the size of her two palms toward herself and saw several metal spheres ranging from pinheads to the size of her thumbnail. All of them glowed with pale blue or white light. Imbued motive forces. These alone represented a substantial outlay of cash.

"I said, don't touch," she warned Miller, who was examining some sheets of paper tacked to the wall.

Miller held up his hands in a mocking gesture, suggesting harmlessness. "I'm just looking. Besides, none of this means anything to me. I'm just a simple businessman."

"I doubt that." Veronica couldn't believe the words that had escaped her mouth. Well, she'd wanted to be more assertive.

She picked over a few more of the baskets and found tiny gears, scraps of unshaped metal, some miniature tools she recognized as part of a standard Deviser's kit. Many of the baskets contained broken pieces, bits of failed Devices probably. She stirred a pile of stubby needles with the eyes on the pointed ends and wondered why he'd kept so many flawed pieces. "There's nothing here," she said, feeling disappointed.

Miller looked over her shoulder. "I don't know what you were looking for," he said. His voice sounded different, almost as if he were concealing excitement. Veronica eyed him, but he was looking at the needles, not at her. She couldn't guess what he'd seen that had him worked up, and she was afraid to pry, not because of her diffidence, but because it might be better for her to pretend she hadn't noticed. If Miller had discovered Ian's secret, he wouldn't be likely to give it up without a fight.

She turned her attention to the sketches on the wall. They were mostly incomprehensible, certainly no finished Devices she was aware of. Wheels, and belts, and some kind of treadle, but even with her limited understanding of Devisery she knew the pieces could belong to any Device requiring constant input of motive force. She removed the pages from the wall and folded them away inside her shirt. Howard might make something of them. Assuming he wasn't the murderer.

"I'll send someone to clean this place out," she told Miller. "The motive forces are valuable, and the other stuff...I'm sure a Deviser would want it."

"I don't know," Miller said, his grin once again calculating. "Ian was behind on his rent. Maybe I should take some of this as compensation."

Veronica sighed. "How much?" she asked, taking out her pocketbook.

"Fifteen guilders."

"*Fifteen—*"

Miller held up his hands defensively. "We had an arrangement. He was somewhat...irregular in keeping up his end of the deal. He may have gotten more than a little behind."

Veronica counted out three gold coins and winced at the resulting leanness of her purse. She slapped the coins into Miller's outstretched hand and thought about calling him a greedy opportunist. But even her newfound courage didn't extend to outright rudeness. Instead, she said, "Thank you for your assistance."

Miller stirred the coins with his finger before pocketing them. "Have you spoken to Pauline Kensington?"

"I don't know who that is."

"She was an associate of Ian's. A financial backer. If you're looking for information about his Devices, she might be able to help. I know she arranged to sell the Devices I couldn't use."

Veronica gaped. "That's...unexpectedly helpful of you, Mister Miller."

Miller chuckled. "It's the least I can do for royalty." He sobered in the next moment. "But if you do find the Device, I want a shot at it, understand?"

"Why is it so important?"

Miller shrugged. "I just don't like missing an opportunity. Keep that in mind, Lady North."

He showed Veronica and Jonas outside and said, "Good luck, Lady North, and my condolences. Ian wasn't really a friend of mine, but I understand losing someone you care about." For a moment, he looked almost human. Then he grinned, and waved a farewell, turning back toward his office.

Veronica watched him go. "That man frightens me," she said to herself.

"Lady is frightened?" Jonas said. "I'll protect you!"

"Thank you, Jonas. It's nothing. Let's go back to see your aunt."

She turned in time to hear a familiar voice say, "Lady North. What are you doing here?"

It was Tyndale.

1 2

Fear flashed through Veronica, guilty fear that she'd been caught doing something wrong. She reminded herself that she had every right to try to find Ian's Device and that Tyndale had no authority over her in non-scholastic matters, and faced Tyndale with her head held high. "Ian had a workshop here. I want to find out what Device he invented."

Tyndale continued walking toward her. He was dressed in proper gentlemen's attire, pressed trousers and frock coat and neckcloth, and looked more out of place on Stowe Road than she did. His expression was as impassive as usual, but beneath his hat, his glass-green eyes glinted with a deeper emotion. "You concealed this information from me," he said, coming to a stop a few paces away. "Did I not tell you to stay out of this?"

"You did. I'm not trying to track down a murderer. I just want to know about the Device. It could be Ian's legacy." Beside her, Jonas shifted his massive weight. She was afraid to look away from Tyndale to see if her large companion was upset.

Tyndale's lips thinned, but when he spoke, his voice was as dispassionate as ever. "Whoever killed Mister Frost wanted that Device. There's no way to disentangle the search for that from the search for his killer. Why did you not tell me you knew where this workshop was?"

"I...didn't think of it when we were talking." That sounded so stupid. She tried to cover her embarrassment by saying, "I'm sorry for the oversight, but I really don't think it matters that much, since you clearly learned its location on your own."

Tyndale's voice sharpened. "And is there anything else you've neglected to tell me?"

The guilty feeling redoubled. Ian's keys were a weight dragging down her pocket. If she handed them over, she really would have no way to find Ian's Device. But she wanted even more for his killer to be found. She dug the key ring out of her pocket and extended it to Tyndale.

Finally, Tyndale looked angry. "Lady North," he began, then visibly calmed himself. "Lady North," he went on in a somewhat calmer voice, "this could constitute obstruction of my investigation. You had no right to these."

"I told you I had them, and you didn't ask for them," Veronica said. She hated that her voice was trembling, and made herself look Tyndale in the eye. "In all the turmoil, I forgot about them. If it was obstruction, it was unintentional."

Tyndale's jaw was clenched tight. "You are—" he said, then clearly changed his mind. "Has it occurred to you," he said instead, "that you could be my primary suspect?"

Veronica's mouth fell open. "I?"

"You were the first to find the body. You might have killed

him and then reported the murder to throw me off the trail—after all, what killer would be so bold as to present herself for investigation?"

Veronica's heart pounded so hard her pulse throbbed in her skull. "But I didn't kill Ian! How can you possibly believe that?"

Tyndale's expression was back to being impassive, and now it frightened her, the way he looked at her as if she were a problem rather than a person. She felt dizzy, and wished she could sit down, because she was afraid she might fall down instead.

She put a hand on Jonas's arm to steady herself. "Lady all right?" Jonas rumbled. She nodded. The last thing she needed was for Jonas to think Tyndale was a danger to her.

"In a murder investigation, one must suspect everyone," Tyndale said. He ignored Jonas, which either said he was intelligent or a fool. "But as it happens, I don't believe you did it. You have no reason to want Mister Frost dead, and I don't think you have the strength to overpower a man half your age or to deliver a blow with such force as I saw inflicted on the body. But your actions are exactly those of someone trying to cover up her guilt."

"I just want—" Veronica's voice rose sharply, and she breathed in a deep breath to calm herself. "Ian invented something he was excited about. If it really was an important breakthrough in Devisery, I want the world to know about it. That's all. I'm not trying to interfere with your investigation, and I'm not trying to conceal my guilt, because I'm not guilty."

Tyndale shook his head, slowly, in the manner of someone trying not to let his frustration overwhelm him. "Lady North, I told you to stay out of this. I didn't think I needed to specify exactly what that meant, because I judged you intelligent and sensible."

"I'm not silly, and I'm not stupid," Veronica retorted, anger and embarrassment overcoming diffidence for once.

"Then why did you not realize that your actions might interfere with my investigation? Have you seen the workshop yet?"

"I have. Whatever is there didn't mean anything to me."

Tyndale let out an impatient breath. "I needed to see that workshop without someone else disturbing it."

"I didn't disturb it." Immediately, Veronica remembered taking the papers off the wall. She almost didn't mention them; Tyndale hadn't yelled at her yet, but if she revealed she really had taken something, it might prove too much even for his forbearance. She reminded herself that her personal embarrassment meant nothing when it came to finding Ian's killer, and reached inside her shirt. "I did take these off the wall. I was going to show them to Master Varner and see if she could make anything of them."

The rustle of paper sounded explosive in the dead silence that followed. Veronica couldn't bring herself to look at Tyndale. She just held the papers out toward him and felt a tug as he took them from her hand. "This qualifies as a disturbance," Tyndale said. "Sweet heaven, Lady North, have you no common sense at all?"

The frustration and anger in his voice made her want to run away. She hated confrontation and hated it more when it was her own stupid fault that she'd fallen into it. But she refused to give this man the satisfaction of knowing he'd driven her to tears. "I'm sorry," she said in a small voice that even to her sounded weak. "I wanted—"

The memory of Ian's body flashed across her mind. She had

wanted to do something for her friend. She hadn't meant any harm and she certainly...yes, she didn't deserve to be yelled at for her perfectly innocent actions. The thought that Tyndale hadn't actually yelled only registered with her briefly before she raised her head.

"I am sorry," she said, cursing the remaining quaver in her voice, "that you didn't think it was necessary to explain to me what your investigation entailed. I am sorry you didn't realize that I might not divine that my wish to find the missing Device would interfere with that investigation. I acted in good faith and out of a desire to do something for a friend. And I refuse to feel guilty about that."

Tyndale's eyebrow went up. "Are you saying this is my fault?"

"Shouldn't it be? I am, after all, not a law-speaker and have no experience with a murder investigation." More memories surged, distant ones, and she crushed them ruthlessly as she always did.

To her shock, Tyndale smiled, just a thin twist of his lips, but unmistakably a smile. "You didn't like me saying that, did you? Even though I meant no insult?"

Veronica shook her head. "It doesn't matter how I felt. You were right."

Tyndale nodded. "I apologize for not giving you more credit. You're right that I should have been explicit about what my investigation would entail and what would constitute inter-ference. There is nothing shameful about your desire to find that Device. But I hope you understand now why it's important you not involve yourself. I know very little about what I'm looking for, which means any evidence could be essential. And it means even something as small as removing these—" He shook the papers lightly, making them rustle again— "could make a huge difference in my finding this killer."

"I understand now. I hope—"

"Don't worry yourself." Tyndale sighed. "You might as well show me the workshop, and save me the trouble of inquiring around."

"Mister Miller might not be so generous with you," Veronica agreed.

"Who is Mister Miller?"

"The man who leased the workshop to Ian. He has a manufactory here. But I think he knows something about the Device he wanted to keep secret."

Now Tyndale closed his eyes, and his lips pressed briefly into a taut line. "You—" he began, his voice raised almost in a shout. Veronica cringed involuntarily. She'd made such a mess of things.

"All right," Tyndale said a moment later, his voice calm once more. "I think you should tell me *everything* you have learned, and who you've talked to. And I warn you, if you fail to mention anything I find out later—"

"You can't have me arrested, Master Tyndale." She hoped that was true.

"No. But I will be extremely disappointed. And you might have to live with the knowledge that you've helped a killer go free." Tyndale's impassive expression made his words sound sinister. Veronica swallowed a sudden lump in her throat.

"The workshop is right here," she said when she'd regained control of herself. "Jonas, wait outside, please? We'll just be a moment."

Once inside, Tyndale prowled the workshop like a tiger, slowly moving around the table and examining the baskets and boxes closely. Veronica was certain he saw more than she had. She stood by the door, hoping not to interfere, though she knew it was too late for that.

Tyndale then spread the papers on the table and looked closely at each. "What did you make of these?" he asked.

Startled, Veronica said, "Nothing. That is, I can see they're part of a larger Device, but I don't know enough about Devisery to identify it. That's why I wanted to show them to Master Varner."

Tyndale grunted, she thought in acknowledgement. He folded the papers and put them away inside his coat. "Tell me about this Mister Miller," he said.

"He looks like a thug, but he's smarter than he looks," Veronica said. "I think he was telling the truth when he told me he and Ian had a good business relationship. Do you think he might be the killer?"

"I told you, I suspect everyone," Tyndale said. "He might have wanted more of a share in the business than he already had. Or Mister Frost's Device might have threatened his business."

Veronica blinked. "I don't understand. Surely...that is, it sounded as if Mister Miller wanted new Devices."

Tyndale shrugged. "People have begun making progress on a Device that will do the work of a loom. That sort of thing can put traditional weavers out of business. If Mister Frost's Device was of interest to a businessman involved in manufacturing, it might have affected Mister Miller's existing affairs. I can't think of a better motive for murder than trying to protect one's livelihood."

"That's remarkably cynical," Veronica said, then blushed at how critical she'd sounded.

"It's only truth," Tyndale said. He leaned against the table, his arms crossed over his chest, and regarded her closely. "Now would be a good time for you to reveal anything else you've kept from me."

Veronica decided not to take issue with his attitude. She had, after all, inadvertently gotten in his way. "I gave you the keys. I assume you learned about this workshop from Howard?"

Tyndale nodded once.

"Then you probably know there are two other workshops, one in Brookside and one in Aurilien. Howard didn't tell me where they are. I told you what I know about Mister Miller—you will probably learn more from talking to him than I did." She cast her mind back over the last eighteen hours. "I honestly can't think of anything else, Master Tyndale. I promise I'll tell you immediately if I do."

"I believe you." To her surprise, Tyndale sighed, removed his hat, and ran a hand through his hair, the least controlled movement she'd ever seen from him. "Will you swear not to delve into this mystery any further, if I promise that Mister Frost will receive credit for the Device once it's discovered?"

His unexpected cooperation surprised her further. "I promise. And I really am sorry."

"You have a point that I wasn't as forthcoming with you as I should have been." Tyndale smoothed his hair and straightened his coat. "This isn't just about the integrity of my investigation, Lady North. There's still a killer out there, and when one has killed once, the next murder is that much easier. Your continued involvement could put you at risk."

That chilled her. "I...hadn't realized."

"Well, you know now, and I hope the knowledge will spur you to greater caution." Tyndale gestured for her to precede him out of the workshop. "Though if you employed that man to bring you here, I suppose that indicates you are already thinking cautiously. Who is he?"

"Jonas Aysboro. He's the nephew of the woman who owns the stationer's. And I brought him as a guide, not a bodyguard."

They stepped outside, and Tyndale looked at Jonas, who was once more playing with his squeaky toy and was indifferent to Tyndale's regard. "I see," Tyndale said, in a tone of voice that angered Veronica on Jonas's behalf.

"Just because he's big doesn't mean he's violent," she snapped. "But he'll defend me if I'm in danger."

"I meant no insult," Tyndale said. "Now, go back to the Scholia, Lady North, and leave the investigating to me."

Veronica nodded and turned away. She could tell Tyndale was watching her go, probably because he feared she would disobey him if he wasn't alert. The thought burned within her, and she sped up. Soon she and Jonas left Stowe Road, and Tyndale, well behind them.

Having returned Jonas to the stationer's shop, Veronica trudged back to the Scholia. Her anger had gone cold, leaving her once more uncertain of herself. The idea of doing nothing, of waiting for whatever Tyndale might accomplish with regard to Ian's missing Device, frustrated her, especially since she was sure he cared more for finding the murderer. Which was right, of course, and Veronica knew catching Ian's killer mattered more than some mystery Device. But she wished she had come up with something to convince Tyndale to let her help. She'd already discovered much on her own.

But Tyndale's last words about her being in danger from the killer sobered her. Until then, she hadn't absorbed the reality that whoever had killed Ian was more than likely someone associated with the Scholia—someone she might encounter without realizing. And if it was someone she didn't know to distrust, that person might hurt or kill her if they thought she was a threat, and she wouldn't be able to defend herself.

She sighed and walked faster. She was hungry—it was past noon—and she had afternoon responsibilities. She hoped they would be enough to distract her from the nagging feeling that she'd done the wrong thing in agreeing so readily to Tyndale's terms.

13

*A*t three o'clock, she entered Lyton Hall and climbed to the second floor where the law library was. She'd been inside the room only once, on her initial exploration of the campus, and had not been impressed. Compared to the Royal Library, still housed in the palace, it was small, barely filling a room only three times the size of her little sitting room. The books were new, arranged in groups where the spines all matched. It gave the law library the look of a stage set for a boring opera where people sang about dry legal matters, though the Opera House wouldn't smell of paper and dust as this room did.

Carlton was already there, seated at a table. A few other students sat here and there, reading or making notes. The spaces between them were great enough to prevent eavesdropping, if anyone had been inclined to eavesdrop on what would surely be boring conversations. A short stack of books lay near

Carlton's right hand, all of them fat and with the page edges unmarked by use.

"Lady North, have a seat," Carlton said. He moved the chair next to him a few inches, but didn't stand to hold it for her. That relieved Veronica's mind. She wanted him to treat her like a student, not like the former Consort.

"I didn't ask which law class you're taking," he went on, "but I guessed it was the second fundamentals class, because the first one would have listed these books." He tapped the stack.

"Yes, that's right."

"Well, these are the ones you'll want to refer to when something doesn't make sense. I've marked the places where they reprint important foundational documents—anything legal experts relied on in writing later works." Carlton flicked a slip of paper that protruded from the pages of the top book. "Did you have specific questions?

Veronica handed him a folded sheet of paper. "These are the things I felt most confused by."

Carlton scanned the page and grunted acknowledgment. He picked up a pencil and began scribbling. "Here are some specific references you can look at, listed by book—I'm afraid I can't give you exact page numbers. I'm not *that* good, whatever Master Tyndale apparently thinks."

A thought occurred to Veronica. "Why is Master Tyndale teaching such a low-level class? I'd have thought he was too important for that, given how many upper-level classes he teaches."

Carlton grimaced. "They make all the Scholia masters teach a few beginner classes. It's supposed to keep them in touch with the students. And it's not like they do more than lecture, so I doubt it's a hardship. Don't feel sorry for Tyndale. He doesn't deserve it."

He sounded so bitter Veronica asked, "Why is that?"

"He's hard on everyone, regardless of who they are or whether they deserve it. I—" Carlton shut his mouth. "It's not important. Anyway, it's not like it will matter to you, given that you're not studying law. What *are* you studying, if you don't mind my asking?"

"Architectonics."

"That seems out of place for someone like you."

Irritated, Veronica said, "People keep telling me that. I'm not sure why it's so surprising."

Carlton smiled. It was the first time she'd seen him do it, and it made him look even handsomer. "I'm sorry, that was rude. It's just such a practical field, and one doesn't think of the Dowager Consort needing to do anything practical."

"That's what Ian said, too." A pang of sorrow shot through her. She wondered how long it would take before mention of Ian didn't hurt like a knife through the chest.

"You mean Ian Frost?" Carlton's smile fell away. "I heard he died. Were you friends?"

"We were."

"Then I'm sorry for your loss." He sounded distant, like he'd already lost interest in the conversation.

"You weren't friends, were you," Veronica said. "Was it...it was over Samantha Wilde, wasn't it?"

Carlton's eyes narrowed. "As if I had anything to worry about from someone like him."

"Someone...like him?" Veronica knew this was gossip, but his dismissive tone angered her, and she couldn't help prodding him further.

Carlton laughed a short, barking laugh that earned him a glare from the nearest student. "He only cared about Devisery, not about Samantha. She should have dumped him months ago. But she thought it was funny to torment me by not making our relationship exclusive."

"That doesn't sound like Samantha."

"Then you don't know her well enough." Carlton laughed again. "Maybe now he's out of the picture, she'll stop playing the field."

"That is a cruel and horrible thing to say about both of them," Veronica said hotly, making the irritated student glare at her instead. "Ian is *dead*. Are you saying you wanted him that way?"

The words had barely left her lips when she realized what they meant. But Carlton didn't have anything to do with Ian's Device, so he wasn't the killer...except Tyndale *had* said he suspected everyone...suppose she was wrong about the killer's motive?

Carlton shook his head. "I don't want anyone dead. But I'm not going to pretend to be broken up about it when we weren't friends."

Veronica watched him closely. He wasn't meeting her eyes, and he sounded distant again—two signs that someone wasn't being entirely truthful. Impulsively, she said, "I suppose that's only honest. Did you know he was on the verge of a breakthrough with a new Device? So his death is doubly tragic. Not that that matters to you, either."

If she hadn't been watching so closely, she wouldn't have seen Carlton twitch before regaining his calm. "I hadn't heard, but I doubt it was anything important," he said. Was his voice a little too calm? "Frost was always on the verge of a break-through, and nothing ever came of those."

"This was different. I think. But it's true, I wouldn't know." Her heart's pace had increased either from excitement or fear. She was sure Carlton was not being forthcoming with her. If only she were Tyndale, who she was certain would be able to turn the conversation in a useful direction! "I only heard," she said, pretending not to look at him, "that his workshop in Saunders Hall wasn't the only one he had. Don't you think he must have been on to something, if he was so secretive?"

"Or he was paranoid," Carlton said. He was back to being calm again. Veronica considered her options and decided not to push. The only other thing she could say was that Ian had been murdered, and that wasn't something she was allowed to give away, even if it might startle Carlton into revealing he'd done it.

"I suppose we'll never know," she said. "Now, about this text by Carruthers..."

She kept Carlton busy for half an hour, but never found a way to turn the conversation back to his relationship with Ian or the missing Device. Eventually, Veronica gathered up the books, thanked Carlton, and walked back to Patience House. She felt low in spirits and discouraged. Carlton had been so dismissive of Ian and Samantha both, and Veronica wasn't sure what disturbed her more, that Carlton and Ian hadn't liked each other or that Carlton had described Samantha as a rapacious tease. That wasn't at all the Samantha Veronica knew and liked. It had to be Carlton's spitefulness and jealousy speaking.

She wasn't sure, either, whether to tell Tyndale her suspicions of Carlton. On the one hand, she'd promised not to obstruct his investigation anymore, and withholding evidence

—if this was evidence, which she doubted—would qualify as that. On the other hand, all she knew was that Carlton hadn't liked Ian and had wanted him out of the way. She had no proof that he was the kind of person who might take direct action to make that happen. And she didn't want to throw around accusations that might hurt an innocent person.

She set the books on her table and sank onto the sofa, closing her eyes and stretching out muscles taut from hunching over notes for half an hour. On a third hand, Tyndale knew Carlton much better than she did, and he would know what his personality was like. It was probably Veronica's duty to let him know there was a different line of inquiry he could pursue. But not today. She wasn't up to facing Tyndale again today. She didn't care if that made her a coward. It could wait until tomorrow.

THAT NIGHT, THE LUCKY STAR TAVERN WAS MORE CROWDED THAN ever. Its warm interior, welcome on a chilly Autumn night like this, smelled of beer and sweat and the beef stew Margo, the tavern owner and cook, always made on Fifthday. It smelled delicious even though it was made of the tag ends of meats from earlier in the week and vegetables gone slightly wizened. People jostled one another in a friendly way, not taking offense at a stray elbow or a heavy foot, as if the crowding made the evening better rather than worse. Veronica was grateful to be with a group of friends, all of whom were more assertive than she was. She might never have found a seat else.

Bec commandeered a round table in one corner, briskly

shooing away the courting couple sitting at it, and sprawled loose-limbed in one of the seats. "Really, the nerve of some people," she said, glaring at the retreating couple. "Thinking they can take up a whole table when it's just the two of them."

Veronica sat next to Percy and was immediately shoved closer to him by Bridget, who apologized. "There's going to be a lot of us, and we'll need to squeeze close," Bridget said.

Veronica nodded. The chairs were filling up fast with students, all of them laughing and greeting each other loudly. She knew only a few of them, but they all addressed her informally, like she was one of them. After a few minutes, it even felt true.

"Randolph, you get the first round," Percy shouted. "Everyone settled? Then let's have a go at the school song!"

Veronica sat in mute amazement as the entire table burst out in a tremendous noise that might have been music. The students sang in different keys and tempi, some apparently racing others to get to the end first and cheering themselves when they "won." She made out scraps of lyrics occasionally, but for the most part, it was a terrible discordant noise that nevertheless seemed to please the singers by how they slapped one another on the back and laughed. For a moment, Veronica felt like an outsider again, ignorant of their traditions. Then she told herself to stop maundering. All of them had been in her position once. In a few seasons, she would be the one singing.

Laughing, Bec put her arm around Veronica's shoulders and hugged her briefly. "I know, it's terrible," she said, "but we always start a gathering that way. It's tradition." She accepted a mug from Randolph and gulped down half its contents in one go. Wiping her mouth on her sleeve, she added, "And tradition must never be broken! Up the Scholia!"

"*Up the Scholia!*" the rest shouted.

Percy shoved his chair back and stood, awkwardly due to how closely he was pressed on both sides. "Let's remember Ian Frost," he said. "He was a good friend and a clever Deviser—"

"Whose Devices never worked!" someone else cut in.

More laughter. Percy saluted the speaker with his mug. "Or worked too well. Don't forget the automatic nose hair trimmer!"

"He was destined for greatness, though," a woman on the edge of the crowd who hadn't found a chair said. "Never gave up no matter how many failures he had. Blandings swore we'd all look back someday and be honored we'd called Ian friend."

Percy nodded. "Let's drink to Ian," he said, "and hope he hears us, wherever he is in heaven."

The group went silent as everyone, Veronica included, drank deeply. Veronica liked the ale she'd been handed. Ale wasn't something served at the palace, and she'd been surprised to discover she had a taste for it. She set her mug down and listened to the background noise of the rest of the pub. So many people talking, laughing, celebrating—and here she was to honor the memory of a friend. It was hard to stay melancholy in a place like this.

"Stories!" Bec shouted, slamming her mug on the table. "I'll go first. There was a time—maybe two years ago? Doesn't matter—when Ian had this idea that he was going to invent a better light Device. He worked at it for hours, messing about to get it to burn brighter or longer or something. Lots of explosive failures, I remember. And he succeeded! Of course, it turned out to need about ten times the amount of motive force for about twice as much brightness, so it wasn't practical. We teased him about it, but all he ever said was, 'If we assume we already know everything, we'll never learn anything.' He lived by those words."

A murmuring went up around the table, people nodding in agreement. "And another thing—" a portly young man began. Veronica took another drink and listened to the humorous story about Ian and some practical joke. The storyteller kept losing the thread of the story and made numerous digressions, and Veronica found his tale impossible to follow, but she made herself look attentive anyway.

She wished she'd known Ian long enough to have stories to tell. They'd spent a lot of time together over the last four weeks, but it was all boring stuff, and the interesting stuff, like how he'd been murdered, wasn't hers to tell.

"I'll get the next round," she said when the tale wound to a halt and everyone had given the teller an awkward laugh.

"No, you're stuck back here," Bridget said. "You can pay, but we'll send Marie to fetch. Marie doesn't mind, right?"

Marie indicated that she didn't mind at all. Veronica finished her ale and had the mug snatched away from her and replaced all in one motion. She surveyed the crowd as the current storyteller wound up her anecdote, which was funnier than the last, and said to Bec, "I don't see Samantha. I thought she'd come."

Bec's laughter died away. "I didn't," she said bluntly. "She and Ian were over."

"Yes, but she told me...that is..." Veronica stumbled over her words and took a drink to cover her confusion. "I thought, from what she said, that she regretted how she'd treated him."

"I don't think Samantha Wilde ever considers anyone but herself," Bridget said. "I know she's your friend, Veronica, but she's sort of carelessly cruel to anyone who doesn't matter to her."

"And she played Ian and Carlton Dunn off each other," said a woman Veronica didn't recognize. "I always thought it was Ian's one weakness, that he couldn't see what she was really like."

Veronica didn't know how to respond. She wanted to defend her friend, but she was acutely aware that she hadn't known Samantha as long as these people had, and what if she was mistaken? "I think," she began.

"It's Carlton who ought to feel like a jerk tonight," Percy said. "I don't know that he and Ian ever resolved their issues. They were always arguing, Carlton getting up in Ian's face about how he wasn't worthy of Samantha, Ian standing his ground and accusing Carlton of unwarranted jealousy. If I were Carlton, I'd be eaten up by remorse."

"Carlton never feels remorse no matter how he uses someone," Bec said. "He used to wheedle me into copying his essays for him because he couldn't be bothered to improve his handwriting. I'm pretty sure he has no soul."

"You would know!" shouted a man who'd just joined the group and who hovered on the outskirts, pressing forward so the people in front of him leaned into the table.

Bec waved a hand. "I'm not saying my judgment is perfect. And Carlton *is* handsome. But I've learned my lesson about being swayed by a pretty face."

"Hey!" Percy exclaimed.

Bec kissed him soundly on the lips. "Pretty is one thing. Devilishly handsome is another."

"Nice save, Bec," Bridget said.

Veronica realized there was another absence. Howard

wasn't there. Worry crept over her. Howard shouldn't isolate himself, and if anyone needed to celebrate Ian's life, he did. "Is Howard—" she began, but someone else started telling a loud story, and her words were swallowed up.

She remembered her suspicions about Howard being the murderer. Tyndale hadn't said what had come of his interrogation, naturally, and Veronica felt irritated by that. Her not being part of the investigation was one thing, but Howard was her friend, and if Tyndale suspected him, she deserved to know, if only so she could stay away from him.

Two more rounds passed. The stories grew wilder and less plausible. Veronica drank enough to feel dizzy, an effect made worse by the warmth of the pub. Her worries about Howard and Samantha faded as she was wrapped in a beer-scented cocoon, surrounded by friends, safe and warm.

"All right, all right, but try this," someone was saying. "What if it wasn't an accident?"

Veronica woke as abruptly as if she'd taken a bucket of ice water to the face. "What accident?" she said, her words running together. Her tongue felt thick and her muscles were as loose as melted honey.

"No, see, not an accident," the man said. Veronica knew him as a student from her art history class, but she couldn't remember his name. "Don't you think it's funny that Ian was able to fall hard enough to kill himself? I've seen his workshop. There's not enough room to move, let alone get up the speed—"

"Tha's enough," Bec said. Her words were even more slurred than Veronica's. She waved an empty mug in the speaker's direction. "Not supposed to talk about death. S'posed to talk about life, Marcus. And my mug is empty. Tha's a crime, an empty mug."

"You mean you think someone killed Ian?" the woman draped over the speaker's shoulders said. "Why would anyone kill Ian? Everybody liked him."

"Not Carlton. Not Ginger Hartford. Not—"

The woman shushed him with a finger to his lips. "All right, not everyone. But killing—"

Veronica felt she should stop this line of discussion, but her head was fuzzy and she was afraid if she spoke, she would only make things worse. Someone else was talking, and to her surprise, she realized it was herself. "Just an accident," she was saying in her slurred voice. "Nothing to do with his Device."

"Hah!" Percy said. He looked and sounded moderately less drunk than Bec. "His Device! Wonder if it was worth killing for?"

"No—" Veronica began, feeling desperate.

"Imagine that," Bridget said dreamily. "He invents something that turns straw into gold, and somebody steals it and coshes him over the head. Or I guess it could be the other way around."

"Are you all still going to Ravensholm?" Veronica said loudly. If rumors like that spread, Tyndale might blame her. And they would interfere with his investigation. Or the other way around. Her mind seized on the one thing she could remember that might distract them. "The project is still there even if Ian isn't."

Percy belched and waved a hand in front of his face. "Project's there. We've been pulled off it. Grief, you know. Plus Ian was important to building some of the Devices that go into the bridge."

"But if his Devices were never successful—"

Bec leaned over and breathed a beery breath into Veronica's

face. "He was fine at building other people's Devices, so long as he didn't invent one himself or try to alter the existing design. Which he always did. Tha's what I loved about Ian, he never gave up."

"Even if someone stole his design. I bet that's what happened." It was the original theorist, Marcus. Veronica wished she could make him disappear. Or maybe it didn't matter. They were all drunk; probably they'd forget this conversation in the morning. Though *she* wasn't likely to, so what were the odds of everyone here conveniently forgetting such a compelling theory?

Bec snapped her fingers, or tried to; it took her about five attempts to make a satisfactory snapping noise. "I bet you're right," she said. "Ian wasn't climsy. Clumsy. Somebody killed him and stole his Device."

"That's stupid," Veronica said, and regretted it instantly when Bec turned on her.

"You found his body," she said angrily. "Why didn't you tell us the truth?"

"I did. It was an accident."

"I'm going to find out who killed Ian," Bec declared, "and then I'm going to punch him straight in the eye." She swayed once, then sagged, her head coming to lie on the table, her fist letting go of her mug. Ale spilled everywhere.

Veronica decided it was time to go. The stories had stopped flowing, and most of her friends were either in Bec's state or singing lewd songs with great vigor. She stood and shoved past Bridget, who said, "You're not leaving, are you?"

"I feel sick," Veronica said, which was true; her stomach felt like she'd filled it with acid instead of good beer. "I need fresh air."

"I should walk with you," Percy said, though he made no move to get up. With as wedged between people as he was, getting up might have been impossible.

"It's not like there's any danger. I'll be fine. I'll see you all tomorrow." Veronica made her way around the table and forced a path through the taproom, which wasn't as full as before, but was still very crowded. Someone pinched her bottom as she passed, and instead of being outraged, she was amused. Fifty years old should be past the point where anyone was interested in a pinch.

Outside, the chilly air struck her over-warm body like a slap. She sobered instantly, though she could tell she still wasn't fully in command of her faculties. She tilted her head back to look up at the sky, wishing she knew how to read the stars to tell what time it was. She'd left her watch in her rooms and had no idea whether it was before or after midnight. It didn't matter. Tomorrow was Endweek, a holiday from classes and tutorials, and she decided she was going to sleep late and let her worries over Ian's murder slip away.

Knightsbury's main street, home not only to the Lucky Star but to a host of other pubs, was still busy even at this hour with men and women strolling along, some in groups, others in pairs. As far as she could tell, she was the only lone pedestrian among them. That made her tipsy self feel sad, and she indulged in a moment's grief over Landon, dead nearly five years now. She'd stopped missing him quite so much after Elspeth had come to Aurilien to take the Crown, what with her fresher grief over her dead son and then Elspeth's cheery presence. But occasionally his loss would hit her like the ache of a broken tooth, forgotten until an incautious jab starts it hurting again. She'd needed him, and he'd left her. She didn't know if that made her angry or just sadder than before.

She left Knightsbury behind and trod the verge of the highway, vaguely fearing some night carriage or post rider overrunning her in the dark, unlighted space between the city and the Scholia. The stars were brighter now in the absence of a moon or the lamps of Knightsbury, and once again she tilted her head back to look at them and immediately had to look down when she tripped over her own feet.

She thought about the possibility that the rumor of Ian's murder would spread. If Tyndale blamed her for it, she would... well, she'd think of something that didn't require yelling or being sarcastic, neither of which she was good at. But she wasn't going to let him criticize her when she'd done her best to quell it. Though he hadn't yelled at her at all that day, even though yelling might be considered justified. He'd been polite and honest and even complimentary. She still couldn't reconcile that man with the harsh-tempered, mean-spirited Tyndale everyone kept telling her he was.

All the Scholia buildings were lit, if only by lanterns over the doors, when she arrived, shivering and wishing her cloak were heavier. It was as if someone knew most of the students were in Knightsbury and would need help finding their way home. She found the door of Patience House locked, fumbled with her keys until she opened it, then fumbled more locking it again from the other side. Then she staggered up all the stairs to her room and fell onto the sofa. She shouldn't stop there. She should go to bed. She'd end up tired and aching again. But her muscles refused to move.

Someone knocked on her door. "Veronica?" It was Samantha.

Veronica groaned and pushed herself upright. She fumbled with the Device light, then turned it down when its full brightness hurt her eyes. Samantha stood at the door in her brightly colored dressing gown. Her eyes were red-rimmed and her mouth trembled.

"Is it true?" she said.

"Is what true?" Veronica said, too drunk still for courtesy.

Samantha swallowed. "That Ian was murdered?"

14

*V*eronica gaped. "What are you talking about?" Gossip was fast, but surely it wasn't *that* fast.

"I heard it from Renie. Everyone's saying Ian couldn't have been killed by a fall like that. That someone murdered him to get his new Device. Is it true?"

Veronica stepped back and gestured to Samantha to enter. "How would I know?"

Samantha shrugged and took a seat on the sofa. "You found him. I guess I thought, maybe you'd seen evidence...oh, I don't know what I thought."

Veronica sat beside her. Well. That meant the rumor wasn't just spreading among Ian's friends. She wondered where it had started. No, that didn't matter to her, because she'd promised to stay out of the investigation. Tyndale would figure it out. Suppose the murderer had started the rumor? That made no sense. Whoever it was would benefit more from everyone believing it was an accident that had killed Ian. She was still too drunk to think straight.

"I didn't see anything about his wound that looked like murder," she said, perfectly truthfully.

"But it makes sense, doesn't it? That someone wanted his Device—if it really was a breakthrough, suppose it was worth a lot of money?" Samantha leaned back and tilted her head so she was looking at the ceiling. "Can you imagine? A murderer, here in the Scholia!"

"We don't know that it was murder," Veronica said, wishing she could push Samantha out of her room and get rid of the rumors that way.

"We don't know it wasn't," Samantha countered. "I think the Scholia should call in an investigator. The guards from Knightsbury wouldn't have any idea, but a proper investigator from Aurilien—"

"I'm sure the Scholia will think of something, if they decide it's true. It's still just rumor."

Samantha eyed her closely. "Are you all right? Veronica, are you *drunk*?"

"Just a little," Veronica protested. "We had a celebration at the pub, of Ian's life. There's nothing wrong with drinking a little."

"No, it's just I never imagined you being even the least bit tipsy." Samantha rose. "I'll leave. You probably need to sleep it off."

She paused in the doorway. "I hope it's true," she said fiercely. "I hope it was a killer and not an accident. Because then I'll have someone to blame." She shut the door behind her before Veronica could respond.

Veronica lay flat on the sofa with her long legs dangling over the armrest and tried to get the world to stop spinning. Tyndale could hardly blame her for this. She'd done what she could to stop the rumors, with about as much success as anyone could against gossip, which was to say, very little. Now the Scholia would have to reveal that they had someone investigating, and Tyndale wouldn't be able to conceal his activities. And the murderer, who before had been secure in believing everyone thought Ian's death was accidental, would now be twice as canny. Veronica felt the chances of finding Ian's murderer were dwindling to nothing.

Her eyelids felt so heavy, like sandbags were weighing down on them. Groaning, she pushed herself up and climbed the stairs to her room. She poured herself a glass of water, drank thirstily, and collapsed into bed without removing more than her boots. Everything else could wait until morning. She hoped.

VERONICA WOKE WITH A HEAD THAT ACHED FAR LESS THAN IT probably should and a mouth that felt lined with sandpaper. She drank another large glass of water, swilling the last of it around her mouth, and felt a little more human. Her body ached nearly as much as her head, and she felt weary despite having slept—she checked her watch Device—nearly nine hours. More evidence that she wasn't as young as she once was.

She changed into the most casual dress she owned and a pair of shoes more comfortable than fashionable and hurried to the refectory, hoping she hadn't missed breakfast entirely. The refectory was half-full of students who were as bleary-eyed as Veronica. Most of them picked idly at their food and conversed in low voices, filling the refectory with a dull, egg-scented hum.

On Endweek, the usual serving rules were set aside in favor of a more free-form model. Veronica joined the short queue of diners standing outside the kitchen, and eventually received a plate containing a spinach omelet and a pile of steaming hashed potatoes. The smell didn't tempt her stomach, but she figured that was normal after the night she'd had.

She sat in her usual place and took a bite of potatoes and thought about what she might do that day. Read, possibly, something not related to any of her classes. She had a mathematics assignment that was due on Secondday morning, but she still had time to finish it tomorrow.

Someone dropped into the seat across from her. "That smells awful," Bec said. She lowered her head to rest on the table, pressing her forehead into the table linen. "Everything smells awful. Why'd you let me drink so much?"

Startled, Veronica protested, "But I didn't—"

"Ignore her, Veronica, she always blames everyone but herself for her rare benders," Percy said. He held two plates laden the way Veronica's was and hooked his chair away from the table with his foot. "Sit up, Bec, you need food."

Bec groaned, but sat up. Percy set his plate and hers down and sat beside her. "You look like you were more sensible than we were," he told Veronica. "Sleep well?"

"Sort of." Veronica poked at her omelet. It was rich with spinach, diced tomatoes, and sautéed mushrooms. She pushed her plate aside and took a long drink of water. "I need a rest day."

"No reason not to take one," Percy said, loading his fork with omelet and potatoes and taking a bite almost too big for his mouth. "I'd say you deserve it after the last few days." He elbowed Bec. "Eat, woman."

Bec nudged her pile of potatoes with her fork. "Veronica's not eating."

"I hate mushrooms," Veronica said curtly. She waited for the inevitable comment. But Bec just shrugged and forked up omelet from her own plate.

Veronica ate a few more bites of potatoes, but they had gone dry and tasteless. Eventually, she pushed back from the table. "I'll see you at supper, I guess," she said.

"See you then," Percy said. Bec nodded. Her mouth was full, and her earlier objections to the food had vanished.

Veronica crossed the yard to the bethel without really noticing where she was going. The day was as clear as yesterday, the sun bright, and she'd stopped wincing at the light. But her mood was still low. Ian dead, herself forbidden to do anything to help bring his killer to justice or find his missing Device, mushrooms...

On a whim, she entered the bethel, whose door stood open. Its cool dimness comforted her, though she still felt nothing particularly special about the place. A few people knelt along the sides of the room, and two young women sat at the front pew, their heads close together, though they were too far away for Veronica to hear if they were speaking.

Rather than take a place at one of the individual niches, she sat at the end of a pew about midway between the door and the dais and clasped her hands in her lap. She had no intent to pray or even to meditate, something Elspeth had tried to teach her that Veronica had been uncharacteristically too impatient for. So she sat and let her mind wander.

She couldn't imagine how the rumor that Ian had been

murdered had started. Given that the Scholia had kept it a close secret, it really was the sort of thing only a drunk student would come up with. But Renie didn't drink, and she didn't go to taverns, so anyone she heard it from would have been as sober as a stone. It was too strange.

She considered, briefly, taking the information to Tyndale, and just as quickly discarded the notion. He would find out on his own, and it was only her impatience and her remaining irrational desire to help that made her even think of it. She should stay silent, let Tyndale handle it, and wait for things to run their course.

Tyndale interested her. From what all the other students had said, she'd expected rudeness, abrasiveness, and a complete indifference to the feelings of others. But he'd been polite, and he'd apologized to her more than once, and he hadn't yelled even though he'd clearly wanted to and she'd possibly deserved it. Granted, he liked d'Arnot's sculptures, and she couldn't believe anyone with good taste in art could be all bad. But even aside from that, she didn't think he was awful. It was tempting to invent a tortured past for him, something that would explain his rather distant behavior, but Veronica knew better than to romanticize real people. It only led to embarrassment or heartache.

She bowed her head and contemplated her fingers, loosely laced together. What must Ian be seeing now in heaven? Veronica's religious beliefs, as casual as they were, still included the knowledge every Tremontanan had that heaven existed and was bound to earth by the lines of force. Even after Landon's and Francis's deaths, though, she hadn't given any increased thought to the nature of the afterlife. She didn't like the idea that her dead might still be watching her, because how awful if their heavenly existence was tied up completely in an obsession with the living world? But she did like to imagine father and son together, learning to know each other in a way that had been impossible in life. Landon and Francis had been so different, and they'd always been awkward around each other, using Veronica as a go-between to provide that connection. It would be wonderful if they'd finally come to terms now that they no longer had her to rely on.

Veronica closed her eyes and composed a wordless prayer, an informal phrase or two that was all she'd ever been comfortable sending heaven's way. *Watch out for Ian,* she thought. *He wasn't ready to go, and that must have made him miserable, having to leave behind so much unfinished business. Grant him peace.*

She waited for some acknowledgment that her prayer had been heard, but felt nothing but a cool breeze from the open door. That didn't disappoint her. Receiving a response from heaven would have terrified her.

She rose and left the bethel, not looking at the worshippers in their niches. A few clouds had gathered in the western skies while she was inside. A storm was coming; she could smell rain in the air as well as see the darkened horizon. She loved reading indoors while it rained, and the tower bedroom was particularly nice in how it sheltered her without dimming the sound of a storm. She remembered discussing old Master Golden with Tyndale and smiled at the memory of that class. Reading for pleasure had been something that had crept up on her after Landon's death. How astonished Master Golden would be that Veronica read books voluntarily now.

In that spirit, Veronica hurried to Covington Hall, where the literature school maintained a small but significant library of modern fiction. She borrowed two books and returned to

Patience House. The storm was advancing more quickly than she'd thought, and the wind had picked up, whipping the dark storm clouds toward the Scholia like a rancher herding cattle to market. The smell of rain on grass was strong, and Veronica inhaled deeply and felt the last of her bad mood disappear.

Mistress Holyoak pounced on her the moment she opened Patience House's front door. "Lady North," she said, her mouth pursed in her usual sour-lemon expression, "I am not accustomed to playing hostess to our residents. In future, please tell your guests to meet you elsewhere."

"I beg your pardon, Mistress Holyoak. What guests?" Veronica hated how humble she sounded, but Mistress Holyoak's hostility never failed to make her cringe inside.

"There is a *woman*," Mistress Holyoak said, managing to make the word sound like something vaguely obscene, "waiting for you in the east drawing room. I explained that you were out and had not confided in me the hour of your return, and she very rudely told me she would wait!"

That didn't sound rude to Veronica, but she nodded politely. "I wasn't expecting anyone, or I'm sure I would have warned you. The east drawing room? I'll go to her at once." She hurried away before Mistress Holyoak could launch into another tirade about the irrational expectations of hospitality some people had.

The east drawing room, filled to bursting with overstuffed sofas and chairs with mismatched upholstery, was the smallest of the public drawing rooms in Patience House. It was also the coldest, lacking a fireplace and boasting three large, imperfectly-sealed windows. Gusts of wind blew through the cracks surrounding these even when it wasn't stormy, which meant when Veronica opened the door, a sharp breeze greeted her, making her shiver. Whoever this woman was, she must really have irritated Mistress Holyoak.

The woman was seated on one of the too-soft sofas when Veronica entered, but rose without the difficulty most visitors had in getting off the deep cushions. Her dark skin and rippling black hair made her look like Veriboldan nobility, but when she spoke, her accent was that of northwestern Tremontane. "Are you Lady North?"

Veronica extended her hand. "I am. May I have the pleasure of your name?" It was a trifle too formal, but the woman's demeanor, cool and commanding, made Veronica feel as if she were greeting a queen.

"Pauline Kensington," the woman said, clasping Veronica's hand in a brief, firm grip that said she disliked having her time wasted. "Ian Frost's business partner."

Irrational guilt stabbed Veronica's heart. Ian's partner. Miller had mentioned her as someone who might know about Ian's Device. For a moment, she imagined excusing herself so she wouldn't break her word to Tyndale. Then common sense asserted itself. She had no idea what Kensington's presence meant, and walking away without even speaking to the woman would be rude. For all Veronica knew, Kensington wanted to share condolences over Ian's death and had no interest in talking business.

"It's good to meet you," Veronica said, "though I wish the circumstances were better. I'm sorry about the room being so cold. The chatelaine..."

"She's a nasty piece of work, if you mean the woman who greeted me," Kensington said. "I'd think I'd given her offense if I'd said more to her than my request to speak to you."

"I'm afraid with Mistress Holyoak, that's enough. We can go elsewhere...I'm sorry, but I don't know what you have in mind."

"This is fine. I'm from Stolling in Daxtry, nearly on the border. Cold and storms are in our blood." Kensington seated herself again, and Veronica hastily took a seat across from her. *She* was cold, her dress inadequate to the chill of the room, but she didn't like to disrupt her guest.

"Garold Miller told me you'd come asking about Ian's workshop," Kensington said. "Why are you interested?"

"Ian was my friend. He told me he'd had a breakthrough on this new Device he was going to show me the night he...died. I thought, if he'd succeeded in inventing something, it might be worth completing the Devisery. As a memorial to him."

"So you're a Deviser?"

"Oh, no. But there are Devisers here...someone might be able to finish his work."

Kensington looked at her with narrow eyes. "I wouldn't have thought the Dowager Consort would stoop to theft."

Veronica's mouth fell open. "I beg your pardon?"

"That Device," Kensington said, "belongs to me, in the event of Ian's death. I funded his research. If it can be completed, any profits from its manufacture revert to me."

"Oh. I'm—" Veronica closed her mouth on *sorry* and regarded Kensington more closely. The woman's pose was relaxed, her arm resting on the arm of the sofa, but her shoulders were tense and her eyes fixed on Veronica as if willing Veronica to feel the weight of her words. Impulsively, Veronica said, "Then you have documentation of your business relationship? Contracts?"

Kensington shifted. "Of course," she said, not blinking.

"Not that it matters, since there's no Device, but...you know,

Ian never mentioned you? So it's fortunate you have papers attesting to what you've just told me. Otherwise I'd be forced to wonder if *you* were the thief."

Kensington's hand closed into a fist. "Are you accusing me of lying?"

"Certainly not. I would never be so rude. I *am* accusing you of attempting to take advantage of my innocent wish to see my friend immortalized for his Devisery." Veronica leaned forward. "I have no need of money, Miss Kensington. I'm sure you realize that. And right now, Ian's Device is only a possibility. But I'm sure if it's discovered, and it's viable, the question of profits can be visited then. And if you were Ian's friend, you ought to be less concerned with how you personally can benefit from this tragedy and more interested in preserving his memory."

Kensington's mouth twitched upward on one side. "I apologize," she said. "You looked like someone who's easily cowed."

Veronica didn't say that normally, that was true. She didn't know what had gotten into her, except that boldness seemed to come more easily when it was on behalf of anyone but herself. "What do you *really* want, Miss Kensington?"

Kensington relaxed her fist. "I was hoping you knew more about the Device. You know how secretive Ian was. He kept the Devisery scattered throughout several workshops, with the information about how it all fit together nowhere but in his own suspicious head. I'm just the finances, Lady North. I know very little about Devisery. But I hoped, if I could collect everything he'd amassed, someone might be able to make sense of it."

"That was what I thought, too. But—"

Kensington looked at her expectantly when she didn't immediately finish that statement. "But, what?"

Veronica couldn't think how to explain about the theft from the Saunders Hall workshop without revealing that Ian had been murdered. "But I'm not the one who has power over his workshop here," she said. "You should make a request of the Scholia."

Kensington's expression went hard. "They brushed me off. Said Ian's affairs were in flux and I had to prove I had a valid relationship to him. But it felt like a blow-off. Does that mean it's true he was murdered?"

"I—" Veronica wanted to laugh at the thought of how irritated Tyndale would be that his carefully concealed investigation was coming apart in the face of gossip. "I'd heard that rumor. I don't know if it's true."

"If it is, someone might have stolen the Devisery. And that would explain why the Scholia officials were so cagey." Kensington looked like she wished she could batter those officials into compliance with her will. "This is disastrous."

"Do you know what the Device did? Ian wouldn't say."

Instantly Kensington's demeanor went wary. "I don't know," she said, and she was clearly lying. "And if I did, I wouldn't tell you."

"Why not? It's not as if I can do anything with the information."

"Ian had a number of projects in development, all of them with manufacturing potential. If other Devisers knew what he was working on, it would give them ideas for what direction to pursue. I can tell you this Device had tremendous implications for its field. If he made it work, it would mean a fortune—for him, for me, for whoever he sold it to." Kensington shook her head. "If someone killed him, I hope the bastard pays. Ian and I weren't close, it wasn't that kind of relationship, but I respected his genius. Not to mention the financial loss I've taken."

"I wish there were something I could do to help," Veronica said.

"You could speak to the Scholia on my behalf," Kensington said. "Ask them to give me access to his workshop."

"I don't know what good that would do. I'm just a student."

Kensington laughed. "You're Lady Veronica North. You are hardly just a student. And from what I've seen of the Magister, your title and rank are more than enough to have him fawning over you, whatever you ask."

The idea disturbed Veronica. She'd tried so hard to be nothing more than a student, to not take advantage of the benefits she might squeeze out of the Scholia. But she remembered how Lansing always tried to give her preference, how readily her wishes were granted when it came to extra tutelage or resources, and she knew she'd failed. "I can ask," she said. "Where can I reach you?"

Kensington reached into a satchel propped against her legs and withdrew a blank book and a pencil. "Here's my address in Knightsbury, and my office in Aurilien. I'll be in Knightsbury for another week or so. Send word if you have any success with the Scholia Masters." She tore a sheet free, folded it, and handed it to Veronica.

Veronica tucked the paper into her sleeve without reading it. "I'll do what I can, but please don't get your hopes up," she said, conscious that it was Tyndale, not the Scholia, she would have to convince.

"I have faith in your persuasive powers, Lady North," Kensington said with a rather cynical smile. She stood, and Veronica rose as well. "Thank you for your time."

"Thank you for being honest with me," Veronica said.

Kensington shrugged. "You're not what I expected. I thought, from what Miller said, you'd be easy to cow. He looked so pleased about it, I thought he'd gotten the better of you. But I'm guessing not."

She left the room, and Veronica trailed her down the hall to the front door and watched her walk away across the yard. Easy to cow? Veronica had believed that of herself, as well.

"Lady North—"

Veronica shut the door on the rising storm and said, "I beg your pardon, Mistress Holyoak, I was lost in thought and did not consider the weather."

Mistress Holyoak glared at her. "You should remember to think of others before yourself, Lady North. It's the courteous thing to do."

Veronica looked down on the woman and felt a laugh bubbling up inside her. She'd spent her whole life thinking of what other people would think or say or do, and turning herself inside out to please them, to prevent confrontation and keep the peace. Now, instead of the anxious worry Mistress Holyoak usually filled her with, she felt only calm. *Not easily cowed.* "I appreciate the lecture," she said pleasantly. "I naturally know *nothing* of courtesy or good manners. How kind of you to put me straight."

She left Mistress Holyoak sputtering in angry confusion and sailed away, head held high, to her rooms.

Once there, she tossed her books on her bed and changed her clothes for something warmer. She really needed to either go into Knightsbury to hire a seamstress to make her a winter wardrobe, or send to Aurilien for her cold-weather things. She wasn't sure she owned anything warm enough for an upland winter, but sewing new clothes could take so long. On the other hand, it would be fun to make a new acquaintance. Miss Wattlesford could give her a recommendation, she was sure.

But as important as that was, something else took precedence. Veronica had to speak to Tyndale immediately. Maybe Kensington's information wasn't very important, but that was three people now who'd heard rumors that Ian was murdered. Tyndale probably already knew about the rumors, but she wasn't going to take the chance and have him find out she once again was concealing information. Even though she really wouldn't be. And she wanted to tell him what she'd learned from Carlton, though, again, it might not be important. Veronica didn't want to take on the added burden of trying to guess what Tyndale would find important.

She threw on her cloak and locked her door behind her. So much for a leisurely afternoon of reading. But the need to act fizzed through her bones, and she felt a rush of pleasure at being able to do something for Ian that even Tyndale couldn't object to. She hurried through Patience House and into the rising storm.

15

Not knowing where Tyndale might be at that hour on Endweek, Veronica decided to try Godfrey Hall first. She wondered if Tyndale worked through the rest day, or if he gave himself a respite. She guessed the former. He struck her as someone who didn't have much of a personal life. Though, again, it might be a mistake to make assumptions about someone she barely knew.

Rain began falling when she was halfway to the administration building. She pulled her cloak's hood farther over her forehead and ducked her head against the chilly drizzle. New warm clothes were definitely in order. Once the storm was over, she would go into Knightsbury and speak to someone. The thought of getting new clothes cheered her.

No one else loitered in the halls when she entered Godfrey Hall, though there were lights coming from beneath a few doors, including the one to the main office. Veronica went straight to the stairs. She didn't think she had to tell anyone what she had in mind, as the Masters' offices were more or less public territory. Outside, the rain lashed the stained glass windows positioned at each landing. The storm muted their bright colors and cast odd shadows through the glass. Veronica loved the sound of the storm, though she knew that was only because she wasn't outside being drenched.

She rapped at Tyndale's door, then knocked again when there was no immediate answer. Reflexively, she tried the knob; locked. She scowled and glanced down the hall to where rain beat against the window. The storm was in full force now, and Veronica hated the idea of running all over campus in it. She thought about going back to Patience House until the rain diminished, but realized Justice House was closer to Godfrey, and she'd get less soaked going there. Sighing, she trotted back down the stairs, snugged her cloak around herself, and sprinted for her goal.

Wind battered her, propelling her rapidly along like a hand between her shoulders. The heavy raindrops felt as large and hard as pebbles flung up by a speeding carriage. She let out a little shriek and ran faster, ducking her head so she almost ran past Justice House in her blindness. She staggered to a halt beneath its shallow portico that gave very little protection against the storm and pounded on the door.

It felt like forever before the door swung open and the elderly doorkeeper peered out. "Yes?" he said, as calmly as if the storm wasn't raging around them.

"I'm looking for Master Tyndale," Veronica gasped. "Is he here?"

The doorkeeper regarded her warily. "It's Endweek," he said, as if that explained everything.

"So is he here, or not?" Veronica demanded. She felt dampness spreading across her back as rain saturated her cloak. "Please, master doorkeeper, I'm freezing."

The doorkeeper paused another eternal moment. Then he swung the door open and beckoned. "Can't let you freeze," he said, and his eye twitched. Veronica belatedly recognized it as a friendly wink. Her face felt too frozen to respond with more than a slight smile.

"Master Tyndale doesn't see students on Endweek," the doorkeeper said. "You should know that."

"I didn't know that. I'm sorry. I'll go...though do you mind if I wait until the storm passes?"

"Nothing wrong with you waiting a bit." The doorkeeper peered closely at her. "It's Lady North, isn't it?"

"Yes."

"Didn't know you were one of Master Tyndale's students."

"He's not my tutor. I'm taking his second law fundamentals class. But this isn't about classes, it's..." Veronica realized in time that she couldn't reveal her true purpose. "Something else," she finished, feeling stupid.

"Huh," the doorkeeper said. "I suppose...why don't you wait here, and I'll let Master Tyndale decide." He stumped away, his gait slightly uneven as if one leg were shorter than the other. Veronica removed her cloak, which was only making her wetter now, and draped it over one arm. A Device the size of a shoebox hung on the nearest wall up by the ceiling, pumping out gusts of warm air she welcomed. She caught her breath and looked around.

Justice House didn't have the large entrance Patience House did; the little room wasn't much bigger than Veronica's bedroom. Heavy, dark paneling made it feel smaller, but it also enhanced the warmth, so welcome after running through the freezing rain. One door, shut now, led to the doorkeeper's room. The other exit was an arched opening through which Veronica saw a hall, dimly lit by lamp Devices at intervals between other doors. A narrow carpet patterned in golds and reds unrolled along the hall and ended beneath her feet. She realized her soaked shoes were leaving a mark and stepped off the carpet onto the varnished floorboards.

Aside from the low whirr of the Device, the place was silent, enough that Veronica gradually became aware of the sound of her own breathing. The silence made her feel like an intruder. She shivered at the thought of going back into the storm. She might be an intruder, but she was a *warm* intruder.

She saw movement at the end of the hall that resolved into the doorkeeper, followed by Tyndale. He was dressed as casually as he had been the night of Ian's murder, in a shirt unbuttoned at the neck and a rather plain blue waistcoat and trousers not as sprucely pressed as usual. He didn't look annoyed that she'd invaded his residence, merely said, "Lady North. Would you join me in the drawing room?"

Veronica followed him a short way down the hall to a door on the left, which turned out to be a sumptuously decorated drawing room that looked like it might have come from a mansion in Aurilien fifty years ago. Its furniture had the same baroque look as the Magister's, all elaborate carvings and curlicues, but the sofa was comfortable, and the room smelled deliciously of violets, which relaxed Veronica.

Tyndale took her sodden cloak from her and spread it over the back of a nearby chair. "I hope your coming out in this storm doesn't mean something dire," he said, sitting opposite her.

"It's about Ian's mur—"

Tyndale held up a hand for silence. "Just a moment, Lady North." He rose and crossed to the door, which hung ajar, and closed it with a faint but definite *click*. "I apologize for the impropriety, but I would prefer not to be overheard."

Veronica hadn't even considered that it might be wrong for her to be alone with Tyndale, and wondered if accusations of improper behavior were common enough for him to be concerned about her reputation. Or was it his reputation he worried about? She suppressed a smile at the thought that she might endanger his reputation at her age and said, "Did you hear the rumors? People have started talking about the possibility that Ian was murdered."

Tyndale's eyes narrowed. "Dear heaven," he said. "That was fast."

"I didn't have anything to do with it."

"Of course not. That never occurred to me. You're far too circumspect." Tyndale leaned forward slightly. "I don't suppose you know where the rumors started?"

"Not exactly. The students at the Lucky Star last night—we were having a memorial for Ian, and one of them suggested it. But he was fairly drunk. I thought it wouldn't go anywhere, because who takes drunks seriously? But then I heard the rumor again from someone completely sober. So it has more than one source."

Tyndale's jaw was set tight. "I really did believe I'd have more time before that idea came to someone. This means I'll have to work more quickly."

"Because now the murderer knows he or she isn't safe."

"Precisely." Tyndale shook his head. "You really didn't need to come out in the rain to tell me this, Lady North. I would have learned of it on my own."

Stung, Veronica said, "You were the one who told me I shouldn't conceal things from you anymore."

Tyndale smiled. "I meant that it's freezing out there, and the information isn't so important that you should risk your health, not that I don't appreciate your efforts."

Impulsively, Veronica said, "You've apologized more than once for saying things I misunderstood. Maybe you should consider your words more carefully so there's less chance of them being misconstrued."

Tyndale's eyebrow went up. He laughed. "Maybe I should. It's a fair criticism."

Veronica blushed. "I didn't mean it as a criticism. Just an observation."

"I know. But you have a knack for putting me in my place. It's not something I'm used to."

She felt even more awkward at this. Quickly, she said, "The rumors weren't the only things I wanted to tell you about. Ian's business partner Pauline Kensington came to see me this morning about his Device. And before you say anything, let me repeat that *she* came to *me,* and I'm not trying to impede your investigation."

"I didn't think otherwise. What did Miss Kensington have to say?" Tyndale's expression had gone intent and searching again.

"That the Device was potentially valuable, and that the Devisery might be worth killing for. That is, she didn't say that, because as far as she's concerned, Ian's death was accidental, but that was my inference. She did say she tried to get permission to go through Ian's workshop here and the Scholia Masters turned her down."

"That was my influence. I don't want anyone poking around when I'm still not sure what was taken."

"I wondered. But I was thinking, if she knew what Ian was doing, she might have valuable information. If she saw the workshop, I mean."

Tyndale shook his head. "That's true, but it would mean bringing a stranger in on my investigation, and for all I know she's the murderer and wants to remove or destroy evidence she left behind."

Veronica nodded. "I see. I hadn't thought of that."

"I'm glad you're not as cynical as I am. It's refreshing."

She blushed again. His close regard made her feel uncomfortable, like he could see through her all the way to her bones. "I'm afraid it just makes me gullible."

"I suppose that's possible, but I doubt it." Tyndale sat back and rested his hands palm-down on his knees. "At this point, I have to decide whether it's worth it to make the investigation public. If it rattles the murderer, that might be a benefit."

"But it will mean more people getting in your way."

"It might be a worthwhile tradeoff."

"But—" Veronica suddenly remembered her conversation with Carlton. Her suspicions about the young man felt stupid now that she'd spoken with Kensington.

"But, what?"

She shook her head. "It's nothing."

"About the murder? Let me decide whether it's nothing, Lady North. Please."

She let out a deep breath. "I was wondering how certain you are that Ian was killed over his Device."

Tyndale's eyes narrowed. "Did you have an alternate theory in mind?"

"I don't know. It's just that I spoke with Carlton Dunn yesterday, and he wasn't at all upset about Ian's death. I know there was bad blood between them over a woman, and I thought...but it's ridiculous. Just because Carlton hated Ian is no reason to believe he killed him."

"And yet something about that conversation made you wonder."

Veronica nodded. "It felt as if Carlton wasn't being completely forthcoming. I don't know that that means he is the murderer, but maybe it means he knows something important."

"That's possible," Tyndale said. "I'm afraid I don't know Mister Dunn very well. We have a history of misunderstanding between us, and he dislikes me enough that our relationship is professional and rather strained."

"But you recommended him as a tutorial assistant."

"He's good at the law, if a bit uninspired in his thinking. Very thorough. He's said he's interested in teaching rather than public law-speaking, and I thought helping you would provide him with necessary experience." He shrugged. "What did you think of his assistance otherwise?"

"He was very helpful. You're right, he knows the material."

"Then I'm glad it worked out."

Impulsively, Veronica blurted out, "You're not at all what everyone says."

To her surprise, Tyndale laughed. "You mean, humorless, spiteful, and prone to sarcastically eviscerating anyone who dares speak to me the wrong way?"

Veronica thought her head might pop from blushing so hard. "I didn't say that."

"I know how I appear, Lady North. And I admit my reputation is earned. I'm frequently impatient with students, and I dislike having my time wasted. It turns out being sharp-tongued dissuades casual inquirers." Tyndale looked as if he were reminiscing about past encounters and found them amusing.

"But doesn't it bother you that people are...well, they seem almost afraid of you." Veronica wasn't sure why she was pursuing this line of conversation, she felt so awkward, but her curiosity drove her harder than her anxiety about being pushy and rude.

"I find I'm happier not caring what other people think." His amusement vanished, and now his reminiscent look turned dark. "Their opinions hardly matter so long as I know myself to be honorable."

"That's not at all my experience."

Tyndale raised an eyebrow again. "Oh? And how should I live differently?"

His sarcastic tone, so unexpected, made her stammer, "I...didn't mean you...that is, I'm sure you know your own mind."

Tyndale's expression changed, becoming impassive once more. "I apologize. I'm not good at taking criticism."

"It wasn't criticism. I just meant that things have always been different for me." Veronica rose. "I'm sorry, I've kept you too long."

"Lady North," Tyndale began, then fell silent. Veronica stood still, because it was the kind of silence that said he wasn't done speaking. "I remember you, you know," he finally continued. "Lady Veronica Chastain, the girl who captured the heart of the Prince. You were the talk of the Scholia. I thought you were hopelessly stuck-up."

Veronica's mouth fell open. "You thought—why on earth would you think that? I don't recall meeting you before coming here." She sank back down into her seat, outrage overriding embarrassment.

"You didn't seem to have many friends, and you hardly ever spoke to anyone. I thought it meant you felt yourself above the rest of us. But then there was a day when I encountered you—it wasn't even a real encounter, we didn't speak—but I saw you with Prince Landon at the Museum of Aurilien, and you were looking at one of the statues, *Helen in Umberan,* I think. And you looked so happy. I realized then that you were just desperately shy, and in love, and I was ashamed of how I'd judged you."

His candor, and the compassion with which he spoke, struck her to the heart. She couldn't think of anything to say.

"And you've heard the worst of me, and you didn't make assumptions even though they were justified. You're a much better person than I am," Tyndale went on.

"That was thirty years ago. I assume you've improved with age," Veronica said, managing a smile.

"I'm not sure of that, but your approval warms my heart." Tyndale smiled briefly before resuming his usual impassive expression. "Thank you for bringing all this to my attention, though I can't say I'm happy at your continued involvement— and I know you didn't mean it," he added quickly when Veronica began to protest. "I would prefer you stay well away from this. So long as I don't know who the murderer is, you could be in danger."

"I know, and I'll be careful. I promise I don't mean to stay involved, but people keep coming to me."

"You have a restful presence that encourages confidences." Tyndale stood, prompting Veronica to rise as well. She ducked her head so he wouldn't see how his compliment had flustered her. "And I'll look into Mister Dunn's whereabouts the night of the murder. I think you're right that it's coincidence, but there's no sense overlooking possibilities."

"I hope I'm wrong."

"*I* hope to make a discovery, any discovery, before rumor turns into disruption." Tyndale opened the door and gestured for her to precede him.

"Are you making progress? Or should I not ask?"

Tyndale smiled. "It's only been two days, Lady North. But... I'm cautiously optimistic."

He saw her to the front door and bade her farewell, adding, "Take care, Lady North," in a tone of voice that clearly indicated he meant a warning as well as a casual goodbye.

The rain had diminished to a freezing mist that her cloak, still not fully dry despite the warmth of the drawing room, failed to protect her from. Veronica hurried back to her rooms, where she turned both heating Devices to full, started water boiling for tea, and cut herself a thick slice off the honey wheat loaf she'd bought last time she was in Knightsbury. Then she gathered up her quilt and wrapped herself in it before settling on the sofa with one of her borrowed books and the buttered bread. But instead of opening the book, she sat staring at the brass and wood Device as if she could see the heat radiating off it.

Now that she was safely away, her conversation with Tyndale, the latter half of it, left her feeling confused and embarrassed, though he'd been perfectly polite. It was the way he'd seen through her, how quietly and straightforwardly he'd reminded her of those long-gone days. She *had* been terribly shy back then, far worse than now; it had been a shock when Landon singled her out for his attention. She hadn't thought she was anyone a Prince might be interested in.

But now, the thought of Landon didn't steer her down well-trodden paths of memory. Instead, she remembered

Tyndale's expression when he'd spoken of himself, how beneath the amusement had been a sort of bitter disdain. How awful, if he'd fallen into habits he despised. She knew well how hard it was to break habits of thought you'd had a lifetime to develop.

It surprised her to discover that she enjoyed his company. They'd spoken more like...well, not friends, really, but age-mates rather than student and Master, and she'd felt comfortable instead of anxious. She had plenty of friends among the students, but she was always distantly aware of the gap in their ages. If she wasn't a student, she and Tyndale might become friends. Of course, if she wasn't a student, she likely would never have met him, and it wouldn't matter.

She opened her book and made herself focus on the words. She'd done what she promised, and now she would stay out of it and leave the investigation to Tyndale.

Someone knocked on her door.

Groaning inwardly, Veronica went to the door, trailing her quilt behind her. "Samantha," she said. "Is something wrong?"

"Of course not. Should there be?" Samantha didn't look distressed, just alert as always.

"I suppose I just expect terrible things after the past few days," Veronica said. "Come in."

"Oh, I won't stay, I have a biology study group in half an hour. It's just that Mistress Holyoak gave me a message that someone's asking for you." Samantha made a face. "I think the dormitories ought to employ runners, since Mistress Holyoak thinks it's beneath her to go trotting after the students. Even though it's technically her job."

Veronica turned off the burner and left her blanket and book on the sofa. "Do you know who it is?"

Samantha shrugged. "I didn't recognize her. Some student, probably."

But when they arrived in the antechamber, it was empty. Veronica knocked on Mistress Holyoak's door. "Was there someone asking for me?"

Mistress Holyoak's habitual glower deepened. "You shouldn't expect me to play hostess to your guests, Mistress North. I know I've told you that before."

Veronica controlled her irritation and wished she were the sort of person who could easily rebuke others. "I'm sorry for your trouble, Mistress Holyoak. I wasn't expecting anyone. Did she leave a message?"

"I left her waiting here while I went about my business. I assume she left when you took your time about coming down." Mistress Holyoak turned and went back into her room, not quite slamming the door behind her.

"Well, that's typical," Samantha groused. "She's so awful. You're way too polite, Veronica."

"Do you remember anything about the visitor? Maybe she's one of the students in my study group. What did she look like?"

Samantha pursed her lips. "Very pretty. Young, maybe only barely an adult. Like I said, I didn't recognize her. Brown hair, big brown eyes, a heart-shaped face, the sort of girl people fall instantly in love with." She said the last with an air of disdain, as if falling instantly in love was shameful.

The description sounded familiar, but Veronica couldn't put a name to it. "I suppose if it's important, she'll come back," she said. "Do you want some tea? I was making some for myself. It's so cold today."

"Love some," Samantha said. "And we can catch up on the latest gossip. Did you know Harold Brewer and Lord Percival

Logue broke up again? I give it two days before one or the other goes crawling back."

"I think Percival can do better," Veronica said.

"Is that a noble's perspective?" Samantha teased.

"No, it's that Harold can't keep his eyes to himself," Veronica said.

"That's the cattiest thing I've ever heard you say. I like the new you. What prompted the change?"

Veronica remembered, unexpectedly, Tyndale's candid gaze and quiet voice. "I'm not sure," she said, but she was suddenly certain she knew.

16

Morgan Lane in Knightsbury struck Veronica as being inappropriately named. Lanes were narrow, winding passages, possibly somewhere rural, but Morgan Lane was a wide, busy street paved with tiny red bricks in chevron patterns. Run-off from the storm trickled through those patterns, making the street glimmer like a watercolor painting. Veronica was grateful for the sidewalk, raised some three inches above the street, that made a barrier between pedestrians and the wet bricks and the water rushing through the gutters.

Miss Wattlesford had been happy to provide a recommendation for a seamstress even though Veronica hadn't bought anything at the stationer's that day. Morgan Lane was only a few streets over from Miss Wattlesford's shop, and Veronica had found it easily, without resorting to asking for directions. The dressmaker's shop, Eulalie's, bore a distinctive brass plaque displaying that name beside the door, and a variety of dresses and gowns in the latest style hung in a wide multi-paned window next to the door.

Veronica stopped a moment to admire Miss Eulalie Robbins' work. Miss Wattlesford had assured her Robbins did plain work as well as fancy, but Veronica, looking at the beautiful gowns, had some misgivings. Well, she was here, and she might as well ask. Presumably if Robbins wasn't interested in Veronica's business, she would know someone who was.

She pushed open the door and heard, not a tinkle of bells, but a deep single-toned chime that sounded Device-generated. More gowns hung on the walls of the showroom, chosen to coordinate with one another as well as showing off the seamstress's varied skills. A few white chairs upholstered in rose silk brocade to match what was visible of the walls stood in artful groupings throughout the room next to spindly-legged tables. The effect, gowns on the walls aside, was of a tea shop rather than a dressmaker's. Aside from Veronica, the room was empty, though the curtain in a doorway opposite shifted slightly as if someone had just gone through it.

Veronica carefully wiped her feet on the square of floral carpet, also rose-pink, just inside the door and took a few steps on the ruddy brown floorboards toward one of the dresses, a pale blue muslin with white ribbon waistband and long, gauzy sleeves. It was a Spring dress, not suitable for the current season, but it tempted Veronica anyway.

The curtain parted, and a sweet-faced young woman with curly red-blonde hair emerged. "Good afternoon. How can I help you?"

"I'm in need of warm clothing, and Miss Juniper Wattlesford recommended this shop. Though I'm not sure—"

The young woman made a dismissive gesture. "These are

just advertisement. I do all sorts of clothing. I take it you're interested in plainer garb?"

"Are *you* Miss Eulalie Robbins?" Veronica asked, trying not to sound astonished. This woman couldn't be more than twenty-five.

"I'm Miss Eulalie, yes." Miss Eulalie smiled impishly. "Expecting someone older?"

"From what Miss Wattlesford said, yes. Though only in the sense that she said your shop was long-established." The young woman's confident demeanor made it impossible for Veronica to think of her as anything but *Miss* Eulalie, as if she really were sixty years old.

"It is. The first Miss Eulalie was my grandmother. I'm Eulalie Robbins III." Miss Eulalie gestured to a chair. "Please, sit. Would you care for some refreshments while we talk about your needs?"

"I—all right," Veronica said. She was conscious of the niceties of polite society, though part of her felt she was abusing the woman's hospitality when really all Veronica wanted was several warm shirts and three or four pairs of trousers.

Miss Eulalie disappeared into the back again. Veronica settled herself in a chair, which was less comfortable than it appeared. So the dressmaker was cleverer than her apparent age suggested. Too comfortable a chair meant customers would overstay their welcome.

When Miss Eulalie returned, it was in the company of a very handsome young man, younger even than Miss Eulalie, who bore a tea tray with a steaming pot and a small plate of iced cakes. He set the tray on the nearest table, bowed, and left the room.

Miss Eulalie poured out hot, dark tea for Veronica and

herself. "He's my brother," she said. "People always wonder if I hired him for his looks, but in truth, he's trying to make a name for himself as a musician and only works for me to pay his bills."

"I see," Veronica said, silently embarrassed that she had wondered about Miss Eulalie's motives. She sipped tea, and said, "I should introduce myself, since you've been so hospitable. I'm Veronica North."

Miss Eulalie choked a little on her tea. "The Dowager Consort in *my* shop? Good heaven. Don't you—I beg your pardon if this is presumptuous, but don't you have dressmakers in Aurilien?"

"It's just Lady North, please. And I'm currently a student at the Scholia, which is why I've come to you. Winters in Aurilien are less cold than here in the uplands, and I'm afraid the changing weather caught me off guard."

"I can imagine." Miss Eulalie took a long drink from her cup. "Well. Then you'll want me to do the sewing rather than have me pass it off to an assistant—"

"Why is that?"

Miss Eulalie, surprisingly, blushed. "Oh, people of rank, they don't...generally they want the services of the master and not her apprentices."

From what Veronica knew of her own class, she could understand that. "It doesn't matter to me. I've always thought quality is quality regardless of someone's credentials."

"And yet you're studying at the Scholia." Miss Eulalie reddened again. "I'm sorry, that was rude."

Curious, Veronica set down her cup. "I don't understand."

Miss Eulalie made another dismissive hand-wave. "People respect the Scholia stamp. A Scholia-trained law-speaker, for example, is considered better than someone who learned his trade elsewhere, never mind his actual skills. I don't mean any offense, and certainly the Scholia education is rigorous. But I've known a few Masters who gained privileges simply by virtue of having taken the robe."

"I'm not offended. I've noticed that as well. I've always thought it worked the other way around, as well—the robe is a sign of a thorough education."

"That's true, too." Miss Eulalie took a large bite out of a cake. Veronica thought it might be to give herself time to change the subject. Sure enough, when she finished chewing, Miss Eulalie said, "Providing you with clothes will certainly go faster if I'm not the only one sewing. What did you have in mind?"

"Oh…" Veronica plucked at her sleeve. "Perhaps half a dozen shirts, heavier than this, but in much the same style, in various colors or patterns. And trousers—three pairs should be enough."

"That's no problem." Miss Eulalie stood. "I'll take your measurements, and then Gareth will bring out the samples book and we can discuss fabrics."

Miss Eulalie measured Veronica with a knotted cord that whipped around her dizzyingly fast. She wrote nothing down, just muttered to herself as she measured bust, waist, and inseam, then went into the back room. Veronica ate a cake. It was a little dry, but the icing was just the right combination of sweet and tangy. She washed it down with more tea and eyed the blue dress again. It was terribly impractical, but she really liked it.

When Miss Eulalie returned, she once again had the handsome young man in tow. He held an enormous, bulging book filled with fabric squares. "You favor pastels, I can see," Miss Eulalie said. "Good choice, considering your coloring. Bright colors would make you look washed out, but this—" She tapped a square of pale yellow wool— "this will draw attention to your eyes." She detached the square from the book and dropped it into her lap.

In half an hour, Veronica had chosen fabric for shirts and some heavy twilled cotton for trousers. Miss Eulalie shooed Gareth away and gathered the swatches into her hand. "We can have the lot ready by Fifthday next," she said. "I hope that's not too long."

"I know what kind of effort sewing takes," Veronica said. "My couturier in Aurilien isn't as fast as you. Though he also doesn't usually make anything but gowns."

"Plain sewing like this isn't as labor-intensive, true." Miss Eulalie ran a hand over the pale yellow wool at the top of the stack. "I'd like to find a way to streamline the process, perhaps do some of the cutting in advance. But with people being all different shapes and sizes, that's not very practical."

"Everard—my Aurilien couturier—he says there aren't as many differences as people think. He's of the opinion that ready-made clothing is a possibility, if people are willing to accept that the clothes won't be a perfect fit."

"Oh, it's possible," Miss Eulalie said. "It's just not economically sensible. It takes so long to sew even an ordinary shirt, it makes more sense to put that effort into a job for a paying customer rather than taking a chance that a random stranger will want it."

Veronica nodded. "I hadn't thought about that, but you're right. And speaking of paying, how much do I owe you?"

"Half now, half on delivery." Miss Eulalie suddenly smiled, a broad grin that made her look even younger than she already did. "I still can't believe the Dow—"

"Really, I'd prefer it if you called me Lady North," Veronica said.

"Oh? Certainly. It's just so exciting. I never thought I'd have the least connection to royalty, and here I am…" Miss Eulalie shook her head in wonderment. "I'm sorry, I didn't realize I'd be so overawed. You're not at all what I would have guessed."

Veronica smiled. It was hard to take offense at the young woman's genuine excitement. "Expecting someone haughty and stiff-mannered?"

"Well, yes! But that's really all anyone knows of the nobility, how they appear at a distance. I'll know better than to make assumptions now."

Veronica rose and extended her hand. "Your work is lovely," she said. "I will have to call on you if I ever need something more formal. I love that blue dress."

"Yes, it's a shame the woman I sewed it for decided it wasn't to her taste." Miss Eulalie made a small grimace. "And she wasn't the least bit noble, just a merchant's wife with more money than sense. At least it makes for good advertising. Some of my finest work."

Veronica walked over to it and fingered the soft muslin. "It probably wouldn't fit me," she said, half to herself.

"No, it's far too short for you," Miss Eulalie said. "And this is the wrong season for it, anyway. But…" She eyed Veronica speculatively. "Altering the skirt into a row of descending panels would allow me to add some length. And I could easily take it in at the bust and waist. If you really want it, that is."

"I really do," Veronica said. "And Spring will come around eventually, right?"

"I like a woman who looks to the future," Miss Eulalie said.

FIRSTDAY DAWNED CLEAR AND BRIGHT, WITHOUT A HINT OF THE previous day's storm. For the first time in days, Veronica felt rested and cheerful. Even memories of Ian didn't do more than sadden her briefly. She felt certain Tyndale would catch the murderer and find Ian's Device, and Ian's genius would be memorialized properly. It was the kind of day where she felt she could take on the world.

That lasted as long as the end of her law class. Master Tyndale's lecture went completely over her head, referring to some legal expert Veronica had never heard of who everyone else in the class was clearly familiar with. She scribbled desperately, hoping her notes would make sense later, and rose at the end of class with discouragement wrapped around her like a cloak woven of iron mesh and despair.

She watched Tyndale leave in his usual abrupt manner. He hadn't caught her eye or done anything to indicate their newfound accord. It made sense, because he was a Master and she was just a beginner student, but she felt bereft all the same. Masters Herewiss and Averill Cates were as thronged with students as ever, and Veronica's problem was no doubt too complicated for a casual answer.

She detoured past the refectory and stopped at Temperance Hall to leave a note for Carlton Dunn. He'd been helpful the first time, and Veronica was certain he knew all about this mysterious legal expert.

Dinner was a boisterous meal, as if everyone else felt cheered by the weather too, and Veronica regained some of her spirits. Bec and Percy entertained their friends with stories of their early courtship, which had apparently been fraught with misunderstanding. "And he thought I was Genifer Howe," Bec told Veronica. "I don't know where he got that idea. She's about six inches shorter than I am and skinny as a lamppost."

"It was an honest mistake. You've both got brown hair. And Daryl said, 'she's the girl with brown hair,' like there was only one of those in the world," Percy retorted.

"Anyway, it all worked out in the end. Carlton and I broke up, Percy swooped in and picked me up as neatly as you please." Bec blew Percy a kiss. "I thought it would only last a few weeks. You know what it's like when you've just broken up with someone."

Veronica, whose only real relationship had been with Landon, nodded anyway.

"And we've been together two seasons now," Percy said.

"That short a time? You act like you've been together forever," Veronica exclaimed.

"We'll be married come next Midsummer," Bec said. "It does feel like forever. Abstinence is *hard*."

"I believe it's worth it," Percy said primly.

"You're also more religious than I am," Bec said, slugging him lightly on the shoulder. "But I'm not complaining. I believe it's worth it, too. And I admit I'm happier than I've ever been."

"You're much better off than you were with Carlton," Bridget declared. "The two of you were constantly fighting."

"Oh, Carlton loves drama," Bec said airily. "It's why he and Samantha are so well suited. Big, dramatic arguments and then big, dramatic reconciliations."

Veronica hadn't seen any of that in Samantha, who if anything was prone to calm deliberation about everything from classwork to her wardrobe choice. But challenging Bec on her assessment of Samantha was more conflict than Veronica was comfortable with.

"He's a very good teacher," she said instead. "Master Tyndale recommended him, and he's quite patient and knows his subject."

"Tyndale," Bec said with a grimace. "I still can't believe you dared speak to him, Veronica. He eats beginning students for breakfast."

"He's really not like that at all," Veronica protested. "He's been polite and helpful every time we've spoken."

"You've talked to him more than once? Voluntarily?" Percy's grimace matched Bec's.

Veronica could hardly explain about the murder investigation. "We...we've crossed paths a few times, that's all."

"Maybe it's because you're both old," Bridget said. "He might respect that."

"Bridget, you're impossible, you know that?" Bec said. "Veronica's not old."

Bridget blushed. "I didn't mean it that way. I meant you're the same age."

"I understood," Veronica said, amused. "And I think you might be right. We have things in common an ordinary student wouldn't."

"Let's stop talking about Tyndale and Carlton before my meal curdles," Bec said. "Has anyone seen Howard recently?"

"I haven't seen him since..." Veronica realized uncomfortably that she'd last seen Howard on the previous Fifthday, the morning after Ian's death. "It's been a while."

"I'm worried about him," Percy said. "He took Ian's death harder than any of us."

"I'll check in on him after dinner," Bridget said. "See if I can't get him to join us for supper. He shouldn't be alone."

"Definitely not," Bec said. "He wasn't at the memorial, was he? Granted, he's not much of a drinker, but I thought he'd be there."

Veronica drained her glass of water and stood. "I'm sure he's fine," she said, trying to regain some of her earlier cheer and feeling once more discouraged. Howard was sweet, and he was clearly grieving, and she wished she were the sort of person who knew how to help with that. "I'll see you later. I hope Carlton has some free time today. The law class lecture was beyond me."

She remembered in that moment that she should have had Ian to commiserate with, and her own grief hit her like a spike to the chest, flashing pain that was over almost before it began. She pushed in her chair and left, hoping no one could see her cry.

Someone had pushed a note under her sitting room door while she was gone. She unfolded it and saw Carlton's familiar spiky handwriting: *Lyton Hall library 3:30 today*. The thought of more classwork after a full day of learning tired her, but she didn't have a choice if she wanted to pass Tyndale's class. Which she did, and never mind her growing desire to prove to Tyndale that she was capable of handling anything he threw at her. That was silliness. Tyndale didn't care about her academic progress any more than he did any other student's.

She tossed the note on the table and brushed out her hair, pinning it up again securely. A thought occurred to her. Suppose Tyndale had discovered Carlton had the opportunity to kill Ian? She might be going to a meeting with a murderer.

Veronica shook her head violently to chase away those

ridiculous thoughts, then had to push a few pins back into place. If that were the case, Tyndale would have had Carlton taken in charge, or at least warned her to stay away from him. She was getting worked up over nothing.

She gathered her books and her satchel and locked her door behind her. Engineering class, and then a review with Carlton. Normal, everyday things that had nothing to do with murder. She wished her oppressive mood would let her appreciate them.

17

*C*arlton was once again waiting for Veronica when she arrived at Lyton Hall that afternoon. "Have a seat," he said.

"I appreciate your help. I hope it's not too much of an inconvenience."

Carlton shook his head. "Tyndale is right that I can use some experience teaching, much as the words 'Tyndale is right' burn in my mouth," he said. "And it's an interesting challenge, figuring out the assumptions later classes make. I don't know that anyone realized the second law fundamentals class leans so heavily on the first."

"It's not terribly bad, or wasn't until today. Has everyone heard of Magda Albright but me?"

Chuckling, Carlton said, "Everyone who's studied law in the last twenty years. Her work on the bounds between negligent tort and intentional tort was groundbreaking."

"And I last studied law thirty years ago. No wonder I was

lost." Veronica sighed. "Please at least tell me there's not an ocean of reading involved?"

"No, just the one book. And it's not even a primary source." Carlton slid a slim volume across the table. "This is a summary of Albright's writings, organized by legal subject. I think you'll find that clarifies everything, if the lecture you had problems with is the one I think it is."

"Thank you." Veronica put the book into her satchel. "I'll have time to read it tonight."

"We should probably meet again after you've read it to go over the concepts and connect them to your notes. You do take notes, don't you?"

Veronica smiled at his slightly derisive tone and decided not to take issue with the implied insult. She didn't know if he was doubtful because she was old, because she was female, or because he was used to other students not treating the fundamental law lectures seriously, but he had a point, because she'd only rarely seen the other students in Tyndale's class writing as he lectured.

"I do," she said, and extricated her blank book from the satchel to hand to him. Carlton flipped through its pages. His expression gradually went from skeptical to impressed.

"Very thorough," he said, handing it back. "And your handwriting is much better than mine. I can barely read my own notes sometimes."

"I had a tutor when I was twelve or thirteen who insisted on neat handwriting." Veronica smiled in memory. "She would make me recopy my work if it was the least bit sloppy. It was quite the encouragement, the threat of having to rewrite an essay I'd spent hours on already."

"I can imagine." Carlton gathered up the rest of the books

and papers on the table. "So, shall we meet, say, Haransday afternoon at this time?"

"That sounds perfect." Veronica put away her blank book. "If you're sure it's not an imposition."

"Not at all."

Veronica watched him out of the corner of her eye as he continued putting things in order. He sounded different than he had at their first meeting, more casual, more confident. "You seem to be in a good mood," she remarked, hoping she didn't sound too nosy.

"It's a beautiful day, and I've always liked the start of a new week." Carlton's smile verged on smug, and Veronica was suddenly sure there was something he wasn't telling her. Her first instinct was to say nothing. Carlton's secrets weren't any of her business. On the other hand, he'd behaved so strangely when she'd brought up Ian before, and she couldn't help feeling, despite what she'd told Tyndale, that Carlton was up to something shady.

She cast about for something to lure him in. "So do I. It's been so awful the last few days, what with Ian's death and all that."

She expected Carlton to respond with something surly. To her surprise, he looked even smugger for a moment before his expression became bland and noncommittal. "I won't say I'm personally grieving," he said, "because you'd know I was lying. But I can admit Frost's death was a loss for Devisery."

"What makes you say that?" Veronica made herself sound as innocent and ignorant as possible. Then she feared she'd oversold herself. But if Carlton found her sudden simpering unbelievable, he didn't show it.

"Everyone knows Frost was on the verge of a major breakthrough," Carlton said. "It's a shame no one will ever know what it was."

There was a definite note of triumph in his voice Veronica couldn't understand. "But surely someone could put together what he'd done already?"

Carlton shrugged. "Possibly. But Frost was paranoid. Kept all his work in hidey-holes separate and secret. I doubt anyone could find all of them."

"That is a shame," Veronica agreed. Her mind worked like mad. Carlton's emphasis on the impossibility of anyone finishing Ian's work sounded exactly like the words of someone who knew the opposite was true. Which suggested that Carlton had some kind of secret advantage—perhaps the kind resulting from having stolen some of that work himself.

Veronica made herself breathe slowly and kept her movements regular and unhurried. "I'll see you in two days," she said, and with measured steps that in no way indicated she was fleeing, she left the law library. Then she hurried down the stairs and out into the courtyard, where Carlton wouldn't be able to attack her if he'd somehow figured out what she'd concluded.

She realized she was walking toward Justice House and made herself stop. In the cool air of afternoon, with the sun shining brightly off the spires of the Scholia, her intuition seemed ridiculous. She had no evidence aside from Carlton's smug demeanor and innocent words that he was the killer. None of that was enough for Tyndale to question him, or take him in charge, or convict him at trial. She was being foolish.

On the other hand...suppose she was right? She shouldn't let her fear of appearing foolish stop her from following her instincts. And her instincts screamed at her that Carlton was guilty of something. Maybe it was only that he'd happened upon Ian's lab after the murder and had stolen the Device, or whatever Ian had wanted to show her. That was no more unlikely than the possibility that he'd killed Ian.

Veronica resumed her journey. She'd tell Tyndale, and leave it to him.

Unfortunately, the doorkeeper wouldn't let her in. "Instructors' consulting hours are from eight to nine in the morning and from four-thirty to five-thirty in the evening, five days a week," he told her. "No exceptions."

"But—" She felt wary of protesting too hard. She'd already made herself conspicuous with her requests to see Tyndale out of normal consulting hours; suppose the doorkeeper became suspicious and drew conclusions about Veronica's real motives? Or, worse, believed Veronica and Tyndale were conducting some kind of illicit love affair? "I'm sorry, I'll come back later," she said.

She now had about forty-five minutes with nothing to do. On a whim, she decided to see if Howard was at his dormitory. She felt vaguely guilty that she hadn't thought of him at all since they'd talked Fifthday morning. Well, it wasn't as if she hadn't been busy.

The majordomo at Fortitude House said, "Mister Peterson isn't receiving guests at the moment." He looked as if Veronica wasn't the first person he'd told that to.

"I see. But he's there, and he's all right, isn't he?"

"He hasn't left since yesterday morning. And I'm not responsible for the well-being of the residents."

The majordomo's attitude irritated Veronica. Without thinking, she said, "You ought to care about the students in your charge. Suppose Howard was sick, or hurt himself? Wouldn't you feel even the least bit responsible?"

The majordomo looked slightly taken aback at her vehemence. "Naturally one doesn't wish harm to any of the residents, but—"

"I should think you'd be very upset if your negligence meant one of the students didn't receive proper care and attention," Veronica went on. "I realize it's none of my business, since I'm only Howard's friend and not his dormitory supervisor, but I would *hope* you at least check up on him occasionally."

"I—" The majordomo's back straightened fractionally. "I assure you, Lady North, Mister Peterson is perfectly well. And I will endeavor to make certain he remains that way."

"Thank you," Veronica said in her haughtiest royal manner.

She decided to return to her rooms to wait out the remaining time. Sitting on her sofa, she had to laugh at herself. What had gotten into her? She was never bold. Apparently, that wasn't true so long as it was her friends she was being bold about. It felt good to use her title and status to help someone. Hopefully the majordomo would make good on his promise, and Howard would eventually come out of his funk and rejoin the world.

She lay down on the sofa and disposed her long legs over the armrest. She should take a short nap. She wasn't very tired, but she felt, after repeated denials, she'd earned the rest. She put one arm over her eyes and let herself relax.

When she woke, blinking, the room was darker than she had expected. She held her watch Device close to her eyes. 5:47. She'd missed her opportunity, and had almost missed supper.

Scowling, she tidied her hair where it had become mussed

during her nap and headed for the refectory. Her news could wait until morning. It wasn't as if Carlton was going anywhere.

Howard was seated at the table beside Bec when she arrived. He looked almost as bad as he had the other morning. Veronica wanted to ask him if he even owned a comb, but that would have been cruel. She settled for saying, "It's so good to see you! How do you feel?"

"Terrible," Howard said in a pale, fragile voice, almost a whisper. He wouldn't meet her eyes. "I haven't been sleeping well, and I keep forgetting to eat."

Veronica didn't know what to say to that. "I'm glad you remembered tonight, anyway. We've missed you."

Howard shrugged. "I tried to get into Ian's workshop. I was hoping I could figure out what he was working on. But the Scholia locked it down tight." He sighed. "I guess it doesn't matter. I don't even have a tenth the skill Ian had."

"Don't be so hard on yourself," Bridget pleaded. "You and Ian were so different in your approaches. Ian was willing to try a hundred ridiculous things in the hope that one of them would work out. You choose one project and follow it to its end. It's why you actually complete things."

"And if anyone could finish Ian's work, it's you, Howard," Percy said. He cast a despairing look at Veronica, clearly uncertain of what he was saying and begging her to step in.

"It's true," Veronica said. "I'm sure if you could get all the pieces together, you'd know what to do next."

"Master Tyndale wanted to know where all Ian's workshops were," Howard said dully. "I think the Scholia wants one of their Masters to do the work. They don't care that I was Ian's friend and business partner."

"Tyndale?" Bec said. "Why would Tyndale care?"

Unease crept over Veronica. "I'm sure," she began.

"Yes, why would he have anything to do with it?" Percy said. "Unless something shady was going on."

"I don't see how that follows," Veronica said, trying to stay calm.

"Tyndale was a criminal investigator before taking up the instructor's position here," Bec told Veronica. "Maybe Marcus was right, after all. What if Ian was murdered?"

"But that can't be," Bridget said, her eyes wide. "Why would anyone kill Ian?"

"For the Devisery," Bec said. "Howard, you said it was important, right?"

Howard raised his head. The furious expression he wore stunned Veronica, who'd been about to protest, into silence. "If Ian was murdered," he said, his voice low and vicious, "I'll kill the bastard. Killing someone brilliant so they could steal his work—I swear I'll kill him."

Veronica gave up. Any more protests on her part would only go ignored, or worse, clue in her friends that she'd known the truth all along. She sat silently listening to the others spin theories about what had happened and why, and hoped they wouldn't find her sudden silence suspicious.

"Veronica, you're so quiet, are you all right?" Bridget asked.

Veronica nodded. "It's just so dreadful," she said. "I don't know what to think."

Bec gasped. "Veronica, you found Ian's body. Suppose he'd only just been killed? You might have passed the killer in the hall and not known it!"

"Or you might have arrived sooner and caught the bastard in the act," Percy said. "Who knows how close you came to being a second victim?"

Veronica shuddered and pushed her plate away. "I'd rather not think about it."

"Let's stop talking about death," Bec declared. "In the morning, I'm going to the Magister and demanding he tell the students the truth. I'm sure the Masters know more than they're saying. And if Ian was murdered, we deserve to know."

The others murmured agreement. Veronica stood. "I hope it's not true," she said, wishing she weren't such a coward and hadn't lied to her friends all this time. But was it cowardice if she was just doing the sensible thing? "I'll see you all in the morning."

It was still early, but she got into her nightdress anyway and took the book on Albright to bed with her. Fortunately, the text was clear and interesting, not dry, and she finished reading it well before ten. Then she lay in bed with the light Device on and stared at the ceiling. How complicated life had become. She wondered if the Magister would admit to having concealed Ian's murder just because Bec demanded it. Bec was persuasive, but the Magister was unlikely to let that sway him.

She turned off the light and let her troubled thoughts take her into an equally troubled dream she didn't remember the details of come morning. It nevertheless left her feeling dreary, a terrible contrast to her cheery mood the previous day.

Tyndale wasn't available when she presented herself at Justice House a little after eight. "He's got a lot of people wanting a moment of his time. I could give him a message," the doorkeeper suggested.

Veronica considered what message she might send that wouldn't give anything away and came up empty. "That's all right," she said. "I'll speak with him later. It's not very important."

And it didn't feel important anymore, she reflected. A night's rest had been enough to convince her her suspicions of Carlton were foolish, borne of a desire to solve Ian's murder. Her friends all said Carlton was dramatic and self-important, and maybe they were right. In which case, his behavior on Firstday was perfectly normal.

She trudged off to the refectory. She'd promised Tyndale she would stay out of the investigation, and here she was looking for ways to involve herself. She decided to forget the whole thing for now. She should focus on her studies and on helping Howard come out of his funk. Everything else could wait.

THE LAW LECTURE ON HARANSDAY WAS FAR MORE comprehensible now that she'd read about Albright, though Veronica was still grateful she would meet with Carlton that afternoon. Again, Tyndale behaved as if she wasn't there, and again Veronica felt irrationally snubbed. She reminded herself that they weren't friends, that students and Masters shouldn't be friends, and she'd built up their few interactions into something that didn't exist. Logic didn't comfort her.

Howard was at dinner that day. He looked better than he had in a while; he'd combed his hair and changed his clothes, and his eyes looked less bleary. "I've made progress on Ian's workshop," he told the others. "I've made a case for being Ian's partner on his projects, and they've promised to give me access to the workshop in a day or two."

"Why not now?" Bec wondered.

"I bet it's the murder investigation," Percy said. "They're still examining the evidence."

"They can examine all they like if it catches the killer," Howard said. He sounded so angry he seemed nothing like himself. Veronica's heart ached for him.

"What about the other workshops?" she asked, hoping to distract him. "Couldn't you visit them?"

"Aurilien's too far away. I'd miss classes," Howard said. "And I haven't had a chance to go into Brookside or Knightsbury. I figured I'd start with the closest workshop, move out from there."

Veronica felt relieved that he hadn't tried to access the other workshops and come up against whatever prohibitions Tyndale had set up. "That makes sense."

"Anyway, I feel more confident than I have since...you know," Howard went on. "It's not impossible. I'll figure out Ian's Device. I just need time."

"That's the spirit," Bec said, clapping him on the shoulder. "Veronica, you're not leaving early, are you?"

"I have a study group meeting before our engineering class," Veronica said, shouldering her satchel. "And another meeting with Carlton after it. It's a busy day."

"Don't work so hard, you'll get dull and uninteresting," Percy teased.

Veronica smiled and waved goodbye.

It *was* a busy day. Her study group was more than usually distractible, which frustrated Veronica. She'd emerged as the group leader, against her wishes, but she was organized and good at the subject and, she had to admit, most of them responded to her the way they would to their mothers. Inwardly she fumed at this reminder of her age. She never felt old except on cold mornings when her joints ached—and when trying to get the study group members all pointed in the same direction.

She left her engineering lecture feeling extremely disinclined to do any more studying, but she'd promised Carlton, and she hated to waste his time by not showing up. The air was chillier than before, and she wished she'd worn her cloak. Two more days, and she'd have warmer clothes. The idea perked her up considerably.

She trod the stairs to the law library without realizing, at first, that the building was more crowded than usual. Murmuring students and a few black-robed Masters in red stoles thronged the second floor hall, congregating around the door to the law library. Veronica slowed her pace. She hoped whatever was going on wouldn't disrupt her study session. Maybe she and Carlton would need to use a different room. Though she couldn't imagine what could possibly have turned the quiet, boring law library into a hotbed of excitement.

The murmurs became more intelligible the closer she drew, though she couldn't make out more than a few words: *found him...unbelievable...don't know what...* She ended up on the outside of the crowd, unwilling to raise her voice or push her way through. She settled for tapping someone on the shoulder and saying, "Is something wrong? What's going on?"

The student turned, looking at her with an expression somewhere between excitement and horror. "It's Carlton Dunn," he said. "He's killed himself."

18

*V*eronica sucked in a horrified breath. Then she pushed past the student and into the room, saying, "Excuse me—pardon me—please let me through." Surprisingly, it worked. The crowd shifted, and Veronica made her way through them until she was in the clear.

The crowd had halted some ten feet from the table where Carlton lay facedown, sprawled with one arm limp over his head. It was the exact pose Ian had been in when Veronica found him, and for a moment, confusion made her head whirl. She blinked away memories and made herself look at Carlton's body. A stack of books beside his head shocked her back to the present. That made no sense. He'd come prepared to teach her, and then...?

"Move aside," a familiar voice commanded. Veronica felt hands grip her shoulders and shift her gently to one side. Tyndale, dark and imposing in his Master's robe and red stole, strode past and placed a hand on Carlton's throat, though it was clear he was past saving. "Who arrived first?"

A dark-skinned woman near Veronica hesitantly raised her hand. "I thought he was sleeping," she said, sounding near tears. "I didn't know—I tried to wake him." Her teary voice turned into loud sobs. "We're not supposed to sleep in the law library!"

"You're not to blame," Tyndale said. He surveyed the crowd with a slow deliberation that said he actually did blame every one of them for gawking at death. His gaze lit on Veronica, paused infinitesimally, and then moved on without acknowledging her. Veronica swallowed. He had not looked even the least bit friendly.

Tyndale lifted Carlton's hand and removed the piece of paper beneath it. "Did any of you read this?" he said, not raising his eyes from the paper.

No one responded. Tyndale looked at the woman who'd spoken, the one who'd found the body. "You read it," he said flatly. "I'm sure some of the rest of you did as well. Is it too much to ask that you not spread rumor around?" He grimaced. "Of course it is. I will nevertheless caution you that whatever you *think* you've seen here is not the whole story. And that Mister Dunn is deserving of some dignity, even in death. Now, all of you, leave this place, and try to restrain yourselves from gossiping more than you absolutely have to."

His biting scorn dispersed the crowd more quickly than a polite request. The murmuring started again, but this time Veronica wasn't listening. She moved with the others, but only as far as the door, where she made herself insignificant and waited for the room to clear. Being insignificant had always come easily to her.

Tyndale was examining the body when it was finally just the two of them in the library. She approached him cautiously, like a deer wary of potential predators. He seemed not to notice her, but when she was within a foot or two of the table, he said, "Did I not make it clear that you were to leave?"

Veronica swallowed again and resisted the urge to flee. "I was to meet him here now," she said. She hoped her anxiety wasn't audible. Another scornful remark from Tyndale, and she would run.

Tyndale looked up. "You had a scheduled appointment?"

"Yes. We're studying—oh, it doesn't matter now, does it? But he's got everything set up for our study session, so why would he kill himself?"

"I don't know," Tyndale said grimly. He pinched the bridge of his nose and squeezed his eyes tight shut. "But the suicide note is very clear."

"It still doesn't make sense."

Tyndale opened his eyes, and she felt pinned in place by his glass-green gaze. "What makes no sense," he said, "is that in his note, Mister Dunn confesses to the murder of Ian Frost."

Stunned, Veronica gaped at Tyndale. "Then he did do it."

"Or someone wants me to believe he did it. But I can't imagine how that person coerced Mister Dunn into writing a suicide note before poisoning him."

Veronica's gaze was drawn to Carlton's face. His features were distorted with pain, and his lips were stained black, as if he'd vomited something vile before dying. Memory struck so hard she felt she might be sick. "Poison," she whispered.

"Lady North, are you well?"

Tyndale sounded concerned, not at all as indifferent as he'd been the past few days, and the simple inquiry brought tears to

Veronica's eyes. "I'm not going to faint," she said, commanding herself rather than responding to Tyndale. "It's just...poison. It's so horrible."

"Of course. I hadn't thought—" Tyndale put a hand on her arm. "You should leave. There's nothing more you can do for him."

She nodded, but made no move to leave. "What will you do?"

Tyndale sighed and released her. "There's no way to contain this," he said. "Too many people saw the body and read the note. The entire Scholia probably knows now that Mister Dunn killed himself in remorse over murdering Mister Frost, which means the truth about Mister Frost's death is also now public knowledge. It means my investigation just became a thousand times more difficult."

"But...what investigation? It's over. Carlton—" Veronica wished she'd told Tyndale her suspicions. She didn't want to conceal anything from him. "I thought...he behaved so strangely—"

"When was this?" Tyndale's voice went sharp.

"Firstday. At our last study session. I tried to get word to you, but you were busy, and so was I, and...I told myself it was just my imagination."

She braced herself for an outpouring of scorn, unable to look him in the eyes. Instead, she heard him sigh. "Don't blame yourself," he said. "Remember we both believed Mister Dunn's involvement was coincidental. Telling me more wouldn't have saved him."

"So you believe he killed Ian."

"I don't know what I believe. Too much of what's happened is impossible."

Veronica watched Tyndale turn Carlton's hand so it was in its original position, then fold the suicide note and put it away inside his Master's robe. "Carlton can't have killed himself," she said. "And yet nothing else is possible."

"Precisely." Tyndale shook his head. "You should leave. Others will be arriving shortly, chief among them the Magister, who will want to know why I didn't contain this."

"But how could you? It's not as if you could have known what would happen."

"The Magister is rarely rational when there's a threat to his fief. I imagine he will blame me for not discovering Mister Dunn was the killer before he could take his life." Tyndale shook his head again. "I can't entirely blame him. I wasn't fast enough."

"You did as much as anyone could have expected," Veronica said hotly. "It's not fair for him to expect a miracle."

Tyndale's lips quirked in a smile. "Fierce in defense of others, eh, Lady North? I thank you, though your confidence in me is misplaced. Go back to your dormitory. I'll handle things from here."

Veronica cast one more glance at Carlton's blackened lips. Her gorge rose. Nodding mutely, she turned and almost ran from the room.

But her stomach failed to completely rebel, and by the time she reached Patience House, she felt well, if emotionally exhausted. The halls were full of women talking in loud voices about Carlton's death, all of them declaring opinions in the certain way of people who had no idea what had really happened. Veronica dodged them and locked herself in the sanctuary of her rooms. The idea of going to supper in a few hours revolted her. She told herself the furor would have died off by then and made herself some peppermint tea. She drank it looking out over the fields behind Patience House and wishing life were as tranquil as an empty field.

When she entered the refectory, her prediction that things would have settled turned out to be completely wrong. Bec pounced on her before she reached her seat. "Have you heard?" she exclaimed. "What am I saying? Of course you've heard. Everyone's heard by now. Carlton Dunn, a murderer!" She shuddered dramatically. "To think I used to kiss him. I want to be sick."

Veronica couldn't think of anything to say. She took her usual seat and folded her hands in her lap. Maybe she could get through this meal without saying anything incriminating.

Bec dropped dramatically into her chair. "It's just awful," she went on. "I know we were speculating on Ian being murdered, but I didn't think we were *right*. And that it was Carlton..."

"I heard he drank poison and went into convulsions right in front of Roberta Connant," Bridget said in a low, conspiratorial voice. "I never would have guessed Carlton Dunn could feel remorse about anything. I guess I was wrong."

"*I* heard Tyndale took the suicide note like he wanted to keep this a secret," Percy said. "As if the whole Scholia doesn't know by now."

"I'm glad he's dead," Howard burst out. His face was pale, but two red spots high on his cheeks said he was anything but calm. "I hope he died in agony. It's what he deserves."

"*Stop it!*" Veronica shouted. The entire end of her table, both her friends and several nearby diners, went silent. Another terrible outburst welled up inside her, and she clenched her fists tight to control it. "Stop talking like that," she said in a low, intense voice that didn't go farther than her immediate circle. "Nobody deserves to die like that. You don't understand. You don't know what it's like, seeing that—" Tears choked her final words, and she stared at her plate, willing memories away.

"Veronica," Percy said, then fell silent again.

"This isn't about Carlton, is it," Bec said. "Something else happened."

A horrible strangled laugh escaped Veronica's throat, so unexpectedly at first she thought it had come from someone else. "You don't know? I thought everyone did. It wasn't all that long ago."

Bec jerked. "Sweet heaven," she breathed. "I'd forgotten. The King. Oh, heaven, Veronica, I didn't think."

"What are you talking about?" Bridget said.

"King Landon died of poison," Bec said. "Veronica, I'm sorry—"

Veronica held up her hand. "It's all right. I'm sorry for shouting. It's just—" She took a deep breath and wiped her eyes with her other hand. "It's not the same, I know, but seeing Carlton lying there brought it all back. I'm sorry."

"You saw Carlton's body?" Percy exclaimed. "Ian's body, Carlton's body—dear heaven, Veronica, it's amazing you haven't broken down entirely."

Veronica laughed weakly. "I guess I'm tougher than I thought."

"I didn't know the King was poisoned," Bridget said. "I lived in Eskandel until three years ago and we never got more than the barest news of the home country. What happened? Or—no, you don't want to talk about it. I'm so stupid sometimes."

"It's all right," Veronica repeated. "Landon's death was a horrible accident. Poisonous mushrooms harvested and sent to the palace, perfectly innocently." That was one thing everyone was certain of after that long, terrible investigation—it had been unintentional. Otherwise heads would have rolled. "Landon was the only one who ate them—Francis was with friends that night, and I hate mushrooms. He ate them, and a little after midnight he woke me up with his vomiting, and then..."

They didn't need the details. How agonized Landon's weeping had been as the poison tore his insides apart. The blood and the vomit all over the commode. How his last words to her had been unintelligible. She'd gone over those sounds in her head for weeks, trying to turn them into some final endearment, something to dull the pain of watching him slip into a coma and then into death.

"There was nothing Dr. Merris could do," she explained. "She was a competent healer, but the poison acted so fast, by the time she arrived, it was damaging new organs as she healed others. Nothing any of us could do. He died late the next day." And life had gone on, and now, it seemed, she was the only one who remembered. Landon had not been a very effective King, so maybe it made sense that he was forgotten now. But she'd loved him, and his death had ended so much of her life she couldn't quite believe it hadn't affected anyone else the same.

"No wonder you hate mushrooms," Bridget said.

"*Bridget*," Bec said, exasperated.

Bridget turned scarlet. "I'm never going to speak again. Veronica, I'm sorry. I didn't mean—"

"I know. And yes, if I hadn't hated mushrooms before, I would have after that." Veronica wiped her eyes again. "I feel stupid, actually, making Carlton's death all about my personal tragedy. It was a horrible shock."

"And it's perfectly reasonable it affected you like that," Percy said.

Howard put his hand atop hers. "I'm sorry I said that," he whispered. "You're right. I shouldn't be glad anyone's dead. But Ian...no, it doesn't matter. His killer is dead, and we can all move on."

Veronica nodded. Deep inside, she knew she was still being a coward. But she'd as much as promised Tyndale she wouldn't spread rumors, and telling them all her suspicions about Carlton's supposed suicide would qualify. She felt wrung out and exhausted, and she couldn't bear explaining that she'd known Ian was murdered from the start. "I'm going back to my rooms," she said, standing.

"But you haven't eaten. Veronica, you can't not eat." Bec reached out a hand to stop her.

Veronica picked up the roll from her bread plate. "I don't think I can manage more than this."

"Take mine, too," Bridget said, pressing it on her. Veronica took it automatically.

"Get some sleep," Percy said. "Things will look less dire in the morning, I promise."

Veronica smiled and left without saying anything. She knew it was a lie. The worst day was always the second one, when the shock had worn off but the terrible thing had still happened, and you couldn't get away from it no matter what you did. But Percy meant well, so she didn't correct him.

She nibbled one of the rolls as she walked back to Patience House, tiny bites that wouldn't sit like lead in her stomach. Carlton dead, an impossible suicide. The thought that he'd meant for her to find his body as she had Ian's struck her and made her stomach burn. She barely knew Carlton, so why would he have wanted to torture her like that? No, it was just coincidence. He'd gone to the law library, arranged books for her to study, written a suicide note, and killed himself. Unless he'd written the note elsewhere and brought it with him. Either way, it still made no sense.

Mistress Holyoak wasn't there when Veronica opened the front door. The way Veronica was feeling, she might have torn into the woman if she'd spoken even the slightest hostile remark. Instead of making Veronica uncomfortable, the idea of lashing out made her feel better. She didn't know who she had become if she could even contemplate confronting anyone. The last six days had affected her more than she'd realized.

In her sitting room, she made more peppermint tea and sat at the little table, sipping and nibbling. The tea soothed her spirits, the yeasty warm bread soothed her stomach, and when her makeshift meal was over, she felt calmer.

Someone knocked on her door. "Veronica? Are you there?" It was Samantha.

Veronica rose, but stopped halfway to the door. She didn't want to talk to anyone, not even Samantha. Especially not Samantha, who would be grieving more than anyone over Carlton. A pang of guilt shot through her. She should want to support her friend, give her someone to talk to and maybe a shoulder to cry on. But she was so overwhelmed herself, she didn't feel she had the emotional resources to help anyone.

She stood there and listened to Samantha knock once more. Then the room was silent. Veronica told herself she would talk to Samantha in the morning. She told herself it was the right thing to do. She climbed the stairs, undressed, and fell into bed, wishing she were anyone but herself.

19

Veronica drifted through the next day in a haze. She only barely heard the words of her instructors. Samantha hadn't come back the next morning, and she wasn't at breakfast or dinner. Her absence added to Veronica's sense of guilt that she had done everything wrong. It was irrational, she knew, but she couldn't help feeling if she'd behaved differently —if she'd told Tyndale her suspicions about Carlton—he might have been captured before he could kill himself.

Her mind kept circling back to impossibilities. Carlton had been prepared for a study session. He'd killed himself while waiting for her. The two things were incompatible. If the second was true, why go to all the trouble of making things ready? But if the first was true, then somehow, someone had managed to kill him and make it look like a suicide. Impossible.

By the end of Master Varner's Devisery class, when Veronica was walking back to her rooms, her head ached and she wanted nothing more than for the week to be over. But there was still Fifthday to get through, and her tutorial with Lansing. She groaned aloud, prompting nearby students to look at her strangely. She didn't care if they thought she was strange. Tyndale was right; there was something liberating about not caring what others thought.

She hadn't seen Tyndale since the previous afternoon and wondered what he was doing. With Ian's killer revealed, his investigation was over. He might still be trying to find Ian's missing Device, but Veronica doubted the Magister wanted his top law instructor wasting his time on something anyone might do, starting with Howard.

It startled her to discover that some of her dissatisfaction arose from knowing she wouldn't encounter Tyndale in a non-instructor capacity anymore. It wasn't as if their previous encounters were pleasant, although parts of them had been enjoyable, like when they talked about art or the old Scholia. There was no reason for them to be friends, and she shouldn't wish for that, not when she already had so many other friends who weren't uncomfortable and sarcastic.

That reminded her about Samantha again. Veronica walked faster. She should see if Samantha was all right. It had to be awful for her, losing Carlton in such a terrible way, just as Veronica had lost Landon. Granted, Samantha's relationship with Carlton wasn't a twenty-five-year marriage, but that didn't mean her heart wasn't seriously involved.

She knocked on Samantha's door. No one answered. "Samantha?" Veronica knocked again. "It's Veronica. Are you all right?"

She was about to walk away when the door cracked open. "Veronica. I'm not up for company right now," Samantha said. She'd been crying, and her dressing gown hung open over her wrinkled nightdress. Her brown hair straggled over her shoulders, tangled and lank as if it needed washing. Her appearance stunned Veronica. She hadn't thought it possible for anyone to let herself go so completely in one day.

"Oh," Veronica said awkwardly. She was terrible at knowing what to say to a grieving person. "I thought...it's just that I know what it's like, sort of...but I don't want to burden you further."

Samantha closed her eyes. "You can't possibly know what I'm going through."

Even more embarrassed, Veronica said, "Not exactly, no. My husband died...was poisoned...but maybe that's too hard for you to talk about."

Samantha looked at Veronica. Her dull eyes looked a little sharper now. "I'd forgotten," she said. "Come in."

Unlike Veronica in her tower, Samantha only had one room, but it was twice the size of Veronica's sitting room and had more windows. Samantha had hung curtains to divide the room in half, providing herself with a tiny space for a sofa and Device burner as well as a bedroom. Currently, the curtains were pulled back so the whole room was visible. It was as untidy as ever, with clothes strewn across the sofa and the end of the unmade bed and mismatched shoes lying where Samantha had kicked them off. Veronica, who loved tidiness, never felt entirely comfortable in Samantha's room, but it suited her exuberant friend.

Samantha gathered up a handful of shirts and half-slips from the sofa and tossed them on her bed. "I'm afraid I don't have anything to offer you. I was going to go into Knightsbury for tea and so forth tomorrow, but now it all seems so pointless." She sat on the sofa and curled her legs beneath her.

Veronica sat at the other end of the sofa. "It's all right. You shouldn't feel obliged to entertain me. You must feel simply awful."

Samantha nodded. "I had no idea Carlton was so disturbed. We'd...oh, it's terrible, but we'd argued earlier this week, and I hadn't seen him since Firstday. It's always better to give Carlton time to cool off." She wiped tears from her eyes. "I'd actually left him a peace offering at his dormitory, some cakes he's—he was fond of. Oh, heaven, if I had just humbled myself sooner!"

"Don't think that way," Veronica exclaimed as Samantha's tears became a noisy flood. "There's always the what-ifs. Carlton—" She couldn't quite bring herself to say *Carlton killed himself because he felt guilty over killing Ian* when she wasn't fully convinced herself that was what had happened.

"And he killed Ian," Samantha said. "That's even worse. It's all my fault they were fighting. Veronica, am I a tease? I didn't think I was leading them on—I thought their feelings were as casual as mine." Her expression pleaded with Veronica to say something to make everything better.

Veronica had never felt so uncomfortable in her life. "I don't think it's teasing if you happen to enjoy the company of many men," she said, fumbling to put her thoughts into words that wouldn't hurt Samantha more. "You've always been very clear —at least, when we've talked before—that you don't want to have a serious relationship yet. You shouldn't blame yourself if other people didn't believe you really meant that."

"But I still feel guilty." Samantha wiped her eyes again. "I can't bear to leave this room. Everyone's going to look at me—I know what they'll whisper where I can't hear."

Veronica straightened. "They whispered about me, too," she said. "There were so many rumors about what happened to Landon, and a lot of them centered on me. They said I killed him, because wasn't it strange that I happened not to eat the very food that poisoned him?" Memories gripped her again, memories of those horrible days when her heart was broken and the world believed she was a monster. "And they kept on whispering even after the official investigation said it was an accident. And then it passed. I doubt anyone but me remembers now there was a time when half the kingdom judged me and found me guilty of killing the man I loved more than anything."

Samantha's face reddened to match her eyes. "I heard those rumors. I...they made such a dramatic story. I'm sorry I ever believed them."

Veronica wiped her own eyes. She hadn't realized she was crying. "But that's how I know this will pass. It's hard, agonizingly hard, the first few weeks, because the world ought to offer you sympathy in your grief and instead you get only slander. At least you haven't been accused of murder."

Samantha laughed, a gulping, painful sound. "Yes, that's something. I'm not a murderer, just a slut who plays men off against each other."

"Don't say that," Veronica insisted, gripping Samantha's hand. "You'll have enough people criticizing you, you shouldn't add to that by being hard on yourself."

"You're right." Samantha squeezed Veronica's hand. "Thank you. You've been such a good friend." She laughed again, and this time it was a more natural sound. "How strange that we should end up friends. In the normal course of things, we would never have encountered each other."

"And I'm so glad we did," Veronica said. "Now, I think you should get dressed and go to supper." She almost invited Samantha to sit with her, but that would make for a tense, strained meal, with all her friends disliking Samantha as they did. It reminded her of when she'd been young and had two best friends, Grace and Emily, both of whom behaved as if Veronica were their personal property and who couldn't stand playing together. How odd that some things never changed.

She left Samantha and returned to her own rooms. Already she felt more cheerful and alert. She was normally so solitary, she sometimes forgot that even she needed companionship. And—she suddenly remembered why Fifthday was important. Her winter wardrobe would be ready. That cheered her even more, the idea of bringing home that beautiful gown. And the winter clothes, of course, but thoughts of the gown, even if it was completely unsuitable for this time of year, lifted her spirits.

She spent half an hour tidying her rooms. The task reminded her of Samantha's...yes, it was a sty, and Veronica refused to feel uncomfortable at the uncharitable thought. Surely Samantha's mood would improve if she didn't live in a constant mess? Whereas Veronica's neat chambers soothed her.

She examined the contents of the tea caddy. More peppermint tea was needed, and she ought to stop in at Miss Wattlesford's establishment for a box of pencils. Well, why not make tomorrow a pleasure outing? She would go into Knightsbury after her tutorial, maybe treat herself to dinner at a café, and hire a carriage to bring herself and her parcels back. The pleasant thought didn't dispel her gloom, but it allowed her to push it to the far recesses of her mind where it wouldn't trouble her. Tomorrow might turn out to be a lovely day.

ON THE STREET OUTSIDE WATTLESFORD'S, VERONICA TUCKED her box of pencils into her satchel and breathed in the warm, fresh air. The day had turned out to be one of those early Autumn days that felt more like late Summer, the sun warm in a cloudless blue sky, the air still but for occasional breezes stirring the scraps of paper and few dead leaves that littered the street. The leaves, and the way the breezes smelled of apples and wood smoke, were the only things that dispelled the illusion.

She strolled along Knightsbury's main street, smiling and nodding at the other pedestrians. Most of them smiled back. It was that kind of day. And none of them knew who she was. Veronica had been surprised, and slightly disturbed, at how much she enjoyed anonymity. It wasn't as if she was ashamed of being the former Consort, or that people intruded on her time when they knew her identity, because people in general were too overawed to approach her. That was it. Those people smiling and nodding at her thought she was one of them, not someone deserving of special treatment. She'd never had that before. And she liked it.

She turned right at the next corner onto Sophia Street as per Miss Wattlesford's directions. It was the same way she and Jonas had gone to find Ian's Knightsbury workshop, though Veronica wouldn't be going that far today. Her goal was the Cinnamon Tea Shop and Café. Veronica had thought it an oddly specific name—she didn't know if it was smart to advertise one's shop so narrowly—but Miss Wattlesford had assured her it was the best café in Knightsbury, and Veronica trusted her judgment.

Unlike the main street, the businesses lining Sophia Street stood far back from the road, leaving broad areas of sidewalk that the business owners took advantage of by setting up outdoor displays in the space between the store fronts and the curbs. Veronica passed a haberdashery with several display racks bearing fashionable hats and a selection of colorful neck-cloths and a toy shop whose extremely modern store front boasted a large plate glass window instead of the multipaned kind Veronica was used to.

Reminded of the toy shop in Stowe Road, she stopped to examine the store's wares. Painted wooden blocks in garish colors made a scattered pile next to a couple of porcelain dolls dressed like fashionable women and a rocking horse complete with leather saddle and bridle. They looked expensive, but to Veronica they lacked the heart she'd seen in that other shop. She laughed inwardly at herself for being sentimental. It was only that she'd liked the storekeeper that she wanted to find his wares superior.

"Lady North! What a surprise."

Startled at being addressed, Veronica turned. "Oh! Mister Miller!"

The craggy-faced man made her an elegant bow, a gesture completely out of character for the man Veronica judged him to be. "I wouldn't have guessed you'd be in the market for children's toys," Miller went on, smiling slightly.

Veronica ignored the taunt in his words. "Just admiring the merchandise. You're not interested in dolls, are you?"

She couldn't believe the words had escaped her lips. How rude of her to meet sarcasm with sarcasm! She opened her mouth to apologize, but Miller laughed and said, "That's put me in my place and no mistake. My apologies, Lady North. I'm not one for friendly small talk."

"Neither am I." Veronica laughed, somewhat self-consciously. "I suppose that puts us on a more equal footing."

Miller lifted his fine hat and scratched his balding head, disordering the few strands of gray hair disposed across it. His sharp blue eyes fixed disconcertingly on her. "And what brings you to Knightsbury this fine day?"

"Just running errands. I was on my way to the café there." Veronica nodded at the Cinnamon Tea Shop, two storefronts farther along Sophia Street.

"So, not business." Miller's expression had gone impassive. "At the risk of being accused of forwardness, may I buy you dinner? I've a matter to discuss with you, in case you were thinking I'm in a courting mood. Strictly professional."

Awkward embarrassment seized Veronica. She hadn't had dinner alone with a man she wasn't related to in years. While the thought that Miller was romantically interested in her hadn't crossed her mind, she did wonder at his invitation. Professional? The only professional thing they had in common was Ian's Devisery. And if Miller knew something...

She told her anxieties to hush and made a rapid decision. "All right, Mister Miller. Strictly professional."

Miller grinned, but made no move to offer her his arm. That reassured her even as it raised more questions.

The café had a few tables on the sidewalk, half of them occupied, but Miller steered Veronica gently inside. "I'd rather not have an audience," he said.

Veronica nodded and let him hold her chair for her at the small table in the corner farthest from the windows. Two sheets of heavy linen paper presented the café's dinner offering in a lovely calligraphic hand Veronica admired with a semi-professional's eye. The Cinnamon Tea Shop adhered to the old-fashioned tradition of offering a single dining option rather than an assortment of choices. Veronica found it charming. Miller scowled slightly upon reading the paper, but said nothing.

Shortly, a woman clad in a sober gray dress with a white frilled apron brought them plates of small puffy rolls stuffed with thin-sliced roast chicken, tiny quiches that smelled deliciously of ham and cheese, and palm-sized cups of tomato bisque. Veronica took a tiny bite of soup and savored the sweet-tangy taste.

"This isn't enough food to keep a man going," Miller grumbled.

"It was your offer, Mister Miller," Veronica reminded him. To her surprise, his irritation didn't make her feel embarrassed or prompt her to apologize for the meal. On the contrary, she felt as if she had control of their interaction. It was a liberating feeling.

His next words shattered her calm. "Do you know a Scholia student named Carlton Dunn?"

Veronica's spoon hit the edge of her bowl with a loud *tink*. "Carlton Dunn?" she said, stupidly.

"That's what I said. Do you know him?"

She almost blurted out *He's dead*, but an unexpected thought of what Tyndale would do in her situation held her tongue. "I do," she said. "Why do you ask?"

"Let's just say I have an interest in his character," Miller said. He picked up his soup cup and raised it to his lips, watching her closely. Veronica wasn't thrown by his deliberate display of bad manners. He meant to throw her off balance. Well, she might be awkward and uncomfortable in social settings, but she was also the former Consort, and she had years of experience at formal dinners and suppers with dining companions from four countries. She was used to not batting an eyelash when someone did something gauche at the dinner table.

"He's a good student, I know that," she said calmly. "I'm afraid I don't know him well. Did you have need of legal advice?"

"So he's a law student?"

Veronica felt a hint of unease that she'd given away too much. She'd assumed Miller knew *something* about Carlton, but she was beginning to suspect this was a fishing expedition. "He is. He's been helping me with a class."

"Interesting," Miller said. He slurped his soup again and set the cup down.

Veronica cut a morsel from her chicken roll and ate it, staring Miller down. Not knowing what he knew left her feeling out of her depth. But there was still that tiny Tyndale-voice in the back of her head, saying *Don't give away more than you have to.* Miller asking after someone at the heart of the mystery of Ian's murder had to mean something.

She decided to push, gently. "You surely couldn't have known you'd run into me here," she said. "Is this coincidence, or something else?"

"Coincidence," Miller said. "A surprising coincidence."

"Yes, that you'd meet someone who happens to know Carlton. That *is* a surprise." Veronica took another bite. Her heart beat as rapidly as if Miller were chasing her instead of sitting quietly across the table from her. She wondered if Tyndale felt this way every time he interrogated someone.

Miller picked up his chicken roll and took a large bite. His eyes narrowed. "This is good."

"Don't sound so surprised. I'm told this is the best café in Knightsbury." Veronica patted her lips with her napkin.

Miller finished chewing and set the roll down. He continued to regard her with that narrow-eyed stare that would have reduced Veronica to a quivering wreck had she not had Tyndale's steadying words ringing through her head. "All right," he said. "You know more than you're saying. And you've guessed I'm the same. I'm willing to be straight with you if you'll be straight with me."

"I don't know what—"

"Don't play games, Lady North. I'm a master of trickery and manipulation when it comes to business." Miller cracked the heavy knuckles of one hand, one at a time. The gesture was contemplative rather than sinister. "I could wring it out of you, but I'm a gentleman, however I may seem, and I'd rather trade knowledge for knowledge. Agreed?"

Veronica nodded, though she didn't intend to tell him everything she knew. She told herself he would do the same.

"Very well," Miller said. He reached into his coat and withdrew several sheets of dirty, cream-colored paper folded into a sheaf. "Last Firstday, a young man came to my office wanting to sell me these. He was furtive enough I would have known something was up even if I hadn't recognized him. He clearly thought he was anonymous, the fool." Miller let out a short, sharp bark of a laugh. "I make it my business to know all the players in Knightsbury, the...let's call them the dark side of the trade."

"You mean thieves," Veronica said.

"You'll notice I didn't use that word. These are more like businessmen who don't truck with legalities. I've dealt with my share of them, though I've always managed to stay on the right side of the law. So I knew this was Eddie Logan even though he didn't give his name." Miller unfolded the papers, but didn't give them to Veronica. "Take a look."

Veronica examined the first page. "It's a schematic," she said. "Part of a Device." Her eye caught a familiar scrawl at the bottom of the page, and her heart, which had nearly settled into its normal rhythm, sped up again. "Ian Frost. Those are Ian's notes!"

"I recognized the style as well as the signature." Miller put the pages back inside his coat. "I also knew there was no way a low-level crook like Logan could have gotten his hands on them. That meant he was working on behalf of someone else."

"But how does that lead to Carlton?"

"Not yet, Lady North. It's your turn to share." Miller's blue eyes gleamed as he smiled. "Let's just stipulate that I know Dunn is the one who sent Logan to me. Did Dunn kill Ian Frost?"

Veronica hastily ran through options in her mind and settled on the one that gave the least away. "Carlton Dunn confessed to killing Ian, right before he committed suicide. He must have stolen the notes."

Miller's eyes widened, but his face remained impassive. "Killed himself?"

"I assure you it's true. I saw his body."

"You certainly find yourself at the center of terrible things, don't you, Lady North?" Miller rubbed his jaw, which today was fully clean-shaven. "Killed himself," he mused. "That changes things."

"It's your turn," Veronica said. "How did you end up with the notes? Which are, by the way, stolen property and don't belong to you at all."

"You can try to prove that," Miller said complacently. "I worked closely with Frost, and who's to say these weren't in the workshop I rented him? But that's irrelevant now," he added, cutting off Veronica's protest. "I'll tell you honestly that I paid for these, fair and square, so don't go thinking what I know you're thinking about me beating Logan senseless. Even though he would deserve it. I'd call the man a rat if I didn't know so many fine rats."

Veronica stifled the impulse to demand he hand the notes over. "When was this?"

"Haransday morning. Well after I'd had Logan followed and learned the name of his backer. I handed over the cash, and Logan gave me the notes."

Veronica frowned. "But...shouldn't that have been it for you? Why would you care who really stole the notes?"

Miller shrugged. "I found I didn't like the idea of Frost's killer profiting from his death. Frost and I weren't close, but I respected him, and he was well on the way to making me a fortune."

"So you were going to the Scholia today to find Carlton."

"I was." Miller finished his chicken roll in one large bite and went to work on his quiche. "But then I saw you and realized I had a chance to gain more information before I confronted Dunn. And now it doesn't matter."

Veronica nodded automatically. Her mind had seized on part of Miller's story that made no sense. "May I ask how much you paid? Or is that private?"

Miller laughed. "You're the most formal person I've ever met, Lady North. Are all the nobility like you? Because I can't imagine you people ever get anything done, what with sidestepping the issues all the time."

Veronica ignored his mirth. "Was it a lot?"

"Enough," Miller said. "Five hundred guilders."

"*Five hundred*—" Veronica sputtered.

"That's nothing compared to how much I'll make if I can find someone to actually build the damn thing," Miller said. "But yes, it's near enough to a fortune for a Scholia student. Aren't they traditionally supposed to be poorer than barrel dregs?"

"I don't know Carlton's finances." Even if he'd been wealthy, five hundred guilders was significant money. "But I don't understand why he would accept money from you and then kill himself later that afternoon."

"That's assuming Eddie Logan didn't run off with the cash," Miller said. "If Dunn was poor, or if he owed someone money, and Logan took it all, Dunn might have felt suicide was the only option."

"I suppose that's true. I didn't see the suicide note, so I don't know if that was his motive." Veronica idly took a bite of quiche. It was cold and the eggs were slightly hard, but the seasoning still tasted wonderful. She still didn't think she should tell Miller her suspicion that Carlton had been murdered, but she couldn't think of any other way to squeeze more information out of him.

"How did he kill himself?" Miller asked.

"Poison," Veronica said curtly. She didn't want to dwell on that at all.

"Huh." Miller rubbed his chin again in thought. "Not a pleasant way to go."

"It's not."

He gave her another narrow-eyed look. "I suppose you'd know," he said. Veronica tensed, ready for more commentary on people who died of poison, but Miller said nothing more.

They finished their meal in silence. Veronica didn't feel any more enlightened than she had that morning. True, this Eddie Logan might have cheated Carlton, and Carlton might have killed himself over losing the money, but Veronica didn't think that was likely. Between his newfound fortune and the smug look he'd worn on Firstday, she was more than ever convinced that his suicide made no sense.

"It's been enlightening, Lady North," Miller said when they were ready to leave. "You've saved me a trip to the Scholia. My feet aren't what they used to be."

"I don't know why you didn't ride, or take a carriage," Veronica said.

Miller's eyes glinted. "No, you don't."

This sounded ominous, but Veronica couldn't think of a response that wouldn't be pushy. Once again, she wished she were a different sort of person. One who could be rude without falling to pieces.

Outside the shop, Veronica held out a hand. "I'll take those notes, please."

Miller laughed, a hearty sound that had passersby's heads turning to stare. "Come now, Lady North, don't you know me at all?"

"They don't belong to you. And you don't know anyone who can make use of them." Veronica's hand trembled slightly, and she cursed her nerves.

"Not yet," Miller said. "But...I'll make you a deal, Lady North. These weren't the only pieces of the puzzle. Logan as much as said outright that there was more where this came from. I think Frost had some kind of prototype, either of this—" He tapped his coat, making paper rustle— "or of some smaller piece. Something important. If you find the rest, I'll hand over what I have in return for getting first crack at whatever the finished Device is. Fair?"

"It's not fair, but I don't see that I have much choice," Veronica said. "But you won't stop trying to find it yourself, will you?"

"Ah, so you do know me, after all," Miller said with a wink. He tipped his hat to her, said, "Good afternoon, Lady North, and...good luck," and walked away down Sophia Street the way he'd come.

Veronica waited for her heart to slow, then she turned and hurried away in the opposite direction. She had to tell Tyndale what she'd learned. No, she had to pick up her wardrobe, and *then* she would tell Tyndale. She didn't like the look in Miller's eye at the end, the one that said he hadn't been entirely forthcoming. Well, she hadn't been forthcoming with him, so maybe that was fair. But as she glanced over her shoulder at Miller's retreating form, an unexpected urgency rose up within her. She felt she'd entered a race she had no chance of winning.

20

---

*H*aving safely stowed her new clothes in her wardrobe and smoothed the fine muslin skirt of the blue gown one last time, Veronica set out to find Tyndale. Despite it not yet being four o'clock, she tried Justice House first, thinking his Fifthday schedule might be different, what with having no lectures. But the doorkeeper shook his head when he opened the door and saw her.

"He's not here," he said before Veronica could even open her mouth. "Try his office in Godfrey. You're awfully persistent for someone who's not even one of Master Tyndale's students." He smiled, revealing the glint of a gold incisor.

"I do have his second law fundamentals class," Veronica protested. She felt as if the doorkeeper had accused her of illicit behavior.

"Never had a beginner student think to approach Master Tyndale before you. You do know he's got assistants? They're the ones you should go to for help."

"I'll do that, thank you." Veronica hurried away. Behind her, the door shut as firmly as if the doorkeeper were shooing her away. Embarrassment made her cheeks hot. Now she was sure the man believed she was enamored of Tyndale, or something equally humiliating. She told herself to stiffen up and walked swiftly to Godfrey Hall, not looking at anyone who passed. They probably wouldn't be able to know of her embarrassment just by looking, but she'd had her fill of being stared at with the doorkeeper.

To her surprise, Bec stood in the hall outside Tyndale's office when she arrived. "Veronica! What are you doing here?"

Confusion tangled Veronica's tongue. She didn't want to give away her real intent, and she didn't want to lie to her friend. "I...it's to do with something we discussed earlier," she stammered. "Why are you here?"

"Tutorial." Bec leaned casually against the wall. "I don't know why you're voluntarily putting yourself in Tyndale's way. He's got assistants who are much nicer than he is. Ellen Averill Cates in particular is a great instructor, and very patient."

"I know, but this is...something only he can help with." Veronica felt herself shriveling under Bec's skeptical gaze. "Isn't this a little late in the day for a tutorial?"

"He rescheduled several of us today. I think he's dealing with the aftermath of Carlton's suicide, though why he's involved, I don't know." Bec scratched the side of her nose idly. "Probably has something to do with how he was Carlton's tutor, too."

The door opened, and a male student emerged. He was scowling and refused to meet anyone's eyes, just hurried away toward the stairs. Veronica couldn't see Tyndale from where she stood, but she heard him say, "Miss Grayson, please come in."

"Lady North is here. Did you want to see her first?" Bec sounded eager, as if she were hoping to delay the moment she'd have to step into the lion's den.

There was a pause, and Tyndale came to the door. He cast a glance Veronica's way that found her completely uninteresting. "Lady North's business isn't urgent," he said in his usual impassive way. "Please wait, Lady North. Or you might return in half an hour."

"No, it's—I'll wait," Veronica said. Immediately she felt like an idiot. Why under heaven had she volunteered to stand in the chilly third-floor hallway of Godfrey Hall like a sappy hanger-on, hoping for a moment of the great man's time?

Tyndale nodded and gestured to Bec, who glanced once at Veronica before entering the room. The door swung nearly shut behind her. Veronica remembered what Tyndale had said about closed doors and moved a short distance away so she couldn't inadvertently overhear anything.

She waited. Students, a few Masters, and one woman in a blue stole with three black bands went in and out of other doors down the hallway. None of them paid any attention to her. Growing bored, she walked back down the hall to the stairs and leaned on the rail above the stairwell, looking at the stained glass window over the landing. It depicted a tree bearing jewel-colored pears nestled into glass leaves of every shade of green, emerald and moss and jade, with a hand reaching up to pluck a fruit. Learning as a tree from which knowledge could be harvested. It was a common enough theme in the early North era, when the Scholia was young and there weren't any other major institutes of learning in Tremontane. Veronica had always found the image appealing, if a trifle overused.

She returned to her post outside Tyndale's office in time for the door to open and Bec to emerge. "Thank you, Miss Grayson. Lady North, I appreciate your patience. Won't you come in?" Tyndale still sounded perfectly impassive. Veronica wished she could read his expressions. He might well be annoyed with her, but she wouldn't know it until he unloaded sarcasm on her.

She entered and took a seat in front of the desk. This time, Tyndale shut the door entirely. She wanted to make a joke out of it, ease the tension she felt, but she felt suddenly as if her entire sense of humor had dried up.

"I'm almost afraid to ask what brings you here," Tyndale said, seating himself behind the desk. "Though at least our encounters are never boring."

"No, never that," Veronica said with a half-smile. "I need to tell you something I learned about Carlton."

Tyndale's face went even more impassive. "That's unnecessary," he said. "Mister Dunn admitted to killing Mister Frost and then took his own life in remorse. There's nothing more to say."

Veronica gaped. "But...what about his scheduled meeting with me? And I've—"

"Lady North," Tyndale said, his voice rising slightly, "the Magister has made it very clear that he's satisfied the investigation is closed. A killer has been brought to justice, more or less. My services are no longer required."

"You can't believe that."

Tyndale arched an eyebrow. "Can I not?"

Veronica shook her head. "Wait until I tell you what I learned, though. The Magister—"

"That's *enough*," Tyndale said. It wasn't quite a shout, but Veronica flinched at his intensity. "Nothing you have to say will change the fact that this is *over*. Why is it you are so determined to insinuate yourself into this debacle? Do you not have fame and prominence enough? Or have you found Scholia life so boring you must invent conspiracies where there are none to be found?"

Veronica's face felt numb. Every fear she'd ever had of being thought ridiculous and unimportant, every memory of saying and doing the wrong thing, came crashing down upon her all at once. "I didn't," she whispered, and caught herself before it could come out as a sob. She stood and turned her back on Tyndale, fighting for control. There was a painting she hadn't seen before on the wall opposite the desk, a Sommers, probably another copy. There was no way Tyndale could afford an original Sommers.

She stared at it, tracing the lines of the landscape with her gaze. The painter had captured the bleakness of the northern Eskandelic landscape so well, the ruddy hills going darker with distance, the acacias that grew in thin, spreading clumps along the narrow river. She remembered traveling that wasteland once and how she had marveled at its stark, unexpected beauty. The memory was tainted by how awful she felt now. She'd been such a fool.

She heard Tyndale's chair rasp against the carpet as he pushed back from his desk. "Lady North," he said, his voice quiet again. "Lady North, I apologize."

She couldn't turn and face him. If she did, she would burst into horrible, messy tears, and humiliate herself even more. Not that he would care, since he was likely used to making people cry. The humiliation would be all her own.

Footsteps sounded, and Tyndale put a hand on her arm. "I can't—Lady North, there really is nothing more to be done. It doesn't have anything to do with you. I am sorry for—sweet heaven, will you please look at me?"

She shook her head and willed her tears to subside. The painting was still clear in her vision, which meant she'd succeeded in controlling herself. "I should apologize for wasting your time," she said. Her voice sounded remarkably clear considering how miserable she felt. "You've been more than kind in humoring me."

Tyndale swore, a blistering word that made Veronica blush. He put his other hand on her shoulder and turned her to face him. "I deserve that," he said bitterly. "I should never have spoken to you that way. It was cruel and untrue and I regret so much—"

"You really needn't apologize," Veronica said. "I understand. It's over."

Tyndale's eyes, so fierce, glinted green as glass. He looked, not impassive, but in the grip of some strong emotion. His hands still held her tightly, preventing her from running, though she couldn't have moved in any case. "It's over," he said. Then he pulled her to him and kissed her.

She let out a gasp muffled by his lips on hers. His kiss was hard and felt desperate, the last kiss of a condemned man, and it sent a surge of longing through her that was part physical and part heartbreaking sorrow. She raised a hand to her lips as he withdrew, his eyes still fierce with that unnamed emotion. "Oh," she said faintly. "Oh, my."

The emotion drained from Tyndale's face. He released her and took a step backward. "I apologize," he said, so formally it broke her heart all over again. "I should not have...that is, I was wrong to...Lady North, please accept—"

She took his face in her hands. "Shut up," she whispered, and kissed him back.

He only hesitated a moment before putting his arms around her and drawing her close enough that she could feel his heart beating in time with hers. Her hands slid down the side of his face and slipped behind his neck, brushing the short, soft hair there. She didn't know how she could ever have forgotten this feeling, the thrill of lips touching lips, hands caressing bodies, but it was all coming back to her now. For a moment, she remembered the first time she'd kissed Landon, but Tyndale's body felt nothing like her lost husband's, his arms around her were strong and firm, and she gave herself over to discovering someone entirely new.

Tyndale moved from kissing her lips to kissing her cheek. "We can't do this," he said, though he didn't stop.

"Why not?" Veronica murmured, kissing the place where his neck met his shoulders and breathing the scent of him in, fresh pine and old paper and an unfamiliar dry musk she felt she might drown in.

"Because kissing a student will lose me my position." Tyndale kissed her mouth again. "And when they find out you were a willing participant, you'd be expelled."

"It would almost be worth it," Veronica said, and was shocked at herself.

Tyndale chuckled and stepped back just enough that kissing was impractical, though he didn't remove his arms from around her waist. "It would," he agreed. "Oh, Veronica. I've wanted to do that for so long."

The sound of her name, her given name, on his lips made her shiver with delight. "I think I wanted it too, though I didn't realize that's what brought me to you, over and over again. Mas

—" She laughed, self-consciously. "I don't even know your first name."

He smiled in a rather self-deprecating way. "It's Harrison. Go ahead and laugh."

Her eyes widened, and she clapped a hand over her mouth to hold in a giggle. "As in, Harrison Cammerton? The King?"

"As in exactly that. My parents were history buffs and very fond of that era."

Veronica bit her lip so she wouldn't smile. "I guess it could be worse."

"It *is* worse. I have a sister named Emelina and a brother named Maximilian."

Now she did laugh. "All the Cammerton royalty. You must have been teased mercilessly as a child."

"All the way through primary school and up until I reached the Scholia, where no one cared about my embarrassing name." Tyndale—Harrison—smiled and touched her cheek, so gently. "But I love the way it sounds when you say it."

"Mmm. Harrison?"

"Like that. Exactly." He kissed her once more, his lips lingering on hers, then withdrew farther, clasping her hand to keep from separating them entirely.

Veronica twined her fingers with his. "What do we do now?"

"About the two of us? I have no idea. I'm quite serious that a relationship between an instructor and a student is extremely forbidden." He tugged on her hand and led her to sit, then resumed his seat behind the desk.

"No, I meant—" Belatedly Veronica remembered what she'd come to his office to tell him. Her former embarrassment had vanished completely, supplanted by memories of kissing and touching and... She cleared her throat. "It doesn't matter. You said the investigation was over."

"I said that because the Magister instructed me in no uncertain terms that I was to leave it alone." Harrison ran his fingers through his hair in an impatient gesture, so out of character it made her smile. "Even though nothing about this makes sense."

"Then you do want to hear what I learned."

"Veronica, I could listen to you speak all day without counting it a hardship. But yes, if you've learned something about either of the student deaths, I want to hear it. Particularly if it allows me to give the Magister a poke in the eye." He looked so grim Veronica felt chilled. She shook off the feeling and leaned forward.

"I ran into Mister Miller in Knightsbury," she began. "And I don't know whether to be angry or pleased about it."

She told him everything that had passed between her and Miller, including her guesses about what he might be concealing. "It infuriates me that he has Ian's notes," she concluded, "but I suppose they're at least safe with him for now. But don't you think it's strange that Carlton would kill himself just as he came into, well, nearly a fortune?"

"Mister Miller could be right about Mister Dunn owing money he couldn't repay." Harrison was leaning back in his chair with one elbow on the arm rest. He propped his chin in his hand and added, "As it happens, I intended to look into Mister Dunn's finances for something just like that. But the Magister closed the investigation before I could manage it."

"You could still look," Veronica insisted. "I'm sure you could do it without anyone noticing."

Harrison smiled. "You have such unwarranted faith in me."

"It's hardly unwarranted if you've succeeded all the other

times." Veronica felt annoyed at his sudden diffidence. "I trust you. The Magister should too."

"The Magister," Harrison said in a ponderous voice, "dislikes the kind of notoriety that murder and suicide bring upon an institution. He's afraid the scandal will affect the Scholia's chances of receiving the endowment."

"What endowment is that?"

"The one the Magister has been pestering the Crown for ever since the new campus opened. The one that will grant the Scholia land and income enough to support itself without the need for fundraising and petitioning the Treasury every year for more money." He shook his head. "I'm certain the Queen will never grant it, because it's a huge amount, more than I'm sure the Treasury can bear. But Donald Montgomery is nothing if not optimistic, and he's as ambitious as he is venal. I'll deny saying that if you repeat it."

"Who would I tell?" Veronica slumped in her chair. She felt excited and weary at the same time, eager to fall back into Harrison's arms for more kissing and just as ready to return to her rooms and sleep for a year. "So there really is nothing to be done."

"About Mister Dunn? Possibly." Harrison now looked pensive. "There are only two possibilities. Either Mister Dunn killed himself, or he was murdered. The physical evidence points to the former, but everything else says the latter is the truth. And if so, I have a duty to find the real killer that trumps the Magister's desires."

"I hadn't thought of it that way, but I suppose you're right."

Harrison fixed his gaze on her again, once more impassive. "Especially since anyone who killed Mister Dunn likely murdered Mister Frost as well."

A chill ran through Veronica at how easily he spoke those dire words. "I hadn't thought of that, either."

"I know. You're remarkably free from guile for someone so intelligent. It's one of the things I find most admirable in you."

Veronica blushed. "I've always thought of it as a curse. I'm far too trusting."

"You strike a perfect balance between trusting and cynicism as far as I'm concerned." He smiled again and leaned across the desk to take her hand. "Veronica—"

Someone knocked on the door. Veronica snatched her hand away just as Harrison jerked back. They both laughed, rather self-consciously, Veronica thought, and Harrison stood.

"Come to Justice House on Firstday during the evening instructors' hours," he said quietly, though Veronica was sure no one could hear them through the door. "I should know more by then."

"What happened to me not being involved?"

Harrison shook his head in mock despair. "You seem to keep getting involved no matter what I do to protect you. We might as well embrace your destiny."

He stopped her before she could open the door and kissed her swiftly, the lightest touch of his lips on hers. "And as to the other thing," he whispered, brushing a strand of hair back from her face, "I don't have any idea what to do. But I don't think I can bear to go back to where we were before this afternoon."

Veronica nodded in agreement. She drew in a deep breath and hoped she looked composed and not disheveled. Harrison opened the door and bade her a polite "Goodbye, Lady North, and I hope that answers your question." Then she was in the hallway, and the door was shut, and she felt bereft again despite her memories of how he'd touched her, how he'd looked at her.

She walked slowly out of Godfrey Hall and back to her rooms, reliving those kisses almost without trying to. What a surprise—and yet it really did feel as if she'd been waiting for that moment ever since she'd first stood in his class and asked a forbidden question. She realized she was smiling a rather silly smile and made herself stop. How unexpected, at her age, to find romance again when she'd thought herself well past the possibility. Unexpected, and beautiful.

In her room, she sat on her bed and regarded the blue gown hanging on the wardrobe door. Had she been thinking of a second youth when she bought it? It didn't matter. She felt twenty-two again, just starting out in life, and after the horrors of the past weeks, it was a feeling she sorely needed. She hoped no one mentioned Master Tyndale at supper, because she wasn't sure she could conceal her emotions.

She flopped backward on her bed and lay staring at the ceiling until giggles escaped her. What a strange, wonderful day this had been. Even the knowledge that a killer might still be out there couldn't take that away from her. She rolled off the bed and began to change her clothes for supper. She felt so full of secrets it was a wonder they didn't carry her away. At least this time, she had one secret that filled her with joy.

21

"You're awfully quiet, even for you, Veronica," Percy said at supper that day. "Something wrong?"

Veronica jerked out of her daydream. "Just...a little tired," she lied. "It's been a long week." She'd been thinking about Harrison and how long it was until Firstday. An eternity, really.

"I'll say," Bec exclaimed. "There's been a year's worth of excitement crammed into a single week. It feels like forever since Ian—" Her mouth shut abruptly.

Silence fell at their end of the long table. Veronica traced circles in the last of her gravy with the tines of her fork. It did feel like forever, and at the same time it felt like no time had passed since Ian had sat beside her for the last time.

Percy cleared his throat. "That reminds me," he said. "Howard hasn't shown up for meals since Haransday."

"He's been behaving strangely ever since Carlton's death," Bec said. "You know what he's like. Always looks like he's afraid he'll be accused of something. But when I told him Carlton killed himself, he went so still I thought he'd had a stroke."

Bridget leaned forward. "I saw him yesterday," she said, clearly glad to have something else to talk about. "He said he was busy with working on Ian's Device. Apparently they finally let him into the workshop."

"Well, that's something," Veronica said. "Though I hope he's not too busy to eat."

"We'll have to keep an eye on him," Bec declared. "Wouldn't it be something if he figured out the Devisery, though?"

Veronica pushed her chair back. "I'll go check on him now."

"You interested in going to the pub tonight?" Percy said.

Veronica hesitated. "All right," she finally said. What she wanted to do was have an early night for more daydreaming. But that was self-indulgent, the behavior of a child, and letting her new romance interfere with her usual activities would only make her miserable in the long run. "But I'll meet you there. I should finish some assignments first."

"Bah. That's what Endweek is for," Bec said. "You're far too responsible."

"If I do it now, I'll have all day tomorrow free," Veronica pointed out.

"Which is exactly what I mean. The midterm holiday is only a week away, and nobody is taking classes seriously now. You should break the rules once in a while. Do something that *isn't* sensible."

Veronica wanted to laugh. "I'll put that into my schedule," she said with a smile, and the others roared with laughter.

The sun had fully set when she emerged from the refectory, and she wrapped her cloak tightly around herself against the growing chill. Autumn wasn't her favorite season, though she loved its characteristic smells. She always felt as if the world were slowly dying as it headed toward Winter. Spring was better, everything waking up and becoming new. Right now she was about as far from Spring as possible. And yet her usual melancholy at the changing of the seasons was a distant memory. She smiled and touched her lips. What a small thing to make such a tremendous difference.

The majordomo at Fortitude House flinched slightly when he saw her on the doorstep. The way he looked at her amused her, his air of steeling himself against an attack. "You're here about Mister Peterson," he said. It wasn't a question.

"I am. Is he in?"

"He is, but he's not receiving guests. And before you ask, he looked perfectly healthy to me, last I saw him."

Veronica suppressed a smile. "It's very kind of you to check on him."

The majordomo scowled. "As if I had a choice," he muttered. Veronica pretended not to hear him.

"Well, would you please tell him that Lady North was asking after him," she said, and turned away as the door shut decisively on her. She wasn't sure she shouldn't have pushed, since Howard might have fallen back into his funk, but between the majordomo's assurances and what Bridget had said, he was probably just deeply involved in Devisery.

When she returned to Patience House, she met Mistress Holyoak stumping along the hallway toward the entrance. Her habitual irritated expression deepened when she saw Veronica. "Lady North," she said, sounding exasperated. "I have told you repeatedly how I feel about being expected to entertain your guests. You ought to be here when they arrive."

"I'm sorry, Mistress Holyoak. I wasn't expecting anyone, or I would have been here to greet them. Is the visitor here now?"

"The young woman left." Mistress Holyoak eyed Veronica suspiciously. "Wasting my time, it's a wonder I put up with it."

To her surprise, Veronica didn't feel the usual stomach-knotting dread and discomfort she did when Mistress Holyoak unloaded her disdain upon her. She wasn't that much taller than the woman, but now she felt as if she towered over her. Why, she wondered in amazement, had she ever let Mistress Holyoak cow her? She was the former Consort—no, even better, she was Veronica North, and she didn't deserve this treatment.

"Mistress Holyoak," she said without a single tremor in her voice, "you put up with it because it is your *job*. I'm beginning to wonder why you took this position if you intended to be so resentful of your duties. Perhaps you need to hire assistants, if you feel yourself inadequate to your responsibilities."

Mistress Holyoak's mouth fell open. "Well, I never," she said. "How dare you suggest that I'm unfit? You nobles, sailing in and lording it over the rest of us—"

"That's quite enough," Veronica said. She hadn't spoken very forcefully, but even she could hear the tone in her voice that demanded respect. "Mistress Holyoak, your continuing antagonism isn't acceptable. I've been polite, and I've been accommodating, because that's how I was raised. But I will no longer put up with you abusing my good nature. Tomorrow morning I intend to speak to your superior about your behavior. We'll see what Mistress Keane thinks, shall we?"

Mistress Holyoak's face, which had been ruddy with anger, paled noticeably. "You wouldn't dare."

"Why not? She's responsible for making sure all the dormitories are run properly. Who do *you* think she'll be sympathetic to? Because I'm sure you've been almost as nasty to everyone else who lives here. Maybe it's time for a change."

"You think," Mistress Holyoak breathed, "that because you're the Dowager Consort everyone will bow to your whims? I should have expected something like this."

"Yes, you really should have," Veronica agreed cheerfully, "because your abusive behavior has brought this on yourself. It's just your bad luck I have the ability to do something about it, because you are absolutely right that the Dowager Consort commands respect. Good night, Mistress Holyoak. And don't expect anyone to help you pack."

She turned on her heel and sailed away in the direction of the stairs. Behind her, Mistress Holyoak called her a nasty name. She hesitated, decided it wasn't worth acknowledging, and continued on her way. Her heart beat lightly and rapidly, but for once it wasn't anxiety making it race. It was exhilaration. She'd never stood up to a bully before, and she certainly had never won a confrontation before, ever. That was, of course, because she'd always backed down before a situation came to a fight. And she hadn't had to yell, or swear, or do anything aggressive. She'd just had to take a stand.

Safely in her room, she leaned against the door, feeling utterly exhausted. Then she laughed, long and loud, almost unable to control herself as the wild emotions of the day emerged in mirth. It was nice to believe her new romance had something to do with the change, but she was sure it had been a much longer time coming than just this afternoon.

She wondered if her mystery caller was the same young woman who'd appeared and then disappeared the other day. Whoever she was, she appeared to be even shyer than Veronica.

Or, shyer than Veronica used to be. Well, either she'd eventually show up when Veronica was present, or she'd decide her business wasn't that important, and either way Veronica had no control over the situation. Which meant she didn't need to fret about it.

She turned on the Device light over her small table and lit the burner. She would finish her mathematics assignment and sketch out plans for her study group's next engineering project, and have some peppermint tea while she did so. Then she really would have all of Endweek free. She had no idea what she would do with that freedom, but in her new independence, just the thought of it was more than enough.

HOWARD WASN'T AT BREAKFAST THE NEXT MORNING, BUT NEITHER was anyone else when Veronica entered the refectory. She'd gone to the pub with her friends, and they'd had a rather late night. This time, Veronica hadn't had more than a single pint, and had woken at her usual time feeling fresh and unhampered by a hangover. It was likely her friends couldn't say the same.

But as she approached the kitchen to get her food, she saw Howard emerge from the line with his plate. "Oh, Howard!" she exclaimed, hurrying toward him. "I've been worrying about you!"

Howard jerked. A sausage rolled off his plate and hit the floor. He ignored it. "Veronica," he said, his face going slightly red. "I was going...I meant to eat in my room."

"I thought that was against the rules. Taking the refectory dishes out of here, I mean." Veronica bent to retrieve the sausage, then thought better of it since she didn't have anywhere to put it. "Come, let's sit. Bridget said you have access to Ian's workshop now. I want to hear all about it."

Howard let her steer him to their usual seats before she joined the line to get her own meal. He was so reluctant Veronica half expected him to be gone when she returned. But he was still sitting there, ignoring his food, when she sat across from him. "You should eat," she told him, taking a bite of delicious flat cakes with honey. "This is so good. I've never had a better appetite than when I came to the Scholia."

Howard picked up a sausage link and dipped it absently in a puddle of honey before taking a dripping bite. "I'm not very hungry."

"Well, eat anyway. You have to keep your strength up." Veronica took another bite. "Now, tell me what you've learned."

Howard reddened again and stared at his plate. "Nothing much yet."

"That's all right. It might take a while to make sense of Ian's notes. Did you go to Brookside or Knightsbury yet?"

"The Scholia brought the contents of those workshops here. It's a lot to go through." He still wasn't meeting her eyes.

"Do you think—" In time, she realized that even though everyone by now knew the contents of Carlton's suicide note, they didn't necessarily know that the Scholia had been aware Ian's death was murder from the start. So she decided not to ask if he thought the murder investigation had discovered anything from Ian's workshops that Howard could use. Instead, she said, "Did they retrieve the rest of the notes from Mister Miller?"

Howard's head came up abruptly. "Garold Miller? What about him?"

Veronica felt uncomfortably as if she'd taken a wrong step. She couldn't remember anymore who knew what. But surely if

Howard had access to Ian's things, he needed to have the stolen notes as well? She decided to take a chance, if a sideways one. "I think Mister Miller has some of the notes from the Knightsbury workshop."

"Does he? How would you know?" Howard's voice went razor-sharp.

"Oh...I spoke to him..." Veronica felt she was digging herself in deeper. "Anyway, I thought the Scholia might have retrieved those, too."

"I don't think so. Miller. Huh." Howard's gaze went distant. "Why did you speak to him? About what? I don't see why you'd even know who he was."

"It's really not important, Howard," Veronica said, casting about for a change of subject. "Maybe you could go to him directly, if you think he still has the notes."

"If he has the notes...that means he got them from Carlton." Howard sounded distant now, too. "I can't believe..." He shoved his half-empty plate away and stood. "I have to take care of something. I'll see you later."

"What are you going to do?" Veronica asked.

"Don't worry about it." Howard's distant air was gone, replaced by a strange agitation. "If Carlton—never mind. Good-bye, Veronica."

"But, Howard—" It was too late. He was already headed for the door.

Veronica took another bite and silently cursed herself, then blushed at even thinking those words. She never used coarse language. Surely it didn't matter anymore if Howard knew Carlton had sold the notes to Miller. And yet she felt she'd made a huge mistake.

Howard's behavior puzzled her. That hadn't been his usual

distracted air, the sense she always had when talking to him that he was on the verge of apologizing for his existence. He'd been sharp and focused when he spoke of Miller, even as he was clearly thinking about something else. This abrupt change in his behavior worried Veronica. It didn't fit with how she expected him to behave when he was deeply involved in new Devisery.

She finished her meal and cleared her plate and Howard's, then headed for the back rooms of the refectory. Her encounter with Howard had almost made her forget her threat to Mistress Holyoak the previous night. She felt full of flat cakes and right-eous indignation. It was past time someone did something about the abrasive chatelaine, and right then Veronica felt like that someone.

She found Mistress Keane, head of housekeeping, in her office and poured out her list of complaints in a polite but firm way. Mistress Keane, who'd begun the impromptu interview in an attitude of slightly servile helpfulness, grew gradually stiller as Veronica continued. When Veronica finished, she said, "Lady North, we've never had any complaints about Mistress Holyoak before. Are you sure this isn't a personal issue?"

"I'm sure the residents don't want to stir up trouble. And while it's true Mistress Holyoak reserves much of her animosity for me, she is rude to the others and slow to respond to complaints. I can't imagine her behavior is representative of the face the Scholia wants to show the world, can you?"

Mistress Keane's eyes narrowed. "No," she said, "it is not." She rose. "Thank you for bringing this matter to my attention, Lady North. I assure you I will take your complaint seriously."

"I appreciate it." Veronica regarded Mistress Keane closely. She did have the appearance of someone who intended to come down hard on her subordinate. That satisfied Veronica immensely.

She spent the rest of the day reading and going for a walk, not to Knightsbury, but all the way to Brookside. Brookside was a quiet village, not at all like the exuberantly young Knightsbury. Most of its small buildings still had old-fashioned thatched roofs, even some of the businesses along its narrow main street. There were very few shops and only two taverns, one of them a full-sized inn and the other apparently the residence of the tavern owner. People eyed her suspiciously, even when she smiled and nodded. She wondered if Ian had faced the same suspicion in setting up his workshop here.

On a whim, she retraced her steps to the second, smaller tavern and pushed the door open. It was only about two o'clock in the afternoon, but the place was already mostly full of patrons who all looked up at her entrance. Veronica reminded herself that she was now calm and collected and not easily intimidated and marched over to the bar.

"Half a pint, please," she said. When the silent barkeeper slid the mug over to her, she added, "And I was wondering if you had business dealings with my friend, Ian Frost? He was a Deviser, and I know he had a workshop here in Brookside."

The barkeep stared at her with a level gaze. His fingers drummed on the scarred, dull wood of the oak slab that formed the bar. He said nothing. Veronica's nerves started to get the best of her. "I don't know if it was here, or at the other tavern…I don't suppose you could help me?"

The drumming never ceased. The barkeep's gaze darted to his hand, then fixed on her again. Suddenly Veronica understood. She took a silver five-stave piece from her pocketbook and slid it across the bar. The barkeep made it disappear, and suddenly his face became more animated. "Asking after Mister Frost?" he said. "He's a popular fellow now he's dead."

"I'm sure others have been here. A gentleman with blond hair, perhaps?"

"Him, and the squirrely fellow." The barkeep made a gesture about shoulder-high to Veronica. "He was here a bunch of times. The gentleman only once. Didn't like the look of him."

"The look of the...squirrely fellow?"

"Nah, the city prat. Had a look that said I wasn't worth his time." The barkeep scowled. "But you don't say no to the Scholia, even if they are all prats."

Veronica suppressed a smile. As fond as she was of Harrison, she couldn't deny his manner could be off-putting. "I see," she said. Then, curious, she asked, "When was How—the squirrely fellow here last?"

The barkeep drummed his fingers on the oak slab again. Sighing inwardly, Veronica handed over another silver coin. It was like feeding one of those carnival Devices that worked only when you inserted a coin. "It's been a few days," the barkeep admitted, scooping up his bribe. "Haven't seen him since last Endweek."

That was strange. Veronica was sure Howard had said he'd tried to get access to the Brookside workshop only a few days ago. "You're sure?"

"Of course I'm sure." The barkeep prodded Veronica's mug. "You want another?"

Veronica drained the last of her ale and shook her head. "No, but thank you for answering my questions. I appreciate your help."

"Frost was a decent renter. Sorry to hear about his death. You weren't his mother, were you?"

The barkeep's sudden dismay amused Veronica, as did the notion that anyone as fair-haired as she could have produced a son as dark as Ian. "No, just a friend." She nodded at the other patrons and left the tavern, still thinking hard.

Howard's behavior now struck her as odd even for him. And she was sure he'd lied to her about the Brookside workshop. But he could have no reason to lie about pursuing Ian's line of research, because everyone knew he'd been Ian's partner and was the logical choice to be his successor.

She walked most of the way back to the Scholia, mentally going over what she knew. Carlton almost certainly killed and made to appear a suicide. Howard behaving strangely. His reaction to Carlton's death. He couldn't...no, surely Howard couldn't have anything to do with Carlton's death? It was an intuitive leap over a bridge missing half its planks, but the idea made her feel as cold as if she knew it was true.

Veronica shook her head and kept walking. She would tell Harrison about Howard's behavior and let him look into it. He knew far more about the investigation than she. And maybe he would tell her the idea was impossible, and she could stop suspecting her friend of murder.

22

*V*eronica knocked on the door of Justice House at four-thirty precisely the next afternoon and waited. When the doorkeeper peered out at her, she said, "I'm here to consult with Master Tyndale."

"I thought you were going to see his assistants instead," the old man said. He scratched his head, disordering his thinning white hair.

"They sent me back to speak to him," Veronica lied shamelessly. She thought about telling the doorkeeper her business was none of his, but decided that level of defiance would draw more attention even than a beginning student daring to take up the great man's time.

The man shrugged. "It's your funeral," he said, opening the door wider so she could enter. "Though maybe he won't go so hard on you, you being royalty and all that."

"I hope so," Veronica said.

The doorkeeper ushered her down a long, dark-paneled

hall hung with portraits of Masters and Magisters. Veronica covertly examined their backgrounds as she passed. Still all identical. She couldn't imagine why the Scholia had spent so much money on the campus buildings and then skimped on portraiture. Well, it wasn't as if these were painted by master artists.

They reached an open space, really little more than a widening of the hall, which was lined on two sides with ordinary wooden chairs like the ones in Harrison's lecture hall. "Wait here, and Master Tyndale will call for you when he's ready," the doorkeeper said. He gestured at the far end of the hall, where stairs led up to a dimly-lit landing. Between the sitting area and the stairs, several doors stood close together as if the rooms they led to were very small. "I don't know as he's come down yet."

At that moment, Veronica heard footsteps on the stairs, a quick, light rhythm she recognized. She schooled her features into what she hoped was as good an indifference as Harrison's habitual expression and seated herself. Presently Harrison appeared on the landing. He wore his Master's robe and stole as he had during the lecture that morning and looked as indifferent as he always did. Veronica's heart beat more rapidly at the sight of him. She hoped the doorkeeper wouldn't notice her agitation.

"Lady North," he said when he neared them. "I understand you have a question."

"Yes, Master Tyndale, and I hope it's not too much trouble." Veronica felt an urge to giggle and stifled it ruthlessly.

"Not at all. Please join me." He gestured toward one of the doors.

Veronica shot a glance at the doorkeeper. His watery brown

eyes fixed on her, but he didn't look suspicious. She hoped that would stay true.

Harrison held the door for her to enter. The room was as small as she'd imagined, with only two chairs on either side of a narrow desk. Both desk and chairs were so plain she felt she'd stepped into some other building, somewhere far from the lavishly decorated Scholia. "Why—" she began.

The door clicked shut, and Harrison's arms went around her, drawing her close. "Later," he said, and kissed her, his lips warm and urgent on hers. Desire swept over her, a wave of delicious heat that thrilled through her body, and she returned his kisses eagerly, no longer caring what the doorkeeper suspected.

After what felt like forever, she rested her head on his shoulder and said, "I thought we weren't supposed to do that."

"We aren't. I never knew I had such poor self-control." Harrison held her more tightly. "Seeing you in the lecture today…"

"You never once looked at me."

"I couldn't. I didn't think I could keep my composure." He ran one hand slowly down her back from the nape of her neck to just above her waist. "I gave myself one look, just before I left the lecture hall, and then I was useless all the rest of the day, waiting for this moment."

She laughed, quietly in case someone else was waiting outside. "And I've daydreamed about you almost every moment since I left your office. What a couple of young idiots we are."

Harrison laughed with her. "Instead of the adults of mature age we know ourselves to be?" He lightly kissed her forehead, then released her. "Have a seat, and we'll talk."

"About the investigation, I assume. Have you learned anything new?"

"Nothing very useful, I'm afraid." Harrison sat across from her, frowning. "I did some digging—some covert digging—into Mister Dunn's financial affairs. He was not a gambler, and his lifestyle was not an extravagant one that might suggest he incurred great debt. On the other hand, his family is not wealthy, and they have sunk much of what few resources they have into Mister Dunn's Scholia education."

Veronica nodded. "So he's not personally in debt, but he might have wanted extra money to help his family."

"Precisely. Which means he had a motive for killing Mister Frost, if his intent was to steal the Devisery and sell it." Harrison tilted his head back briefly as if looking for heaven's guidance. "But that minimizes his motive for suicide. If he cared enough about his family to want to help them, he was unlikely to then kill himself, leaving them mourning."

"Unless he really did feel guilty over killing Ian. Though..." Veronica hesitated.

"Though, what?"

In a rush, she said, "Carlton didn't strike me as someone who felt remorse over things. And most of my friends share that opinion. Some of them know him much better than I did. So I don't feel that's the answer."

Harrison nodded. "It's not proof, but I don't like to disregard intuition in a criminal investigation. Sometimes it's the mind's way of making sense of facts that otherwise don't fit. Though I never base an accusation purely on intuition, which would be irresponsible."

"I understand." Veronica intertwined her fingers to still their nervous fidgeting. "But speaking of intuition, I should tell you about Howard Peterson."

Harrison's eyebrow arched. "You suspected him before."

"Yes, and I was sure his odd behavior was just grief. But now he's lied to me—maybe not about anything important, but I can't understand why he would do that."

"Tell me."

She listed for him Howard's strange behaviors since Carlton's death, ending with how he'd lied to her about the last time he'd been in Brookside. Harrison listened with his usual impassive expression. "You're right that that's not actionable," he said when she finished. "But it bears looking into. You said Mister Peterson became agitated when he learned Mister Dunn had had possession of the notes? Which, by the way, you probably shouldn't have told him."

Veronica sighed. "I was afraid of that. It just slipped out."

"It's all right. This mess is growing complicated enough I'm not sure even I can keep all the details straight."

"I'm sure that's not true. Anyway, yes, he suddenly became very curt with me, and then he left in a hurry."

Harrison tapped a finger against his lips. "I wonder," he said. "Now, this is all supposition, but...if Mister Peterson killed Mister Frost and stole the notes, intending to develop the Devisery himself, and then Mister Dunn found out about the murder and blackmailed Mister Peterson into giving him the notes..."

"Then Howard would have a reason to kill Carlton, either in revenge or to get the notes back." Veronica shook her head. "But that still doesn't explain how Howard got Carlton to write that suicide note."

"It solves only half our problem. And, as I said, it's all supposition." Harrison ran his fingers through his hair in a gesture Veronica was coming to recognize as indicating frustration with a complex puzzle. "And now we come to the really bad news."

"You frighten me."

Harrison gave her a wry half-smile. "The really bad news is that the Magister got wind, somehow, of my poking around. He called me into his office yesterday and read me a strong lecture on how I was to stop immediately or risk losing my position."

Veronica gasped. "He can't do that!"

"He most certainly can. And will, if he's afraid enough of what trouble I might bring upon the Scholia. I told you Donald Montgomery is utterly committed to protecting this institution."

"Yes, but to the point of permitting a murderer to get away free? Surely he must see how wrong that is!"

Harrison shook his head. "He seems to be under the impression that this disaster has solved itself. One man kills another out of greed, then kills himself when his remorse becomes too great. Neat and tidy."

Veronica snorted in derision and then felt embarrassed at her unladylike behavior. Harrison only smiled. "Your passion for justice is admirable," he said. "But in this case, I'm inclined to let the Magister have his way."

Veronica sat up straight in her chair. "No!"

"Veronica, I don't like it any more than you do. But any further investigation I do will be difficult to conceal. And I can't find a murderer if I've been expelled from the Scholia premises. It might be better to let this sit for a while and allow the murderer to believe he or she is safe. Then..." He spread his hands wide, palm up, to indicate anything was possible.

"I suppose you're right. But what if someone else is killed?"

"I don't see why that would happen. The Magister is right

about one thing; this debacle seems focused on Mister Frost's Devisery, and knowledge of that is out in the open now. If Mister Peterson is the murderer, he's gotten what he wants and has no need to kill again."

"Unless he's *not* the murderer, and he's the next one in danger."

Harrison grimaced. "I hoped you wouldn't think of that. Don't worry. I intend to watch Mister Peterson carefully—that's something I can do without arousing suspicion. Whether he's the killer or a potential victim, I don't intend to let him out of my sight."

"That seems like all we can do."

"It is, for now." Harrison reached across the desk and took Veronica's hand. "As to the other matter...it's not safe for us to meet privately on campus. It already looks strange that I've given a beginner student my attention. So it will have to be Knightsbury. I'll look into places we can go where no one will notice."

Unease had crept over Veronica as he spoke. What he described sounded so furtive, it made her uncomfortable. "I... don't know if that's a good idea."

"It's the only way we can have privacy, Veronica."

She withdrew her hand from his. "I mean I don't know if it's a good idea that we...Harrison, you said you could lose your position for having a relationship with a student."

"Only if they catch us. And I have extensive experience in concealing my movements."

Her heart felt leaden, each slow beat shaking her body to its core. "I don't want to risk it."

Harrison sat up in his chair. "You don't want to risk it? Isn't it my risk to take?"

"You also said they'd expel me. We both have so much to lose, Harrison. Isn't it better we...we stop now, before things go too far?"

His glass-green eyes suddenly looked as shallow and empty of emotion as they had the first day she'd seen him. "So you're saying this has all been an act. Something you had no intention of pursuing."

His words struck her like a knife piercing her leaden heart, a dull ache rather than a sharp pain. Almost she stood and fled. But she knew enough of human behavior to know when someone had lashed out in an attempt to turn their own pain outward so it wouldn't hurt so much. "Stop that," she said sharply. "You know it's not. You're hurt and disappointed and you only said that so I'd be at fault. I know you didn't mean it, but if you keep talking like that, you really will destroy whatever this is between us."

Harrison's expression didn't change. He blinked once, then let out a slow sigh. "Sweet heaven," he said in a low voice. "You're right. About everything. Veronica, I apologize. Please forgive me."

She nodded. "Landon used to do that to me, early on," she said. "And I would always crumple under his sharp words, and that would fill him with remorse for hurting me. It took time, but he learned not to turn his pain and embarrassment outward. And I learned not to be so easily crushed."

"Sarah and I never learned that lesson. We'd fight, and then we'd be silent for days, waiting each other out." Harrison sighed.

Veronica felt uncomfortable again. "Sarah. She was your wife?"

Harrison eyed her narrowly. "You've heard the gossip. That she left me because I'm impossible to live with."

"I have. I didn't believe that was the whole story."

"It's not." Harrison finger-combed his hair back into place. "It was a mutual decision. We'd grown apart, and we were fighting more often than not. But our youngest wasn't an adult yet, and we agreed to control ourselves for a year or two, for her sake. Then Sarah told me she'd met someone else and she wanted me gone."

He smiled that wry, self-deprecating smile again, and its bitterness broke Veronica's heart. "And the children all chose to stay with her after the divorce when I adopted out. Not one of them wanted to take my side. I don't think I've ever felt so worthless and insignificant. It took years, and an embarrassingly ill-judged affair with a colleague, for me to come to terms with it."

Veronica realized she'd been holding her breath and let it out slowly. "How long ago was the divorce?"

"Ten years."

"So...does the Scholia permit affairs between Masters? Is that why you're still here?"

"That was before I took this teaching position. I was a criminal investigator and law-speaker for a guild in Aurilien. It's why I came here, actually—I needed to get away from my colleague, for both our sakes."

"I'm so sorry. That's a terrible thing to happen to anyone."

"And it's why I lashed out at you just now. I'm afraid I fear being rejected, which may be part of the reason I enjoy keeping others at a distance. And you..." He looked away from her at the wall, which was bland and unadorned with anything that would justify his attention. "I'm not very rational where you're concerned."

"I feel the same. Harrison, I care about you. I never thought I'd feel this way again, not after losing Landon. But it's not..." She wiped her eyes and hated herself for crying like a lovesick young adult. "We haven't made any promises. We need to let this go before it breaks both our hearts."

"It may be too late for that." His smile made it partly a joke, but only partly. He let out a deep sigh. "You're much wiser than I am. All right. Lady North—"

"Oh, *please* don't say that!" Veronica begged.

Harrison raised an eyebrow again. "It's all or nothing, Veronica. Do you think we'd be able to keep our resolution if we're intimate in even that small way?"

Now the ache in her chest was sharp and terrible, impossible to get away from. "You're right. I'm sorry."

Harrison rose and extended his hand. "Lady North, thank you for your assistance. I'm sorry we couldn't solve either of our problems in a satisfactory way."

Veronica clasped his hand and wanted to burst out crying at how strong and firm and comforting it was. But that was all over. "I hope I was able to help, Master Tyndale."

"If you feel you need to transfer to another class, I can arrange it. You wouldn't be at a disadvantage."

She shook her head. "Not yet. Unless my presence is too difficult for you."

Harrison smiled. "I think I can contain myself, now that...anyway."

Veronica stood and let go of his hand. "I'll tell you...no. I'll send a message if I change my mind."

He nodded and opened the door. "I hope that answers your

question, Lady North," he said for the benefit of the two students seated in the waiting area.

"It does. Thank you for your time. I won't trouble you again." Veronica hurried past the waiting area, hoping her eyes weren't still red from crying. She left Justice House without seeing the doorkeeper and made it all the way to her rooms without encountering anyone she might need to talk to. Then she locked her door, sat on the floor with her back against it, and sobbed.

This was stupid. She was a grown woman, sensible and not prone to letting her desires rule her life. An affair with her instructor, even if they didn't sleep together, was against all the rules as well as being slightly dishonorable, because suppose he gave her preferential treatment? No, breaking it off was the right thing to do. And it didn't matter how it hurt. She was old enough to know the pain wouldn't last.

But in her heart, she would always think of him as Harrison.

23

She made herself go down for supper, though she first spent some time restoring her face so it wasn't ravaged by tears. The last thing she needed was for her well-meaning friends to try to ferret out what had made her miserable.

She needn't have worried. Howard was missing, again, and all the talk was about him. "I don't know where he went," Bridget said. "The majordomo at his dormitory said he'd gone out earlier today and hadn't returned. So it's not like he's moping in his room."

"I guess it's good he's getting out," Percy said. "It does him no good to hide away from the world."

"He's probably just obsessed with the Device. I bet he's holed up in Ian's workshop right now." Bec took a bite of mashed potatoes. "These are better than usual."

"Maybe we should take him something to eat," Veronica suggested. Her motives weren't pure; she wanted to see if

Howard displayed any more signs of guilt. She shouldn't pursue the investigation anymore, she knew, but it made the terrible ache in her chest less painful to have something else to think about.

"I bet I could get the cook to make up a box for him. He's got a soft spot for students who are suffering. Always wants to cure them with good food and a pat on the shoulder." Bec glanced toward the kitchen. "I'll ask when the meal's winding down."

"That would be a nice gesture," Bridget said. "And I'd like to know if he's made progress. It's exciting to know Ian will live on in his Devisery. Well, not really live on, obviously, he's dead, but—"

"We get it, Bridge," Percy said, sounding amused.

Veronica ate potatoes, trying to keep her mouth full so she'd have an excuse not to speak. She felt worn out, bludgeoned by the events of the previous week and a half and ready for life to go back to normal. Pre-Harrison normal.

"What's everyone planning for the midterm holiday?" Percy said. "Veronica, are you staying here? It's a long trip back to Aurilien just to turn around again almost the moment you arrive. We do have a lot of fun here when classes aren't in session, if that helps."

"I haven't decided," Veronica said, grateful for an ordinary, non-emotionally laden question. "I miss my family, but you're right, a four-day round trip journey for only two or three days at home is a bit much. And traveling is exhausting."

"I love traveling," Bridget said. "Staying at inns, seeing the countryside. I guess it's harder on you because of your age, though, isn't it? You must get so tired."

"Bridget, you're impossible," Bec said. "You make Veronica sound like she's seventy."

"She's right, though," Veronica said. "Riding in a carriage all day leaves me so achy. You three shouldn't get old if you can help it."

"We'll have to work on that," Percy said with a grin.

"Maybe the biology students know the secret. They're always messing about with concoctions." Bec stood. "I'm done eating. Let me see what I can wangle out of Cook."

The others had cleaned their plates by the time Bec returned with a wrapped bundle. "Cook's accommodating so long as you don't try to steal his dishes," she said. "Let's go."

The cold air outside smelled of snow. Veronica tilted her head back and looked at the stars for a few seconds. They were sharp-edged and clear, little specks of light undimmed by clouds. "I wonder if we'll see the first snow tomorrow."

"Could be. I can feel it in my bones," Percy said. "We usually get snow around this time, when Autumn's nearly half over. But I don't think it will be tomorrow. Maybe Haransday."

Bec led the way through Saunders Hall to the basement stairs. Someone had fixed the malfunctioning light Device, and it and its twin shed a bright, clear light over the steps. It was impossible to fear anything in such a sane, well-ordered environment. Even so, Veronica lagged behind until she was at the rear of their little group. Part of her feared seeing Ian's workshop again, and she didn't know if she was more afraid of finding it still disordered or that it had been restored to its usual pristine condition. Either way, it meant Ian really was gone.

Bec knocked on the door, then opened it. "Howard?"

The lights were on inside. Howard looked up from where he was tinkering with a contraption made of a metal framework studded with gears and pulleys and several woven belts webbed between them. He jerked in surprise. "Bec," he said. "What are you all doing here?"

"Brought you food so you wouldn't starve," Bec said. She plopped the package on the table, well away from Howard's work. "Are you making progress?"

"You didn't have to do that. I'm fine," Howard said.

"You don't look fine," Bridget said. "You look as if you haven't slept in a while. Can't you stop long enough to eat?"

Howard glanced at each of them in turn. When his gaze settled on Veronica, she thought she saw him twitch. But he didn't say anything, just pulled the package across the table and opened it, releasing the delicious aromas of roast beef and mashed potatoes.

Bec magically produced a knife and fork imprinted with the Scholia crest from her sleeve. "What Cook doesn't know won't hurt him," she said when the others exclaimed. "I'll put them back tomorrow. Besides, how else is Howard supposed to eat those delicious mashed potatoes?"

Howard took a few bites of his meal, then set it aside. "I'll eat the rest later."

"Howard," Veronica said.

"I said I'm not hungry," he retorted sharply. "Thanks for caring, but I'm really busy. This Device is complicated."

"What does it do?" Veronica asked. Rather than being hurt by his harsh words, she felt cold. Howard wasn't behaving like an innocent person.

"I don't know yet," Howard said, not looking at any of them. "I know what some of the pieces do, but I don't know how to fit them together yet. Which is why it's so important I be left alone to work all this out."

"Well, fine, if you're sure," Bec said. "Let's leave the genius to work, everyone." She didn't bother concealing her anger, but Howard didn't react. He turned his attention back to a couple of tiny gears it looked as if he was having trouble getting to mesh.

Bec stormed out, followed more slowly by the others, with Veronica still bringing up the rear. "I like that," Bec said. "That's the last time I do anything nice for him."

"Come on, Bec, you know how Howard gets," Bridget said. "He always feels he needs to prove himself, especially by comparison to Ian. Or—well, he used to."

"He'll be fine," Veronica said. Behind her, the key turned in the workshop door's lock.

SHE'D HOPED SECONDDAY WOULD BE EASIER THAN FIRSTDAY, IF only because she didn't have a law lecture. Instead, she found herself watching every blond-haired Master in a red stole, hoping for a glimpse of Harrison. She hated her weakness, but she told herself this was temporary, just a part of grieving over her lost romance that had barely had a chance to develop.

So she made herself go to all her classes and take exhaustive notes. She met with her engineering study group and managed not to shout at them when they went off on tangent after tangent about everything but engineering. Their casual burbling about their love lives infuriated her. The intensity of her reaction startled her. She was never seriously angry about anything, and yet she wished she could slap Hermione and Robert for talking about the women they were seeing and how happy they were.

By the time supper rolled around, she was even more emotionally exhausted than she had been the previous day. She wasn't hungry and didn't want social interaction, but she wanted even less for her friends to think something was wrong and try to tease the details out of her.

The meal tasted like bland water, though her nose insisted the rich barley soup was delicious. She ate as much as she could bear, slowly so no one would think anything was wrong, and listened to Bec and Percy argue in a loving way over some disagreement they'd had. Veronica hadn't listened to the details. Tomorrow, she'd have to sit in Harrison's lecture hall and watch him in full awareness that she would never kiss him again. And since the seats the students had chosen the first couple of days had become their unofficial assigned seating, she'd be front and center for him to see, too. Maybe she needed to change classes, after all.

"—and that's why it doesn't matter whether we share the same taste in books," Percy concluded, with the air of someone who'd just made a telling point. "It's all about our differences."

"Veronica, tell him he's wrong," Bec said.

Veronica, startled, said, "Wrong?"

"Yes, about how it's more important couples have interesting differences than that they have everything in common." Bec leaned forward, away from Percy's attempt at a rebuttal. "You were married for twenty-some years, right? So you know better than we do how to keep a marriage going."

"Unless she and the King fought all the time," Bridget said.

"*Bridget.*"

"I'm serious! You didn't, did you? But you might have. I'm just saying no one can tell from the outside where a marriage is in trouble." Bridget's earnest face was pink with embarrassment, but she held her ground.

"Landon and I had disagreements, but not very often,"

Veronica said. "We were married for twenty-five years, almost, and nobody manages to last that long in a marriage without hitting rough patches. But we learned, early on, how there's always something you can apologize for, even if you're not primarily at fault."

"That's not true if the marriage is abusive," Percy pointed out.

Veronica nodded. "Yes. I'm talking about an ordinary relationship where both people are reasonable and not inclined to deliberately hurt each other." She remembered what Harrison had said about his marriage, and a lump formed in her throat. She swallowed and went on, "It's just that if one person gets angry, and the other gets defensive, those are both bad reactions that can be apologized for. It doesn't have to be one person backing down from the other. Does that make sense?"

"Yes, but that's why it's so important that you have enough in common that you don't have those misunderstandings in the first place," Bec said.

"I don't know if that's true," Veronica said. "Landon and I were very different people. He was bold, and I was shy. But we... I think we were the solution to each other's problem. He needed reassurance, and I needed support. So it was our differences—" She blinked back tears she didn't know why she was crying. "It was our differences that made us strong."

"I was right," Percy said smugly.

"I didn't mean to make you cry, Veronica," Bec said, uncharacteristically solemn. "I'm sorry. I didn't realize how hard it was for you to talk about the King."

Veronica shook her head and wiped her eyes. She was certain the man she was mourning was not Landon. "It's nothing. I'm just so tired, I think I'm quick to cry right now."

"Perfectly understandable," Percy said. "You should make it an early night. See if you don't feel better in the morning."

"I'll do that," Veronica said. She pushed her chair back. "I'll see you all in the morning, then."

She gathered up her cloak from the cloakroom inside the refectory's front door and wrapped it around herself. The cold, damp smell in the air was stronger now, and Veronica thought Percy had been right; they'd see snow before morning. Normally the thought would have cheered her. She didn't love late Autumn or Winter, but the first snow was always so pretty, before it turned to slush and the novelty wore off. Maybe in the uplands, snow stuck long enough to stay pretty, unlike in Aurilien where the cold months were mostly gray and depressing.

Despite the cold, she walked slowly back to Patience House, passing Honor House without more than a glance for the carved lion head over its front door. Why a lion to represent honor, she'd never bothered to ask. The animal over Patience House's front door was a bear, which seemed an even less likely symbol.

Two people, a man and a woman, stood in the shallow portico of Patience House, their faces half-cast into shadow by the Device lighting the door. The sound of an argument drifted toward Veronica on the crisp, cold air. She slowed her steps even more, not wanting to intrude. Then she realized the man was Howard.

Curiosity propelled her forward, dispelling her reticence and her feeling that she was snooping. The woman he was speaking to was young, probably not yet twenty, and she was a stranger. That wasn't odd, given how many Scholia students there were and how few of them Veronica knew. But as she drew closer, and the woman's face came into focus, Veronica felt as if she'd seen her before.

The argument cut off as Veronica neared, well before she could make out words enough to know what they were fighting about. "Howard, is everything all right?"

Howard jumped and put a hand on the girl's shoulder. He looked so furtive Veronica knew something was up. "It's fine, Veronica," he said. "Everything's fine. Ar—she was just leaving."

Veronica regarded both of them. The girl didn't look like she intended to go anywhere. Howard's hand on her shoulder seemed more a restraint than anything else. "I'm sorry, I don't know your name," she said, ignoring Howard to indulge her curiosity. "I'm Lady North."

"I know," the girl said. Her voice was soft and as lovely as the rest of her, and Veronica's feeling that she'd seen her before intensified. "Lady North, it's you I've come to see."

"It's not important, Ariane. I've already told you everything you need to know." Howard released the girl and made a little shooing motion like a mother hen shooing her chick away from danger.

Memory clicked. "I remember you," Veronica exclaimed. "You're Garold Miller's daughter. I saw you at his office."

Ariane nodded. "I've been trying to reach you, but you were always gone, and that terrible woman made me feel I was doing something wicked in waiting for you. You were the one who brought news of Ian's death. I hoped—" Tears filled her eyes, making them as liquid as a fawn's. "I hoped you would tell me more."

"But surely Howard...he must have given you details."

Veronica felt increasingly uncomfortable at the girl's obvious distress.

Ariane shot Howard a look. "He says it will only make me upset. But...you're a woman, Lady North. You must understand how I feel."

Suddenly Veronica did understand. "You were in love with Ian," she said.

Ariane nodded. "I need to know what happened. How he died. Howard won't say more than that he was murdered. Who would murder Ian, Lady North? Everyone liked him. Even my father liked him, and he doesn't even like himself. It can't be true."

Veronica tentatively reached out, feeling as if she were approaching a skittish, wounded dog, and took Ariane's trembling hand. "It's true. Ian was murdered. But I think Howard is right. Knowing the details won't change anything. It won't bring Ian back."

Ariane's face crumpled into tears. She threw herself at Veronica and buried her face in Veronica's chest, sobbing. "He was all I had," she murmured. "He can't be gone. He just can't."

Awkwardly, Veronica put her arms around the weeping girl and hugged her. She was reminded of Francis's occasional tantrums, when he was small, that always devolved into sobs and pleas to be held and comforted. She didn't know why she'd always been so reluctant to hug her own son. Hugs made her uncomfortable, made her feel as if the other person needed something she was incapable of supplying. But now, holding Ariane and patting her back soothingly, she felt more confident than she ever had in the face of tragedy.

"I'm so sorry," she whispered. "I know. I lost the man I loved, too." Lost both of them, she realized, and was startled almost out of her skin to realize she loved Harrison. Surely it was too soon, they barely knew each other, and yet she felt in her bones it was true. No wonder she'd been exhausted and miserable. "I promise it gets easier."

"I'll never forget him!"

"No, you won't. But the pain will fade, and eventually you'll be able to remember Ian the way he was when he was with you. I promise it's true."

Ariane lifted a devastated face to Veronica's. "I don't know if I can bear it."

"Of course you can. You must be strong, or Ian wouldn't have loved you." It occurred to Veronica that she didn't actually know if this feeling Ariane had had for Ian was reciprocated, but she didn't feel bad about possibly lying to the girl, since the truth would only hurt her more.

She became aware of Howard still standing nearby. He'd moved to the edge of the portico so furtively she suspected him of wanting to flee this awkward encounter. His face was fully in shadow, but she thought he looked uncharacteristically impassive, as if Ariane's tears didn't move him at all. Veronica felt impatient with him. Even Howard shouldn't be so self-absorbed he couldn't spare sympathy for someone who was grieving. Someone he clearly knew, based on Ariane's words and the way they'd looked while they were arguing.

"It will get easier," she repeated, releasing Ariane and taking a step away. "Now, I think you should go home. It's cold and dark—Howard, you should escort Miss Miller back."

Ariane's expression became puzzled. "I'm not Miss Miller," she said, with an almost childlike confusion. "I'm Mistress Frost. Ian was my husband."

24

"*I* beg your pardon?" Veronica exclaimed.

"Ian and I were married three—almost four weeks ago," Ariane said. "It was a secret from everyone because my father would never have approved. But I'm an adult," she said defiantly, as if Ian were right there and Veronica had threatened to forcibly separate them. "I can make my own decisions. And Ian promised to take me away from that awful place."

"I see," Veronica said. She felt faint. Ian secretly married to this girl—it should have been impossible. She didn't know why he hadn't even told his closest friends, except... "I thought...I beg your pardon, Miss—Mistress Frost, but you did know Ian was involved with another woman?"

"Please just call me Ariane, Lady North. It feels so much more friendly, and Ian always said you were his good friend." Ariane wiped her eyes. "And I know all about Samantha Wilde. Ian said I was so much nicer and prettier than she, and he always got so flustered when her name came up, I knew he was embarrassed at having liked her. So I tried not to mention her. But she was nothing to him." She smiled then, and the expression was so at odds with her innocent face, so *adult* a smile, Veronica was taken aback. "I made sure he never had any regrets."

Veronica began to feel it would be a mistake to underestimate this girl. Woman. If she was married, that made her a woman no matter how childlike she appeared. "I see," she said. She thought back on Ian's red-faced silences whenever Samantha's name was mentioned, how he'd insisted the two of them were over. It was certainly possible he'd been embarrassed rather than secretly still in love.

She looked over at Howard, who had moved even farther away. "Howard, come here," she said sharply. "Did you know about this?"

A look of guilty fear flashed across his face and then was gone. He glanced at Ariane, then faced Veronica again. Then he sagged like a puppet with its strings cut. "I found out last week, when Ariane came looking for you."

"Then why didn't you tell us? Howard, this girl has been grieving. Don't you think she could have used the support of Ian's friends?"

Even in the pale light of the Device, Veronica could see beads of sweat forming on Howard's forehead. She couldn't understand what had made him so agitated, unless—but if he'd killed Ian and Carlton, surely confronting Ariane wouldn't be enough to make him break down?

She made a decision and hoped it wouldn't hurt Ariane terribly. "Howard, you need to tell the truth now. All of it. I don't care if it's painful, you can't go on keeping secrets. I'm sure...I'm sure whatever you've done, you had reasons." She didn't actually believe that, but she knew Howard well enough to guess he would shut down entirely if she reminded him of the punishment for murder. Deep inside, her heart was screaming a warning at her that he was a murderer, that he might be desperate enough to attack her, but she stood her ground, hoping a bold front would protect her.

Howard shuddered. His fists clenched, and he stared at the ground between them. "It's not fair," he said, the words sounding as if they were being dragged out of him. "I worked with Ian on *everything*. I was his *partner*. I should have been the one, not this...this girl who seduced Ian so she could get out from under her father's thumb!"

Confused, Veronica said, "The one who what?"

"I did *not* seduce Ian!" Ariane shouted. "I loved him, and he loved me. I don't understand why you couldn't be happy for us!"

"Because you're his heir!" Howard shouted back. "That Device belongs to me, or should do. I've figured it out, I did all the work, but you're the one who will get all the profits!"

Understanding dawned. Veronica drew in a startled breath. So Howard was guilty, all right, just not of murder. "You lied to Ariane," she said. "You concealed the fact that the Device was complete, or would be soon, because it's Ian's Device, and as his widow, it belongs to her. You wanted the money."

"I wanted the credit," Howard said bitterly. "That's even more important. But yes, I deserve to make a fortune, after all the work I did. Why should this silly chit of a girl reap the benefits when all she ever did was lie on her back—"

Ariane slapped him. "Don't you dare cheapen our love," she snarled.

Veronica caught Ariane's wrist as she raised her hand for

another blow. "Stop it," she said. Both Howard and Ariane stiffened, but they stopped glaring at each other. "Howard, you'll get the credit for completing the Device. And I don't know much about patents, or Devisery, but I can't imagine you shouldn't have something from it. After all, Ian never did figure out how to make it all work, right?"

Howard turned his sullen glare on Veronica. "It doesn't work like that," he said, but he sounded uncertain.

"Well, like I said, I don't know much about it. So I don't know how it works. But I'm sure we can think of something."

"We? We're nothing." Howard laughed. "Garold Miller will swoop in and claim it all on behalf of his daughter."

Ariane gasped. "He can't," she said, gazing imploringly at Veronica. "I can't go back to living with him. He's cold and awful and he hates me because I remind him of Mother. Please, Lady North, help me!"

Veronica looked from one distraught face to the other and wished she didn't feel quite so old by comparison. "If you're Mistress Frost and not Mistress Miller, you adopted into Ian's family when you married, and your father has no claim on your estate," she pointed out.

"Yes, but you don't know him," Ariane insisted. "He'll figure out something. You have to stop him."

Veronica wasn't sure about the chances of her stopping Miller from doing anything, but the thought left her feeling tired rather than frightened. "It's possible," she said slowly, thinking it through, "he'll be satisfied with the profits from purchasing the rights to produce the finished Device. It's what he wanted, after all."

"But he—"

"That's enough," Veronica said. "Either you're an independent married woman, or you're a helpless child. It's past time you decided which of those you want to be. How do you think Ian would feel, knowing his wife didn't have the courage to stand up for herself?"

Ariane straightened. "He'd be so disappointed."

"That's right. So stop crying and complaining and help me think." Veronica's gaze fell on Howard. Curiously, she asked, "What is it? What does the Device do?"

Howard shrugged. "Nothing, yet."

"But you said you figured it out!"

"I did. But I can't get the timing to work. I'm so close, Veronica. If I were Ian, I'd intuit the solution, but I'm just me. I have to run test after test—but I swear it will work."

Veronica felt like throttling him. "Howard," she said with dangerous calm, *"what will it do when it's finished?"*

"You probably won't be impressed," Howard said. "It doesn't seem like much, but I promise—"

"Talk, Howard!"

He shrugged again, making his neck disappear into the collar of his greatcoat. "It's an automatic sewing Device."

Veronica sucked in a breath. "You can't be serious."

Howard misunderstood her. "I swear it's important, Veronica. I know it's not glamorous, not like a self-propelled wagon or something to take heat out of a room, but—"

"You don't have to explain, Howard. I see the implications." Did she ever see the implications. This would revolutionize clothing production. Revolutionize the economy of Tremontane. "Sweet heaven. Ian really was onto something. And you made it happen. Howard, don't you see how wonderful this is?"

Howard's tentative smile looked pained, as if he wasn't yet

convinced that anything in this mess was wonderful. "You think so?"

"*Howard*. It's amazing. And I swear I'll make sure you get both credit and the fortune you deserve."

Howard's smile faltered. "But you...you aren't a Deviser, or a law-speaker dealing in patent law, or—"

"I am the former Consort, Howard. I can do anything." She'd never felt so certain of that in her life.

"That's true," Howard said, hope dawning. "You can."

"But what about me?" Ariane said. "Ian promised I wouldn't have to live with my father anymore."

Veronica felt a moment's exasperation with the girl. She reminded herself that Ariane was young and self-absorbed as most young people were. "You'll inherit Ian's portion," she said. "It should be enough...what do you want to do, anyway?"

Ariane brightened. "I want to move to Aurilien and open a chocolate shop," she said. "It's what Ian said I could do once the money came in. I've always wanted to have my own little shop where people could sit and talk. Can I do that?"

Privately, Veronica wasn't sure Ariane had the gumption for a business endeavor, but who was she to judge? "You absolutely can," she assured her. "But for now, you have to return home— no, I know you don't want to, but until the Device is marketable, you have no money to support yourself. You have to be brave a little while longer, Ariane—unless your father is abusive?"

Ariane shook her head. "He's just unpleasant and bossy. He thinks he can still tell me what to do even though I'm a married woman. A widow, even."

"But he doesn't know about you and Ian, Ariane. You aren't being very fair to him. I think you should tell him about your marriage soon—though probably not until you've told him about the Device. That will soften his heart considerably, I judge." Veronica patted her shoulder. "Howard will take you back, and I'll be in touch. And if you need anything, you know where to find me. Just don't be afraid of Mistress Holyoak, all right? She can't hurt you." With luck, Mistress Holyoak wouldn't be in a position to do anything to Ariane. Or to Veronica.

"Thank you, Lady North!" Ariane threw her arms around Veronica, who responded not quite as awkwardly as she once might have. "I knew you were the one to talk to!"

"Thanks, Veronica," Howard said, a little sheepishly. "I'm sorry I was stupid. Friends?"

"We've always been friends, Howard," Veronica replied. She decided not to tell him she'd suspected him of murder. "I'll talk to you tomorrow, all right? You can explain what's left to do before the Device is functional, and I'll ask—" She shut her mouth. Of course she couldn't ask Harrison's advice. "I'll find someone in the law school who understands patent law, and we'll start working on those details."

"I'm looking forward to it," Howard said. "Come with me, Ariane. We'll borrow a carriage."

Veronica stood on the doorstep of Patience House and watched them walk away toward the stables. She shivered, then couldn't stop shivering. She was much colder than she'd realized.

Mistress Holyoak didn't appear when Veronica opened the door. She breathed out in relief and hurried to her rooms, where she turned the heating Devices to full and stood for a moment with her hands over the one in the sitting room, flexing them to restore circulation. So Howard wasn't the murderer. A tiny, Harrison-like voice in her head pointed out that she couldn't be sure of that, but it was easy to ignore. Besides, Howard's erratic behavior fit more with him concealing information than with him being guilty of murder.

She flopped onto her sofa and tilted her head back to stare at the ceiling. It was painted pale blue and made her feel even colder. She got up and slowly climbed to her bedroom, feeling tiredness set back in. She'd been alert while dealing with Ariane and Howard's crisis, but the excitement hadn't dispelled her weariness, just displaced it for a while.

She put on her nightdress and crawled beneath her blankets, shivering while her body gradually warmed the freezing sheets. A fleeting thought of having someone else in her bed with her, warming her, set her heart pounding for a few beats before she controlled herself. She curled into a ball and hugged her knees.

This hadn't been a physical fling, easily discarded and almost as easily gotten over. Veronica thought back through all her interactions with Harrison, starting with the moment she'd stood up to ask a question in his lecture hall. She couldn't put her finger on when it had happened, but it was obvious now that she'd been drawn to him from the start. All those times she'd defended him to her friends...seeking him out because of the murder, then seeking him out because she wanted his company...their first kisses in his office had been powerful not just because she'd gone five years, nearly, without romantic intimacy of any kind, but because she loved him.

It had taken her a year to realize she cared more deeply for Landon than she did anyone else, and another three months to recognize that feeling as love. And after that, it had been another three years before she'd learned Landon really did love her instead of seeing her as a dynastic obligation as she'd always assumed. Veronica hadn't believed she would ever fall in love again, but whenever the idea crossed her mind, she'd figured a new romance would pattern itself after the old. But what she had with Harrison—what she'd had, past tense, she corrected herself—was so different, and so unexpected, it was no wonder she hadn't known the truth.

She was grateful she hadn't realized she was in love when they'd said their final goodbyes. If she'd even suspected there was more to their relationship than attraction, she might have agreed to Harrison's proposed affair. That would have been disastrous. Veronica was under no illusions about how difficult it was to keep important secrets. She'd seen too many people's lives ruined by lying and stealing and infidelity to want to walk that road.

Warmer now, she uncurled and tucked the blankets under her chin. It didn't matter. They couldn't be together, and whatever she felt for Harrison would eventually fade, though not as quickly as she'd imagined. She let herself cry a few self-indulgent tears before her weariness claimed her, and she slept.

VERONICA WOKE FEELING MORE RESTED THAN SHE HAD IN DAYS. For a few blissful moments, she didn't remember anything about the last few days. Then memory asserted itself, and her heart constricted with the knowledge that it was broken. She would have to see Harrison this morning and pretend he meant nothing to her. To her surprise, she didn't weep. If she was lucky, her heart had already begun to mend. She was sure she wasn't that lucky.

Snow had fallen the previous night, blanketing the buildings and the yard and eliminating every trace of the gravel paths. When Veronica emerged from Patience House to attend her first lecture, students had made their own paths, trampling down the snow into a thick dull crust. It wasn't beautiful, but it wasn't slush, either, and Veronica stood a moment watching people walk past and admiring the tiny icicles no bigger than the first joint of her pinky that hung from every eave. Winter might not be so terrible.

She reached Lyton Hall earlier even than usual and settled into her seat. She was alone in the lecture hall except for a couple of young men who sat close together and stared at her as if she was still a novelty. When she glanced their way, they quickly turned their heads and pretended not to notice her regard. Young people could be so silly.

The lecture hall gradually filled. Veronica doodled in the margins of her blank book, wishing she'd dared skip this class. The lectern in the center of the platform loomed large at the edges of her vision. Harrison must be tall indeed not to be dwarfed by it. Of course he was tall; they were the same height. She was being as silly as the young people.

The room was nearly full. The women sitting on Veronica's left had their heads together for some murmured conversation Veronica didn't try to overhear. She traced another near-perfect circle and filled it with smaller circles. If the bell didn't ring soon, she would go mad, run screaming from the room and fling the contents of her satchel across the courtyard.

The great bell atop the bethel rang at that moment. Veronica straightened and told her stupid heart to stop hammering at her. She was a grown woman, not a silly child, and she could look at Harrison without falling to pieces.

But the door at the back of the platform didn't open. No

Harrison entered the lecture hall, black book in hand. Veronica looked at Master Herewiss, sitting on the front row all the way to the right, and at Master Averill Cates, sitting two places down from him. They were looking at each other, though Veronica couldn't see their expressions from her seat. Then Herewiss moved to sit beside Averill Cates, and the two of them put their heads together. They were probably talking, but a murmur of voices had risen to drown them out, filling the lecture hall as students speculated on what could have caused Master Tyndale, of all people, to miss the opening bell.

"You think he's finally cracked?" the woman immediately on Veronica's left whispered to her friend.

"Maybe the Magister got fed up with his behavior and fired him," the friend whispered back.

"That's never going to happen. Maybe his poisonous tongue got him in trouble with someone who beat the stuffing out of him, and he's too embarrassed to show his face."

Veronica bit her lip to keep from snapping at the women. All their suppositions were impossible, but there was a real reason Harrison might be in trouble with the Scholia, and that was if the Magister found out he was still investigating the deaths. Veronica didn't know the Magister well, but she knew men and women like him, quick to react out of fear when their lives or livelihoods were threatened. Even so, it wasn't likely the Magister would terminate Harrison's position without providing an alternate instructor. Students paid too much for this education to put up with erratic instruction.

Five very long minutes after the bell rang, the door slammed open. Harrison strode through, his stole flapping with the speed at which he entered. Veronica had begun coming up with increasingly awful and improbable scenarios, and she was so relieved to see him she didn't remember to be flustered.

Harrison slapped his black book on the lectern loudly enough to cut across the remaining chatter. He didn't look at Veronica at all. "Today we will discuss the standards for sentencing," he said, his voice as unemotional as ever. "The first codified rules for determining the type and length of a criminal sentence were laid out by the Veriboldan legal authority Han La, who wrote..."

Veronica took notes, but her heart wasn't in it. Harrison sounded impassive, but his jaw was set tight and his eyes had a depth to them that meant he was very upset about something. Her nerves began twanging. If the Magister was aware of Harrison's ongoing investigation, he might have punished Harrison some way other than firing him. Veronica didn't think it would be easy to replace Harrison mid-term, and maybe the Magister had taken that into account. But she didn't know what that punishment might be and had no way of guessing.

She made herself focus on the back of Master Averill Cates' head to keep her thoughts from spinning around and around her suppositions. The woman had styled her hair in an elaborate braid that from this distance looked like a single fat strand woven into an intricate pattern. Veronica tried following it to its end, got distracted, tried again. She made a few more notes. Would this lecture never end?

Finally, the bell over the door jangled, and Harrison finished his sentence, slammed his book closed, and disappeared through the door at the back of the platform. Veronica put her book and pencil away and fastened her satchel. That had been the most harrowing hour of her life, not counting when she'd given birth.

She crossed the yard without staying on the gravel paths, her thoughts still distracted. She wished more than ever she could talk to Harrison. Anything that made him so angry had to be terrible indeed.

A young man in Scholia colors, red and black, stood at the refectory door. He appeared to be searching the crowds for someone. When his gaze lit on her, he came forward and saluted her. "Lady North," he said, "the Magister would like a moment of your time in his office."

"What, now? It's dinnertime," Veronica said.

"Even so, my lady." The young man bowed. "I'm afraid I'm just an aide, and the Magister didn't confide in me his intent. Do you know the way, or would you like a guide?"

"I know the way. Thank you." Veronica watched him run off, but didn't immediately follow. Surely Harrison wouldn't have implicated her in his investigation? And yet she couldn't think of any other reason for the Magister to summon her.

She took firm hold of herself and gave herself a mental shake. This summons didn't have to be about anything awful. It was more likely to have something to do with her bequest. Or possibly the Magister wanted to enlist her help in petitioning Elspeth about the endowment. But a chill, deep inside her, told her it wouldn't be that simple. Something was wrong.

She walked at a normal pace across the courtyard to Godfrey Hall, her feet crunching on the packed snow. Her boots had held up to the Autumn weather so far, but her toes were cold, and she told herself she should get thicker socks, or wear two pairs. It was easier to think about than speculating on what might await her in the Magister's office.

The Magister's secretary didn't react as if Veronica was in trouble. "You're to go right in, Lady North," she said, and immediately returned her attention to the stack of papers in front of her. That made Veronica feel less nervous. If it were something truly dire, it was likely the secretary would have caught wind of it.

She entered the office and gently closed the door behind her. The Magister stood at one of his enormous windows, looking out over the courtyard. "What a mess," he said without turning around. "All those footprints. The gravel paths will be ruined come Spring."

"That hadn't occurred to me," Veronica said. "I suppose all those people, walking wherever they want…"

"Exactly." The Magister turned and sat behind his desk, gesturing for Veronica to sit opposite him. He shifted some pens and an inkwell, rather nervous gestures, Veronica thought. She glanced around rather than stare at him and potentially make him more nervous. The room was more cluttered than when she'd been there last, with a couple of lidless wooden crates, far rougher than any of the baroque furniture, pushed into a corner next to the sideboard and a stack of cardboard folders on the corner of the desk. As Veronica had always considered the Magister tidy to the point of obsession, this struck her as odd. But she herself was too nervous to draw any conclusions.

Finally, the Magister's gaze fixed on her. "Do you know why I've asked you here, Lady North?"

"I don't, Magister."

His eyes narrowed. "There's nothing you'd like to tell me?"

Veronica, puzzled, shook her head. This didn't sound like it was related to the investigation.

The Magister laced his fingers together and rested his hands on his desktop. "If you're honest with me, this will be much easier. I ask again, is there something you'd like to tell me?"

"Magister," Veronica said, her nerves failing her, "I really have no idea what you're talking about. Have I done something wrong?"

"I see," the Magister said. "I'm sorry you've chosen not to be open with me."

"I *am* being open with you! Please, just tell me. What should I have said?"

The Magister let out a deep breath. "You should have confessed," he said, "to carrying on an affair with Master Harrison Tyndale."

25

"What?" Veronica exclaimed. "But I—was someone *spying* on us?"

She knew immediately that had been the wrong thing to say. The Magister's frown deepened. "Then you do admit to it."

Veronica's heart hurt from beating so hard, both from fear and anger. Who had dared...oh. The doorkeeper. He'd been right outside the tiny meeting room in Justice House when Veronica and Harrison had been kissing and talking stupid romantic talk. She could easily imagine him pressing his ear to the door to listen in.

An unexpected fury swept over her. "I don't know what you think you know," she said, her voice shaking, "but it's not what you believe."

"I know you and Master Tyndale have spent a great deal of time in one another's company over the past few weeks," the Magister said. He picked up a pen and restlessly tapped its nib against the desk. "And you were heard speaking to each other in a way that proved your romantic attachment."

"I can't believe you would give credence to evidence gained illicitly."

"How else should I have learned of it if you concealed your actions? Lady North, this is a serious situation. Instructors and students are forbidden to enter into liaisons. It's unprofessional and dishonorable and leads to favoritism. It compromises the reputation of this institution."

"We haven't done anything wrong."

The Magister's pen stopped tapping. He leaned forward. "Lady North," he said, "if you believe your rank puts you outside the rules, I assure you that is not the case. I will not have this Scholia be a laughingstock as we enforce the rules only when it suits us. I don't know how you can continue to protest innocence when you've been caught, but it's shameful of you."

Veronica rose. She clenched her hands to keep them from shaking. "It's true Harrison and I share deeper feelings than those of teacher and student," she said. "The details are none of your business. But we never did anything to reproach ourselves for, and we broke the relationship off because we knew it was against Scholia rules. Ended it completely."

"And yet you are still in Master Tyndale's law lecture."

"That isn't against the rules."

"It doesn't help your case, Lady North." The Magister stood as well. He was a few inches shorter than Veronica, but he stood as if he towered over her. "I have already told Master Tyndale that his position here will be terminated as soon as we can find a replacement. I am seriously considering expelling you as well."

"That is so unfair," Veronica breathed. "We did the right thing, and you're punishing him for a few days of breaking the rules?"

"We can't show leniency. That leads to chaos. Everyone believes their sins shouldn't be punished so long as they didn't actually mean any harm."

Veronica glared at him, at his stern visage and grim mouth, and realized the truth. "This is because Harrison wouldn't stop investigating the murders," she said. "You weren't satisfied with ordering him to stop. You want him gone so he can't bring any more shame down on the Scholia."

"Do not make unwarranted accusations, Lady North. You don't understand the situation at all."

"I understand that you're taking advantage of a technicality to get rid of a troublesome Master," Veronica shot back. "Your best law instructor, too. Replacing him is going to be a nightmare. Pardon me for not commiserating."

"Watch yourself, Lady North. Your position here is tenuous. I choose to believe you were seduced—"

"Excuse me?" Veronica demanded. "My part in our relationship was—"

"Don't say anything that will force me to expel you," the Magister warned. "Dowager Consort or no, you don't want the scandal that will ensue. I—"

The door opened. "Magister, there's—" the secretary began.

"I've said we weren't to be interrupted, Dorothy," the Magister said. He sounded calmer than he looked.

Dorothy didn't hesitate. "Yes, Magister, but it's the bursar, and you said he was to be admitted immediately he arrived."

The Magister swore under his breath. "Wait here," he told

Veronica. "This isn't over." He strode from the room after one last glare at her.

Veronica remained standing, still shaking, after he'd left. How dare that petty, greedy little man threaten her? And yet he had all the power. The knowledge that she could be punished for giving up the man she loved burned inside her. Damn him and his pride. She didn't blush at thinking the profanity. If there was ever a time for profanity, this was it.

She sank back into her seat and glared at the Magister's chair as if he were still sitting in it. There had to be something she could do to convince him. Harrison shouldn't lose his position just because the Magister was afraid.

Five minutes passed, and the Magister did not return. Veronica grew bored and achy from the uncomfortable antique chair. She stood and stretched stiff muscles, then prowled the room, examining the baroque lines of the cabinets and chairs. The Magister ought to be ashamed at having forced the Treasury to pay for his expensive antiques. It wasn't as if they were necessary to his job.

She walked from one end of the window bank to the other, trailing her fingers along the windowsills and looking out over the snow-packed courtyard. Her watch told her it was almost noon and dinner would be about to start. She was too angry and afraid to feel hunger.

Her foot kicked something hard. She looked down and saw the two lidless wooden crates that were so out of place in the Magister's baroque den. A paper lay atop the contents of one of them. Idly, Veronica picked it up. *Sort for personal effects to return to Mister Dunn's family*, it read.

Interesting. These were Carlton's things. Why they were in the Magister's office, she didn't know, but if they contained anything relating to his "suicide," possibly the Magister hadn't wanted them out where they could be tampered with.

Veronica lifted the scarf that lay beneath the note. She was snooping, yes, but at the moment she didn't care. It wasn't as if Carlton was in a position to protest the invasion of his privacy. And the Magister wasn't likely to become more angry with her no matter what she did.

This couldn't be all of Carlton's worldly possessions. There was the scarf, and a box that proved to contain a selection of tie pins, all of them tasteful, and some notebooks and textbooks in the first crate. And a folded piece of paper, lying flat against one of the crate's sides. Veronica unfolded it.

I can't go on like this, it read. *I acted rashly and a man is dead.*

It was the suicide note. Veronica reflexively folded the paper, averting her eyes. Then curiosity got the better of her, and she unfolded it again. She read another line—and stopped. Her heart, which had finally calmed down, sped up again. She examined the paper closely. Surely someone had noticed what was wrong with the note?

She swiftly went to the door and had her hand on the door-knob when the door swung open, hitting her arm and making her exclaim in pain. "Lady North," the Magister said, "you weren't leaving, were you? I told you, our conversation is not over."

"I have to see Harrison at once," Veronica said.

The Magister's scowl returned. "Lady North, have you no shame?"

Veronica rolled her eyes. "This is not about me, it's about Carlton Dunn's murder. I need to find Harrison immediately."

Instantly, the Magister's demeanor went cold. "Mister Dunn committed suicide. I didn't think you would stoop to entertaining wild speculations just to distract me from the issue at hand."

Veronica thrust the paper at him. "Didn't anyone look at this suicide note?"

"Lady North, are you out of your mind? Many people looked at it. Or are you questioning its validity as Master Tyndale did?"

"Of course I am," Veronica said. "This isn't Carlton's hand-writing."

Just then, the great bell atop the bethel tolled noon, signaling the start of the dinner hour. It was such perfect timing Veronica felt it had rung in vindication of her.

The Magister's eyes narrowed. "You *are* out of your mind. Of course it's his."

"No, it's not." Veronica dug in her satchel. It was overfull, as usual, with blank books and too many pencils. Impatient, she strode to the Magister's desk and upended the satchel over its gleaming surface. Pencils bounced everywhere; blank books slid across each other in an untidy pile. Veronica sorted through them until she found her law book. She roughly shook it, and a loose sheet of paper fluttered out.

She snatched it up and returned to where the Magister still stood by the door as if rooted there. "*This* is Carlton's handwrit-ing," she said, shoving it at him. "He wrote that while I watched him."

The Magister took the page. "There are two handwritings here. This is hardly proof."

Veronica felt like strangling the man. "Mine is the other one. I wrote a list of questions I had about my law class, and Carlton wrote references where I could find the answers. It's his handwriting. And it looks nothing like what's on the note."

The Magister took the suicide note and held the two papers side by side. "It still means nothing," he said. "Some people's handwriting improves when they want it to. This matches the handwriting on every assignment Mister Dunn turned in this term. It's definitely his."

Exasperated, Veronica said, "No, that just means whoever wrote the note wrote his—"

Her face went numb with shock. "Oh, dear heaven," she whispered. "I think I know who killed him."

"Lady North, you're delusional. You should go to the infirmary." The Magister didn't sound very certain. Veronica ignored him.

She snatched the suicide note out of his hand and pushed past him, running for the outer door. The secretary looked up, then quickly looked away, reddening as she had not before. Veronica realized she and the Magister hadn't spoken very quietly when discussing Veronica's sins. So her "affair" with Harrison wasn't a secret any longer. It didn't matter. She had a killer to catch.

She ran down the stairs, her knees twinging as they usually did when she descended stairs too quickly, then dashed along the corridor, shoving past people without even a sidelong apology until she reached the administrative office. At this time of day, it was fuller than usual of students taking advantage of the dinner hour to handle their non-academic business. For a moment, Veronica hesitated, thwarted by the sea of petitioners. Then she drew in a deep breath and plunged into the crowd.

She pushed her way past several students, all of whom protested at her rudeness, until she reached the wide counter that divided the room in half. "I need to find Master Tyndale," she panted. "It's an emergency. You must have his schedule."

The man behind the counter looked at her skeptically. "His schedule is posted in Lyton Hall. If you're his student, you should know that, Lady North."

Veronica felt like screaming. "I don't mean his class schedule, I mean—look, can you tell me where he has his dinner? Or whatever it is he does during this hour?"

The man shook his head. "That's not available to students. The instructors don't need to be plagued with questions on their private time."

Veronica leaned forward. "What's your name?"

"Gavin Beltrane, Lady North." He looked surprised that he'd responded so readily.

"Gavin Beltrane," Veronica said, "who am I?"

Gavin swallowed and glanced quickly to either side as if he thought this was a trick question. "You're...Lady North, of course."

"I am the Dowager Consort, Gavin," Veronica said. "I rank so far above you you'll need a stepladder a mile high to come close to where I stand. Now, tell me where to find Master Tyndale, or heaven help me, I will see you ruined."

Gavin blanched. "He should be dining at Justice House," he whispered.

"Thank you, Gavin. I appreciate your help," Veronica said. The politeness was an afterthought. Urgency flooded her veins and made her thoughts buzz so rapidly they were a white blur.

She turned to find the crowd behind her had gone still. All of them were watching her in varying degrees of fear and awe. For once, Veronica felt no anxiety at being stared at. She swept out of the room, her head held high. No one got in her way.

She ran as fast as she could for Justice House, slipping twice on the packed snow and catching herself before she could fall.

The door was locked, as usual. She yanked on the knob anyway and pounded on the door so hard it made her fist tingle.

The door creaked open slowly. "You don't have to—oh," the doorkeeper said.

"Yes, it's me," Veronica said. "You eavesdropped on me and Master Tyndale, didn't you? And then you ran like a rat to the Magister and told him everything you thought you knew."

"It's you should be ashamed," the doorkeeper said, lifting his chin defiantly though his face was red with embarrassment. "We have rules for a reason."

"You should have listened to the whole conversation, if you meant to be a thorough-going snitch." Veronica itched to slap him. "You missed the important part."

She shoved past the doorkeeper into the tiny entrance chamber. "Where's your dining room? I need to speak to Master Tyndale."

The doorkeeper laughed. "Brazen, aren't you? Well—"

She rounded on him. "Spare me the lecture. Just tell me where it is, or I will open every door in this place until I find it."

"You wouldn't dare," the doorkeeper said.

"Watch me," Veronica retorted. She took two steps toward him until she could loom over him as she had the Magister. "You forget to whom you are speaking."

The doorkeeper flinched as if he'd suddenly remembered she was no ordinary student. "It won't do you any good. He's not here."

Veronica, taken aback, said, "Then where is he?"

"He went into Knightsbury. Didn't say why. I don't know where in Knightsbury and I don't know when he's coming back, so don't come over haughty with me." He swallowed. "I was just doing my duty."

"I fail to see how it is your duty to spy on a Master," Veronica said coldly. "If anyone should be ashamed, it's you." She was sure she couldn't wait in Justice House for Harrison's return, not with the hostile doorkeeper still hovering nearby within reach of the flat of her palm. "Tell Master Tyndale he's to join me at Patience House as soon as he returns. It's urgent. And if I find out you didn't give him that message or delayed it in any way, I will not rest until I see you fired. Are we clear, master doorkeeper?"

The doorkeeper swallowed again. His antagonism had vanished as he shrank in on himself, visibly alarmed at her threat. "Yes, Lady North. And...I'm sorry."

"You certainly are," Veronica said, and slammed the door behind her.

She trudged back to Patience House. She wanted to protect her precious evidence by meeting with Harrison in her rooms, but he wouldn't be allowed past the first floor. It would have to be in one of the sitting rooms, insecure and too public, as soon as he returned. She didn't think she could bear the agony of waiting. But the alternative was to take a carriage into Knightsbury and wander the streets crying Harrison's name, and that was pointless as well as ridiculous. She would just have to wait.

The entry hall was once more empty when Veronica let herself in. On a whim, she knocked on the chatelaine's door. Presently, it opened, and a strange woman looked out at her. "Lady North," she said. "Can I help you with something?"

"Who are you?" Veronica asked, too overwhelmed for politeness.

"I'm Miss Armant, the new chatelaine." The woman smiled at Veronica. "Mistress Holyoak had to leave unexpectedly. I hope that's not a problem."

"Of course not," Veronica said, managing not to let out an exultant whoop. She was overwhelmed, not mad. "I'm sure it will be lovely getting to know you."

"I look forward to serving the ladies of Patience House," Miss Armant said. "Now, if there's nothing else...?"

"Actually, there is. I'm expecting Master Tyndale sometime soon." She hoped it was soon. "Would you show him to the east drawing room when he arrives? And send someone to my room to fetch me there?"

"Are you sure you wouldn't prefer another room? That one is freezing." Miss Armant looked as if she felt Veronica deserved better, not because she was the former Consort, but because she was a person. Her concern cheered Veronica.

"No, I think I need somewhere cold for this," she said. She hoped the chill and the draft in the east drawing room would ensure their privacy. For this, they needed it more than ever.

She hurried down the hall, rubbing her arms as if she was already waiting in the cold drawing room. Harrison couldn't take more than an hour, could he? Even if he was a slow eater. She wondered why he'd gone into Knightsbury for dinner. Maybe the news about their relationship had already spread, and he didn't want to be stared at. She could hardly blame him. She couldn't imagine the Magister's secretary wouldn't tell everyone she met, either. The idea of facing her friends, who'd always been so vocal about their dislike of Harrison, filled Veronica with a different kind of dread. She could imagine what they'd say. Well, if Harrison presented the Magister with a murderer, maybe they'd be too busy talking about that to criticize her.

She ascended the stairs quickly, meeting no one on her way. Everyone must be at dinner. Her stomach chose that moment to growl at her. Apparently it hadn't gotten the message that she was too anxious for food.

She couldn't believe the evidence had been there the whole time. If only she'd arrived at the Lyton Hall library five minutes earlier the day Carlton died, she would have seen the suicide note then, and everything would have turned out so differently. She glanced at the note again, at the unfamiliar but graceful handwriting. Maybe she was wrong, but she couldn't help remembering something Bec had said once about her relation-ship with Carlton. If that were true, then only one person could have murdered Carlton and Ian both.

"Veronica!"

Veronica froze. "Samantha," she said, turning around slowly. "Why aren't you at dinner?"

"I was, but I have the worst headache," Samantha said. She stood in the doorway of the washroom Veronica had just passed, rubbing her left temple. "I thought I'd make myself some tea and see if I can't get it to go away before my next class."

Veronica made herself stand very still, though she didn't know why she thought that would help. Samantha surely couldn't intuit what was going through Veronica's head at the moment.

Her hand closed more tightly on the suicide note, which she hadn't put into her pocket. Samantha's gaze flicked to it. Her eyes narrowed. "What's that?"

"Nothing. Just some notes." She silently willed Samantha into her room and out of sight. Glancing down at it, she realized she was holding the note so the writing was clearly visible. She folded it quickly and began to tuck it away.

Fast as a snake, Samantha was at her side, grabbing her

wrist. "Just notes?" Veronica was too slow to prevent her snatching the paper away. It tore as Veronica tried to hold onto it, leaving Veronica with one corner.

Samantha opened the paper and read its contents. "This is Carlton's suicide note," she said. "Why do you have this?"

Veronica couldn't think of any excuse to give. "It's not important. You should go get that tea."

Samantha fixed her eyes on Veronica's. She was shorter, but more heavily built, and her grip on Veronica's wrist was hard and painful. "I wonder," she said, "what you think you know."

"I don't know what you're talking about," Veronica said. She tried to wrench her wrist away, but Samantha held her fast. "Let go, Samantha, you're hurting me."

Samantha's smile wasn't the least bit friendly. "I think it's time," she said, "we had a little talk."

26

*V*eronica yanked away from Samantha, again with no results. "I don't understand," she lied. "Why are you doing this? And why do you care about the suicide note?"

Samantha began walking toward the southwest tower, towing Veronica along with her. "I think you know why," she said. "You're wrong, whatever you believe, but I can see why you think you're right. Let's just sit and chat."

Veronica thought about screaming. So far, Samantha hadn't done anything to threaten Veronica with actual violence. It was barely possible Veronica could bluff her way out of this situation, but only if she kept her head now. She stopped struggling and followed Samantha to the tower door.

Once inside, Samantha took the key from Veronica's hand and locked the door, then slipped the key into her pocket. "That's better," she said. "I'd rather we weren't disturbed, don't you agree?"

"I'll make tea. I have something for a headache," Veronica volunteered.

Samantha laughed. "Do you know, it's almost gone now? Excitement seems to have rid me of it. But I think you should definitely make tea." She let go of Veronica's wrist and sat on the sofa, the suicide note crumpled in one hand.

Veronica turned on the burner and set the kettle to boil. She stayed near it, as far as she could get from Samantha that wasn't up the stairs. "I'm not sure I understand. Are you not feeling well? Because you're talking nonsense."

"Veronica," Samantha said. "Oh, Veronica. You figured it out, didn't you?"

"Figured what out?" Veronica said, feeling desperate.

In a flash, Samantha leapt from the sofa and shoved Veronica into the bookcase. Books fell, and the statuette of *Giselle* wobbled and hit the ground by Veronica's feet. "Don't act stupid," Samantha snarled. "You think I killed Carlton. And if you think that, you believe I killed Ian, too."

Veronica kept her gaze fixed on Samantha, hoping she didn't look as terrified as she felt. She'd been so stupid. "I don't think anything. Let me go."

Samantha smiled again. "You weren't fooled by the note. How did you figure it out? I've been copying Carlton's papers for him since last Summer term. As far as anyone knows, that's his handwriting."

Veronica gave up. "He made notes for me when he helped me study."

"Did he? Such a small thing." Samantha released Veronica and stepped away. "And now you think I killed him."

Veronica rubbed her shoulder where she'd banged it against the bookcase. She assessed her chances at reaching the door before Samantha caught her. Samantha's attention seemed directed inward, but with her pacing the sitting room, they weren't good chances. Veronica took a sideways step toward the door. Samantha's head came up. The look in her eyes frightened Veronica. It made her friend, if she was still that, look nothing like herself.

"Sit there," Samantha ordered, pointing a finger at a chair next to the table. "I don't want you getting any ideas about leaving in the middle of our conversation. Who did you tell?"

Veronica sat, keeping her eyes on Samantha the way she would a deadly snake. "The Magister. He knows everything."

Samantha laughed. "That old fool? He doesn't care if a thousand students die so long as his precious Scholia survives. I bet he didn't believe you."

"Of course he did. I showed him Carlton's handwriting. His real handwriting." But she hadn't mentioned Samantha's name because she'd been so shocked by the realization. She hadn't told anyone the identity of Carlton's killer. Her message to Harrison had been vague. And no one except Miss Armant, who had no reason to suspect danger of Samantha, knew where Veronica was. She'd been even stupider than she'd realized. Her only hope now was to keep Samantha talking until someone came to summon Veronica downstairs to meet Harrison. Which could be hours from now. Veronica felt sick.

Samantha glanced at the suicide note. Then she pressed the corner of it to the hot burner and waited for it to catch fire. "The Magister may believe your story that someone other than Carlton wrote this note," she said, "but now you have no proof it was me. And without proof, it's just your word against mine. Even the word of the Dowager Consort isn't enough to convict someone of murder."

"It's still a strong witness," Veronica said. "And once Master Tyndale learns the truth, he'll find other evidence. You have to give yourself up, Samantha. It's just going to be worse if you...if you do anything else." She didn't want to give Samantha ideas by telling the woman not to hurt her.

Samantha's attention was still on the burning paper in her hand. When it burned down nearly to nothing, she shook out the fire and popped the remaining corner into her mouth. Chewing, she said, "You're so considerate. It's why I like you. I wish it hadn't been you who found out the truth. Really, it was the perfect plan. Though it would have been more perfect if Carlton hadn't tried to blackmail me over Ian's death."

Veronica let out a shallow, long breath. "Why would he do that? He should have—" She shut her mouth. She wanted to keep Samantha talking, not antagonize her with reminders of the justice she deserved.

"Carlton always was a fool. Though a handsome fool." Samantha smiled in reminiscence. "He knew I'd killed Ian, and he threatened to expose me if I didn't pay him off. So greedy."

"And you poisoned him and made it look like suicide."

"Nobody ever realizes the kind of access we biology students have to all sorts of poisonous substances." Samantha's smile widened. "Though it's hard to poison someone without them realizing. I gave him a dose of something relatively harmless that made him ill, then offered to give him the antidote if he swore never to tell what he knew."

Veronica's gorge rose. "And the 'antidote' was the real poison."

Samantha applauded. "I knew you were smart. Oh, Veronica, it's been so hard not being able to tell anyone how cleverly I managed all this. It was the perfect plan."

Now Veronica was sure Samantha was mad—a very well-concealed, sociopathic kind of madness. She remembered all the times they'd sat together, all the times she'd comforted Samantha in her apparent grief, and anger began to take the place of revulsion. She concealed her rising fury and said, "So you did kill Ian. Why? Did you want his Devisery that much?"

Samantha looked at her as if she were the mad one. "Why would I want his Devisery? He dumped me, Veronica. Told me it was over, that he'd met someone else and we were done. How dared he do that? I'm the one who's supposed to do the dumping. I tried to find out who the other woman was, but he was too cautious. I think he knew I was dangerous. He just didn't know what to fear."

"I see," Veronica said. "So you went to his workshop and killed him. I must have just missed you that night."

Samantha grinned like a child and bounced a little on the balls of her feet. "No, don't you see, that was the clever part! I dosed him with strikewort over the course of a couple of weeks. It destroys the lungs from the inside and looks like a perfectly natural death. I just had to wait him out."

"But...Ian was killed by a blow to the head. Not poison."

The grin fell away. "That was Carlton's stupid interference. Apparently he went to Ian's lab to warn him to stay away from me, like the strutting peacock he was, and Ian died in front of him. Carlton guessed what had happened and of course immediately jumped to the conclusion that I was responsible. And the fool decided he could make money twice—by selling the Devisery and by blackmailing me. He told me he bashed Ian's head in to make it look like a break-in. Then he took Ian's notes and came straight to me."

Veronica nodded. "I understand. That really was stupid. He

had no proof you'd poisoned Ian. But you didn't need to kill him. You could have turned him in. As far as anyone knew, he was Ian's murderer."

"I don't let men dictate my life, Veronica, you know that." The kettle began to whistle, and Samantha nodded at it. "Why don't you make us some tea? All this talking has made me thirsty."

Veronica rose from her seat and busied herself with the tea caddy. Her mind went frantically over her options. Where was Harrison? She didn't think, after Samantha's story, that she was in danger of being attacked physically. Samantha clearly had a poisoner's mindset. But even if she didn't kill Veronica, she might still escape, and that was unacceptable.

She poured tea with a shaking hand and handed a cup to Samantha. "So why don't you leave? You can escape. No one knows to suspect you yet."

Samantha reached inside her shirt and took out a thin copper phial the length of her pinky finger. "I'm just going to make sure I get a good head start." She unstoppered the phial and dumped its contents, a pale blue powder that glittered in the sunlight, into the cup. Then she extended it to Veronica. "Drink this."

"Are you—" Veronica swallowed the word *mad*. "I'm not going to poison myself!"

"It's not poison. Just a sleeping draught. You'll be perfectly safe." Samantha smiled, a friendly, nonthreatening expression. "I use it myself when I have a restless night."

Veronica looked at the cup, then at Samantha. She knew about Samantha's sleeping powders. She had a deep suspicion this was not one of them. If anyone was likely to carry poison casually on her person, it was Samantha. And there was no way

Veronica would willingly consent to her death, not like poor trusting Carlton, drinking poison he thought would save his life.

She was about to refuse the cup the second time. Samantha couldn't make her drink. Then she realized she'd been stupid again. Just because Samantha hadn't lifted a hand against either of her victims didn't mean she wasn't desperate enough for violence. She was twenty-seven years younger than Veronica and much stronger. And she wasn't going to leave Veronica alive to keep her from escaping.

Stalling for time, she said, "You swear it?"

"Of course. Veronica, you're my friend. I don't want to kill you. I didn't want to kill anyone, but you can see how they forced me into it, can't you?" Samantha's hand on the outstretched cup didn't waver. "Here, we'll trade. You know how I love your tea."

Veronica couldn't think of anything else. She handed her cup over and took Samantha's poisoned one in exchange. Samantha took a long drink. "Oh, that is delicious," she said. "I don't know how you—"

Veronica flung the steaming contents of her cup into Samantha's face and bolted for the door. Samantha screamed. Veronica yanked on the door. It didn't budge. Too late, she remembered Samantha had locked it and taken the key. Then Samantha grabbed hold of her hair and dragged her away from the door. Veronica fought her, clawing at her hands until Samantha let go. She backed away until she was pressed against the door.

Samantha's face was red from burns, and the back of one hand was bleeding. "How could you do that?" she demanded. "I'm your friend. I didn't want to hurt you."

"I'm sure that's not true," Veronica said. "Unlock the door, and run. I won't follow you. You'll have your chance."

"Liar," Samantha said, but without any force behind the word. "Now I'll have to kill you the hard way. I hate the hard way. It's so bloody." She ran at Veronica and slammed her fist into Veronica's stomach.

Pain shot through Veronica's body. She lashed out at Samantha's face with her nails, clawing her again, and managed to dodge a second blow. She twisted to get away from the madwoman and ran for the burner. It had a solid, heat-resistant base—if she could hold it by the base, she could strike Samantha with the heated coil.

Samantha tripped her, and Veronica fell, cracking her left arm against the edge of the table. An even worse pain shattered her forearm, and she cried out and rolled away from Samantha's kick. Cradling her injured arm close to her chest, she scooted back until she was up against the bookcase.

Samantha advanced on her, her bloody and burned face alight with fury. "I can't believe you would betray our friendship," she said. She picked up Veronica's bread knife where it lay on the table next to the remnants of a loaf. "You shouldn't have made me do this."

Veronica's right hand fell on something smooth and cold. She wrapped her fingers around it, registering its contours as the statuette of *Giselle*. Without thinking, she lifted it and swung it at Samantha's head.

The heavy round base connected with the side of Samantha's skull with a meaty thunk. Samantha jerked and collapsed. The bread knife fell from her limp fingers and bounced away under the table. Samantha's head hit the floor, and she sprawled, limp and unmoving, just two feet from where Veronica crouched.

Breathing heavily, Veronica dropped *Giselle* and edged close to Samantha. The thought that she might have killed her was a distant terror, made unreal by the knowledge that Samantha would surely have killed her. She felt along Samantha's head and found a lump forming, then gingerly touched her throat, looking for a pulse. It was weak, but it was there, and Samantha was still breathing. Veronica let out a shaky, relieved sigh.

She stood unsteadily and retrieved the knife, thinking if Samantha were to recover soon, she didn't want to leave the madwoman a weapon. Then she dug through Samantha's pocket for the key. A flash of memory of crouching over Ian's body to take his key ring struck her, and she sucked in a breath and began laughing. She couldn't stop herself. She laughed helplessly, hysterically, until her chest ached and she was shaking again.

Finally, she stood, feeling a hundred years old instead of fifty, and staggered to the door. It took her shaking hand a few tries to unlock the door, but once she was through, she closed it again and leaned against it, breathing heavily. Then she locked the door so there was no chance of Samantha getting free. In passing, she thought about the possibility of Samantha waking and destroying Veronica's rooms in revenge, but she was too weary to worry about possibilities.

She kept her injured arm held close to her chest as she made her way down the stairs. Patience House was as quiet and empty as if this were the fallow time. Of course, it was still the dinner hour. It felt as if that confrontation had gone on forever, but it couldn't have been more than fifteen minutes. Veronica felt another laugh bubble up inside her, but this time she controlled it. She didn't need Miss Armant thinking she was crazy.

Miss Armant found her halfway down the hall from the stairs. "Lady North!" she exclaimed. "What happened?"

Veronica found she didn't know where to start. "Send to Knightsbury for the guards," she finally said. "There's a murderer locked in my room. And I think my arm is broken."

$\mathcal{M}$iss Armant was as sensible and efficient as Veronica had hoped, ordering a carriage to Knightsbury for a detachment of guards, sending to the infirmary for someone to make sure Samantha wouldn't die, and finally summoning the Magister himself. The Magister blustered his way into Patience House five minutes after the guards arrived. "Lady North, if this is an attempt to change my mind," he said.

"Magister, if you can believe that, you are a fool," Veronica said, pain sharpening her response. "Do I look like someone who's lying to get herself out of trouble?" Her hair was a mess, her clothes marked from the scuffle, and she was sure she'd have bruises in the morning.

Just then, Samantha and the guards appeared. The Magister, his mouth open to deliver another criticism, fell silent. Samantha's hands were bound in front of her, and she looked dazed. She didn't acknowledge any of them. Veronica followed the little procession out the door. "I'm going to the infirmary," she told the Magister. "And then I am leaving the Scholia for Aurilien. If I decide to return, I'll let you know."

"But—I told you the decision to expel you is not final."

Veronica stared at him and was pleased to see him flinch. "You needn't bother," she said. "I have grave reservations about any institution so concerned with appearances that it would permit a murderer to go free. And I find you personally repugnant."

She left the Magister sputtering on the doorstep of Patience House and walked into the gathering crowds in the courtyard. Everyone was staring after Samantha and her guards. No one noticed Veronica. That suited her as well as the Magister's reaction.

Veronica had never been to the infirmary, which took up the rear half of the first floor of Covington Hall. The attendant on duty took in her appearance with growing horror and listened to her lies about having fallen with a look of skepticism. But she summoned a doctor, who splinted Veronica's arm in silence. "You'll want to be careful with that for a while," the doctor said when he was finished. "It should be six weeks or so until it's healed. I'll provide you with a sling, and something for the pain."

"It only has to hold until I get to Aurilien," Veronica said. "I'll have the palace healer take care of it."

"You're going home for the midterm holiday?" The doctor stepped back. "That's a long trip for only a few days. There's no healer in Knightsbury, but I'm sure you could find someone in Treston—it's a good deal closer than the capital."

"It's all right. I want to see my family, even if it's only for a day or so," Veronica said. It wasn't any of the doctor's business that Veronica wasn't sure she would return.

She sat on the bed they'd provided her after the doctor left and regarded the room. Only a few of the ten beds were occupied, mostly with sleeping students. The one young man who was awake and had watched the procedure stared at her like a man in a dream, unsure of what he'd seen. Veronica smiled at him, but his expression didn't change. She felt suddenly homesick for a place where no one would look at her as if she was an oddity.

With her arm held snugly to her chest by the sling, she left Covington Hall only to almost run into a trio of students hurrying the other way. "Veronica!" Bec exclaimed. "What happened? Everyone's talking about Samantha Wilde being arrested and you being nearly killed. Are you all right?"

"Just a broken arm." Veronica kept walking, drawing them away from the entrance. "What are they saying?"

"Crazy things," Percy said. He had a firm grip on Bec's hand. "That Samantha tried to kill you. That she killed Ian. What really happened?"

Veronica shivered despite the cloak draped over her shoulders. Thin clouds had risen up to obscure the sun, and the temperature had dropped significantly since that morning. "Can we go somewhere warmer? I'll tell you everything once we're inside."

Patience House was still the center of mad activity despite Samantha being gone, and the refectory was crammed with students who'd had the same idea Veronica had to seek shelter. They ended up in the Lyton Hall law library, which was totally deserted. Veronica sank wearily into a chair far from where Carlton had died. She was surprised to find that the law library otherwise held no horrors, though it was hard not to imagine Samantha handing Carlton the poison he'd willingly drunk.

"Samantha poisoned Ian," she said when they were all settled. "He was dying slowly of it, and it would have looked like a natural death, except for Carlton. He and Ian were in the workshop when Ian died, and Carlton decided to steal the notes and make Ian's death look like the result of the theft."

"That doesn't make any sense," Bridget said. "Or maybe it does. No, I'm right, it makes no sense. Why draw attention to Ian's death? Someone might have eventually tracked Carlton down."

Veronica shook her head. "Carlton guessed what actually killed Ian. He must have known what Samantha was really like, and..." She let out a breath. "I can't believe I was so stupid. You all were very clear about Samantha's nature, and I thought I knew better. I'm so sorry I didn't listen."

"She was good at being nice to the people she thought were important," Bec said, putting a hand on Veronica's. "And I'm sure she actually liked you, so of course you wouldn't see her true self. Don't be embarrassed."

"I know, but...it doesn't matter. Carlton blackmailed Samantha about Ian's murder, and Samantha killed him and made it look like suicide. That's how I figured it out. When I finally saw the suicide note and realized the handwriting wasn't his, I remembered what you'd said, Bec, about Carlton getting his girlfriends to copy out his essays. I knew Samantha was the only woman he'd been close to recently. Everything else followed from there."

"Except it doesn't explain why Samantha attacked you," Percy said. "How did she know you'd found her out?"

"I was stupid." The memory of just how stupid she'd been

made her shiver again, and then she was shaking hard and her friends were all exclaiming over her. "No, it's all right, it's just a delayed reaction," she told them through clenched jaw. "Don't worry about me."

"You could have died, Veronica. We're going to worry a little," Bec said.

"And be grateful you weren't so stupid you told Samantha the truth," Bridget said.

"*Bridget.*"

"It's true, isn't it? Veronica's very smart. And very lucky." Bridget shivered herself. "And—" She stopped, her face going red.

"And, what?" Veronica asked.

The other three fell silent. Percy and Bec exchanged glances. They all had the look of people who were waiting for someone else to speak. Finally, Bec said, "Veronica. You and Master Tyndale? Really?"

It was Veronica's turn to blush. "Really," she confessed.

"But how can you possibly like him? He's terrible," Bridget exclaimed.

"I have to agree with Bridget for once, though I'm sorry she was born without tact," Percy said. "You can't possibly."

"He's not at all what you think," Veronica said. "And I know I said that about Samantha, so you probably think my judgment is suspect, but I promise—" She blinked away tears. "It doesn't matter. It didn't actually go anywhere. So can we just forget about it?"

"Veronica," Bec said, then fell silent. After a moment, she tried again. "Veronica, does the Magister know about this?"

Veronica nodded. "I'm leaving for Aurilien in the morning."

The three burst out in protest. "You can't be expelled for

that, not if you broke it off," Bridget said. "You shouldn't have to go."

"The Magister won't want the former Consort leaving in disgrace," Percy said. "It makes the Scholia look bad. He won't insist you leave."

"It's not up to him. I can't stay." Veronica shrugged, which sent a twinge through her broken arm. "I'm going back to the palace to have my arm healed. I haven't decided if I'm coming back after the holiday."

"You have to come back. What would we do without you?" Bec said.

"Yes, and Howard is so much easier to live with when you're here to keep him in line," Percy said. "Please don't leave."

"Where *is* Howard?" Bec asked, looking around as if she expected him to pop out of the woodwork. "I hope he's not fallen back into despair."

"No, he's fine." Veronica didn't have the energy to explain about Howard and Ariane and the Device. "Though that reminds me I have to speak to someone on his behalf before I go."

"But you'll come back, won't you?" Bridget insisted.

Veronica sighed. "I'll think about it. The Scholia is more corrupt than I imagined, between how the Magister wanted to suppress Har—Master Tyndale's investigation and...well, everything. But I hate to give up on my education a second time."

Bec gripped her hand. "That's a better way to look at it. Go home, be healed, and think it over. Then come back. If Howard really has figured out Ian's Device, you'll want to be here for that."

"That's true," Veronica said.

When the others had left, she went down the hall to

Magister Hanley's office. The head of the law school was in and clearly had not heard any of the commotion, which eased Veronica's mind. He readily agreed to help her with her patent law questions. "I'll set Magister Radholm to work. She's an expert in the field. You're sure you can't give me details?"

"It's a delicate matter. I don't mean to impugn your ability to keep a confidence, but this Device will change the economy forever," Veronica said. "I don't want to risk my friend's future."

"I'm not offended, and you're perfectly right." Magister Hanley winked and smiled. "If it's as important as you say, I'm sure we'll all know the truth before long."

Veronica returned his smile and let herself out.

The bell had tolled for the first afternoon class while she was in Magister Hanley's office, and the courtyard was empty. Veronica trudged across the courtyard back to Patience House. She was missing her engineering lecture, but it wouldn't hurt her ranking to miss just one. She hoped missing tomorrow's classes would be as unimportant, but she couldn't bear staying even one day longer. And if she decided not to return, it wouldn't matter which classes she had or hadn't missed.

There were still students in the halls of Patience House, women who didn't have lectures this hour. All of them stared at Veronica and whispered among themselves, but didn't accost her. She didn't know if they were talking about her fight with Samantha, her affair with Harrison, or just her generally disheveled appearance, but she no longer had the energy to care.

Safely in her room, she stared dully at the mess. Then she wearily began righting furniture and picking up the shattered pieces of the cup she'd flung at Samantha. She put *Giselle* back in her place and was surprised at how heavy the statuette was;

she almost couldn't manage it one-handed. It must have been terror that let her lift it easily enough to strike Samantha. It was also a miracle the statuette's base hadn't crushed Samantha's skull. Now that the crisis was past, Veronica could be grateful she wouldn't have to defend herself against accusations of killing someone.

The idea made her sink onto the sofa, shaking again. She closed her eyes and thought of nothing until the moment passed. Then she climbed the stairs to her bedroom and lay fully-clothed on the bed, staring at the blue gown hanging on the wardrobe.

She hadn't seen Harrison at all since it happened. She didn't even know if he'd returned from Knightsbury yet. She wished he was here and was glad he'd stayed away at the same time. She didn't need the heartache of being reminded of what she couldn't have. Though if she left the Scholia, there was nothing to stand in the way of their relationship, was there?

She closed her eyes again and breathed out, slowly and deeply, until the last vestige of tension flowed out of her. She had been serious about how corrupt the Scholia was. And yet most of the Masters and Magisters had nothing to do with Donald Montgomery's fears and pandering. The students weren't at fault for his actions, either. And she really didn't want to give up on her newly recovered dream. Leaving the Scholia felt like the wrong choice, and yet she didn't know if she could bear to continue.

With indecision ringing through her head, she drifted off to sleep.

VERONICA WENT INTO KNIGHTSBURY THE NEXT MORNING WITH Howard, Pauline Kensington, and Magister Radholm. The round, dark-haired Magister was ten years younger than Veronica and full of exuberant good humor. She also was polite enough not to allude to any of the scandals Veronica had fallen into over the last few days. "That's going to take the world by storm," she said, pointing at the crate by Howard's feet. It took up most of the floor of the carriage and forced the four passengers to sit close together.

"It will," Veronica said. "I hope Mister Miller understands that."

"If he's as canny as you say, he'll appreciate the offer we'll make him," Kensington said.

"He's greedy," Howard said. "I hope he doesn't try to steal it."

"He's greedy, but he's not stupid," Veronica said. "It will be all right, Howard."

The carriage stopped outside Miller's manufactory, and Kensington helped Howard carry the crate into the front office. Flora, the secretary, came to her feet when they entered. "I'll tell Mister Miller you're here," she said, and vanished out the door.

Shortly, Veronica heard footsteps, but it was Ariane and not Miller who entered. The young woman let out a little shriek and flung herself at Veronica.

"You were right about everything," she exclaimed. "Father was so excited about the Device he wasn't even angry I'd concealed my marriage. And he said I could go to Aurilien now instead of waiting! He's even going to pay my way! Of course I'll pay him back, because I hate the thought of being indebted to him, but isn't it thrilling!"

"I'm so glad for you," Veronica said as she hugged the girl, awkwardly due to the sling. She kept her reservations about Ariane's plans to herself. Ariane was an adult and able to learn from her mistakes. And for all Veronica knew, she had a secret gift for business and would thrive in Aurilien.

Heavier footsteps indicated the arrival of Miller. He cast his lowering gaze on each of them in turn, reserving his longest look for Radholm. "Is that it?" he said, pointing at the crate.

"That's it, Mister Miller," Howard said. "Would you like to see it?"

Miller nodded once, curtly. Howard removed the lid, which had had its nails loosened to make that easy, and brushed away the straw the sewing Device was packed in and removed its canvas cover. Miller bent to examine it. "It's not finished," he said.

"There's no case yet, and it will have to be mounted on a table for full efficiency," Howard said. He didn't sound at all nervous. "But it works. Ian's innovation was putting the eye of the needle at the tip and using two threads for the lockstitch instead of one. I worked out how to time the motive force pulses so the upper and lower pieces of the Device work together."

Miller stood. "I'll want to see it work. But..."

"The patents for the individual Devices as well as the Devisery as a whole have been duly registered in Knightsbury," Radholm said. "I'm informed you are interested in investing in the production of the Frost-Peterson Device."

"Who are you?"

"Magister Clare Radholm, law-speaker and patent law expert." Radholm stuck out her hand in a businesslike fashion. "I'm handling legal matters for Mister Peterson and Mistress Frost."

Miller shook her hand brusquely, but he didn't look angry,

just calculating. "I'll expect a reasonable fee for the development," he said. "I'm taking an enormous risk on these Devices. Seamstresses might not want to be put out of business by them."

"So long as we can agree on what 'reasonable' means, I don't think we have a problem," Kensington said. "And you'll have a window of exclusivity on development, which should give you plenty of time to profit before you have rivals."

"I'm sure there's a market for instructional courses in using the new sewing Device," Veronica suggested. "Something you might manage as well."

Miller's eyes gleamed. "That I might, Lady North." He nodded once. "All right. Let's go upstairs and work out a deal."

"Thank you, Mister Miller," Howard said, not quite concealing his eagerness.

"Yes, thank you, Mister Miller," Veronica said with a smile.

Miller turned his attention on her. "I suppose you're responsible for this?"

"It's Howard's Device, Mister Miller."

"And you've been behind him all the way." Miller clapped her familiarly on the shoulder. "Congratulate me on my daughter's marriage. It's too bad Ian didn't live to see this day."

"I agree." Veronica swallowed the lump in her throat. "But I doubt anyone will ever forget his name."

28

Three days later, Veronica sat in the great drawing room of the east wing, staring into the fire that was never extinguished even at Midsummer. She supposed there was some symbolism there. Something about the North dynasty's resilience. Or maybe that Tremontane went on regardless of which family was at its head. At the moment, all she cared about was how it warmed her.

She absently rubbed her left forearm. The healing had been excruciating, but it had only taken a few minutes, and Veronica had been willing to endure a moment's pain in exchange for not having six weeks of aching inconvenience. Almost she wished for the lost days of the Ascendants, when Tremontane had had so many more people gifted with magical healing abilities. Though most of the Ascendants had terrorized the country, so it was just as well they were gone.

It did make her wonder how many people with inherent magic there really were, hiding their talents throughout

Tremontane. Surely most of them had abilities that were no threat to anyone? When she considered how valuable some of those abilities were rumored to be, such as finding lost objects or knowing when someone was lying, she felt it was a shame there was such a general fear of even simple, harmless magics.

She heard footsteps and turned to see Elspeth enter the room. Her niece looked weary, but cheerful. "I'm so glad to have you home," she said. "We've missed you. Did Duncan mention the opera tonight? You're invited."

"Thank you, I'd love to come." Veronica stood and stretched. "I was planning to go for a walk in the garden and then read for a while. It's so strange not to have the demands of classwork and essays regulating my life."

"I understand. I think if I ever had a day off, I wouldn't know what to do with myself." Elspeth continued through the drawing room in the direction of the exit. Veronica picked up her cloak from where it had been warming next to the fire and reveled in the feel of fire-heated wool against her skin.

Snow hadn't yet fallen here in the lowlands, and the garden was wet from the constant rain of mid-Autumn, wet and dreary. Veronica was so glad to be out in the fresh air, she didn't mind how depressing the headless roses and leafless trees were. Today was the first official day of the Scholia midterm holiday, though many students, especially the ones who lived some distance from Knightsbury, left as soon as they could get away on Fifthday. The Scholia seemed so far in the past it was as if she'd already left it forever.

She hadn't yet made her final decision. She'd told Elspeth all that had happened, and Elspeth had been furious. "Donald Montgomery *dared* treat you so disrespectfully!" she'd shouted. "After everything I've done for him. And *spying* on his own people. They make such a big noise about how trusting they are in their students, not giving them curfews and all that, and yet they stoop to eavesdropping! I've a mind to go down there and let the Magister know exactly how displeased I am."

"I won't stop you," Veronica had said, amused despite herself, "but it won't change anything for me. It's still my decision."

She remembered the look Elspeth had given her, the compassionate, knowing look that had shaken Veronica to her core. "What about Harrison Tyndale?" Elspeth had said. "If you don't go back..."

"I know. I'm just not sure I should give up my education for the sake of a man, even one I...care about," Veronica had said. "It's not an easy choice to make."

"Well, I'm on your side and I'll support whatever you decide to do," Elspeth had concluded. "But that's the end of the Magister's hopes for the endowment. Granted, we couldn't afford to give it to him anyway, but even if we could, I certainly wouldn't reward him for his stupid, venal behavior. He can stew in the knowledge that he failed."

The memory of Elspeth's irritation made Veronica smile even as her heart ached. She hadn't seen Harrison at all before leaving. She'd heard from Bec that he had returned late from Knightsbury the day everything had happened and was busy handling the aftermath of Samantha's arrest. It hurt that he hadn't come to see her, though she knew that was impossible. She'd still wanted so badly to let him hold her, to feel his body against hers one last time.

Her toes felt numb and so did her fingers. She flexed both and headed for the door. She needed a cup of hot tea and a good book. Neither of those had ever abandoned her. She remembered pale blue crystals sifting into a teacup and shuddered. The natural philosophy department had tested the residue from the shattered cup as part of the evidence against Samantha. The Master who'd done the testing wouldn't tell her what the substance had been, but he'd looked very ill, and Veronica decided she didn't need to know.

Someone knocked on her sitting room door as she was removing her boots. Her maid Iris entered. "This came for you," she said, extending a card.

Veronica took the card and read, in one heart-stopping moment, the words *Harrison Tyndale, Master.*

"Is he here?" she demanded.

Iris was taken aback by her vehemence. "I suppose so. The messenger said he was waiting for a response."

Veronica rushed to her bedroom and shoved her feet into the first shoes she found. "Thank you, Iris," she said. "I'll go there now."

Iris watched her curiously as she brushed out her hair and pinned it up again. "Shouldn't I do that for you?"

"I don't think I could sit still long enough. It's all right, Iris, I'm used to doing for myself now. Though your work is so much better than mine," she assured the girl as her face fell. It was hard to remember Iris wasn't more than twenty, and very proud of being able to serve the former Consort. Veronica hadn't realized until that moment how much she'd enjoyed her independence at the Scholia, even the small independence of having no maids and cleaning her own rooms.

She ran through the halls of the palace, only slowing when the stitch in her side reminded her she wasn't thirty anymore. Then she walked, sedately, though her insides were skipping about like so many Spring lambs and she was afraid her hair was falling down again.

She paused in the Rotunda, unexpected fear touching her heart. She couldn't understand why Harrison would come here. If he meant to urge her to return to the Scholia...but he'd been dismissed, so why would he care? Unless the Magister had changed his mind once it was evident Harrison had been right about the investigation.

She tipped her head back to look at the ceiling murals of the deeds of Edmund Valant, last of the Valant Kings and a lazy disaster of a monarch who hadn't done even a tenth of what the murals displayed. Veronica had known Willow North's last surviving son, Sebastian, and he'd always said his mother found the murals amusing, which is why she'd never had them painted over. Since they were the work of the famous muralist Garson, Veronica had always been grateful for Willow's robust sense of humor. What an artistic loss that would have been.

The sight of the beautiful art soothed her. Whatever had brought Harrison here, it wasn't his desire to hurt her. She was convinced he would never intentionally do that. She would speak to him, and then make a decision about the Scholia. She hoped it was a decision she wouldn't regret.

The antechamber was empty when she entered it, but two of the doors leading off it were open, and the captain of the guard stationed at the front doors emerged from one of them at Veronica's arrival. "Lady North, you have a visitor. I've asked him to wait here," the woman said.

"Thank you, Captain Dubose, I appreciate it." Veronica waited impatiently for Dubose to open the door to one of the small waiting rooms Elspeth claimed were kept cold on purpose to dissuade casual visitors with unimportant business.

Then Harrison followed the captain into the antechamber, and Veronica had to make herself breathe.

He was dressed formally in coat, waistcoat, and trousers, with his greatcoat over one arm and his hat in his other hand. He looked at her with the same impassive expression he always wore, but his attention on Veronica felt as intense as if he'd kissed her again. He handed his coat and hat to an attendant in North blue and silver, but didn't approach Veronica. The two of them watched each other in silence. Finally, Harrison said, "Lady North. Thank you for agreeing to see me."

"It's my pleasure," Veronica said, feeling as awkward and stiff as if she'd never spoken to him before.

He still didn't move. Veronica's nerves began to get the better of her. "Will you walk with me?" she asked.

"If you wish," Harrison said. He extended his arm to her, and she took it, hiding the thrill that went through her at even that simple touch.

They passed through the Rotunda before Veronica realized she had no idea where they might go for privacy. If he had something unpleasant in mind, she didn't want to hear it in the east wing, and it was too cold outdoors for an extended conversation, not that she knew that was what this visit meant.

And then the perfect place came to her. "This way," she said, steering him off to the left.

"Where are we going?" he asked.

She shook her head. "You'll see."

They walked for about five minutes, gradually moving south and west. The farther they went, the fewer people they saw, until they were alone in a long, empty hallway, their shoes tapping quietly across the white tiles delineated by dark gray grout so the floor looked like a lattice. Paintings hung on the dark red walls, each a masterpiece whose frames alone were works of art. Harrison stopped Veronica once. "Is that *The Lily Pool*? The original?"

"It is. I told you the palace is full of art."

"I know. I just didn't realize how much you meant." He took a step closer to examine the brushwork. "This should be in a museum."

"I agree. But there isn't anywhere with room for it, and Elspeth doesn't have time to commission a new museum, so it stays here for now. I'm sorry."

Harrison shook his head. "You shouldn't apologize to me. It's not as if I'm responsible for the disposition of art throughout Tremontane."

"I just feel slightly guilty at how much I enjoy having it where I can see it whenever I want. When I'm home, I mean." She felt awkward at the sideways allusion to her current predicament, but Harrison didn't comment. "But that's not what we're here for."

"It isn't? That would be more than enough." Harrison let her guide him onward, though he slowed his pace occasionally to admire another painting.

The hallway terminated in a round room with a domed ceiling. Here, the muralist Garson had been at work again, and Veronica had always loved looking at the dome and its depiction of Haran in the Eidestal. Despite her lack of religious feeling, the tale of Haran's journey had always moved her. But the ceiling wasn't why she'd brought Harrison there.

Harrison slipped his arm free from hers and walked toward the statue at the center of the room, moving like a man in a dream. "It's *Xavier*," he said, his voice faint. "Dear heaven. I had no idea how beautiful it was."

Veronica joined him in front of the statue of the warrior, his blade aimed heavenward as if daring the lost gods to come after him. "Look where the sword is pointing," she said.

Harrison turned, his head tilted back. He chuckled. "Is that on purpose?"

Veronica followed the line of the sword to where it pointed directly at Haran on the ceiling. "Harvey d'Arnot carved the statue in place here," she said. "He swore it was coincidence, that he would never blaspheme—though I'm not sure it's actually blasphemy—but I think he meant it to remind the viewer that we are not heaven's pawns. That even Haran could be considered a revolutionary for not being content to go on as people had for centuries before her revelation." She sighed. "I really would like it to go elsewhere, so people can see it, but I'm not sure what that would do to the artistic integrity of the installation."

"When you told me this was in the palace, I was resentful, I admit," Harrison said. "But seeing it now...maybe what you need is some way to direct tours through this wing. I can't imagine moving this anywhere else."

"You may be right. It's a good idea."

Harrison returned to looking at the statue. Veronica watched him instead. She loved the strong line of his jaw and the way his blond hair curled over his ears. She loved everything about him. Anxiety crept over her again. Much as she had enjoyed this moment, she wished he would say what he'd come here to say, and let her get on with her life without him.

"You're staring at me," Harrison said without turning his attention from *Xavier*.

"I am," Veronica admitted. "I'm glad to see you."

"But you're too polite to ask why I've come," he replied. He turned to face her. "I'm glad to see you, too."

Veronica's heart sank. That didn't sound like he cared about her as more than an acquaintance. Clearly he'd come to his senses about the two of them, unlike she, who was foolish and stupid and sentimental. She composed her face in a placid expression that gave none of her inner turmoil away.

"The Magister," Harrison said, his expression still impassive, "was extremely apologetic when I finally met with him the evening after your spectacular capture of Samantha Wilde. He said a number of things that amounted to how he knew I'd been right in pursuing the investigation all along and was grateful the real murderer had been apprehended. Then he told me my dismissal was rescinded and begged me not to leave."

"That's wonderful! Er...is it wonderful? You don't look like you're happy."

Harrison shook his head. "I told him I was resigning, effective immediately."

Veronica's mouth fell open. "You didn't have to do that."

"I did, actually. I didn't want to be accused of impropriety in my behavior."

"I don't understand," Veronica said. "What impropriety?"

Harrison took her hands in both of his. "The impropriety of an instructor courting a student. I assume you're still a student? I suppose, after what I've heard about your interactions with the Magister, that's not a given, but I hope you won't let him drive you away from the Scholia. You're too good for that."

Veronica's face felt numb with shock. "Courting?"

Harrison's wry half-smile made her heart turn over in her chest. "The alternative," he said, taking a step closer, "is going to my knees and begging you to marry me right now. But it's only been a few days since our relationship began, and I thought we should take some time to get to know each other first. And I'll be damned if I go through any more days like I did last week, watching you sit in my lecture hall and being unable to publicly acknowledge how much I love you."

"Harrison," Veronica breathed. Then she threw her arms around his neck and kissed him.

He pulled her as close as he had the first time they'd kissed and returned her kisses with the same wonderful passion she hadn't been able to forget the whole time they'd been separated. "Because I do love you," he whispered between kisses. "You are the most amazing woman I've ever known, and I hope—"

"I love you, too," she said. "In case you were wondering."

His smile broadened. "I was, actually. I didn't think I could bear it if I was the only one."

She rested her forehead against his. "I felt the same. I was so afraid you were here only to tell me...oh, I don't know what I thought."

"I spent the whole journey from the Scholia planning what I would say to convince you to give me another chance. Then I saw you, and everything went straight out of my head. You standing there, so beautiful, like a painting by Maitland—"

Veronica laughed. "Amanda Maitland paints flowers, Harrison."

"I know." He nuzzled her neck. "Tall and slender and pale like a lily, you are. I would give up a thousand teaching positions to have you in my arms for the rest of forever."

Veronica blushed and kissed him harder. "Are you sure you

don't want to marry me immediately? I'm sure Elspeth would be willing to perform the ceremony."

"Married by the Queen? That's an unsettling and compelling thought. But no, my beloved, I would like to wait until Wintersmeet." Harrison withdrew enough that he could look at her with those wonderful glass-green eyes. "I found a place to live in Knightsbury that day, and inquired about positions with local law firms. Though I'm tempted to set up as a criminal investigator on my own. What do you think?"

"I think," Veronica said, "you can do whatever you set your mind to, so long as we're in it together. And Wintersmeet can't get here soon enough."

*V*eronica woke to the sound of Harrison moving around in the kitchen. The delicious smells of coffee, ham, and eggs wafted through the air, and she sat up and felt about with her toes for her slippers. But before she found them, Harrison appeared in the doorway with a large tray that smelled even more delicious up close.

"Breakfast is served," he said. "A special meal for an important day."

Veronica giggled and sat up straighter. "You pamper me."

"Every chance I get." He set the tray on the end of the bed and leaned over for a kiss. "Eat up. We've only got two hours before the ceremony."

Veronica ate ham and eggs with enthusiasm. It had been a relief, when they'd married, that Harrison knew how to cook, and a blessing that he cooked well. Veronica had never cooked a day in her life and was intimidated at the thought of learning how. But Harrison had insisted it was something he enjoyed, and Veronica had turned those duties over to him.

She loved their little house in Knightsbury, even though it made the journey to her Scholia classes more of a chore. Today was the last day she would ever have to worry about that. The thought filled her with mingled excitement and melancholy. She'd worked hard to reach this day, and now she would become a Master, with all that entailed. Another new beginning, this one with a partner she loved more than anything.

Harrison was dressing as she finished her meal. "I can't find anything in the wardrobe," he said. "I'm not sure packing for the move to Aurilien the last week before you graduate was a good idea anymore."

"It was your idea, dearest."

"I know. Sometimes I have bad ideas. Please don't hold that against me." He finished tying his neckcloth and shrugged into his coat.

Veronica came up behind him and put her arms around him. "I want to be there when they finish building my house. It's so exciting!"

Harrison smiled. "Your final assignment. Though what gives me a warm feeling inside is that you coerced the Magister into approving your personal home as your Master's project."

"You've said that at least ten times in the last six months. I think you should let your bad feelings go. It's not as if the Magister has any power over us."

"I'm not as nice as you are. I'm practically known for it." He turned in her arms and kissed her. "Now, get dressed before I forget we're on a schedule today, and take you back to bed and ravish you."

"Later," Veronica said, returning his kiss. "I insist on it."

THERE WAS STILL SNOW ON THE GROUND, THREE DAYS BEFORE Springtide, but Veronica felt as warm as if it was Midsummer. It was an illusion, she knew as she drew her cloak close around her, but everything about the day was so perfect she didn't mind pretending that she wasn't cold. The skies were clear and cloudless blue, the sun radiant, and as their carriage fell into line behind the other carriages bringing guests to the graduation ceremony, she looked eagerly out the window at the tall bethel and the copper bell that gleamed painfully bright at its top.

Harrison descended from the carriage when it came to a stop at the bethel door and gave her his hand. She shook out her black robe and hoped her favorite blue muslin gown she wore beneath it wasn't hopelessly wrinkled. It was more formal than was necessary, as the robe was enveloping enough that she could have gone naked if she'd chosen and no one would know, but she loved how confident it made her feel, even if no one saw it.

Veronica left Harrison at the door with a kiss and walked down the central aisle to her seat near the front with the other graduates. She passed Bec and Percy and their infant daughter, seated with the other visitors, and waved happily at them. Bridget was still in Aurilien, finishing her studies in the Royal Library, but there was Howard near the back, his blond hair its usual untidy mess. She wished briefly that Ian could have been there. Even nearly two and a half years after his death, she found she missed his perspective. Despite her lack of religious feeling, she wished for once that her dead could see her now. Landon would be so proud.

Elspeth and Duncan were already seated in the chairs reserved for the presiding Magisters and visiting royalty. Elspeth saw her and smiled, but made no other movement. Duncan held her hand in his and was looking at his wife with such tenderness it took Veronica's breath away. Well, they'd had their miracle. They deserved every happiness.

The bethel hall quieted as the Magister approached the edge of the dais. "On this day, we celebrate the accomplishments of the Scholia students who have mastered the knowledge of their chosen fields of study," he said, his wispy voice carrying far thanks to the design of the bethel. "In honor of our graduates, we welcome her Majesty, Elspeth North, to address us. All please rise for the Queen."

Veronica stood with the others as Elspeth, with Duncan's help, rose from her seat and made her awkward way forward to take the Magister's place. She rested a hand on her well-rounded belly and smiled at the gathered visitors.

"Thank you for your welcome," she said. "It's gratifying to see so many new-minted Masters joining the ranks of those serving Tremontane. This Scholia's legacy is one of honor and knowledge, and I am grateful for the vision of my ancestor, Kerish North, and that of Queen Willow North who made his vision a reality. You who graduate today have worked hard to reach this point. Some of you will continue your studies. Others will go out into the world and use your skills to make it a better place. But all of you can be secure in knowing you deserve the accolades you receive now."

She turned her gaze on Veronica, and her smile broadened. "You have my personal respect," she said, and though she was addressing all the new Masters, Veronica knew what she really meant. "For some of you, this accomplishment is something no one expected you to achieve. Take pride in your work, and may heaven bless you all."

Applause filled the room as Elspeth sat carefully, with Duncan aiding her as if she was made of spun glass. Veronica could hardly blame him. He'd worn a rather stunned expression the last seven months, and looking at him, Veronica could believe in heaven's intervention in mortal lives. She still wasn't sure she cared about religion personally, but the resentment she'd never fully acknowledged had died the day Elspeth announced her pregnancy.

The Magister was speaking again. Veronica let his words wash over her without listening to them. Despite what she'd told Harrison that morning, she herself had never really forgiven the Magister for his cruel behavior. He'd begged Harrison to reconsider his resignation, had gone so far as to tell them both he would make an exception for their courtship, and Veronica had never been so disgusted with anyone in her life. She'd encountered him only a handful of times since then—it was easy enough for a student never to come to the attention of the Magister—and counted it no loss.

Soon, the heads of each of the schools rose to welcome the new Masters. Veronica stood when her name was called and walked across the dais to receive her red stole. Though there had been sporadic cheering at each of the previous candidates' names, a hush fell over the bethel when it was her turn. The silence made tears come to Veronica's eyes. It was a better accolade than raucous applause.

When the last Master had received her stole, the Magister again stood before them. "Rise, Masters, and be recognized," he said, and *then* the cheering shook the bethel, and Veronica thought she heard the great bell tremble in response.

She left the group to hug both Elspeth and Duncan, then found Harrison beside her, spinning her around for a long, warm kiss. "Master North," he said formally.

"Master North," she responded. He'd adopted into her family unreservedly when they married, saying only that Tyndale had such a poor reputation, he wanted a chance to start over.

"There's a party planned for tonight," he told her, speaking loudly over the noise of hundreds of relatives and friends congratulating the graduates. "We're going to attend, yes?"

"Of course," Veronica replied. "Though I'll want to nap first. I'm not as young as I used to be."

Harrison's smile grew wicked. "Now that you mention it, I think a nap might be in order. We old folks need our rest. Among other things."

Veronica put her arms around him. "Take me home," she said, "and I'll let you show me what those things are."

ABOUT THE AUTHOR

In addition to the Crown of Tremontane series, Melissa McShane is the author of The Extraordinaries series, beginning with BURNING BRIGHT, as well as The Last Oracle series, COMPANY OF STRANGERS, and many others. After a childhood spent roaming the United States, she settled in Utah with her husband, four children and a niece, four very needy cats, and a library that has finally overflowed its bounds, which only means she needs more shelves. She wrote reviews and critical essays for many years before turning to fiction, which is much more fun than anyone ought to be allowed to have.

You can visit her at her website www.melissamcshanewrites.com for more information on other books.

For information on new releases, fun extras, and more, sign up for Melissa's newsletter: http://eepurl.com/brannP

ALSO BY MELISSA MCSHANE

THE CROWN OF TREMONTANE

Servant of the Crown

Exile of the Crown

Rider of the Crown

Agent of the Crown

Voyager of the Crown

Tales of the Crown

THE SAGA OF WILLOW NORTH

Pretender to the Crown

Guardian of the Crown

Champion of the Crown

THE HEIRS OF WILLOW NORTH

Ally of the Crown

Stranger to the Crown

Scholar of the Crown

THE EXTRAORDINARIES

Burning Bright

Wondering Sight

Abounding Might

Whispering Twilight

Liberating Fight (forthcoming)

THE LAST ORACLE

The Book of Secrets

The Book of Peril

The Book of Mayhem

The Book of Lies

The Book of Betrayal

The Book of Havoc

The Book of Harmony

The Book of War

The Book of Destiny

COMPANY OF STRANGERS

Company of Strangers

Stone of Inheritance

Mortal Rites

Shifting Loyalties

Sands of Memory

Call of Wizardry

THE CONVERGENCE TRILOGY

The Summoned Mage

The Wandering Mage

The Unconquered Mage

THE BOOKS OF DALANINE

The Smoke-Scented Girl

The God-Touched Man

Emissary

Warts and All: A Fairy Tale Collection

The View from Castle Always

www.ingramcontent.com/pod-product-compliance
Lightning Source LLC
Chambersburg PA
CBHW051227260626
47162CB00002B/302